Jules Hardy was born [   ]
around London. Follow[   ]
of jobs, including cleaning, labouring, tutoring, mobile
fish-mongering and freelance publishing work. She is a
trained carpenter and now works as a teacher in Bristol
and Bath while studying for a PhD. After publishing
several short stories, *Altered Land* is her first novel.

'A compelling story about a mother's love for her son,
the different ways people survive physical and mental
damage, and the persistence of a dream . . .
Hardy keeps you hooked from the start.
A well crafted, consistent debut'
Arena magazine

'Her extraordinary deep understanding of heartbreak,
trauma and the intricacies of human relationships
conveys itself via a deft handling of her characters,
never judgmental and always compassionate . . . This is
a truly wonderful book: a heart-rending,
heart-lifting tribute to many kinds of love'
Time Out

'[A] stunning debut . . . shifting timeframes and
shocking revelations make this an engrossing read'
Good Housekeeping

'A subtle exploration of the senses'
Lisa St Aubin de Teran

ALTERED LAND

JULES HARDY

POCKET BOOKS

LONDON • SYDNEY • NEW YORK • TOKYO • SINGAPORE • TORONTO

First published in Great Britain by Simon & Schuster UK Ltd, 2002
This edition published by Pocket Books, 2002
An imprint of Simon & Schuster UK Ltd
A Viacom Company

1 3 5 7 9 10 8 6 4 2

Simon & Schuster UK Ltd
Africa House
64–78 Kingsway
London WC2B 6AH

Simon & Schuster Australia
Sydney

www.simonsays.co.uk

A CIP catalogue record for this book is available
from the British Library

ISBN 0-7434-2904-4

Typeset by Palimpsest Book Production Limited,
Polmont, Stirlingshire
Printed and bound in Great Britain by
Cox & Wyman Ltd, Reading, Berks

ACKNOWLEDGEMENTS

Many people have contributed to this novel, wittingly or otherwise, and I suspect they'll know who they are. Far too many to name, unfortunately, so they'll have to accept my thanks here. Those whose work I would particularly like to acknowledge are my agent Maggie Phillips for her good-humoured professionalism, and my editor, Suzanne Baboneau, for the pain-free excisions. But above all my hat goes off to Melissa Weatherill, whose enthusiasm for the manuscript led her to relentlessly badger people into reading it.

For Malcolm and Tessa because I wasn't there;
for my mother and Amanda because they were.

The hospital – its heavy freight
lashed down ship-shape ward over ward –
steamed into the night with some on board
soon to be lost if the desperate
charts were known. Others would come
altered to land or find the land
altered. At their voyage's end
some would be added to, some diminished.

Jon Stallworthy
from 'The Almond Tree'

JOHN

Ian's black hands are stark against white marble as we wrestle Hercules from his plinth, sweating fingers slipping on the capital's volutes (I remembered, Ma, I remembered) made slimy by moss. Even Ian and I struggle to carry the god up the steps of the deck. We edge like crabs down the side of the house, resting the bust on the path every few feet, and then there is the problem of hoisting him into the removal van. I climb into the echoing space and grab Hercules' ears as Ian pushes at his bearded chin. A passer-by trots over to help, a short, skinny man who looks ludicrous next to Ian's bulk. He says something as Hercules thuds on to the van floor and Ian smiles, shakes the man's tiny hand.

Ian disappears round the back of the house as I edge-walk Hercules to the back of the van, to stand among the others: Pan, resting his pipes on shaggy concrete knees; Apollo, looking smug (and where were *his* oracles when you needed them?); Achilles; Narcissus; the wolf suckling Romulus and Remus; a unicorn with a delicate weathered horn; the many gryphons, gargoyles and sphinxes. All of them marking the passage of another year – my mother's birthday gifts to me. There's not much else – a few boxes of books and black plastic bin-bags of clothes, my tool-boxes, routers, drills and workbench.

Ian reappears, carrying the plinth under one arm, as easily

as a roll of carpet, and slides it along the van floor. 'That it?'
he asks.

I find myself tugging hard at the tip of my beard, a sure sign
of something. 'I'm just going to check I've got everything.'
I walk down the path and through the gate out on to the
deck. I wouldn't say it's my favourite (the wooden half-boat
deck with its bowsprit maiden has a special place in my heart)
but it is possibly the best-crafted. It was, after all, a labour of
love – odd to think of that now. I touch the knobbled scar
buried under my hair, carved by a falling lemonade bottle, as
my other hand plays with the worrystone in my pocket. The
green malachite stone has been worried for nearly thirty years,
worried paper-thin, and as I stand in my garden, memorising
every plant, every tree, it finally snaps in two.

I walk back to the van, out into weak May sunlight, and
before I pull down the rolling door I look again at the statues,
boxes and bags. Is that all there is?

The night before my thirteenth birthday I couldn't sleep, kept
awake by the excitement of the thought of going to London
for the weekend. Although she was in her bedroom, I could
hear my mother murmuring on the telephone; the cottage
was so small any sound filled it. I switched on the bedside
lamp and opened my book, only to read the words 'His
heart broke'. I threw down the book, turned off the light and
pulled my heart-warmed blankets tighter around me, thinking,
His heart broke? His heart *broke*? How did it break? Did it
shatter into a thousand pieces? Or did it snap into two bloody
halves, without a sound? Through my open bedroom window
I could hear the sea slapping round the pilings in the creek as
I burrowed deeper into my bed. I could see my breath on the
cold air as I listened to salt-water turning pebbles and rocks.

Looking into the darkness of my childhood room I decided I would never break my heart. I imagined holding it close, warm and silent as a well-kept secret. Gathering myself against the cold, I scooted from the bed, snatched Tub the Ted from the chair and jumped back into my warm nest. Hugging Tub, I prodded the hard bump of his growling mechanism and heard the comforting, thin roar. Suddenly I was embarrassed. I was nearly thirteen and I was cuddling a teddy bear. I dumped Tub on the floor. Childish thoughts.

How was I to know that was the last night of my childhood? Maybe if I had, I would have held Tub in my long, skinny arms all night long.

My wife, Sonja, is from a different world, a Nordic world of snow, soused herrings and long winter nights. She left that world when she was seventeen, her mind her passport; for her mind was, and is, so razor-sharp it would make minced meat of Ockham himself. Sonja could have studied anywhere – MIT, Harvard, Oxford – but the first time I saw her was at King's College, London. An ugly building which seems even now an unlikely place to find beauty. Yet it was there that I saw her for the first time, there that I first touched her hand and noticed nothing unusual. For she left me breathless, boneless and, eventually, she would argue, heartless. I managed, somehow, to speak, to form words and ask her where she was from, what she was studying, as her hand grew hot in mine. She frowned and looked at my lips, as I looked at hers. We smiled and knew then – both of us – that this meeting would last a lifetime. And so it has. It has lasted for the life-time since that moment. It has stretched over twenty years and I have never stopped loving the woman whose hand I first touched in that ugly building.

*   *   *

The first time I took Sonja down to Devon, to my mother's house in Thurlestone, it was a humid August night and we arrived to find her drunk, weaving slightly, her gestures clipped yet indefinite. The three of us sat in the library, searching for conversation as my mother fumbled with her glass, her cigarettes, her lighter. The air was heavy, made boxy by the static of an impending storm. When my mother went to the kitchen for a refill, I followed her and told her my news, told her why Sonja and I had come to visit. I knew my mother had spoken, knew she'd said something because the air moved.

'Sorry?' I asked.

My mother whirled round, furious, gripping a green gin bottle tightly by its neck. 'I said, "She may be beautiful but she's not right for you."'

I looked out at the volcanic arch, which shattered the horizon of the line between sea and sky. A dark slab of granite in the bay, sun blazing through its portal. 'I can't believe that, Ma,' I tried to say but I must have only whispered.

My mother, her glass frosted by ice, smiled her wintry smile. 'You can't even talk any more.'

'I'm going to marry her.'

'Then you're a fool.'

'I love her.'

'Fine. Fine. Love her, then, go ahead and love her. But you don't have to marry her.' My mother scissored around the kitchen, sharp as a blade, picking up oddments and resetting them, slicing them, cutting them up or down and throwing them away. A lime was slashed and sectioned. She came to rest against the hard chrome edge of the cooker, holding her colourless drink against her chest, against her heart of stone.

I considered this. 'I'll marry her anyway.'

I didn't hear Sonja's soft entry, in bare feet on a slate floor. It was my mother's flint-glance that made me turn to see Sonja watching me.

'Special, you don't have to,' she said, and smiled.

'But I want to.' When I said this my voice must have had a touch of amazement: how could it be that anyone would not want to marry Sonja?

My mother tapped me on the shoulder and reluctantly I turned away from Sonja to look at the lipstick-furred edges of my mother's mouth. It was the fine spray of saliva on my cheek – as if she'd just stabbed the lime inches from my face – that made me realise how angry she was. 'There's something wrong with her,' my mother said, gesturing at Sonja with the empty glass.

All these years later I can still feel the spray of my mother's spit and I rub it with my hand. But however hard I wipe, scrub my skin, however often, it's still there, that spray. Because she was right. There is indeed something wrong with Sonja, there always was.

I'm eight years old and I'm standing in the middle of a living room in a shabby Victorian house in Earl's Court, watching my mother, my beautiful, angle-poised mother, grabbing other people's waists, swaying and screaming with delight, swilling drinks (no change there) because the score is 2-2. Then suddenly it's 3-2 and my mother is crying, which is fine because she rushes over to me, kneeling right by the screen, and colourless sloe-scented drink spills down my front as she hugs me while the commentator bawls, 'This is a heart-stopping moment!' Well, it certainly was for me because all I could do was glance down at my scrawny chest and wait for my heart to stop. I watched everyone in

the room as they danced, spilling Watney's Red and cheap
plastic-bottle red wine. I was watching for their *hearts*, and as
I sat right next to the television, which was blaring in my ear,
I heard someone yell, 'They think it's all over . . . It is now!'
And when I turned round it was to see a ball ballooning into
the net as if it were itself an overblown heartbeat.

The first time I touched Sonja, really touched her, was in
her bed in halls, the only place I felt safe then. She put my
hand on her bare breast and smiled. Looked at me and said,
'Burgundy wine.'
    'What?'
    'Wine. Your hand.'
    'I don't get it.'
    'You don't have to.'
    'Right.'
Three weeks later I stood in my mother's kitchen and told
her that I was going to marry Sonja and my mother said that
there was something wrong with Sonja. That stormy night,
after my mother had staggered to bed, we sat out on the deck
with a bottle of red wine and I found out what it was.
    Sonja told me then that she is a synaesthete: someone who
tastes colours, sees music, feels sound, hears pictures, smells
temperature. Her senses have mingled; they play randomly
with each other. One sense is stimulated and another receptor
stretches, like a dog on a hot pavement, and replies.
    'What? Like thinking Wednesday is blue and six? Monday
is yellow and three? That kind of thing?'
    'No, not like that.' She frowned and wrapped her arms
round herself. 'Not like that.'
    'Like what, then?'
    'What you're talking about is to do with language and

experience. You're responding to words, labels, and your experiences of them. Everyone has colours they prefer, numbers they like – maybe because of their shape or something.' She reached for her glass of wine as lightning razzled across the bay, making cliffs and beach jump purple. 'I mean like that – the sky changes and I taste sour lemon. I see the flash and I taste lemon.' She looked away from me, out to sea. 'When it's really bad I don't even see the lightning, I just taste lemon.'

'Jesus Christ.'

She wakes to the alarm on Monday mornings tasting peaches, she listens to opera and sees John Martin's vast canvases. She eats spaghetti and her hands tingle as if a bolt of silk is being pulled through them. Eating in a restaurant is always an interesting experience.

'How was your fish, madam?'

'Wonderful, like aluminium.'

Sometimes it's worse than other times. Sometimes she can't function very well because her vision, her interpretation, of the world is so at odds with the rest of ours. Most of the time it's not so bad. She says that she would rather be a synaesthete than colour blind. But, then, she was always an *optimistic* synaesthete – as I realised when she described my touch as being burgundy wine. And now I understand what she means: my touch is not *like* burgundy wine, it *is* burgundy wine.

I remember looking out at the volcanic arch and thinking, Well, that's just fine.

Twenty years is a long time; it used to be a generation. Sonja and I have lived half our lives together. And all around us people have failed at the one thing they wished to do well – to love someone and to stay with them. So simple. So why is it that over the years friends have come to us in pieces, fragmented wrecks, and cried in front of us, as Sonja makes pictures of their words and I watch their faces and their mouths work? We have always been the constant, the given, the exemplar.

Sonja and I don't have children. I'm not sure when we made that decision; I'm not even sure if it was a decision, a choice. I don't know. I woke up one day and realised we were both forty and childless, realised that all we had was each other. Which was enough for me because if children had arrived they would have brought change and disturbance with them. Our lives would have been bent out of shape, twisted by unfamiliar uncertainties and unexpected fears. Besides, I've never been quite sure what fatherhood means.

I am a carpenter. I shape wood so that it will fit together one way or another, and I sometimes think my mother's disappointed that this is what I do. I left King's College after a year and trained for a City and Guilds diploma. One Friday afternoon I climbed on my motorbike and drove to Sonja's halls of residence, swerving and listing violently at high speed, because I wanted to get to Sonja. (I have always wanted to get to Sonja.) I burst into her room, wearing sawdust-covered dungarees and a motorcycle helmet and asked her to marry me and she said she would. Her friends exclaimed, talked of the romance of what I had done. I didn't have the heart to tell them it wasn't romance; it was loneliness that prompted me.

And now I'm a carpenter in Bristol. I'm not sure how I journeyed down these two decades to arrive here in a huge house with more money than I have time to spend. How did this *happen*? Sometimes I feel my life is like a vast sieve: pour in time and effort, shake, and a cloud of money drifts out. You entertain thoughts such as this if you live with a synaesthete. Nothing is like anything else and yet everything is like something else. A handful of raspberries is the sound of rain falling; the smell of diesel is the sour taste of fried okra.

One evening, many years ago, I sat in the garden of the Highbury Vaults pub, kneading the calluses on my hands, thanking some deity or other for the evening sun, and I began to talk to the man sitting next to me. This was Ian, a metal-worker, a man of steel, a colossus, so muscle-bound I wanted to repot him, to put him in a bigger body, a more accommodating body. I have since always been fearful that he will burst out of his own. He asked me what I was doing at the time, and I told him I was building a deck. He flinched (I half expected his skin to peel open) and said that he was doing the same. We had a few more pints and sketched some ideas on paper. At the end of the evening, when we stood and shook hands, I realised Ian was only an inch or so shorter than me. Absurdly this pleased me, made me trust him. Three weeks later Elemental was born. What else would we call our company? He wrought iron and I shaved wood. Elements. Fashioned elements. And now we build decks for people who can afford them – and they are many – in Bristol and Bath.

It was when we moved into the studio flat in Battersea, just after we were married, that Sonja decided it was time I learned to cook. She'd spent her childhood eating fish in its various guises and was fascinated by the abundance of food in London's shops. Every Saturday morning we'd go walk-about, Sonja armed with a shopping list, and she'd point out fresh ginger, lychees, clemenvillas and asparagus, sharon fruit and Jerusalem artichokes. She tried to show me how to select the best but this wasn't always successful. My huge hand would wrap round an avocado and in the act of squeezing it gently I'd reduce it to green pulp. We'd buy pork belly and calves' liver, venison and guinea fowl – anything but fish. Then over to Fulham and she'd trawl the Italian delis for balsamic vinegar, pancetta and Parmigiano.

Early Saturday evenings, when a bottle of wine had been opened, we'd begin the lesson in the tiny galley kitchen. Sonja skipped the basics like poaching eggs or roasting a chicken. Instead she cut straight to lemon poussins *persillades*, guinea fowl with grapes, fresh tagliatelle with egg and truffle. She tried to show me how to fillet, skin and slice but I only ever ended up slicing myself. The kitchen was so small that I'd stand pressed up behind her, watching over her shoulder as we became increasingly distracted by contact and eventually the lesson was abandoned.

I loved those Saturdays, walking hand in hand down new streets, bags full of wild, unfamiliar food on our backs. Stopping for coffee, watching people marching past as we ate lunch and talked about decorating the flat or where we'd spend the summer. Every Saturday was like a holiday, a present.

When I was a boy – when I was Merboy – all schoolchildren had to take the eleven-plus, the exam that separated the stupid from the intelligent, separated the children who'd have a good life from those who wouldn't. Or, at least, that was how we thought of it. I walked into the class-room one morning and Mr Plunkett, who had a hooked nose and a voice like a foghorn, was laying out papers on the desks.

'Player, put two of these out for each child,' he brayed, giving me a box of pencils. 'And get a haircut soon.'

'Yes, sir.' I followed him round the room, doling out the pencils. 'Sir, is this the exam?'

'Don't ask questions, just do what I asked.'

'Yes, sir.' I carried on, thinking that he hadn't asked, he'd told me; thinking that I wanted to be somewhere else; thinking that I knew my mother wanted me to pass this exam.

Other children began to straggle into the classroom, and I saw some of them turn pale as they realised what the papers were because even then we all knew what it meant: grammar school or secondary modern. Success or failure. We all sat at the desks, alphabetically for once, and when Mr Plunkett called for silence the only sound I could hear was Martin Sawyer, two seats behind me, breathing snottily through his snaggle-toothed mouth.

That lunchtime we stood in tight groups, talking about the questions, not running and shouting, playing football or tag or British Bulldog. Martin Sawyer edged up to me.

'Some of them are tricks, y'know, to catch you out,' he said nasally. 'Like the one about the pound of feathers and pound of lead.' He was scraping at the asphalt of the playground with his shoe. ''Sobvious it's a trick – 'sgot to be the feathers that's heavier.' He looked up and caught me smiling and his face flushed pink under his sallow skin.

Sonja and I went to Paris for our honeymoon – but we might as well have stayed at home since just about all we did was make love all day and night, stopping only to call room service. I lay on the lumpy, unfamiliar mattress the first night, my feet and ankles hanging over the end, unable to sleep. The heat was stifling and even with the long, shuttered windows wide open the air, coloured by the smell of garlic from the restaurant opposite, lay on me as heavily as a blanket. I was thinking

of my mother sitting alone on her deck, no doubt thinking
of me. I felt I'd cut myself adrift from her, felt that she was
receding already in my mind, a well-known island slipping
over the horizon. I hated my mother for not loving Sonja and
I loved my mother for many reasons. I was twenty years old –
too young to forgive her for not loving and old enough to feel
fear for her. Because I knew that she'd sit alone for ever on her
deck, drinking whisky and looking out over the sea, wishing
things could have been different. All that week, as Sonja and I
explored each other's bodies, occasionally dragging ourselves
out to walk the streets and eat, I was aware of my mother's
ghost, not walking beside me but sitting beside her. A young,
beautiful ghost, a different woman, who – I discovered many
years later – didn't exist.

When I was Merboy I lived in a cottage overlooking a creek
in Noss Mayo, in Devon. One day when I was eleven, after
the bus had dropped me at the top of Back Road, a group of
boys came out of the garden of a house nearby, looking sly and
brutal. I knew them, knew they were dangerous, slow-witted
and vicious. I began to trot down the steep hill towards the
creek, my bag bouncing on my back, as they lurched behind
me, cat-calling. I jogged on, the gradient hurting my knees,
the thought of swimming in high-tide waters pulling me down
the hill, knowing I could easily out-sprint the bullies. Then
one of them, Martin Sawyer, thin as a bulrush with buck
teeth and acne, who thought that a feather was heavier than
lead, yelled, 'Who's yer mother been fucking today, then?'
The question flowed down the valley, through the open
stable-door of my mother's cottage, across the dog-leg of
the river and over the sea as Eddie Lamble, fat half-wit,
wheezed his approval.

'It ain't yer father, is it?' Eddie Lamble crowed, his voice like sour milk.

Drawing level with the church, my breath jolting out of me, I could see the river filling the creek but I stopped running. I turned back to face the pack and shrugged off my bag as they thundered towards me.

The sound of Martin Sawyer's nose breaking was extraordinary – the shattering of a pane of glass hidden in a pillow.

Bristol is a city calling for, in fact querulously demanding, decks. Unlike Rome it has more than seven hills; it seems to have an endless number of them, as many as anyone could possibly require. I have staggered up St Michael's – known as Cardiac Hill because of the conveniently placed hospitals – with a belly full of Smiles' Best. I have toiled up Totterdown and, on occasion, sweated my way up Ashton Court Road to Pill. I have even dragged myself up Constitution Hill, drunk at Christmas midnight, when the street was iced over, by hauling myself up on car bumpers. I was feet from my goal when my hand slipped on the steel bumper of an old blue Triumph Herald and, buttery-safe drunk as I was, I slithered down the length of the hill, spinning and giggling, clutching at ice-sleek cars, my coat snagging and tearing. I hurtled through Jacob's Wells and came to rest at the foot of Brandon Hill, fitting neatly into the deep gutter. I lay there stunned and stared at the stars.

It was on Constitution Hill that I built my first deck, a simple, ham-fisted affair. Cheap Malaysian rubber-tree wood, artlessly devised to hold the weight of a stout family as they sunned themselves after Sunday roast. It was a neighbour who saw that pitiful effort and asked me to do the same at the back of his house. If a city is perched on hills, if it boasts shaming wealth built on blood, slaves and tobacco, then decks are good business. A long-windowed Georgian house of two storeys, even-eyed and finely balanced from the street, will be four storeys at the rear. Dropping down with a vertiginous swoosh to an untended garden. How pleasant, how convenient, to have a deck at the kitchen level. This was the notion that seeped into my addled brain as I lay in the gutter at the bottom of Constitution Hill. I didn't know then that it would make me rich and lazy and heartless.

How did I become heartless?

Ian is talented and accomplished. His manners are fine and considered. He can wrestle single-handedly with a set of iron spiral steps, speak French and Italian, he can even do sign language; he can sail, windsurf, play the harmonica and cook. He is handsome and cultured; he is also lonely. We go out every Friday night from work and drink in different pubs because Ian doesn't like to stay in one place for the evening. He thinks that if he keeps moving he increases the chance of meeting the One. Well, maybe. I met the One twenty years ago and I wasn't even looking. I sometimes wonder what people think of us as we sit there, gesturing unexpectedly, me looking like a wild man, the shavings caught in my beard falling occasionally into my beer and Ian with the black-silk dust of iron-working leaving his dark, coffee-coloured face raccoon-like.

Sonja owns a delicatessen off Whiteladies Road, a beautiful, labyrinthine shop full of foreign mysteries. Much like Sonja herself. The delicatessen spreads through the ground floor of a beautifully proportioned Georgian house, fluted pillars with acanthus-wreathed capitals supporting a portico above the customers as they enter. They can tie their dogs there, on one of the pillars. Sonja has had a brass cleat fixed in the restoration mortar and puts out a terracotta bowl of water for the dogs, who gather in numbers, forming a maypole of tangled leads fanning down to the water.

I know this because I often pass the shop on the way from one job to another. If the traffic lights are red I can watch her move in her space, dressed in a dazzling white apron, her doubting grey eyes scanning the delicacies as if she's never seen them before. I never try to attract her attention, I just sit in the truck watching her. I have eyes like a hawk. I can see that the wild boar sausages have gone up from £3.75 to £4.15 a pound. Outrageous.

When we first moved here to Bristol Sonja began to study for a Ph.D. in psychology. Then one evening, six years ago, she came down to my workshop in the basement and announced that she was bored by study, by her life of libraries and libidinous lecturers. She wanted to deal in something concrete.

'Concrete?' I asked, pulling at a jammed router bit.

'Yes. Something in the world.'

My hand slipped and the razor edge of the bit sliced the ball of my thumb. 'You don't have to work. Do whatever you want to do.'

'I want to do something in the real world.' She moved to a stool, picked up the rusty jack saw on the seat, and sat, holding it in her hands.

'Something to do with concrete?' I sucked the blood hard and pressed my undamaged thumb against the cut. Sonja ignored the blood – a commonplace hazard of butchers and manual workers.

'No. I mean something I can hold, something that's corporeal.'

'Right.'

'Something where there's some of *me* in it.'

'Right.' I grabbed a towel and wrapped the wound.

'I want to open a delicatessen. How much money do we have?'

I looked at her beautiful, unexplained face in astonishment. Cerebral Sonja asking about money? 'A lot.'

'Enough to buy a shop?'

'Depends where.'

'Whiteladies Road.'

'Right.'

'So can I do that? I can look into it?'

'I don't know. You haven't told me how much it'll cost.'

She mouthed a figure so colossal, so alarming, that I dropped the towel. 'Bugger me!'

'It's beautiful.'

'So are you and looking at you is free.'

'Ah, come on, Special – be serious. I really want to do this. OK, I've been studying and you've been working, but who ever said that the two weren't the same? They're both work. I'm just so bored with university. I feel like I'm marking time, not going anywhere.' She dropped the jack saw and dust flew from the floor as she walked back up the basement steps and closed the door, stirring dust in eddies.

'Right.' It was Harry who had infected me with this verbal tic, this catch-all word, 'right'. I've never shaken it off.

When my bleeding thumb had staunched, I went upstairs and lay on one of the sofas, a deep, comforting yet lonely bed. I lay and watched car headlights scallop the ceiling. We did have the money, I knew that. She could have her beautiful shop and fill it with delicacies. But there was the rub. Something she could hold, she'd said? Jesus. She holds a tennis ball and thinks of custard; holds a Mont Blanc fountain pen and tastes copper; holds my hand and thinks burgundy wine. I mean, I was struggling – a delicatessen run by a synaesthete? Eventually I slept fitfully, to be woken by daylight, and went to our bedroom. Sonja was sprawled across the mattress, a sheet dangling from one foot, the cotton fabric lapping like milk on the carpet in the dawn light. As I say, live with a synaesthete and the world is no longer your own. It becomes an ocean of experience into which we dip, hoping that what we reel in bears *some* relationship to what others feel.

I touched her heel and she groaned. 'We have the money, honey. Buy it today.' I watched her wake up, watched her encounter her world. It was a Tuesday morning. Was she tasting opals? Hearing mustard seas? Seeing calypso? Who knows? It takes Sonja a long time to connect to the world as we know it. She has a lot of data to rearrange.

She turned to me and smiled, her hand reached out to touch mine and my heart missed a beat. Literally. Missed. A. Beat. There was an absence in my chest. 'I love you, Special,' Sonja said, smiling. And my heart stopped.

Ian and I are both amazed by success. It was not what we sought when we set up Elemental. Of course, we wanted it to work, we wanted to do the things we did best every day – wringing iron and shaving wood. But the degree of success has astounded us. There aren't enough hours in the day, there aren't enough experienced, talented iron-workers and carpenters, and there are too many rich, demanding customers. Our work has featured in trade magazines and Sunday papers, in lush, thick coffee-table books about house restoration and improvement. For our decks are not simply load-bearing, they are works of art. We began simply, with wooden rails, slatted floors and the occasional spiral staircase. But now the decks incorporate fused glass, granite, sand, driftwood, pebbles, columns, second storeys, movable sections. They are a mélange of cedar, pitch pine, hazel pine and teak; mahogany and walnut, elm and lime. I have supplies of purple- and green-heart delivered from the West Indies for decoration. Ian and I comb restoration yards for materials of terracotta and Bath stone, rusted metal and chains. We once built a deck with the pitch pine planks from a Scottish brewery supporting a pulpit and curved rail from a Welsh Methodist church. Let it not be said that deck-builders are without humour. We have even built a deck with a glass floor, on the third storey of a Victorian building in Charlotte Street. What, I wonder, do the people in the garden flat below see when they go out to look at the stars?

Ian delights in linguistics, revels in the intricacies of language, and every week he adopts an orphaned word. Perhaps he likes the sound of it, or the shape of it, and he tries to worm it into every conversation he has. It can be anything – propinquity, jurisprudence, flotsam, banjaxed, jinxed, neoteny – and he'll use it whenever he can. He says, and I think he's right, that we don't use our language, don't explore it. He says we'll all soon be reduced to five hundred words, mere grunts expressing simple desires, Riddley Walker-like. His word for this week is 'incandescent', which strikes me as being a bit too work-related.

The moment my heart stopped I loved Sonja more than I'd ever done. Merely touching her ankle had undone me. She

reached out for my hand and my heart *stopped*. I can remember
feeling as if the ball had hit the net again, as if Geoff Hurst
had kicked that glorious shot into my chest and the ball was
ballooning through me. That is the last thing I remember.
Apparently I keeled over like a felled oak, like Lincoln's
cherry tree, like a Californian redwood – which seems an
appropriate response for a carpenter to have when his heart
stops. My next thought was entertained in a bed in hospital.
I can't remember what the thought was but I think it was that
I was hungry. Sonja was sitting next to my bed holding my
hand and I have always been convinced that she'd never let
it go. She just smiles when I suggest this.

'What happened?' I asked.

'Your heart stopped.'

'Bollocks – I'm thirty-five years old. How can I have a
heart-attack?'

'It wasn't a heart-attack. It just stopped beating regularly.
Something to do with electrical impulses.'

Her eyes were greyer than I'd ever seen them. I realised
that she hadn't slept. 'How long have you been here?'

'I don't know.'

'Go home and sleep.'

She cried at last, her head resting on my malfunctioning
chest, and I could feel all her movements with an intensity I'd
never felt before and haven't since. It was as if I had slipped
into her body. I felt like pulped breadfruit, crushed chestnuts,
pale and malleable, and I understood at last what it was to see
the world as she did. 'Sonja, Sonja.' I lifted her head with my
catheter-snaky hand and her water-washed eyes stared. 'I'm
not going to die. I'm not going to leave you. I am *not* going to
die. Go home and sleep.' She believed me and so she went.

*   *   *

Embedded in the wall of the heart are four structures that conduct impulses through the cardiac muscle to cause first the atria and then the ventricles to contract. These structures are the sinoatrial node, the atrioventricular node, the bundle of His and the Purkinje fibres: the pacemaker mechanisms. It was, apparently, my bundle of His that was causing a problem, short-circuiting the whole shooting match. So they cut my broad, hairy chest right open and put in a pacemaker, a small, shiny dumb-bell of metal. Ian could have made me one sporting curlicues and roundels. Now my sinoatrial node and bundle of His (whose? someone else's?) sit there, unloved and bypassed. Sometimes I wonder if that is why I'm heartless.

Ian came to visit me in the hospital, his face grave and concerned, wiped clean of sweat and iron dust. He laid his huge hand on my chest and when he spoke my thorax vibrated.

'How you doing, Special?'

'Feeling like shit.'

He nodded and produced a bag of tiny kumquats. 'Thought you might be.'

'What's the word for this week?'

'Homeostasis. Difficult to work into a conversation down the Miners' Arms without you there.' He smiled and bit into a kumquat, the fine, minuscule zest spraying my face, reminding me of my mother.

I have conjectured for half my life, since that moment when I touched Sonja's hand at King's College, about her origins. I know she was born in Estonia, that she is Nordic, but she doesn't seem to belong to the north of the world. She generates warmth as if her core is burning; her skin feels bronzed, smells of soft toffee. Where is she *from*? What journeys did her ancestors make? Did they climb the Himalayas and take the direct route, through Pakistan and Uzbekistan, through the swampy heartlands of Russia to Estonia? Or were they romantic stargazers, taking a leisurely, ten-generation stroll along the coasts and waterways of two continents? And as they wandered what made them move on? Move north? Weren't there enough olives, fish and wild boar? What made them toil north through ever colder lands to fetch up in Kingisepp on the island of Saaremaa?

Sonja doesn't care about all this, she shrugs and changes the conversation if I mention it. I'm not fanatical about genealogy, merely curious, fanciful. I'm a Celt, hammered out of the tin mines of Cornwall and the coal mines of Wales. I have black hair and beard, periwinkle eyes and a table of a chest, a barrel of a body. I could beat back a band of Picts and still have time for breakfast. But, as the playwright Robert Bolt would say, a bitch got over the wall somewhere, for I have olive skin which tans in a moment. There must have been a gypsy or an Italian count who dallied in Dyfed or Kernow.

As I say, I'm not fanatical, merely curious because I'm a product of the land on which I live. After all, I'm only three generations from smallholding, goat-tending and tipping my cap. Around me there are fellow Celts, even in this cosmopolitan city. Recently in a gorge near Bristol there was a fall in a cave, soft limestone sloughing down beneath stalactites, to reveal a skeleton, supplicant and long dead, tens of thousands of years old. The gorge is remote, even now, small-town and landlocked. The people who know how to prised the DNA of this long-dead man from his body and took samples from everyone in the nearby villages. They found a perfect match, a shy, diffident school-teacher whose face almost exactly mirrored a projected mask of the dead man. I told Sonja about this and she shrugged and changed the conversation.

When the taxi brought me back from the hospital, pacemaker pulsing silently in my ribcage, my chest hurt. The scar prickled, my ribs felt tender and my heart ached. Ever since I was a boy I'd worried about my heart breaking – I'd never given a thought to it aching and had certainly not imagined it stopping. I sat in the cab and watched Sonja in our front garden, wielding secateurs and trowel, rummaging in a black bin-bag, digging and delving. Her hair was pinned up and she wore a sarong. She turned when I opened the cab door, looking guilty and doubtful (looking like the daughter of a tribe who had crossed two continents). Seeing me she smiled, came to the car and hugged me, fussing over bags and payment, before leading me into the house. Hours later, after we had made very gentle love, after we had taken tea, after I had looked at my post, I went into the garden alone as she ran us a bath. I opened the bin-bags she'd filled and found in them the butchered remnants of every bleeding-heart plant we had.

I wonder sometimes whether Sonja's synaesthesia is a side effect of her family's peregrinations. Perhaps they saw so much that was new, tasted so much that was different, heard so many sounds previously unheard by them, that they carried with them a sensory overload they couldn't name. This is what's difficult with synaesthesia. It has to be described in language because there are no other tools. Even Microsoft Word doesn't have a toolbar that reads 'language, thesaurus, synaesthesia', and if it did what would it say? 'Monday –

peaches', 'Brandy – Rodin's *Kiss*', 'Volcano – hand running over dead coral'? Even then it would be only *one* synaesthete's version of the world.

Sonja once entertained some fellow synaesthetes here and I watched from the kitchen window, feeling furtive, as Sonja served wine and snacks. Then she called me out to join them on the deck and I sat for a while with six people whose worlds matched no one else's, not even each other's. They laughed as they bit into tortillas and talked of deserts and ceramics, snickered as they sipped Chablis and heard 'La Wally', felt wet sand, smelled tamarinds. Overwhelmed, I made my excuses and went to lie on our bed. Hours later Sonja joined me.

'Are you OK?' I asked. 'Have they gone?'

'Yes, they've gone. And no, I'm not OK.'

'Why not?' We didn't touch, just lay there, looking at each other. I know more than most how important it is to *watch* people as well as listen.

'They don't see things like I do.'

'Well, honey, you knew that would be the case. You knew that before you asked them here.'

'I know that. I *know* that. But I guess I was hoping that one of them would feel the same. Would name the same things. Like the guy with short blond hair? When he tasted the wine I was sure he'd say something about straw – it was awful by the way – but what did he say? It reminded him – that's the received argot, it reminds one – of zoysia grass. Bloody zoysia grass. I've never even seen the stuff.'

'I bet one of your ancestors did.'

'There you go again.' She turned on her back and crossed her arms on her chest, the same pose as the skeleton revealed in Cheddar Gorge.

*   *   *

One of our customers once asked Ian and me to design and build a deck shaped like a boat; he said he wanted it to *be* a deck, as it were. He'd been a sailor all his life and couldn't imagine a life on land without a railing and a curved, planed, interlocked floor. His house was out in the country, sliding down the banks of a river, so we built out over the high-tide mark. The deck curved round from the sides of the house, the railings made from old, reclaimed banisters with beautifully turned spindles. Ian contacted a boat-builder and we stripped out the deck of a yacht that was being broken up, and installed the floor so that it dipped away neatly to drain the rainwater. The customer wanted rigging and pulleys installed so we strung these round the edge. He could even run up a pennant on the short mast we slotted into the floor, should he feel so moved.

One afternoon as I was rummaging through the reclamation yard in Wells I came across a bowsprit maiden, faded and unloved in the corner of a shed. She had wild, slightly crossed eyes and the pale blue cloak falling from her shoulders revealed, sadly, only one breast, reminding me of Ellen. But she *was* a maiden and she deserved better than to be tossed in a corner and forgotten. I took her home, sanded her down and arranged to have her vacuum-treated. Then I repainted her cloak and face, although nothing, it seemed, could correct her squint. I repaired the deep crack that ran through her navel and painted her with layer after layer of yacht varnish. I even tried to fashion a new breast for her having found a round of Caribbean purple heart among my off-cuts that was approximately the right size. I'd turn it on the lathe in my basement workshop then run upstairs to feel Sonja's breast, running back down to the lathe while the feeling was still hot in my hand. Sonja might be sitting at a desk doing her accounts, or standing by the Aga cooking, or watching TV, and when she heard my steps thundering up the stairs she'd lift her blouse or T-shirt and carry on cooking, or reading, or whatever. But the maiden's breast was never convincing. It simply didn't work. And long-drawn-out and enjoyable though the project was I had to abandon it. The reason, of course, was that Sonja's breast was full and ripe, made of flesh, while the maiden's was a Michelangelene attempt at a breast – unaccountable to gravity, a half tennis ball stuck near her shoulder. Now that one-breasted bowsprit maiden stands proud on the prow of the deck behind the old sailor's house, looking out over the river rising and falling. Which may not have the marine drama of the Straits of Molucca or the fury of Cape Horn but at least it's something for her crazy eyes to watch.

A few months ago Sonja knelt before me as I was reading and touched my cheek.

'You're not talking enough,' she said, her eyes scanning my face in the same way as they scanned the morsels in the refrigerated displays in her shop. Doubtfully.

'What?'

'You're not talking enough. You're retreating.' She squatted down, in what I think of as her Indian pose, and said, 'Tell me a story.'

'Which one?'

'Um . . .' she bounced on her haunches '. . . the one about the picnic and the lemonade.'

I smiled, despite myself, despite the fact I have told this story a million times, despite the fact I'm the victim. 'OK. So, I'm nine years old and my mother and I are in the cottage in Noss Mayo. We wake up one Sunday morning and the sky is blue, the sun is shining, the Yealm is running high. It is an Indian summer.' For a moment I wondered if Sonja understood more of Indian summers than I ever shall. 'Anyway, Mother takes it into her head that we're going to have a picnic. She boils eggs, cuts slices of ham and chicken, washes lettuce and tomatoes. We're all packed up with loads of little plastic containers and flasks and she's like a dynamo, thinking that's the way normal people live. As we're leaving the house I remember there's a bottle of Corona lemonade in the fridge. I ask if we can take it and she says we can but only if I carry it. So I go and get it. You don't know the bottles but when I was a kid Corona lemonade was the thing. More than Coke or Pepsi. It came in a heavy, dimpled glass bottle with a striped white and yellow label. And the bottle had deposit paid – you had to give one in every time you bought a new one or you didn't get a discount.

'So I grab the bottle and go into the road where Mother's waiting. She's just a ray of sunshine, calling out to the neighbours and waving as we load up the old Morris Minor. She's taken it into her head that she wants to go to Thurlestone and she cruises really slowly past a huge house looking out over the arch in the bay. She points, just like she always does when we go there, and says, "There, pumpkin, is my favourite house in the whole world. Imagine waking up to that view. One day, pumpkin, one day. I'd give anything to live there."'

I stopped speaking for a moment. Does my mother ever remember saying that? Does she ever turn that wish over in her mind?

'Anyway, we get out of the car and start walking down to the beach, across the golf course, and the links are really crowded, balls flying everywhere. All the golfers are yelling, "Fore!" and she covers my head and giggles as we duck down together. Then she's walking ahead of me because I begin to ramble, looking in rabbit holes, turning over stones, looking for lost golf balls. The sun's hot and I feel brilliant. My mother's happy as a sandboy, I'm going to go swimming and then I'll eat as much as I want, food I really like. I begin to flip the bottle in my hands. Y'know, just end over end, even though it's all slippery with sweat. I begin to throw it a little higher and then, as my mother disappears into the dunes, I fling it up into the air, even though the lemonade will fizz out when it's opened. I throw it up as high as I can, and then I look for it. Big mistake. The sun's at its highest, absolutely dazzling. I'm blinded by it and begin to reel about, arms flailing, as the bottle falls. When it lands it knocks me senseless.'

Sonja snorted with laughter, even though it was a picture of my younger self being damaged. I guffawed. 'It took my mother five minutes to realise that I wasn't behind her. When she came back to get me she found I was knocked out and there was blood everywhere. We spent the afternoon in Plymouth's casualty ward, with me being given eight stitches. But as my mother said, rather brightly given she'd been at the wine in the ladies' room, at least we had enough to eat while we were waiting.'

Sonja grinned as I thought that my mother might have been annoyed that we lost the deposit on the smashed bottle.

'More stories,' Sonja said.

'No, no more.' I smiled, then, to take the sting out of the words. 'I'm tired.'

'OK. Thanks. You spoke really well.' Sonja pushed herself out of her Indian pose and kissed my cheek. 'Coming to bed?'

'In a minute.' I picked up my book and pretended to read until she closed the door.

When she'd gone, I dropped the book on the sofa, lowered my chin to my scarred, unnatural chest and thought. Unknown

to Sonja, whenever I told that story I thought of another. I
didn't know why it reminded me, maybe because when I was a
boy I always thought my mother was so self-assured, beautiful
and . . . proud, almost. But I knew that when I was six months
old my mother went to Plymouth Central and caught a train
to Bristol Temple Meads to look for my father, my Celtic,
feckless, handsome father. Her husband. She went to the
department store on Park Street where she'd found out he
worked, and begged him to come back. She *begged*, my mother.
My *mother* begged. And he said, 'No.' He stood in the shadow
of the Victorian buildings on Park Street – where I have since
built decks, built bridges – and he said no. I've never met him
but I have seen photographs and I can imagine him forming
the word 'No', spitting it out on the pavement.

It was Ellen, my mother's closest friend, who told me this
charming vignette. She told me one afternoon when we were
walking the beach in Thurlestone as my mother slept. I'd been
complaining that my mother hadn't spent any time with us,
that she'd just locked herself away in her room. Ellen stopped,
caught my arm and pulled me round to face her.

'John,' Ellen said, 'let your mother alone. Give her some
peace. She needs some time on her own.'

I was cold, I was fourteen, I was scared that my mother
didn't love me any more. I lashed out. 'Why didn't she *make*
my father stay?' I shouted, as sand whipped by January winds
flew around us.

So Ellen told me how my mother had tried to do just
that.

I'm forty years old now and I still haven't fathomed it. My
father left my mother because he was worried that I'd be

imperfect, that I might be deaf or blind or perhaps contorted, crab-like, with webbed feet. Is that sufficient reason? This is the question I ask myself all the time – is it sufficient reason? The answer, just as his was, is 'No'. Because he left before I was even born. He left *while* I was being born, when my mother was in hospital giving birth. I arrived on the eleventh day of the eleventh month, with Scorpio rising to boot, yet even these auspicious signs couldn't persuade him to stay. As I was tussling my way into the world my father was packing his belongings and leaving and when my mother finally made it back to the flat, it was to find him gone. He did, however, have the good manners to return some materials he had taken that didn't belong to him. My mother, balancing me awkwardly on one hip, opened the package he had sent her and the first thing she found was a leaflet on family planning.

It was Ellen who told me this too and I know now she was trying to save me from wasting my life imagining I loved my father, imagining that he deserved to be loved. She failed but at least she tried.

I have many scars – from the Corona bottle, from the various router bits, chisels and drills with which I have wrestled. I look at my body and map out my life by scars. But there are many scars I can't see.

It was months ago that Sonja asked me to tell her the lemonade story; since then she's been distracted, inattentive. Sometimes I see her, as I sit in my truck and she moves around her world; a world of Patum Peperium, Amaretto, Belgian truffles and Parma ham, bread still steaming from Herbert's in Montpelier. The deli does very well, despite my misgivings. Sonja has a handy knack – she buys only cheese that makes her think of silver and burgundy, wine of silk, bread of mares' tail clouds, cold cuts of navy and cotton twills. I hadn't thought of that – that the admixture of senses might be advantageous. But often now when I pass the shop she's not there. Where is she? She has always been the model manager, the first to arrive, the last to leave. She used to snatch her lunch in ten minutes in the stock room, maybe wolfing down a samosa or felafel followed by a slab of chocolate brownie. But now I can't see her when I look for her.

It took three men to pull me off Martin Sawyer's limp body all those years ago, as his blood dribbled slowly over the asphalt of the road in Noss Mayo. Eddie Lamble was long gone. I remember the sound of Martin Sawyer trying to breathe through his mouth, his lips swollen by my fists, as swollen as if they'd been stung by wasps. He looked up at me through closing, purple eyes and sighed and a bubble of blood burst beautifully in the gap between his front teeth, its filmy surface catching the afternoon sun.

Sonja's family are a brooding, blond bunch. I looked forward so much to meeting them, looked forward to impressing them. I wanted to be the attentive son-in-law, mature beyond his years, nurturing and supporting their daughter. They came to visit one Christmas, a couple of years after we were married, and Sonja and I collected them from the station in our second-hand Ford Cortina III estate. I pulled up in front of Temple Meads (trying not to think of the time, twenty-one years before, when my mother had arrived there, preparing herself to beg) and braked in astonishment. There were so many of them, and so many cases. They looked scared, alien in ill-fitting suits and dated skirts. Around them was a lake of luggage.

'Jesus Christ!' I turned to Sonja. 'Are they visiting or defecting?'

'It's the first time they've been away. Don't be rude.' But even she looked a tad glassy-eyed.

It took three trips to transport all the people and cases and boxes. I walked into our tiny flat with the last case and they were all standing in our box-like living room, touching things: ornaments, books, TV, pictures. I thought for a mad moment that they were all *blind*. Why else finger everything? One of Sonja's sisters, Olga, was even touching the walls, turning her fingers round the corners. I decided to take control, slapping my hands together and booming, 'Well, who's for a drink?'

They all stopped their fingering to look at me blankly before turning to Sonja to speak in their own language. I scanned their faces one by one, looking for recognition and found none, so I got a beer from the fridge and went to bed. Hours later Sonja joined me, quite drunk on vodka. She woke me by gently pulling the tip of my beard and kissing me, her tongue hot with lemon-scented raw alcohol.

'Well?' I asked.

'They like you, Special.' She held her hands up to admire the rings she wore – a sure sign of drunkenness.

'How can they? They didn't even speak to me.'

'Well, they don't speak English.'

'Right.'

The next day I went to stay with Ian in his flat. We spent the day fishing at Chew Magna and now that's what I do whenever her family arrive: I make three trips to take them to our house and then I go to stay with Ian. We walk and work, have drinks and visit restaurants. We drive out to Hay-on-Wye, go down to Constantine Bay, maybe go camping in the Gower. It's an easy, silent relationship. Then, when it is time, I go back to the house – which by now smells of black butter, fish and mushroom stew – and run three trips to Temple Meads. Before they slip away, like blond wraiths, Sonja's family bow slightly stiffly towards me and I find myself bowing in return. This exchange is wordless – how could it be otherwise?

One question always bothers me. When I looked at Sonja's family that first time I was struck by how bleached, how angular they all were. Yet Sonja is a luscious woman, with deep blonde hair and grey eyes, her body soft and curved. Did a dog get over the wall? I look at Sonja's mother and her flat, pale blue eyes slide away from my stare.

I've always enjoyed visiting Ian in his workshop; in fact, I go out of my way to drop in on him in his furnace-filled room on Cumberland Road. I like walking in and there he is, stripped to the waist, dripping with sweat, squinting and blinking as it runs into his eyes. He tips his visor on to his forehead, wiping his face with a cloth, and he looks as if he's been wearing the helmet of a diving suit made at the turn of the century, a heavy, curved mask in front of his face.

Today Ian pulls off the visor when I enter and glugs water from a bottle, looking at me strangely, almost speculatively.

'I came to pick up the plans for Hampton Road,' I say. He nods towards the desk and I rummage about among the hammers, bits and tongs until I find the papers. 'When shall I tell her we can start?'

Ian shrugs, wipes his face with a rag. 'Next Wednesday?' He picks up a cold chisel and turns it in his hands. 'Special . . .'

'Yes?'

Ian stares at the blue flame hissing from the solder. 'Nothing. It's nothing.'

'You OK?'

'Yeah, I'm fine.' And I thought he said then, 'It's not me, it's you.' But his lips didn't move.

It was Sonja who taught me to dance. She pulled me to my feet one evening in our first tiny basement flat in Kingsdown, the deposit paid for by my second year of deck-building, and I stood foolish and bear-like as she put a record on the turntable. Then she turned to me and took my hands.

'Watch my feet.' She began to move, graceful and balanced.

I'd always loved to watch her dance but I had never thought to join her.

'Give me your hands,' she said, and took my callused hands in hers. She pulled me to her and guided me round the room. She smiled up at me and pressed herself against the length of my body. Gradually I learned to follow her, to mirror her movements as she danced to the music, to the rhythms.

'There,' she said, laughing, 'you *can* dance, you see?'

I felt stupidly accomplished, proud of doing something a five-year-old could do. That's how Sonja made me feel. We've danced through our life together: tiny, crab-like dances in our early flats and houses, then swirling across the vast polished floors of this house, from room to room, our feet synchronised, hands locked. I've sometimes wondered what people think as they glance in through the windows to see us swooping about, laughing and giggling.

But it doesn't matter now because we haven't danced for months. We haven't really even talked for months. My mind composes words, then the doubts I have about Sonja and her desires rush in, displacing those words, and I stay silent. Sometimes I think she's watching me as I stand with my back

to her, making coffee, slicing bread, reading a letter. I think
she's watching me and I don't know why.

I went to Cumberland Road again today. The tide was low
and the riverbeds were thick with brown mud, stinking in the
sun. It was early on the morning of the equinox, already too
hot. Ian's door was locked so I found my little-used key and
went in to look for the transformer to take over to Hampton
Road. There was a note on the worktop, held down by a
twisted lump of steel and as I reached for it a hollowness
inflated in my heart. I paused, waiting for the feeling to pass,
knowing it wouldn't. I took the note to the door to read it
in the sunlight.

> Special – gone to Walcotts in Bath to collect the pillars
> for H. Road. Can you call Mrs Richards re the damage to
> the door? The team at Alma Vale Rd need 2 x 20m ext.
> leads. I tried to say it yesterday but couldn't. Maybe this
> is better – I think Sonja's having an affair. Sorry. Ian

The hollowness was still there as I thought of the foundations
dug out behind the house at Alma Vale, thought about having
to go to Jewson's to buy the extension leads. I looked again
at the diarrhoea mud of the riverbanks and I knew Ian
was right.

I drove up Whiteladies Road, parked the truck on a
double yellow line and stood looking at the delicatessen.
The Labradors were bumbling about, plump bellies rubbing,
tongues slapping at the water. Sonja was laughing with a
customer as she wrapped a round of cheese and set the
package on the counter. She turned and called out to an
assistant and he laughed too. Sonja was glowing, content in

her space. I realised I hadn't seen her laugh for an age; when
she was with me she wasn't like this. She looked up, saw me
and her face changed, doubt drowned her eyes.

A traffic warden tapped me on the shoulder and pointed
to my truck. 'Is this yours?'

I nodded.

'You'd better move it.'

I shrugged and turned back to the shop to watch Sonja as he
wrote me a ticket and slapped it on the windshield. He walked
away, giving the waistband of his trousers a self-satisfied tug.

'How did you know?' I ask Ian, as we sit outside the
Kensington, pints of Smiles' warming in late-afternoon sun.

'I drive around more than you do. I've often seen them
together. I didn't think anything of it the first few times.
Then it was obvious. I saw them outside Rocinantes and it
was obvious. Something about the way they were sitting, the
way they were talking. I don't know.'

'Well, who is he?'

'How the fuck do I know?' Ian is irritable because he is
shamed by being the messenger.

'Shit.' My hands are shaking, and I touch the lemonade
scar, bumpy and numb beneath my hair. I touch it to calm
myself, a nervous tic that connects me to childhood. I realise
I'm scared. 'I'm scared,' I say. 'I don't know what to do.'

'Ask her about it.'

'How can I ask Sonja that? She won't answer.'

'Ask her anyway.'

And of course I go home and say nothing. Any words I
can conjure up seem unequal to the task of asking Sonja. So
we sit in silence, reading, as the sun falls behind the house,
leaving the deck in shade.

*   *   *

I'm sitting in Ian's car, staring at the pedestrians toiling
up Park Street and along the Triangle. Some are laughing,
walking arm in arm, and I wonder how they do that. How
can they do that when I've forgotten how? Ian slows down
and touches my arm. He says nothing but points across the
road to Brown's and there's Sonja, sitting out on the terrace,
at one of the brushed zinc café tables, holding the hand of a
blond, clean-shaven man.

'Stop!' I shout, and Ian swerves into the kerb, parks
outside the JCR. We sit, saying nothing, watching my wife
with another man. Even with her sunglasses on I'm aware of
Sonja's grey eyes looking at him. There's something strange
about the way he moves, the way he angles his head towards
her, something awry about the way her hand drifts towards
his and brushes it, guides it almost. They gather up bags and
stand, their drinks finished, and a yellow Labrador hauls itself
to its feet, shakes and looks up at the man, feebly wagging
its tail. He feels for the clip on the dog's yellow jacket and
takes hold of the harness.

'Jesus Christ,' I whisper, 'he's blind. He's fucking *blind*.
What does she think she's doing?'

Ian shrugs his massive black shoulders. 'Well, you're deaf,'
he signs.

JOAN

3 April 1999

Spring's late this year and it's very cold tonight. I sit here wrapped in a blanket on my deck, writing in the light-circle of a storm lamp, the ever-present bottle of whisky at my feet. I sit and look out over Thurlestone's moonlit bay, the arch and its shadow dark against the shifting, constantly fracturing silver sea. All round the house behind me I can hear the sibilance of young leaves in the chestnuts, feel the spreading gloom of the plane trees. This is what I do every night: write my journal and drink glass after glass of fine whisky, listening to my trees grow old.

And I wonder, Was I a good mother? I don't know. I really don't know. I can say that I tried to be, that I tried to be the best I could be. But I'm not sure it was enough. When I see John now, which is not often, I wonder at the distance between us. I wonder if that distance, that gulf, opened Moses-like when I walked out of the hospital and he started to scream and I didn't go back to comfort him, to fill his silence. I don't know. I look back at *my* mother's life and it's so alien that I can't even begin to decide whether I was as maternal, as comforting. I was alone, with a son who changed in a moment from a wild, almost dangerous, boy into a nervous, deaf adolescent. I didn't know what to do, and who was I going to ask? Now they have all these help groups, counsellors, support networks, psychotherapists.

Thirty years ago the only people I could have called to say that my son hadn't spoken to me in two months, that he cried and whimpered in his sleep, that his father hadn't visited . . . well, what's the point? I could have talked all night but only to the men in white coats.

What worries me more than these memories, and they worry me enough, is that John seems to be retreating from the world again. The way he did in hospital when he looked at my face and turned his back.

20 July 1976

That policeman who came to the cottage a few years ago, the day when John broke Martin Sawyer's nose, was, if I remember rightly, more interested in me than in John's misdemeanours. They usually were. John sat on the kitchen stool, his legs swinging, an ice pack against his eye, and ignored the policeman's monotonal voice rambling on and on about other, better ways of settling disputes, as John looked sceptical, staring at the floor and grunting every now and then. Finally the man ground to a halt and made the mistake of ruffling John's hair, saying he hoped never to have to see him again. John simply looked at him, making it plain that the feeling was mutual.

'Perhaps we could have a word in private, ma'am?' the policeman asked.

I sent John out into the garden and sat on the still-warm stool. 'Yes?'

'This was a serious assault for someone so young. He's lucky he's too young to be charged.'

I said nothing.

'Do you know why it happened? What started it?'

'No – John won't say.' But I thought I could guess.

'Well, let's hope he's learned his lesson, let's hope it doesn't happen again.' He glanced at his notebook. 'It's not the first time we've been round, is it?'

'No.'

'In fact this is the third time this year.'

'Yes.'

'I believe you live alone.'

'No, I live with my son.'

The policeman glanced through the kitchen window at John, who was squatting down by the small pond in the corner of the garden, swirling the water with his hands. 'I meant that you don't have a husband.'

'That's right.'

'Perhaps he needs a man around, a role model, if you like.'

'Possibly.'

The two of us watched John in the garden.

'The victim is badly injured, as you know. He's sustained a broken nose and fractured jaw as well as a number of abrasions.'

'Martin Sawyer isn't a victim, he's a bully. And I know that you've often been called round to his house, too. In my opinion, if John hit him, he deserved it.'

'Nevertheless . . .'

I stood up. 'I'm sorry to be rude, but I've got lots of marking to do.' I followed the man's dark blue uniform through the tiny hallway, and he stopped, as I knew he would, at the front door, turning his ludicrous helmet in his hands.

'I was wondering if, maybe, you'd like to have a drink sometime? Perhaps we could go to the Ship for a meal?'

'Thank you, but I'm very busy at the moment.' I watched his face change as he tried, tried so hard, to think of a diversionary tactic, a means of lulling me into saying yes, and failing.

'Maybe some other time?'

'Thank you for taking the time to come round.' I nudged him through the door and closed it behind him.

I went back to the kitchen and poured a drink before going out to the garden. 'John, tell me what happened.'

He looked at me, his always startling face unbalanced by a swollen, black eye. 'Nothing.'

'Don't be stupid. The police don't come round for nothing.'

'He was saying stuff I didn't like, so I hit him.'

'Well, that sounds really intelligent.'

John shrugged. 'I'd do it again.'

'Well, try not to, will you? Every time a policeman comes round here he asks me out. It's getting boring.'

And John laughed.

I sat in the cluttered living room after John had gone to bed, the sky still blue at ten o'clock, marking undergraduate essays. But my mind wasn't on it, my heart wasn't in it. The ramblings of eighteen-year-old would-be philosophers, their minds too consumed by ego even to contemplate their insignificance in the face of metaphysics, frankly bored me. I sat back in the chair, poured another drink and thought of John. I knew he meant what he'd said – that he would do it again. And I had a good idea of what, exactly, Martin Sawyer had said to deserve it. Every time this happened, every time John defended my reputation, a policeman came to my house, remarked on my being single and implied that he could become the male of the household. It didn't seem to occur to them that John had a father somewhere. Dai Davies, whose last word to me had been 'No'.

And I'm thinking of what that boy is like now as he studies in the school at Exeter, towering over the other pupils, constantly frowning, his blue-blue eyes uncertain. I suspect he's too nervous, too unsure of himself, these days even to contemplate burying his fist in someone's face, however much he must want to.

23 June 1974

That Saturday afternoon, when John appeared with his sandy plank in the cottage at Noss Mayo, I was sitting at the back of the house in the garden, drinking wine and reading Kant inattentively (is there any other way of reading his impenetrable text?) as I thought of seeing Miles Brandrin that night. I remember listening to John hauling the wood through the house and out into the garden, trailing sand and sea-water. He'd found it, half buried, on the banks of the Yealm near Wembury, and dragged it miles to show me. His face was alive, his eyes dazzling blue, his black hair matted. He lugged it across the grass and dropped it at my feet.

'Look, look what I found! How old do you think it is? Is it hundreds of years old? It looks like it. It might be worth hundreds of pounds.' He knelt down and rubbed the sand from a faded, hand-painted word: 'Merboy'. I noticed then that the veins on his hands and forearms were beginning to bulge, like small, green ropes under his brown skin.

John frowned. 'What's that mean? Merboy?'

'Well, he's like a mermaid, but instead of being a girl he's a boy. It's a boy with a fish's tail instead of legs, covered with silver scales and little fins. A boy who lives in the sea, who swims with dolphins and seals.'

And he looked up and smiled. 'That's me.' Then he sat suddenly and slumped against my legs, rubbing the painted word.

'Had a good day?' I asked, untangling his hair with my fingers.

Merboy nodded as he watched a yacht easing its way to a pontoon strung along the middle of the Yealm. 'I'm going to be a sailor and have my own boat. And I'm going to have air tanks and go diving. I'm going to sail round the world.'

'I know.'

The two of us sat in the hot sun, Merboy dreaming of circling the globe as I dreamed of Miles.

15 April 1999

I'm trying to read in my journal what I wrote about when I first saw John in the hospital. I can barely make it out, my writing is so spidery-drunk. I try to break the cycle – try to avoid the whisky and the introspection that follows. But it always catches up with me. This journal – it's the only thing I talk to now apart from Ellen and I don't talk to her often enough. Not a journal, really. More a memoir. An *aide-memoire* for the times when whisky has destroyed my memories. I have a mound of notebooks in the house which I've filled over the years, filled with trivia, with ideas, snippets from newspapers, letters. Who will ever read them? Why am I preserving my life? I write because, like John, I find it hard to speak to people. We're still so damaged.

There was a wild storm today, gales and lashing rain. Some tiles were lifted and a branch from the plane tree was torn off. It smashed the cloches as it fell. I watched the clouds scud across the bay, so low they brushed the hills. The rain pelted against the windows of the conservatory, endless, a river moving over glass. The sea was grey and white, rocking backwards and forwards, like water in a vast bowl, blankets of spume moving with it. I stared at that grey and white world for hours, and the colours inside the house, when I finally turned away, were so loud they hurt my eyes.

27 June 1999

I drove up to Oxfordshire this weekend to see Ellen. She's still so good for me because even now, after all this time, when I'm with her I don't drink so much. She stays up with me, talks and plays cards, reads, whatever it takes to match my going to bed. She doesn't say I can't drink, has never said that, but she knows I respect her too much to render myself speechless with alcohol. So I have a few glasses, eke them out over the evening, fighting the desire to tip the bottle on its end. We talk but we skirt subjects – her dead husband, my deaf son, her cancer, my face. These are not cheerful subjects for conversation. Instead we discuss exhibitions, books, travel, politics, films – Teflon, hard-edged subjects which omit the personal. Of course, there is the matter of conviction, of preference, of choice. But these things are not what Ellen and I would consider *personal*.

Usually I arrive on a Friday evening and we sit in the kitchen by the Aga and eat a meal prepared and cooked by Ellen: baked beetroot or baby scallops in a cream sauce, corn-on-the-cob oozing organic butter, or poached wild salmon with dill. This Friday it was fresh tuna and lime with a green salad. Ellen cares about food, so I eat, apparently appreciative. What I care about is the two bottles of wine we allow ourselves. How this routine has come about is a mystery, a ritual with no foundation. We drink two bottles of wine on the first night I arrive. Of course, I drink the lion's share but I'm allowed no more. Ellen follows me up the stairs and wishes me good night, fussing until I'm in bed. Anywhere else and I would slip from the bed and go to the drinks cabinet in the library but not at Ellen's. Never again.

The first time I stayed overnight at Ellen's, not long after she'd left the hospital, I did just that. I was thirty-eight years old and I crept from my room, like a schoolgirl, looking into the unfamiliar darkness, an adventure looming, a deception forming. I felt my way down the unfamiliar, crooked stairs, my hands running over the knobbled, sandy walls of the Cotswold house until my toes found carpet and I shuffled through the dark hallway to the library, hoping the dogs would ignore me. One flapped a lazy tongue at my ankle as I passed him sleeping. I knew that in the corner of the room was the matte black triangular corner cabinet left to Ellen by her grandmother and I made my way towards it, only to slam my knee into the corner of a marble-top coffee table. I hopped and rubbed my leg until the pain had passed, then opened the door to the cabinet. I found a bottle of Canadian Crown Royal whisky and slipped it out of its mauve velvet bag before finding a glass. Just one glass, I thought, as the sweet, mashed alcohol hit the back of my throat.

It was, of course, Ellen who woke me, wordlessly, the next morning. She shook my shoulder and stood over me as I surfaced from the lake of fermented grain in which I had temporarily drowned. Ellen is a tall, rangy woman, with one breast and a grip of steel. She grabbed the shoulder of my dressing-gown, pulled me to my feet and dragged me through

the house – I began to appreciate just how spacious it was – and
then she threw me outside the back door, on to the stone path.
I tripped and fell, grazing the heels of my hands and tearing
my knees. She stood in the doorway and in her hand she held
the empty Crown Royal bottle. She lifted it in such a way
that its curving belly caught the morning sun and shimmered.
Then she opened her fingers. The bottle smashed on the path,
scattering shards of glass around me. To be honest I was a tad
touchy about that – about shards of glass flying around me.
Ellen threw a dustpan and brush at me. 'Clear it up,' she said,
and closed the door.

I've never done that again – sneaked through her house to
drink her dry. Because I now respect her too much to do that;
perhaps I respect her fury too much to do it again. I don't
know. She allows me to drink in moderation because, she
says, she can't stop me drinking. And she's right. So, better
to have a few to take off the edge and then go to bed, policed
by my own contrition. Also, she points out, she herself has
a cocktail of drugs she must take each day. As she says, not
by choice but they're still drugs. Seems churlish to deny me
mine. In moderation.

I did eventually ease myself to my feet that morning,
my cut hands and knees smarting, to sweep the shards
and splinters of glass from the path into a dustpan and
dump it in the rubbish bin, whimpering and hating myself
for the sound. I walked slowly back up the path, dressed
in a flimsy, blood-, whisky- and ash-stained dressing-gown,
to the stable door that had been slammed on me and
knocked tentatively. Ellen threw it open, still angered, and
pointed to the sink, where plasters, Savlon and bandages had
been laid out. I dressed my minor wounds as she stood at
the Aga, furiously swirling bacon and mushrooms round a

griddle. She slammed down a plate of tomatoes, toast, egg, sausage, bacon and mushrooms, next to a glass of freshly squeezed orange juice and brewed coffee, single breast jiggling alarmingly beneath her brushed cotton shirt. There was just the one plate. Now, drunks don't eat but I sat there, newly plastered, and ate that breakfast as Ellen leaned against the silver bar of the Aga, her tightly held mug of coffee steaming. I ate the food and drank the juice, held the coffee cup in my hands, sitting at the scarred, stained kitchen table, yearning for a cigarette.

Ellen looked at me, her face set. 'You can only come here if you promise never to do that again.'

'But I didn't intend—'

'Promise.'

'I never meant—'

'Will you do that again if you visit me?'

'No.'

'What? I can't hear you.'

I pushed the chair back and stood opposite Ellen, the crockery rattling on the table. 'Don't ever say that.'

Still Ellen stared. 'Will you ever come back here and creep around my house stealing my booze?'

'No!' I shouted.

'In that case let's go for a walk.'

And I never have stolen her whisky again. Nor do I drink too much in front of her. I don't know what Ellen did to me the day she threw me out the back door but somehow she established a benchmark in my sodden mind.

So – now I eat the wondrous meal on Friday night, eyeing the wine meanwhile. I sleep fitfully because I don't have enough whisky or gin jumping round my blood, and then, after Saturday-morning newspapers, shared crosswords and coffee, we pull on torn, stiff, unwaxed Barbours, ill-fitting Hunter boots and walk the fields around Ellen's house, with the ever-amenable, ankle-licking dogs trotting and sniffing behind.

Ellen – she is tall and rangy, full of energy, full of information, full of good humour and barbed opinions. She makes me laugh and she doesn't give a monkey's fart what I look like. She makes me indifferent to my appearance when I'm with her. Perhaps we should have been lovers, partners, but the idea is laughable. It's never been an option, because after a couple of weeks together we have grated each other so raw that our parting is a relief. Between us there's so much unsaid, so much untouched, that the conversations about the Arthurian legend, the Algonquin Circle, the premium growing conditions for tarragon, wear thin enough to reveal the skeletal hinterland of our lives; their bleached bones, picked clean of carrion, are exposed. That is what is personal. Not religious or political beliefs, nor love and its loss, nor the travails of companionship. What is left is absence. The absence of our husbands, the absence of her breast, of my beauty, of her child, of my Merboy. So many things have disappeared that were once there. We don't often talk about the things that aren't there. We don't often talk about absences. But this weekend we did just that.

We'd tramped the entire Cotswolds on Saturday, or so it seemed to me. It was probably a four-, maybe five-mile walk around Chipping Camden, punctuated by coffee and a brandy in a dark, firelit pub. We were lying on settees, reading, in what it pleases Ellen to call 'the music room' although it has neither, being the smallest room in the house and having no instruments or sound system.

'Ellen,' I said, 'I think John's in trouble.'

She took off her glasses and folded them carefully, slipped them into a case. Sat up and looked at me. 'Why?'

'Because he's not talking. I know he finds it hard to talk but it's a sign when it drops off the scale.'

'What does he say when he does talk?'

'Nothing. He talks about nothing.'

'What do you think is the problem?'

'Sonja. I don't think it's going well. I'm sorry.'

'Don't apologise. Do you want another drink?'

I knew that this was Ellen's way of saying that I could talk, get drunk if I needed to; even get personal if necessary.

She went to the cabinet in the library and brought both of us a drink and then she put a half-bottle of J&B next to my glass. I smiled at her and vowed to myself that I would take only a couple of inches from the bottle.

'So,' Ellen said, 'you think John's in trouble.'

'Yes. He came to visit me a couple of weeks ago and, I don't know – his eyes were different. They were clouded or something. Shifty. And every time I asked him about Sonja he hunched. I know he hunches a lot. But this was different. And then I drove up to see him on spec last week and I went to the deli. He was parked outside, just staring at her. He looked murderous, mad. Barking mad. I knew if I went up to him he'd just ignore me. It was like he couldn't see anyone but her. Something's going on. What should I do?' I twisted on the settee and looked at her.

'Ask her about it.'

'I can't. For Chrissake, I don't feel easy asking her if she takes sugar in her coffee. How can I ask if she's having an affair? Because that's what it must be. It can't be John.'

'Why not? Why can't it be John?'

'Because I know what it's like to be deceived and he's got

the look of someone who's being deceived. I look at him and I see the expression I wore for years. If it was John who was running around, he'd at least look guilty, or maybe I'd have surprised him looking happy and he doesn't. Anyway, he's not capable of doing that, of cheating on her. You know him as well as I do. His life runs on rails, that's what he wants. He's incapable of sleeping with someone else. Sometimes I think he feels he's still being punished and he still doesn't know what for. And, come to that, neither do I.'

'Well, what can you do? If you can't speak to her, what can you do? Joan, John's forty years old. Shit happens. You can't see your children through everything. Let him go. I've spent my life telling you to let him go. John's one of the biggest men I've ever met, in so many ways. Let him go. You can't anticipate everything.'

And this is where Ellen and I stall, because she lost her husband after four years of marriage and her unborn child at the same time. Strangely, even though I didn't know Ellen then, I can picture her in her pale yellow clapboard Connecticut home, the pillared gallery running three-quarters of the way round the house, Christmas lights flashing at long mock-Georgian sash windows. I imagine her younger, more hopeful self waiting by the door for her husband to reappear after a day of blue-fishing out of Atlantic City; imagine Ellen dipping back into the kitchen to stir and baste, then reappearing on the gallery to watch the dark road, waiting for the sweep of headlights. Maybe she wore an apron. Maybe she wore a sou'wester and oilskins. I don't know and she's never told me. But I do know from the few evenings when she got personal that she spent the late afternoon and early evening wrapping Christmas presents for Matt, her husband. She sat awkwardly on the carpet of the newly decorated nursery, pregnancy making her clumsy, cutting and sealing paper, tying ribbons, trying not to look at the clock. Later she lit the dozen tiny gold candles on the green and red wooden candelabra on the window sill and she sat silently in their pale light waiting for him.

Eventually she heard a car slithering on the icy roads nearby and heaved herself to her feet to go down the stairs. She waited by the door as the evening slipped swiftly past and turned to night. Headlights appeared at last, bucking on the long, private drive. Concern died in her, distilled to anger at the lateness of the hour, but then she noticed the dead blue lights on the roof of the car, the blackness and whiteness of it. The unfamiliarity of it. The car stopped on the gravel in front of the door, stopped gently, not spitting stones. Two officers climbed out and she knew from the heaviness of their bodies, by the mud-heavy way they tucked their caps under their arms, not looking at her, she knew why they were looking at the trees, at the lake, at their boots, looking at anything but her.

'Excuse me, ma'am,' the older officer said. Ellen stared at his cropped, grey hair. 'Are you Ellen Matthiesen?' he asked, and at that moment her abdominal muscles slammed shut like a vice round her rounded belly.

Ellen told me this many years ago.

She also told me that her labour lasted three days; three days she spent breathing deeply, sweating, her hands clamped round steel rails, screaming and bellowing. Three days birthing her already dead child. When it was over, when the drama was done and she was reduced to a childless, husbandless woman slowly, or, rather, very quickly, going out of her mind, the grey-haired policeman visited her in hospital. Ellen was lying in bed, scrubbed and scraped clean, staring at the sky. He came into the room, holding his cap, and said nothing. Then he went to Ellen, wrapped his arms round her and held her against his big chest and she held on to him as if she was drowning. He tried to soothe her, stroked her hair. Apparently he was crying too as he held her, disbelieving that so much could happen to a woman in one night.

Ellen and I don't play the oneupmanship-in-misery game but if we did I think she would win hands down.

'I persuaded Matt to go fishing so I could wrap his Christmas presents. I didn't know he'd never come back.'

'I missed the turning over Battersea Bridge. I didn't know it would make a difference.'

Small choices.

10 July 1999

'Ask her,' Ellen says about Sonja. Ask her if she's having an affair, if she's going to leave John. How can I possibly do that? Sonja is a closed circle which spins in its own orbit. After that first night when I met her – when I looked at her and knew something was wrong – I never asked her again what exactly synaesthesia means to her, what it does to her. After she looked at me and said, 'It's not a disability,' and stared my drunken self down with those beautiful grey eyes I just couldn't ask about it again. Is it her foreignness that's her defence? I don't know. I can feel the splintered planks of the deck beneath me, taste whisky burning my tongue. I can see the arch in moonlight, smell my own sweat this hot June night. I'm listening to a car crunch down the lane, changing gear, brakes squealing. What would she experience in my place? I have no idea.

Yet she allows John into her closed circle, allows him

to orbit her world with her. He found a way in and I never thought anyone else ever would. But now I'm sure someone else has. If I could just see her for a minute, a moment, I could look into her eyes and I would know. She never met Merboy, of course, and I wonder what she would have made of him – my salty wild boy. Sometimes I wonder if she is touched by John – if he stirs pity in her. God, I hope not. He doesn't deserve to be pitied. None of us does.

15 January 1977

I went into the attic today to put last year's journals into their box, and I came across that record player I bought John, a present for passing his eleven-plus exam. It looked so small – a brown and black plastic box without any speakers, just a small grille on the side. It only played seven-inch singles and it had a small disc to put over the spindle of the turntable if the record didn't have a centre. I'd forgotten those odd plastic things, like curved triangles, that you had to put in the middle of singles. You had to snap them in with your thumbs. He played the most awful music and it got worse as he got older. I'd give him pocket money, maybe two shillings or half a crown, for washing the car, cutting the grass, or tidying his room, and he'd catch a bus into Plymouth and buy singles he'd play over and over. The cottage too small to get away from the noise. There was one – 'In the Summertime' – that he played again and again, singing along endlessly. It drove me mad. Then, when we moved to this house, I threw away all the records, put the player in the attic and he never asked about it. Why would he?

10 December 1999

The papers are full of end-of-millennium predictions and speculations. The television when I watch it, which is rarely, focuses on nothing else. End of year, end of century, end of millennium. Everyone trying to whip up some *fin de siècle* spirit. There are constant reviews of the century – the Great War, the moon landings, the nuclear mushroom cloud. Sometimes I wish Einstein had been a watchmaker. What madness, really, all of it. Strange, though, to think that I lost one of those years, a whole year, when I lived in that flat in Lambeth, visiting John in hospital every day. My world shrank to catheters and drips, lino floors and endless nights of waiting within the same four beige walls. England joined Europe, Nixon was re-elected, the Israeli Olympic compound was stormed. Ezra Pound and Harry Truman died. Burglars broke into the Watergate complex. The Americans dropped napalm in Vietnam, Northern Ireland smouldered and caught fire. And I stared at John's back for months as the world exploded outside those walls.

JOHN

I lost my hearing on my thirteenth birthday, the day after I discovered that hearts could be broken. My mother woke me at four o'clock that morning, the November sky midnight black, the air still tangy with cordite from the weekend of Guy Fawkes Night. I trod on Tub the Ted when I got up, hopping from foot to foot on the freezing floor. My mother had packed the suitcases the night before and as she tidied the kitchen I splashed some water on my face and dressed, still yawning. My mother made a flask of tea and I carried a bottle of lemonade – very gingerly – out to the car. It was cold, not quite freezing. She idled the car, the engine loud in the pre-dawn black morning, while I fetched the cases and Toulouse, the cat, nearly tripped me, squawking when I stepped on his tail. I forgot to duck as I left the cottage and smacked my forehead on the door lintel, not for the first time. I remember every detail of that early morning, not because of what happened or what we saw but because of what I *heard*. I never thought to turn and look at the cottage, perhaps wave as we left, because I didn't know then that I wouldn't see it again.

The grey, bullet-nosed car with its split windscreen scrunched down the lane running parallel to the creek, swooped round the hairpin of Back Road and groaned up the hill. I remember the whir of tyre rubber, the squeak of the car window being lowered dragging rubber the wrong way, the sound of the gear shaft shifting. Even now I replay my mother's sneezes, her coughs, the voice of the man in the café where we stopped for bacon butties and tea outside Ilminster. I hear my own voice chattering, although the memory grows hazy, and the music . . . sad, lonely songs of the early morning, breaking up on the ether. There's one song I can hear whenever I want because it plays in an endless loop in my memory – after all, it was the last song I ever heard. I don't even know who sang it – a woman's voice. The lyrics still make my chin tremble even now. I can conjure the refrain of 'Is That All There Is?' sung to a wandering string accompaniment. But what's the point of finding it? I'll never be able to hear it again.

My mother and I drove to London, giggling and playing around in the old Morris Minor, singing along to the radio. We were going to sightsee in London and to stay with her friends in Earl's Court for the weekend, sleeping on a sofa in the same room where I had waited for people's hearts to stop. The journey to London was a long one then, single-lane roads and small Devon and Somerset towns to be negotiated, and as the dark miles passed I looked out of the window, chewing my lip, still worrying about my heart breaking.

We drove up the A3, through Roehampton and Wandsworth, my mother increasingly unsure in the heavy traffic. She planned to turn over Battersea Bridge but missed it, went over Albert instead, coasted up Oakley Street, her frown deepening, the middle finger of her left hand constantly touching and pushing the choke button. This drove me crazy, this sub-conscious tic of hers. The only reason she did it was because when I was a young child my idea of a good time was to pull it right out when she wasn't looking. Even now, twenty-eight years after that day, she still does it. It earths her.

'Well, well,' she said, 'howsabout we go to the multi-storey car park near Gloucester Road? Then I don't have to bother about the one-way streets around Earl's Court. We can hop on the tube or a bus, then pick the car up this evening and drive over. What d'you think, pumpkin?'

I hated it when she called me that, and now I would give all I have just to hear the word. 'OK – as long as we can go on a bus.' I loved the Routemaster buses, loved swinging on the white spiral plastic-clad poles on the platform, swinging out into London.

'Hmm. I think I head for Sydney Street.' She turned right on to King's Road and I watched the crowds. People shouted across the street, whistled and hummed. The cars hooted, buses rumbled. I was part of the world. Music pumped from clothes shops. I swivelled round to look at the front of a shop where Levi's jeans hung. I was getting my first pair that day, as my birthday present. A rite of passage – the passage from child to teenager when the cheap, nasty jeans of youth were cast aside and Levi's replaced them.

'What a madhouse,' my mother muttered, as we pulled, at last, into the ugly concrete box of the car park. The man on the radio announced it was eleven o'clock and the two minutes' silence began, during which we were to remember the war dead. I saw people stop in the streets and lower their heads; even London itself seemed to quieten a little. We collected a ticket from the machine and the bar rattled upwards. She was about to turn up the concrete spiral to the next storey when I spotted a car pulling out a couple of lanes down on the ground floor. I flapped my hand. 'There, there.'

'Oh, well spotted, pumpkin!' and my mother smiled her wonderful smile.

I remember every word of this inane exchange because it

was the last I ever heard. Hardly Homeric. Every day I wonder what would have happened if I hadn't seen that car pulling out of that space. We'd have been moving upwards, moving away, climbing the spiral. I wonder what would have happened if my mother hadn't missed the turn over Battersea Bridge. Because the manner of living seconds and minutes mattered, although we didn't know it then.

My mother pulled into the vacant space and stretched, rolling her head on her neck. My heart thumped as I pictured the shops on King's Road in which, somewhere, there was a pair of Levi's waiting for me. I opened the car door, climbed out and stretched. My mother was rootling in her handbag looking for her brass, circular compact. She found it and began to dab at her upper lip in the rear-view mirror as music burst out again on the radio, the two-minute silence at an end.

The curious fact about bombs is that your experience of them is over before the sound waves hit you. No matter how close you are – and I was close – the blast of them is the last thing you experience. Must have been the last sound I ever heard and yet I have no memory of it. My eardrums caved in like the wooden coastal shacks of Japan in the path of a tsunami; they folded and fragmented, floated away down my middle ear, sleek and thin as onion skin. Another curious fact is that your mind and your brain don't know what to do with the information they're receiving about this event – an event so violent, so unexpected. It has no referents, no previous experiences of same. When the world shunted and blew apart, as I thought of Levi's jeans, I didn't know what was happening. I was thirteen years old exactly – what did I know of Sinn Fein? Of Orangemen? What did I know of the barbed wire circling Belfast and the British soldiers crawling, helmeted and fearful, within it? The Celts and the Picts still at it.

I was hurled against the car, which was turning, crumpling in the same direction as I was travelling, slamming my face into jagged metal. Mortar and concrete blocks showered down. A vast, solid section of the ceiling fell and landed on the overturned car, saving us from the cascade of mortar, the catherine wheel of concrete. I was wedged in the space beneath the ceiling, pressed against the chassis, and the exhaust pipe burned the skin on my arm as I lay there, deaf, bewildered and thirteen. My mother was apparently mewing like a kitten, the mirror of the compact embedded in her hand, the glass of the windshield embedded in her face.

The car windows saved my mother's eardrums: they took the force of the blast and imploded with it. She told me once that she lay there, blinded by blood, and heard something of the aftermath. She described it as the dripping of buildings: the fluttering of fragile things, the slump of dangling lumps of concrete, the slithering of broken glass over dust. And it goes on and on. You can, apparently, hear it over the sirens of the emergency services shrieking through the streets, racing to save you. It goes on for hours. There are some objects that are blown apart, some that fly – fire-extinguishers, doors, lift cages and the contents of people's cars, the contents of their lives. Cases, books, clothes and shoes, briefcases and tool-kits, spare tyres and documents, soft toys, blankets, books, letters and notes. These are the things that slither for hours, fragments of lives slipping through debris.

My mother was trapped by twisted metal, imprisoned by the car she loved, her blood pumping through a hundred deep wounds, blinded by blood, temporarily slightly deafened. She called out to me and of course I didn't hear her. I know I cried out too. But we couldn't *hear* each other. I could smell something sharp and seared, an intense, foul perfume. It was

the skin of my inner arm smouldering. My mother thought
I was dead and kept struggling with the weight of tons of
concrete to come to me, to soothe my way out of this world,
whimpering the whole time.

They freed her first, hours later, cut her from the car and
put her on a stretcher to take her to the hospital but she
raved so long and loud (she had no idea how loudly she was
raving) that they tended her there as she waited for me to
be released. I was dragged out of my concrete jungle limp,
broken and confused. Bloodied and very, very bowed. She
says that she looked at my eyes through her slashed lids and
knew something was wrong. My eyes were too bright, as if they
were compensating for something, roving over the aftermath.
We were both yelling incoherently, our lives already changed
beyond recognition.

I spent more than a year in Tommy's. Thirteen months – it
was a tenth of my short life. I slept for weeks as the operations
and anaesthetics wore off, my young body fighting the damage.
And once I had groggily recovered from one operation, I was
wheeled into the theatre again, my mind, my body groaning,
for yet another. I didn't see my mother for weeks but they
were weeks I didn't remember.

When she was eventually wheeled on to my ward I didn't
recognise her at first: she was thin and pale, her sad calves
sagging on her legs, unused and uncared-for. But it was her
face that made me turn my back and face the wall. It was a
maze of scars, a pitted landscape of flesh. Her eyebrows were
twisted by damage, her mouth rearranged by scissions. My
mother had been beautiful and now she looked flayed, so I
turned my back and faced the wall. Then I couldn't even see
her asking me questions.

*   *   *

I watch my wife steady the Blind Man's arm as his dog
manoeuvres him down the crowded steps outside Brown's.
I turn to Ian in the truck and sign, 'I mean that he can't even
see Sonja – can't see her beauty. At least I can do that.' Ian and
I have a habit of signing when the emotional heat is on full.

'What else do you do?' he signs in return.

'I love her.'

Ian passes a hand over his other closed fist: 'Not enough.'
He puts the truck in gear and pulls away from the kerb as the
traffic warden who ticketed me outside Sonja's deli watches
us, confused by the flying fingers.

When I was lying in my bed in St Thomas' Hospital, when I
was not in a theatre, in a surgery, in a bathroom, I thought of
my father. I was only thirteen but I knew that our pictures, our
names, would have been in the papers, on television. But he
still hadn't come. He had left me twice. His absence was twice
noted. Why didn't he come? He must have read about the
bombing, must have seen pictures of the aftermath. Perhaps
the fact we were still drawing breath eased his conscience? I
don't know.

They tried to repair my ears, tried to build me new eardrums. But this was nearly thirty years ago and the techniques
weren't as sophisticated as they are now. They cut my ears
off and with an uncluttered approach to my middle ear they
tried to fashion drums from other soft tissue but the new
tissue became infected and the operation failed again and
again. And, of course, the German measles during my ruined
mother's pregnancy had done some damage – I had a degree
of congenital nerve deafness. Which at least gave everyone –
the nurses, the surgeons, my father – an out, an excuse, a
justification for failure.

The skin grafts on my back, which took the blast, are clumsy but painless. The work on my face, which was slammed into the crumpling door of the Morris Minor as it turned like a wind-blown piece of paper, is better but not smooth and that's why I wear a beard. My scalp is a maze of healed skin. I can indeed chart my life's course by the scars I bear but, as I have said, some of them are unseen.

Of course, I can't forgive them. Because it was, perhaps, at that moment, when my world blew apart, that I became essentially heartless. As the turn of the century approaches I read about the Secretary of State for Northern Ireland trying to deal with the stalling peace process and I think: Fuck you. All these years – twenty-eight to be precise – and nothing's changed. Paisley is still bawling, the Taoiseach is still arguing, Gerry Adams is still sweet-talking the US President. And I can't hear any of them. I have to read the newspaper reports of their inflexible exchanges because I can't hear them. They offered us compensation, the English government, and my mother took it.

Tell me, how do you compensate for the loss of trust? For the essential loss of a mother? For the loss of some of your face and all of your hearing? For the loss twice over of a father who never visited? For the loss of conversation, of music?

Tell me: how much are these things worth?

Sonja has taught me many things – how to dance, how to cook, how to laugh, how to ask people to look at me when they speak. She taught me how to look in the mirror and not flinch, how to think of my father and not drink whisky; how to plant bulbs and tend European oleander. How to make love, how to forgive people for their impatience. She has fought for me in restaurants, in bars, over dinner tables. She even took me, one sharp autumnal day, to the local football club and talked to them as I stood by the car, twisted with embarrassment, shamed almost by my eternally silent world. But they took me on and they looked at me when I asked if they would, so I could watch their lips.

I sit here, on the settee where I fell asleep when I sliced my thumb, when Sonja asked me if we could buy the deli. I stroke the thin, white line of that scar and wonder what else she has taught me. She has taught me to love her, for it seems I am unable to love myself. She tells me over and over that I should be grateful that I have a memory of sound and speech, that it means I can speak, if not hear what I'm saying. She has tried to teach me to be grateful that I can master new words, that I can look at an unknown word and have a stab at it, read its meaning in a dictionary. Try to use it in a sentence. When Ian came to me in the hospital, biting into small, zesty kumquats, I asked him what his word for the week was. 'Homeostasis,' he said and I practised saying it until he nodded and smiled, his cheek bulging with fruit. I wasn't sure what it meant but I could say it.

As I have said, Sonja is an optimistic synaesthete. But I am numbered among the pessimistic deaf. I find it hard, this life of watching people, of constantly asking them to look at me when they speak so that I can read their lips. I grow old, I grow tired. This is a common disposition among the deaf: it takes so much effort to hold conversations that eventually you forget to speak, forget to watch faces, lips.

'You're retreating,' Sonja tells me.

Is that really so surprising? Outside this house people grab my arm or tap me on the shoulder all the time, trying to pull

my attention towards them so I can watch their lips. Drivers
shout unheard insults as I step off the pavement, the television
flickers, the radio chatters, records spin on turntables, CDs
slip silently away and none of it is for me. People laugh and
smile as I frown. Planes and saws move across wood, mallets
hammer without sound, helicopters move across the sky. But
this house, this room, every room, is peaceful. I open the front
door, leave that unheard bedlam behind and Sonja is waiting
for me, smiling, ready to fill the void. Or so it used to be.
The Blind Man can hear. He can listen, have conversations
unpunctuated by silence.

'You're retreating.'

And so I am and I know it. I supervise the building of
decks, I finger my scars, I grind my chisels to razor-like
sharpness, I work in my basement workshop in the bowels
of our house because I cannot survive and talk to Sonja at
the same time. I have, after all, a finite number of resources.
I can keep the money rolling in, can deal with waking and
watching people's lips, but I can't do all this and love Sonja
well at the same time.

Not long after I married Sonja I went to visit my mother and
the two of us sat on the rackety old deck of the Thurlestone
house and got drunk together; a departure from the norm –
usually she was plastered when I arrived. We sat, rocking on
our heels, crouching on the steps of the collapsing deck –
this was before I became a deck-builder – a bottle of whisky
between us, a storm lantern burning on the step so I could
watch her lips move, her fingers sign.

'That wasn't the first bomb I ever heard,' she said, pouring
an inch of raw whisky into her glass. We hadn't mentioned the
bomb for years, crazy as that sounds. We'd ignored it, turned

our backs to it, just as I had done on my thirteenth birthday. I sat very still, glass in hand, watching her.

My mother sighed, and rubbed her upper lip, where the damage had been the worst. 'When I was a little girl, you know, six or seven years old, the raids would never stop. We'd hear the sirens, me and my mother, and go to the shelter down at the bottom of the garden. Plymouth was bombed every night, every bloody night. We'd go to the shelter and Ma would lie on top of me when the bombs were hitting. We had a lodger, because your grandfather was fighting in France and money was tight. She was only a girl, she must have been about sixteen, from the country, by which we meant Cornwall, a farm girl. A farm girl with a thin, pinched face. She worked in the munitions factory. I remember lying underneath my mother and looking at the girl all alone on a bench. She didn't have anyone who loved her enough to lie on top of her. She always looked so scared.' My mother poured another inch of whisky. 'My grandparents lived on Southdown Road and their house took a direct hit but they weren't there at the time. They'd been out walking and sheltered somewhere else. When we went round there was one wall left standing, the windows intact, the curtains still hanging. They were dark brown velvet and they had small holes in them where shrapnel had sliced through them. There was a mantelpiece, still upright, and on it there was an unbroken china teapot, unscathed. Merely rattled. I've got it on my mantel now.'

I didn't know what to say so I poured myself another drink.

'Thing is – what I hated most about that time and it's an odd thing to remember, what I hated most. There was so much to hate.' My mother was bouncing on her heels, her mouth working. Still I said nothing because we never talked like this. 'What I hated most was arriving at school. Not because I didn't like school, I did. There was a cloakroom outside the classroom, where we hung our bags. I made one for you when you went to school. Y'know, for holding pumps and pencils and toys. Whatever. And all of them had a name stitched on them. I can see yours now – blue and white, with your name picked out in red. I've still got it somewhere.' She sipped whisky. 'Anyway. My mother used to take me to school and sometimes we'd even have to go into a shelter on the way there because the bombers were coming. Then we'd get to school and go to the classroom and the teacher would be taking away a bag. Unhooking it from the peg. Looking apologetic. It would be the bag of a child who didn't make it to the shelter.' My mother's lips folded in on themselves. 'What did they do with all the bags, John?'

'I don't know, Ma.'

We sat there, looking over the sea, wondering what they did with the bags of all the boys and girls who didn't grow up to be blown apart by other bombs. Did they burn them? Did they hide them? Did they give them to the parents – those little material sacks full of conkers and marbles, odd socks and damp pumps? Enough poignancy in there to undo the best-prepared, most resigned parent.

We each poured ourselves another drink, bouncing still on our heels as the waves rippled in, moonlit.

I looked at my mother, at her mutilated face lit by blue storm light, and minded for her for the first time in years. She was hunkered, brooding, caged by memories. I've said that I'm only three generations away from goat-tending and cap-tipping. More than that, I'm but one generation away from ration books and no bananas. One generation away from villages with one telephone. I remember black-and-white televisions, remember telephone numbers given as words – Derwent 3427. Remember discovering pasta, an exotic food then. I looked at my mother, her lips working in the moonlight and held my breath because nothing I could do would ever give her back her life.

I have a desk-top computer and a lap-top; I have access to the Net; a mobile phone which I use to e-mail; a pager; a mobile text-phone; a box to subtitle films. I have a wife who sells soft Italian Cambozola cheese for £5.38 a pound and a mother who spent her childhood dreaming of bread and jam and silence. But it was me who ended up with all the silence she could ever dream of, enough silence to last a lifetime.

Sonja and I slipped into the complacent years without noticing that we had. The small flats were long behind us and we bought the six-bedroom house in Clifton. '*Six* bedrooms?' friends asked, in wonder. We liked it, its space, its gardens, the cellar and the indecent spread of light; that was why we bought it. And for cash. '*Six* bedrooms?' friends asked jealously. At the same time, Ian bought his vast loft, ceiling supported by steel columns, overlooking one of the canals. The light shimmers on the ceiling when the sun hits the canal at a certain angle.

Before we moved into Clifton we had the house rearranged, a few walls knocked down, stained glass restored, radiators and Aga installed. The usual. The things you did in the early nineties if you had money. I built the deck and the kitchen, replaced some floors. Sonja chose the colours. I know that she was thinking of me when she made her choices because she chose well, she chose quietly. I would come home and find the hall wheat and terracotta, the bedroom linen and coffee. It is a house of long, deep sash windows and floating fabrics. It is a house large enough to dance in. A house large enough to forget each other in.

As the complacency deepened, so the routines of our lives became more ingrained. I have always woken early, always woken to the memory of my face turning red, worried into wakefulness by the scars I cannot see. I wake in the cast-iron bed made for us by Ian – a madness of curls and spirals, wood bursting from unexpected metal curves. All around me there is quiet space and this is Sonja's masterstroke, creating a house where silence is what is deliberately sought rather than a given. In one corner stands a French-polished, walnut-veneered wardrobe with a smoky, copper-tinted mirror. In two corners of the room are the doughty elm chairs that I salvaged from a skip, stripped and restored. That is all.

I ease myself from the bed, careful not to wake Sonja, and go down to the kitchen to squeeze fresh juice and grind coffee. As the coffee filters I have my shower and dress in check shirt, jeans and Doc Martens – there is, after all, comfort in cliché. (There is comfort, too, in complacency.) I collect the papers from the mat and pour the coffee as Sonja stumbles down the stairs, unwashed, always amazed to be awake. We exchange a floury, sour kiss and she turns, her eyes still puffed half-shut, to the juice and gulps it down. In the summer we go out on the deck with our coffee, in the winter we sit by the Aga in the kitchen. Sonja turns on Radio 4 for the *Today* programme, apparently. We divide the paper and read. I light my first cigarette when I've finished my first coffee. For half an hour we sit and eat the breakfast provided by the deli the night before, pecan and maple twists or brioches or almond Danish. Then I fold the main section and sit back, looking at the blonde, tousled crown of Sonja's head. This is the signal for her to smile vaguely, look up and, in recent years, take off her glasses

'So – what are your plans for the day?' she asks.

I bore her with the on-going sagas and demands of the jobs we are doing. It might be the stock we've had stolen, a bounced cheque, a stonemason caught smoking a joint on the job. Then I say, 'And you?'

She bores me with the details of late shipments, a fungal delivery of Belgian chocolates, the problems of labelling genetically modified food.

I stand and gather together keys and cigarettes, clip my pager to my belt. 'Well . . .'

She stands, moves round the table and I walk out to the hallway, where she leans against me as I unlock the front door. I turn and we kiss again, her hand touches my beard. We separate and she asks, 'When will you be home?'

And maybe I say six, or eight, or nine. 'And you?'

She shrugs. 'Sevenish, probably.'

We kiss again and I leave.

In summer I walk straight to the pick-up, jump in and slide into the day. In winter I stand and scrape off the ice, watching it fall in irritating, dry white lines. And then I slide into my day. I know that when I've gone Sonja stands for a moment in the hall and scratches, yawning, perhaps examines herself in the hall mirror. She tidies the kitchen, then goes upstairs to run her bath. As it fills she chooses her clothes and lays them on the bed. Sonja *floats* into her day, slipping slowly into the scented water and dressing languidly. But once the front door's closed behind her and she strides down the path she's a dynamo. It's just that it takes her engine longer to grind into motion.

We both work six days a week and sometimes I work seven. This doesn't happen often but when it does I think it's my fault for having accepted too much work, or having taken on the wrong crews. I love my work so I don't mind but I know that Sonja minds very much. What can I do?

'Take on less work, do fewer jobs, make less money,' Ian says.

Our evenings vary a little. Usually after we've eaten we sit and read novels or newspapers. We have a television but Sonja generally listens to Radio 4 or to music. I watch football when I can because I don't need subtitles and there's no plot to follow, particularly when England are playing. Sometimes I finish work early and go to the deli to pester her as, hair slipping, she flits about, wrapping and sealing. I try to persuade her to go for a drink, a meal, a coffee and eventually she accedes, grumbling about being rushed. Sometimes we play pool and drink pints and she matches me pint for pint. Or maybe we just walk along Whiteladies to the Triangle and down Park Street to St Nicks or the docks. Once there we might have a drink and catch the bus home. Or we walk up Blackboy Hill to the Downs to look at the sunset clipping the suspension bridge. Sometimes we go to see a subtitled film. At weekends we may have friends over for dinner, or maybe go to their houses. Friday nights I go out with Ian, and Sonja goes out with Clare, a friend from university who lives in Bristol.

Two evenings a week, no matter how late we finish work, Ian and I go to the gym. After I had the pacemaker inserted, the surgeon told me to exercise. More importantly, he told Sonja I should – seeing a lack of enthusiasm on my part – and she called Ian and told him, and he phoned my mother and told her. Then my mother came up to see me and took me to register at a health club. So I do it. Ian needs to work out like a bear needs toilet paper but he does it too. He does it for me (although I have sometimes caught him looking at a number of trim, Lycra-clad buttocks). Always makes me smile – Ian and I walk in, black and white giants, dressed in tatty work shorts and vests, covered with smears of varnish and wood glue, and the young boys in their primrose and black Lycra turn pale and run. Ian lifts weights I can't even move; he can bench-press three hundred pounds. On a good day I can manage two seventy but, as I waste no time pointing out to him, I have to lift it further because I'm taller. He just laughs. He pedals faster, runs further, leans over and ups the levels on my machines. I sweat, I curse, I get angry, and again he just laughs. At the end of a session we sit in the sauna and talk about how we can expand the business, build more decks, about how he will find the One.

Occasionally Ian and I go to Ashton Gate, with some of the carpenters from work, to watch the football. The colours and smells and movements are so distinctive, they're the essence of my experience – the red-roofed stand, the waving scarves and red and white painted faces, terraces littered with cups and papers. The smell of frying onions and microwaved pies, cigarette smoke and sweat. I don't need any cues to know when to yell and shout – every time a player misses from three feet, or falls and rolls in feigned agony. Every time the net bulges with a walloped shot I jump up and roar with the rest of them. I join in seamlessly. When it's over we walk through Greville Smyth Park to the Nova Scotia and sit by the water, or in the snuggery, arguing the finer points of team selection and formation, only to come to the conclusion that it would help if the players could pass to someone wearing the same colour shirt.

It's a small world, as I have said, a comforting world. I have for years, twenty-eight to be exact, avoided the unexpected. I revel in routine, in known parameters, in the predictable. But nothing is predictable now.

My father's father – my unseen, unknown grandfather – was so appalled by his son's actions, by his treachery in leaving a wife and newborn child, that he gave my mother the small cottage on the banks of the Yealm creek in Noss Mayo, Devon. It had been my grandparents' weekend retreat but they were so ashamed that they abandoned it to us, then retreated for ever. To say it was small would be understating the case. It would indeed have been impossible to swing a cat in there, because both of you couldn't have been in one room at the same time. I loved it. Loved to hear the water lapping up the piles as the tide rose, loved to play on dinghies and yachts owned by friends' parents or summer visitors. I'd spend whole afternoons when the tide was right running the short length of the jetty outside the Swan and landing in the water bomb-style, one knee pulled up, clutched tightly by my arms, spray fluming around me. I made friends for a week, for a day, for an afternoon, and bands of us would walk along the estuary, through the bluebell woods, swinging whippy branches torn from buddleia bushes, up and over the small headland and down to Cellar Beach where the world opened, the first of the Atlantic waters booming just past the Tamar. I was the wild boy who could swim like an otter, who would dive from the highest point, the first to try surfing, water-skiing. I was Merboy.

Sometimes I look back and wonder what my mother did all the time. There were days when we would go out together, the two of us, on trips to Polperro or St Ives, days spent looking in the endless clear rockpools of Crackington Haven, full of darting fish small as commas and fleshy, red-cushioned anemones. We'd crouch down by the pools, unmoving, and in the unruffled surface of the water our faces would be reflected, heads nearly touching. We ate hot pasties and saffron buns slathered with clotted cream, huddling under blankets on wind-lashed beaches. We walked the sands of Daymer Bay and Rock, had pub lunches in Padstow and Helston. I'd sit in beer gardens, legs swinging, gurgling the last of my lemonade through a straw, as my mother sat back in her chair, eyes closed, flawless face turned towards the sun, a cigarette burning between her fingers, a sweating gin and tonic leaking its ring on the table in front of her. I watched the men who walked past look at her and look at her again. We visited the Cornish villages where my mother's family had lived – mean and bleak, dying with the end of the tin trade and the closing of the Great Western Railway. Yet, surely, all those days number but a few over thirteen years. What did she do the rest of the time?

I realise now that she drank a lot. Not as much as she did later but seriously and often. I think she read a lot, too, out in our stamp-sized garden, full of old roses, hawthorn and ragged quince bushes. I also think she had a string, a thick rope, of lovers. My mother was beautiful then. When I was a boy I couldn't understand why my father had left – how could he leave someone so beautiful? (Now I know there are many reasons for people leaving others.) My endless, waterlogged days on the river, on the beach, must have suited her. I'd burst into the house at each day's end, covered in sand, black hair stiff with salt, and she would be sitting in her chair, book open, smiling languidly, glass of wine nearby. It was an easy relationship, a relationship without sharp edges. And then, on my thirteenth birthday, we went to London.

*   *   *

My mother's injuries, although horrific, were mainly razoring glass cuts and broken bones. She healed faster than I did, her wounds scabbing over then flaking away to reveal the pits and incisions on her face. Her left eyebrow was twisted, leaving one eye squinting down the remaining days of her life. Her broken ribs, legs and arm were set and the jagged tips melded together. She came to my room every day once she was able, at first sitting in her wheelchair and later limping in to sit in the chair by the bed. Her hair was lifeless and she was pale, broken. She didn't read, she simply sat and watched my breathing back, for that is what I turned to her. It must have been a small back, the spine visible as delicate, shiny bumps moving slightly under the damaged skin. My mild English tan, the tan I held over from one summer to the next, would have faded. At first I was always naked, the sheets held away from my skin by a flimsy frame. The skin grafts were exposed while they healed, and that's what my mother stared at for hours every day. She must have been willing the skin to close, to change from angry red to pink.

I don't know if she spoke to me – how could I know? – but I think she did. I've never asked her. I think she sat and moved her rearranged, frayed lips, framing words in a different way, urging me to come back into the world. As my grafts closed and the frame was replaced by a flimsy blue gown she was discharged but she didn't go home, back to the cottage. She rented a flat in Lambeth and came to see me every day. She was there by seven in the morning and left at eight at night. Each day she would bring something – some fruit, a comic, a poster, Subbuteo, a picture from a magazine, a mobile, a pack of cards, a bottle of Ribena, flowers, a packet of wine gums. She stuck the pictures on the walls, stacked the comics on my table, dangled the mobiles from the beams. By the end of my time there, my room was a boy's Aladdin's cave, full of spinning colours and hundreds of pictures. And all the time she talked to me, unheard, touched my undamaged skin and talked to me.

It was months before I turned to look at her. That much she did tell me. From the time when I glanced at her in the Morris Minor, flapping my hand at an empty parking space, to the time I turned on to my tender back and looked at her healed face, three months had passed.

What had I been thinking as I lay on my side, wrapped in silence, staring at the beige wall? I can still see that wall now, see all its pits and scars, the black scuff marks where the trolley wheels carrying the blood-pressure monitor always scraped. The gouge in the plaster near the skirting-board where something had landed with a crash, which I would not have heard. As time passed the wall filled with pictures – of footballers, of yachts, of waves. My favourite was a poster of men surfing Big Wednesday off the coast of Hawaii. The waves reared tens of feet into the air, almost tumbling back on themselves, but I knew, I always knew, that they would fall and break. And there, balanced on flimsy boards, were two men, specks against the endless blue, arms outstretched, knees bent, black shadows against the raging blue waters. I looked at the men and I tasted salt in my mouth, felt spray turning over me. I must have stared at that picture for hours as my body struggled, for it was not only trying to mend, it was trying to grow. I was thirteen years old and I was growing.

It took a long time for my mind to order itself. At night, or whenever I slept, unless I was snug and safe under the effects of drugs or anaesthetic, I called out, cried, yelled incoherently. I whimpered endlessly, a whimper which was to me ungovernable. I was always scared that I would wake to the pain. The pain was crushing, it crushed harder and deeper than the falls of mortar, more than the weight of the car. My back was a lattice of quilted skin, my arm a burnished pillow of flesh borrowed from my thigh, the pearly pink of conch shells. It was the pain that scared me, because I'd forgotten how it had arrived. No matter how hard I tried, I couldn't work out what I'd done to deserve it.

And then the memories began to seep back as I stared at the wall. The memory of sound hit me one grey, endless afternoon as my mother sat behind me. I remembered the sound of Toulouse the cat squawking when I trod on him, remembered carrying a bottle of lemonade. I reached up and touched the healed scar on my scalp. That afternoon I laboured as I lay on my side, trying to remember where I had been going with the bottle. I knew it was important.

It was once I began to remember, began to think, to struggle with the past, that the pain started to recede – or perhaps it simply became the norm? That it is possible to be wrenched from one state of being to another in an instant, in an intense blast of grey bland Semtex the size of a matchbox, is too much for the thirteen-year-old mind to grasp. There is no language I can use to describe the turmoil, the confusion, of those months as I healed and grew and remembered sound. This confusion left me with many questions and that was why I finally turned and looked at my mother. She didn't smile at me, for what was there to smile about? She just held my hand whilst I cried.

The next day her present was a red spiral pad with matching pencil. She had a blue set for herself. She put the pad on the bed, on my stomach, and eventually I picked it up, turning it in my hands, puzzled. I opened it gingerly, my burned arm tight and ungiving. I picked up the pencil and stared at it, an alien object. I had spent so long thinking of sound, mourning its absence, that I had forgotten I could write. I am ambidextrous, the only trick I inherited from my father (apart from being heartless, that is, but I didn't know that then).

My mother knew better than to write the first note. It was me who had to take the first step back into the world of communication. My fingers felt furry, far away. I took minutes to write the wobbly, arthritic phrase, *Why can't I hear?*

My mother stared at the question for a long time. She had had months to prepare for this moment and yet she still struggled.

You've lost your hearing.
I know that. Why?
You've lost your eardrums.
What are they?
They help you hear.
How did I lose them?
A bomb, in the car park.
Which car park?
In London. On your birthday.

I lay back, tired, my hand aching. I remembered a glimmer of why I had been carrying bottle of lemonade, why it had been dark outside. The pain receded a little more. That's how it is – the brain orders and makes sense of even the inconceivable, and pain's power to confuse diminishes. A while later, when I could, I wrote again.

Can we find them?
Find what?
My eardrums?

What was my mother supposed to write? What could she say? How could she begin to guess how much hope there was in my mutilated body?

No. They got broken too badly.

I closed my eyes. I had travelled across the south of
England, as a grey dawn seeped over hedgerows, heading for
London, wasting my time worrying about my heart breaking?
Just how many parts of my body could break?

How long have we been here?
Four months.
What month is it?
March.
When?
1972.
What happened to your face?
I got cut by glass but it's OK now.
Will it get better?
Maybe.

The next day when my mother came in, she wasn't alone.
A small blonde woman dressed in a white coat came with
her. She took out a pad and wrote on it, tore the sheet off
and handed it to me.

*My name is Miss Handel. I am here to help you, to help you get up
and start moving about.*

I read this and panicked. I wanted to stay in that room for
ever, with my mother. Just the two of us, safe and clean, the
door closed. I shook my head, looked at my mother, who
began to write as well.

*John – I know this is hard but enough time has passed. You have
to get up, begin to move, or you never will.*

I shook my head and began to whimper. Miss Handel
glanced at my mother and wrote another note.

John – I'll come back tomorrow. Think about it for a while.

I tried to scrunch the single piece of paper, failed and
dropped it on to my bed as Miss Handel left. All day my
mother wrote, explaining how I could be normal again,

that life wasn't over, my skin had healed, my bones had set. She wrote pages of notes, explaining that she knew I was scared, that I was frightened of everything, that she would be there . . . on and on. The next day Miss Handel came back and I whimpered again, and for days after that.

But of course there was an end to it. I'd always loved to move, to swim, to dive, run and, of course, to fight. The dream of doing these things again had been planted in my now ever-cautious mind. Eventually I let Miss Handel handle my legs and arms, move my joints, but only after I had written,

In here. In this room with my mother. Not going outside.

And she had nodded and smiled.

OK!

My limbs were stiff and unyielding but they improved. And finally one day, my back taut and protesting, I sat up on the edge of the bed, the pale blue gown open at the back. I looked at my dangling legs for the first time in months. They were ivory white with scars running here and there. They looked pitiful and thin because they were. These were not the legs of a summer-Devon Merboy. I felt my chin trembling, my mouth working, and I cried with shame, with self-pity. My mother came round the bed and gently wrapped her arms round me, held my head against her breasts, and through my misery I could feel hers. The first time in months that I had thought of someone else.

Soon I was shuffling a few steps, and sitting in a chair, my back padded by water-filled cushions. And then they began to come into my Aladdin's cave – the psychologists, the physiotherapists, the surgeons, the ear specialists, to try to persuade Merboy to emerge from his shell. They measured me, tested me, goaded me to do more, to push harder, they tried to make me *mind*, little by little. The eye specialist –

a stern, tall man with grey beard and steel glasses – came with his equipment and motioned for me to sit without even introducing himself with a note. This stung me and for the first time I decided to show off, slipping from my bed and limping to the seat as well as I was able, my back creaking in protest. I was in place before my mother made it half-way round the bed to help me. I looked at her and she smiled, for the first time since my birthday. It was horrible to see the way her mouth was pulled sideways by the small gatherings of skin stitched together to compensate for the tears. But it was a smile I became used to, even though my mother learned quickly to hide it with her hand. When he had finished the tests the Eye Man looked at me gravely and held out his hand for my notebook.

John – I have to report that you have the sharpest eyesight I have ever come across. You could see the needle in the haystack.

Eye Man handed it to me and his sudden smile dazzled me.

One day, five months after I had arrived on the stretcher, maddened by damage, a short, plump young doctor, without a white coat, wearing a spotted red and white bow-tie and red braces, came into my cave, saluted me and sat on the edge of the bed. He had his own notebook and he wrote:

Hello John, I'm Harry. How do you feel today?

OK.

That's good. You're doing very well. You're the big success story of Tommy's.

Who's Tommy?

It's the name of the hospital. St Thomas'. Tell me, what do you like doing best?

Before he gave me this message he held out his hand for my pad of paper, just as the eye specialist had. I frowned, confused. He had his *own* paper. I looked at my mother and she smiled her twisted smile and nodded. I gave him the pad and then he gave me the message. I looked at it, puzzled. I waved my hands at my pad, itching to answer. Harry took the message back very gently from me and underlined the words *Tell me*. I looked again at my mother but her face was impassive. My arms flapped, beat the mattress. I already liked Harry – why was he teasing me? I wanted to cry as he began to write.

John, you have forgotten something, which is fine because you've had a very rough time of it. You have had a terrible time so no one blames you for forgetting this one thing. It's kind of like magic. We know you can't hear. But, John – you can SPEAK.

I read the message and looked at my mother, my mouth slack. Again she nodded. I could speak? It's difficult to understand how it is that you forget that you know spoken language, that you can speak although you can't hear. But I had forgotten. I had, after all, forgotten that I could write. I had also forgotten that I could speak; I had almost forgotten *how* to speak.

So – what do you like doing best? Tell me.

It felt as if the whole world was waiting as I lay there staring at the men surfing Big Wednesday. Many times I felt the word in my mouth, like a bolus of food, and then swallowed it. It lodged behind my teeth and I forced it back and swallowed it, a hard word at the beginning but the ending slipped down my throat. My lips were made of lead, my tongue of sponge. I *had* to spit it out, the world was waiting. I spoke, apparently soundlessly. I looked at my mother and for the second time in five months she smiled.

Can you say that again, John?

'Swimming.'

*   *   *

Apparently the heart is a 'hollow pear-shaped muscular organ placed between the lungs in the middle of the chest that pumps blood through the body, supplying cells with oxygen and nutrients'. So they say. 'The apex pulses with every beat and this is what you feel when you hold your hand to your heart.' Perhaps others do. I'm no longer sure what I feel. 'The adult heart is approximately the size of a fist. In an average adult it is about five inches long and three and a half inches across at its broadest point.' This is not the size of my fist but it may well be the size of my heart. It seems hardly adequate to shoulder the burdens it has been given during my life. Certainly not adequate for Shylock's purposes, since the average adult heart weighs less than a pound.

The heart is described as the seat of all emotion; I realise that now, realised it when they put the metal box in mine. A heart of steel. When a leg is injured you favour the other, when a finger is damaged, the other hand comes into play, when one eye has a stye, the other watches the world. But what happens when your heart is damaged? What do you favour? I'll tell you: you favour yourself.

Sonja is still seeing her Blind Man. I know this because Ian tells me he sees them together everywhere. I know this because she is different. I'm retreating as far as the Severn tide and she says nothing. I think she no longer cares. I don't ask questions in the evenings during our time together on the deck, in the garden, in our living room. I read and I watch her, knowing she wants to be elsewhere.

'Ask her about it,' Ian said. 'Ask her anyway.'

I try to imagine what, exactly, I'm supposed to ask her. 'Do you still love me?' 'Have I done something wrong?' 'Why don't you want to dance with me?' 'Are you fucking the Blind Man?' Every time I phrase that question my heart jumps, misses a beat, and my fists curl. I miss her but how can I ask her that? And what would she answer?

It seems I have forgotten once again how to speak.

It was Harry who took me outside Tommy's for the first time. He came into my room and enunciated, 'GET DRESSED', in such a way I knew it was a command. Dressed? What did he mean?

'What d'you mean?' I asked.

Get dressed. You're going outside for a walk. He wrote the note and threw it at me.

'Outside?'

He smiled for an answer, his white teeth matching the polka dots on his bow-tie. I looked at my mother – still there, still there. She nodded and smiled with one side of her face – this was her shorthand for 'I'm too tired to cover half my face.' She reached beneath the hospital bed for a bag and what did she drag out? What else could she have pulled out other than a T-shirt and a pair of Levi's?

The clothes I had worn while writhing on the stretcher all those months before had been, first, blasted, bloodied and scorched, and then cut from me. I had been naked for much of my stay at Tommy's, as the grafts settled. Then I had spent months in gowns, used to everyone seeing my arse.

My mother and Harry watched me as I fingered the Levi's, stiff and twice-folded. I smiled. Harry winked at me and pulled the curtain round the bed, shooing my mother outside. He bustled around, helping me balance as I put one limp foot into a leg of the jeans, helping my befuddled hands pull the

fly zip, slipping the white T-shirt over my head. I was like a
child, I'd even forgotten how to dress. And then I stopped,
remembering I *was* a child: Merboy.

'Merboy,' I said.

What? Harry wrote.

I shrugged.

'Mirror. I want a mirror.' I hadn't wanted to see myself
before this.

There isn't one, he wrote.

'How do I look?' I asked. I wanted to be the best for my
mother when those curtains were pulled back. I wanted to
be a big boy, a well-dressed boy, a snappy dresser. The jeans
rubbed my scars and it felt odd to have fabric brushing the
skin on my back. I kept plucking at the T-shirt. The shoes on
my feet? They felt heavy, cumbersome. Harry stepped back,
looked at me and turned up his thumb.

'OK?' Harry asked. I nodded and he swirled back the green
curtains.

My mother cried when she saw me. Well, what else was
she supposed to do? She didn't cry gulping, face-twisting sobs,
she'd done that too many times already. No, she cried silently,
still able to write.

You look wonderful. Do you want me to come with you?

'No.' I was standing in my Levi's, feeling different. I was
in clothes and I could communicate. Why would I need my
mother?

OK, she signed.

I looked at Harry and he smiled, opened the door of
my room.

I'd been out of my room before to go to the bathroom, to
go to the physio block – a corridor, a lift. But Harry walked
me to another set of lifts and my hand drifted to hold his.

It was cool and plump. He smiled at me, winked again and punched a button in the wall.

'Could take some time,' he mouthed, and smiled.

I got 'some time'.

The lift arrived and we stepped in, Harry and I. The lift to my physio ward had grey walls, marked by wheelchairs and stretchers. This lift, which was for visitors, was made of stainless steel, distorting mirror surface shuddering. I watched with some interest as a skinny, tall, near-bald boy, wearing trousers far too big for him, shifted from foot to foot, his back twisted, his eyes wide, holding the hand of a man wearing a bow-tie. It took 'some time', long enough for the lift to get to the ground floor, for me to realise exactly who it was. I yelped and tried to pull my hand away from Harry's but he held on with a lion's grip.

The doors opened and there they were – all the nurses, ward sisters, doctors and specialists I had ever seen in my months at the hospital. All the cleaners who had scooted round my room, all the ward orderlies who'd ever brought me food, all the porters who had wheeled me endlessly to and from the theatres. They lined the corridor, clapping, turning up their thumbs, making circles of thumb and forefinger, smiling and laughing with each other, smiling at me.

Harry pointed to the sliding automatic doors at the end of the corridor and raised his eyebrows. He took a small step and I followed him, clinging now to his hand. We walked like emperors, like conquering heroes along the long, polished linoleum floor. Hyacinth, the black cleaner who always wore scarlet lipstick to match her nail varnish, who nearly burst out of her bright pink overalls, who came in every morning at six and sang as she mopped ('Mary Bring the Cattle Home Across the Sands of Dee', my mother told me years later);

Hyacinth, who sat on the edge of my bed five mornings a week, taking my hand in hers and sketching letters on my soft undamaged palm with her gaudy, ring-encrusted black fingers, spelling out questions, jokes, comments on doctors; Hyacinth, who threw back her head and laughed in a way that I imagined I could hear, teeth gold-filled and glinting; Hyacinth burst from the knots of people and stopped me, put her hands gently on either side of my face, looked into my eyes and smiled. She tilted my head – so gently – and kissed my forehead. 'For you,' she mouthed, holding a small, gold-paper-wrapped present. She stuffed it into the pocket of my jeans and melted away into the crowd.

The glass doors to the infinite outside slid back, saving me from another reflection of myself, and Harry and I stepped out. The cold hit me like a slap and I shivered. Harry put his arm round me. He didn't mouth anything, he didn't write anything, he let his arm slip away very slowly and stood back, leaving me to gawp. I looked at the night skyline of London and watched in astonishment, the cold forgotten, as fireworks spotted the sky with false starlight, doubly false as the star-bursts were reflected in the Thames. It was Guy Fawkes Night and London was burning, smoke drifting.

I wanted my mother then and I turned, shading my eyes against the cordite flares, and there she was, eight storeys above me, hanging out of a window. I waved and she waved back. I flapped my hand for the first time in nearly a year, motioning for her to come down, but either she didn't see the gesture or she ignored it, remembering the consequences of my flapping a hand.

It's November here in Bristol, a sharp, unforgiving month. The frost has come early and winds saw at my hands as I work, arms aching in the cold, my padded shirt useless against this weather until I work up a sweat. Sonja and I no longer take our morning coffee out on the deck but sit instead by the Aga, wrapped in silence. Ian no longer sees her sitting with her Blind Man outside Bar Humbug, the City Farm, Torches, wherever they can sit and catch the sun. I wonder where they meet now, as the year draws to an end.

Last weekend Ian said to me, 'Special, I don't believe that you've done nothing about this, man. Said nothing about this. It's been going on for months.' We were in his flat sitting on the floor, resting our backs against the white cotton twill settee, smoking a joint and watching grey bolts of light swivel across the ceiling.

I passed the joint, exhaled, and said, 'I'm afraid that if I say anything, if I bring it out into the open, she'll go. And then what will I do? It's OK for you. You just live your life. But things for me aren't so easy.'

'Easy?' He arches an eyebrow.

'Oh come on, you know what I mean. You live alone. You don't know how it is, being with someone.'

'No, I don't, and I wish I did.'

'I don't know. The thought of her leaving . . . I don't know. It's as if she's waiting for me to make a move. She must know that I know.'

'Of course she does. It is kind of obvious that you do.'

'What d'you mean?' I looked at his lips moving.

'You hardly ever talk, except to me. You walk around like you're treading on eggshells. You walk around like a zombie, if you want to know the truth. As much fun as a turd in a punchbowl. I'm surprised she hasn't left you anyway.'

He held out the joint to me but I got up and walked out, slamming the door so I could feel the rush of air. I walked

down to the river where swans bobbed in the wake of a late
booze-cruiser and I smoked a cigarette, watching my freezing
breath mingle with the smoke. The time, I thought, has
perhaps come. This limbo, this lovelessness, seemed endless.
I wanted my life back, wanted to be complacent, wanted to
be as whole as I could be . . . but what if she left me? What
then? The circular argument revolved within me. I realised
I was tired, tired of the argument, tired of living this silent,
Sonja-less life. Spinning the cigarette butt out into the water,
the swans moving towards the ripples it made, I stamped my
feet to shake off the cold and imagined eggshells splintering.

Of course I apologised to Ian in my shambolic way the next
day. He smiled and waved his hand – nothing, it's nothing; it's
everything, I thought – and he turned back to his furnace.

And here I am today, aching, wrestling with the banister of
a deck on Cotham Grove, forcing it into place, taking short
cuts, wedging spindles with shavings and pegs into hastily cut
holes. My hands betray me, my skills betray me. Mr Bodge has
come to visit – and come to visit in the worst possible place,
for the house on Cotham Grove is owned by Mrs Harpy and
her husband. Aptly named, indeed. She is a strikingly attractive
blonde woman in her late thirties, beautifully groomed, her
clothes rustle and fall just so, in shades of olive and taupe,
cut on the bias. She is always expensively shod, even when
she treads gingerly through the sawdust and shavings, the
dry, smoking puddles of fine Blue Circle cement dust rising
like steam round her ankles, to comment on an aspect of
the construction of her two-storey oak and granite deck, with
its lashings of cherry. She has eyes of emerald, finely angled
bones and a soft voice, apparently, like honey. She is the
psychobitch customer from hell.

I sit on the top step, notice that it shifts a little to the

left (the tenon has been shaved a tad too small) and light a
cigarette, pour coffee from my flask, steam billowing in the
cold air. I lift my right hand, the hand that was thrown against
the burning exhaust pipe of a Morris Minor twenty-eight years
before, and begin to stretch and flex it. In cold weather it hurts,
tends to cramp. I wrap it round the cup to warm it. I sit looking
out at the autumn-blasted garden, dead now, fallen to earth
apart from the laurel tree in the corner. I'm turning over in
my mind the questions I will ask Sonja, picking my words,
examining them as closely as Merboy examined pebbles on
a beach, selecting some and rejecting others. I test the words
for their fit, their feel in my hands and mouth. Which word
should be the first?

It's the slight vibration of the wood beneath my buttocks
that makes me turn, and there is Psychobitch, a cashmere coat
slung casually over her gym-honed shoulders, picking her way
cat-like through my pile of tools. My heart sinks like a coin
thrown into a barrel of diesel, slowly but surely, and I groan
my way to my feet to watch her slightly too thin lips move.

She comes up to me in the misty light and begins to talk.
She knows I'm deaf and she over-compensates for this. She
mouths her words as if she's wrapping her lips like clingfilm
round a plum, as if she's cutting through tough salami skin
with her teeth. 'Mr Player, I'm delighted to see you.'

I spread my hands – the right hand throbbing – and smile
tensely. 'And I you.'

'There are a few things . . . well, many things, that Brian
and I are unhappy about.'

'I'm sorry about that.'

'Why didn't you return my phone calls yesterday?' Her
face pinches and I see in it all the disappointments of her
self-centred days.

Because I'm deaf, you thoughtless git. A telephone is as much use to me as a Tampax. 'I didn't get the message. I'm sorry. My colleague should have called.' A too-gentle rebuke, which passes unnoticed. 'What seems to be the problem?' Usually I have an easy, ursine charm, which disarms the disgruntled. But in Psychobitch I know I've met my match. Knew it the moment that I came to the house for the first time. Knew it when I stood in the hallway and met the Harpys – Harpies? – and smelled for the first time the astringent atmosphere of their expectations in the air.

She laughs mirthlessly. '*The* problem? There's more than one.' She beckons me with a beautifully manicured finger and I follow her as she embarks on an exhaustive litany of regrets on their part. She points to nails and screws set askew, scratches on the rendering on the side of the house where planks have been carried through, empty cement bags that have been piled below the deck's frame. She ushers me into the kitchen and points dramatically to a film of dust that has billowed around the bottom of the door. I am slack-jawed, I am disbelieving, I am, I suddenly realise, absolutely fucking exhausted.

I touch her arm and she shies away from me. Am I that alarming? I catch sight of the two of us reflected in the kitchen window. We're so mismatched we're a Chaplinesque joke. Her silk-lined coat slips from her shoulders, we both reach for it and she backs away as my hand dips near hers. I may be six feet seven inches tall, with a piratical beard and hands the size of a Spode dinner plate, but no customer has ever flinched from me before. I pick up the coat and, amazed by the tenderness of it against my skin, I keep it in my hand. I am – unexpectedly – overwhelmed by a desire for intimacy. I want her to reach out and touch my ugly, scarred hand and smile. I want her to hold me, want her to stand in the kitchen and just hold me tight, stroking my back, kissing my neck.

'Mrs Harpy,' and I'm trying, here, to modulate my voice, to calm her but I have no idea how I'm speaking: when my bones ache my voice slips, 'when I gave you my quotation, how long did I estimate we'd be here for?'

'Four weeks, although I fail to see how—'

I reach out and touch her arm again. 'How long have we been here?'

'Six days. But I still don't know why—'

'In four weeks time this house will look delightful. I promise you. In four weeks time, you can point out any problems you have with the job, if any, and they will be addressed. But, for now, please trust me and let us get on with the job.'

'But—'

'Please.' I hand the coat to her, sad to relinquish its touch, and walk out on to the deck, my hands aching with loss of one sort or another.

When I got home that night my right ear was aching, sending bolt lightning to my skull, beating it Thor-like. I went to bed and Sonja brought me water, ibuprofen, lay next to me and stroked my forehead. For a while I imagined that nothing had changed as I wrestled with the fears that earaches reanimate, bolstered by her presence, warmed by her body heat. I fell asleep, my head throbbing, my heart heavy with the knowledge that everything had changed.

The next morning Sonja phoned Ian, her eyes still slow with sleep, and told him I'd be late, that I was going to see the doctor. She bundled me into T-shirt, padded shirt, jeans, thick socks, DMs and donkey jacket and drove me to the surgery. She sat in the waiting room, flicking through a magazine as I went in. It wasn't Dr MacNeill but a young, unknown locum. I sat in the chair and watched his profile while he glanced through my file. It was as thick as the Bible. He turned to me and I saw fear in his eyes. 'Just send me to St Michael's,' I said. 'Just call and ask for an appointment with Dr Laws.'

He cleared his throat – I could tell because his shirt collar moved – and gestured for me to turn in the chair. He picked up an aural light and replaced the black plastic beak-head of it with another, sterile beak. I turned my head and tensed as he caught my pinna between finger and thumb and began to search my canal. He tried to be professional, tried to be calm, but the maze of scars beneath his fingers, the unending darkness of my ear canal, the feel of my ridged, damaged jaw undid him. He knew then that I was held together by cat gut. His hands were shaking as he wrote a short note on my files. He gripped the edge of the desk and turned to me. 'I'm going to call St Michael's right now.'

'What's wrong?' I asked.

'It looks like a slight infection. Nothing much. But, you know, best to be on the safe side.' He tried to smile, best bedside manner, and his lips twitched.

He was too young for this, too young-arrogant to take a . . . shall we say seasoned?, patient's word for it and too young-vulnerable to touch and see the lifelong damage suffered by some. He bent his head over the phone and talked as I looked at the familiar posters warning me about Aids, smoking, fatty foods, cholesterol, heart disease. I always wondered why there were never any posters warning the unwary about heartbreak.

While the locum talked on the phone, I dunked my

pain-free left hand into the pocket of my donkey jacket and drew out my green malachite worrystone, rubbing it with my hard, callused thumb, an action so thoughtless, so practised, I was surprised to find it between my fingers when I reached out to take the locum's note. Ambidexterity is a boon and my right thumb and forefinger snapped up the stone and began to worry it.

Hyacinth gave me my worrystone: she danced out of a crowd, kissed me and slid a small, gold-wrapped present into my pocket. Later, back in my room, I pulled it from my pocket, wrinkled and squashed. I tore off the paper and there it was, small and tombstone-shaped, with a slight polished indentation. Wrapped round it was a note, written in sloping capital letters: 'GOOD LUCK SPECIAL! I THINK MAYBE YOULL NEED THIS ONCE IN A WILE!' I showed my mother the stone and she turned it in her hands as I undressed, carefully sliding the jeans over my scarred, white legs.

'What is it?' I asked, hopping from foot to foot.

It's a worrystone, she wrote.

Already she was working it between her fingers, mindlessly.

You rub it when you worry, rub it like this. Her thumb slipped back and forth over the indent.

I read Hyacinth's note again. 'What's a wile? Why does it only happen once?'

My mother looked at me and smiled her half-smile.

It happens a lot more than once in a lifetime.

I go back into the waiting room at the doctor's and Sonja looks up from a magazine. We walk out together, her arm threading through mine.

'Well?'

'I have to go to St Michael's. It's nothing, but the guy was a locum and he panicked.' I smile down at her in reassurance. 'He called them and they're expecting me.'

Sonja drives me there and I persuade her to go home, go to work. I do, after all, know my way around the ENT clinic, can walk it in my sleep. I make to get out of the car and Sonja grabs the sleeve of my jacket, pulling me round to kiss my mouth. She tugs my beard and mouths, 'G'luck, Special,' and smiles. My heart soars, electricity crackling across my pacemaker. For a moment she looks like the Sonja I met at King's College, the Sonja I have lived with for twenty years. She drives off, waving through the open window until she turns a corner.

Dr Laws, the registrar, ushers me straight into his surgery and examines my ears, his mouth pursed, his bifocals glinting. 'It's a mild infection, John. Nothing to worry about.' He writes a prescription and hands it to me. I begin to stand but he touches my hand and motions for me to sit. He takes off his glasses and folds them, pinches the bridge of his nose, then looks directly at me, stern and forbidding, reminding me of the Eye Man in Tommy's all those years ago.

'John, do you remember when you were, um, a young boy and they tried to make you some eardrums?'

I blink and swallow because the question conjures up the picture of a pale, thin boy on a hospital bed, crying for days as the infected tissue itself wept, oozing pus out of his ear canals. I nod, unable to speak.

'Well, that was a long time ago and things have changed, methods have changed. The surgery has improved beyond measure. I looked at your file while I was waiting for you, and I think you should consider having cochlear implants.

Before we do that we'd have to attempt myringoplasty again. It's essentially the same idea – making you new eardrums from the soft tissue of your neck. And then when that's healed, we'll try the implants.' He must see the fear in my eyes. 'John, I wouldn't recommend this unless I believed it would work. I've known you, what, fifteen years? I know what scares you. It's something of a miracle that you have survived at all.' He sighs and shakes his head a little. 'But the thing is, John, the thing is, I know you're remembering the last time – when it went wrong.' His eyes scan my face and I nod again. 'When they operated on you then, your body was young, it was badly damaged, you were fighting Lord knows how many infections. I'm not saying they shouldn't have done it, but . . .' He arches his eyebrows slightly. 'Anyway, what's done is done. You're now a forty-year-old man, and a rather imposing one at that. Your scar tissue healed decades ago. You're fitter now than you have ever been. You're a big man, John, a strong man. It will be different this time. Hand on heart.'

'Will I hear again?' My hands are gripping the arms of the chair, fingers deeply denting the padded leather.

Dr Laws pulls a sheet from the folder that details my sad aural history and holds it out so that we can both see it. It's a graph I've looked at many times, mapping the sounds I can hear. On one side is the graph showing what I hear when I wear the headphones over my ears and the lines for both left and right are flat, following the horizontal axis. Nothing. I hear nothing. Next to it is another graph, the same as the first, mapping what I hear when the sounds are transmitted through my skull, bypassing my pointless, drumless ears. Dr Laws taps the lines with a pen. 'Look, you can hear about thirty with your left and thirty-five with your right. The residual hearing left after the German measles damaged you when you were a foetus.' Jesus Christ, I think, I was under attack before I was even born. I look back at his ascetic, careworn face. 'There is a possibility – a *possibility* – that if these operations, the myringoplasty and the implants, are a success you will be able to use the aural faculties you possess. You may hear this much.' And he taps the graph with the pen. 'Not only that, you would stop getting these infections.'

I stare at the thin lines joined by black dots, trying to imagine what it would be like to hear thirty and thirty-five.

'Go away and think about it John. Talk to Sonja about it. As with all operations, there are risks. Ask her to call me if she wants to. At home if necessary.' He writes his home number on a yellow Post-it and hands it to me.

I stand, my mind sparking with possibilities and doubts, reeling a little as I try to order my thoughts. I shake the doctor's hand and walk slowly to the door. He catches me as I open it, tugs my sleeve. 'One more thing – it might help you make up your mind.'

'What?'

'Even if you can't hear, even if that doesn't happen, as long as there are no perforations, as long as the eardrums are whole after the myringoplasty, there *is* something you'll be able to do.'

I'm puzzled. 'What? What will I be able to do?'

And Dr Laws smiles a wolfish smile. 'Swim, Special. You'll be able to swim.'

It was Hyacinth who nicknamed me Special. She sashayed into my room early one morning, before my mother had arrived, pushing her mop and bucket before her, and I could tell she was singing by the way her mouth was moving, her high-held buttocks twitching. My fingers plucked at the thin

blanket on the bed as I watched her. I'd never seen her
before; she radiated energy, and something else. Took me
a while to recognise what it was – happiness. I hadn't seen
that for some time. Hyacinth ignored me for minutes and
then, in an exaggerated pantomime, pretended to see me
for the first time. She pushed aside the mop and bucket,
came over to the foot of the bed, picked up the clipboard
hanging there and flipped the pages, pursing her mouth and
frowning. She looked again at the cover page and laughed,
her teeth flashing gold, then came to perch on the edge of
the bed.

'Hello,' she mouthed.

'Hello,' I said, intrigued.

'How are you?'

'OK.'

She said something else but my lip-reading wasn't well
developed then and I lost the words. I picked up the pad
by my bed and held it out to her but she brushed it aside and
motioned for me to give her my hand. She held it for minutes,
rubbing it with her thumbs, watching my face, learning my
face, she told me later, so that she would know each day how
I was feeling. Then she turned up my palm and traced a letter
on it. My skin tingled. I watched the shape form.

'M?' I asked. She nodded and traced again.

'Y?' Another nod. And then she drew a line across my skin,
scraping it with her nail.

'I?' Doubtful. She shook her head, held her thumb and
forefinger apart.

'Space?' I asked, and she nodded, laughed. I laughed
with her.

'M . . . Y. My! My!' I shouted, suddenly understanding,
delighted to have solved the problem.

'Yes, my – my.' We laughed again.

She traced out the sentence, 'My name is Hyacinth.' I tried to say the name, watched her mouth and copied it, over and over, until she clapped her hands and rocked on the bed. 'Yes! Yes! Hyacinth.' Only, of course, I was saying 'Hyacint' just as she did.

Then she traced, 'I HAVE A NAME FOR YOU.'

'John Player?'

She shook her head, and traced, 'SPECIAL.'

'Special?'

She nodded and pulled a cigarette packet from her pocket. She held it out to me and there, embossed on the black packet in gold letters, were the words John Player Special. I was enchanted, kept turning the packet in the light of the bedside lamp, watching the letters change colour. I laughed again, enjoying the feeling, my pain forgotten for the first time, and it was then that my mother walked in, to see me laughing aloud, an enormous black woman sitting on my bed, holding a packet of fags.

When I woke the next morning the first thing I saw was a poster, trimmed of its picture of cigarettes, pinned above the picture of the men surfing the rollers, the poster black and gold. 'John Player Special,' it said 'for when you want the best.' My mother had asked, cajoled and eventually bullied the tobacconist on the corner of her road in Lambeth to pull it down from his window and give it to her. She had come in early so it would be in place when I woke up. Minutes later Hyacinth walked in, bawling, 'Mary Bring the Cattle Home Across the Sands of Dee', shocking my mother, who was snoozing, into sudden wakefulness. Hyacinth saw the poster and roared with laughter, slapping her huge chest with her jewelled hands. My mother and I joined in.

Hyacinth did that – made my mother and me laugh out loud, together.

I leave Dr Laws and walk out of St Michael's Hospital, standing in the ambulance bay at the entrance, swaying, unbalanced by the unexpected. The hospital's patients give me a wide berth as I contemplate what to do. I can walk home, gather my tools, put them in my truck and do some work *chez* Psychobitch. Or I can walk to Whiteladies and take Sonja out to lunch. I stuff my hands in my bagged, stretched pockets and walk down Tyndalls Park Road. As I walk, I turn my world over and over in my mind. A few days before I had decided to ask Sonja, as Ian badgers me to do, about the Blind Man. Indeed, I'd selected the very words with which to ask her. Yet and yet . . . this morning she had called me Special rather than John for the first time in months. She had tugged my beard, she had kissed me. And now this – an invitation to allow someone to lop off my ears, slicing through old scars, in order to snip at my neck and try again.

But if I could hear . . . ? Would that make a difference?

The clouds part, blow away, and I am walking down Tyndalls Park Road with a sharp blue sky around me, leaves falling, wind biting and fresh. Surely, *surely* I can change, cease to be a silent curmudgeon (Ian's word of the week) and become Sonja's lover again? A group of slim-hipped students, toting bags and skateboards, reel out of Woodland Road, nearly crash into me as I walk. They shrink back, startled. Good Christ – I scare people I don't even know. Was I talking to myself? I don't know. I can't hear.

I pass the BBC buildings, my mind thrashing in a thousand traps, and walk the length of Whiteladies until I find myself outside Sonja's deli. I stand there, under the portico, my hands bagging the pockets I force them into, thumb and forefinger rubbing the worrystone. Labradors come to me, their slow legs stumping, tongues lolling, licking and smiling. I ignore them, worry Hyacinth's stone. Sonja comes out, rubbing her upper arms in the cold.

'What happened at the hospital?'

'An infection. I've got antibiotics.'

'So – are you going to work?' She is bewildered. Doesn't know what to do with her hulk of a husband. She glances again and again up and down Whiteladies. 'John?'

So I'm not Special any more? I have reverted to a John. 'They want to operate again.' I'm shivering.

'I'll get my coat.' Sonja goes back into the deli and shrugs on an old donkey jacket of mine. It reaches her knees and the arms are rolled back over and over but I love to see her wear it because I always feel as if it is me wrapped around her. I watch her write a long note, her brows creased, and hand it to one of the assistants, who shoves it into his jeans, nodding agreement with her instructions. I know now that she has been planning to meet the Blind Man, that I have scuppered her plans. I shiver again as I rub my thumb on the malachite. I THINK YOULL NEED THIS ONCE IN A WILE! A black Labrador licks my hanging hand and it is all I can do not to punch its stippled black snout. What is wrong with me?

Sonja comes out of the shop, looks at me and grabs my hanging hand, holds on to it. I looked down at her beautiful, troubled face.

'Where do you want to go? Home? Out?' she asks.

'Out.'

We begin to walk, both her hands holding one of mine, awkward, but it's fine by me. We walk along Whiteladies Road, up Blackboy Hill to the Port of Call, saying nothing

of import. We settle at a table, food ordered, pints of Smiles'
Best in front us. Sonja looks at me and speaks. 'Why do they
want to operate?'

I tell her what Dr Laws has said. I try to be factual, try to be
dry and medical about my options. But she, Sonja, the listener,
is one of my options. It's for her that I'd do it, have my ears
sliced off again. But that is the dark part of the equation that
I can't tell her. The Port of Call is a dim, lamp-lit pub, a place
of niches and bolt-holes, yet it isn't dark enough, labyrinthine
enough, for my choices to hide in.

'Dr Laws said that if it works, if I don't have any perforations in my eardrums, I can swim again. Even if I can't hear
I may be able to swim.'

'Well, John, that's wonderful.'

I want to pick up my pint of Smiles' and throw it somewhere. 'Yes.'

'So – will you do it? Have the operation?' Sonja looks like
a mildly interested cousin, three times removed, but I think
she has realised that among the thousand traps my mind has
laid itself there are some waiting for her.

'Well, I have to be assessed, apparently. Some tests that
work out if I'm the right stuff. Because some people have
it done and think they'll hear everything and they don't.
Or maybe they're not physically OK. You know. The way
I look at it, I never heard much anyway, so . . . yes, I'll do
it if I can.'

In the gloom I see a darker shadow cross her face, as one
of the traps slams shut, snaring her options. I know she won't
leave me until I am whole again. And I know, too, what her
next question will be.

'So,' she says, lowering her grey eyes to stare at her beer,
'did Dr Laws say how long you'd have to wait?'

'No, he didn't. You could ask when you phone him.'

'Yes, I could, couldn't I?' She stares out of the window, mentally rearranging the calendar of her life, listening to her options squeal as they are squashed one by one under the heel of my decision.

Harry of the spotted bow-ties, lurid braces and smooth, chubby face, was a child psychologist, specialising in psycholinguistics. I know that now but when I was in Tommy's I thought he was just a nice man who came to see me a lot. Which, in a way, was true. Years later Harry wrote to me at school and told me that he took me on as a personal crusade after a case conference when he heard of my injuries, my silence, my constantly turned back. When he heard that I was an only child, with no father and an eternally damaged mother. When he heard that the degree of my trauma was so severe, so extreme, that I hadn't said a word for five months and seemed incapable of speech. That I'd forgotten, it would seem, how to live, how to love, how to speak. He said he sat in the conference room and his chest tightened until he felt he couldn't draw breath. When the surgeons began discussing how they intended to break my legs again and reset them, he made his excuses and left the room. He walked the long linoleum corridor, scene of our later triumph, and wandered around outside the hospital, smoking cigarettes, waiting for his chest to ease. Once it had he went back to the main entrance, crossed to the reception desk and asked for pen and paper, took off his white coat and came to my room. He sat on the bed and wrote, *Hello, John, I'm Harry. How are you today?*

He has since said that, like my mother, he noticed the mad brightness, the openness of my eyes, roving everywhere, rarely blinking. He noticed that my hands moved all the time, rubbing, fingering, fidgeting. I was compensating for my hearing, trying to learn as much about the world as I could through my other senses. He also said that when he heard the first word I spoke, 'Swimming', his breath was squeezed once more by a constricting chest. Harry has a heart of gold, a huge heart, but even he didn't have heart enough to tell me then that I would never swim again.

The Elemental office is a grey, cheerless unit in a light-industrial area of Bedminster. A couple of months ago Ian and I received a letter from the Department of Education and Employment asking if we would take on an apprentice as part of some scheme to reduce unemployment – if we took on a young, long-term unemployed person and trained them, they would be paid a trifling weekly sum by the DEE. 'What d'you think?' I asked Ian, handing him the letter.

He read it and wrinkled his nose. 'I dunno. What can we teach them?'

'The rudiments, I guess. Teach them how to get up for a reason?'

'You decide.' He put the letter on the desk and dangled his truck keys from finger and thumb. 'Remember you've got to collect the order from Robbins.'

'Yeah. D'you need anything?'

'No. I'll catch you later.' And off he went, to wrestle with iron in the firelit cave of his workshop.

That night I asked Sonja what she thought of the scheme. She was cooking, moving around the Aga, slicing onions, skimming the purple scum from a pan of simmering red kidney beans. She was making her chilli con carne, a dish hot enough to make even the most spice-jaded palate extremely thoughtful.

'I think it's great,' she said, wiping away onion-induced tears with the hem of her T-shirt. 'I took one on about a year ago and she did really well. She's working in Planet Earth now and earning three times as much.'

I picked up my beer and sluiced it round the bottle until froth formed. 'You didn't tell me.'

'You didn't ask.' Sonja moved away to the Aga and threw chunks of pork into red-hot fat, jumping back as it spat at her.

A flash of anger sizzled through me. Well, good Christ, I can't come home and ask every conceivable question on the off-chance that it's happened. 'Hi, were you mugged today?' 'Was there a multiple pile-up outside the shop?' 'Has there been an earthquake in Japan?' 'Who is the Blind Man?'

'So, you think we should do it? Take on one of these people?' I asked.

She brushed a strand of hair away from her eyes with the back of her hand. 'Yes, I do. I mean, there's the problem of the pay – you get them for nothing and they get something like fifty quid a week, which seems like exploitation to me. After all, it's only a fiver more than they'd get for lying in bed all day. But, but . . . Elaine did well out of it.'

'OK, then we will.'

And so it was that Darren Whiteside came, for a short while, into our lives.

It was Harry who taught me the rudiments of lip-reading, pushing me every day to improve, to be faster, to be more engaged. He knew that this was the time to do it, before I began to forget, began to expect less of the world. It is a strange sensation, to be newly deaf. For when you open your mouth to speak, nothing happens, there is no sound, and yet it seems there is, because the listeners nod and smile, shake their heads and reply. Simply because you do not hear sound does not mean there is no sound – an aural Schrödinger's cat, which is all ears. Harry tried to explain this to me, more, I think, to show me that he understood me rather than the reverse.

John – think of your bedroom at home. I expect it's full of things. Books, clothes, pictures, he wrote.

'Shells,' I said. 'Lots of shells and pebbles. And bits of boats.'

Right. Lots of things. You haven't been in your room for a long, long time.

I nodded hard, trying not to think of my bedroom in the tiny cottage in Noss Mayo, for if I thought of it it would become a part of this, a part of the bomb and its consequences. I wanted it to remain separate, unsullied.

You haven't been in there, you haven't seen it, or picked up the pebbles, or slept there for a long time. But that doesn't mean it doesn't exist. It does. Just like your speech. Even though you can't hear it, it still exists.

I nodded again, closing my eyes, trying to keep out the familiar pictures. My mother, sitting as ever by my bed, picked up my hand and held it.

So what we're going to do, you and me and your mother, is make sure you can talk and that you can listen. But instead of hearing with your ears you're going to hear with your eyes. And what did the doctor say about your eyes?

I smiled. 'That I *could* see the needle in the haystack.'

Right.

So every day I shuffled out of my room, helped by my

mother, and went up in the beige battered lift the five storeys to Harry's room. It was tiny, filled with books and papers and ringed, tannin-stained china mugs balancing on piles of magazines. Harry would be sitting there, hands tucked under his pale double chin, smiling, a blackboard and chalk behind him. I was given passages to read aloud, I'd watch Harry speaking single words, then phrases and then sentences. I practised fricatives and aspirates, practised saying 'church, 'thing', 'thump', 'shirt', 'funny', words that worked my lips.

Harry's approach was, I now realise, holistic. Not only did I have to be able to use my eyes to hear, I had to be able to speak clearly, not be allowed to become lazy so my words slurred and jumbled. I had to learn to read people's faces as well as their lips, be able to read their whole bodies. I had to be able to write clearly, know how things were spelled so I could crack the shell of their sound on my teeth. He taught me to modulate my voice, taught me not to shout (I had been yelling for months) but rather to pitch my voice like a ball at the right height for the listener to catch. He had to make sure that I was learning all these things equally so that I was armed as well as I was able. Harry was a gentle man, a gentle teacher. Like Hyacinth, he had learned to read my face and he knew when I was struggling, when I was bored, when I'd slipped away and was thinking of other things. But he was relentless: like the others he made me *mind*, so that I would ask people to repeat things, ask them to turn their faces to me, rather than mentally shrugging and turning away from conversation.

My mother would sit during these hours, watching every move. The curious thing was that, although her lips had been pulled awry and her mouth swivelled a little, when she spoke I could always understand her, could understand her every word.

When the lesson ended, I'd go and stand at Harry's window to look at London, look at life outside the glass. The trains pulling out of Waterloo, the cars, floors below, fighting the wheel of a roundabout, people crossing the roads, planes flying into Heathrow. In the distance I could see the Post Office Tower, the skyscrapers of the City. In the far distance I could still see London – it went on for ever.

Then they broke my legs again and I retreated into my familiar shell of pain, wondering how much more of me there was to break.

I waited three-quarters of an hour for Darren Whiteside on his first day. It was half past eight when the door opened and he sauntered in, sour and resentful. He stood, looking at me sitting at my desk, his hands dangling by his side.

'Darren Whiteside?'

He nodded, looked around the office.

'You're forty-five minutes late.'

He shrugged. Looked down, said something.

'What?'

He said something about buses.

I stared at him. He was wearing a cheap, electric blue Umbro football shirt proclaiming him to be one of England's finest football players, which wasn't anything to boast about. He wore jeans eight sizes too big for him, slung round his hips with a loose belt, a reversed baseball cap and a pair of outsize Nikes, laces undone. As I looked at him he unwrapped some gum and began to chew it, mouth open. He was tall and thin, looked malnourished. His face was pale and spotted, his hair greased back, cut in a wedge shape, hanging limp in a straight line above a bristled neck. His eyes were sludge-coloured and narrow. Darren Whiteside was a spike, the kind of youth no bouncer in Bristol would let into a pub or club under any circumstances. Yet he looked familiar. I was confused – he reminded me of someone but how could it possibly be anyone I knew?

'Tomorrow you get here at quarter to eight, like everyone else.'

He sighed, looked at his shoes, out of the window, moved back and half sat on the window-ledge, crossed his ankles.

'I said tomorrow you get here at quarter to eight.'

No response.

'What jobs have you done before?'

He talked for a moment at his shoes.

'Pardon?'

Again he mumbled.

'Darren, I'm deaf. If you want to talk to me you have to look at me so I can lip-read.'

He looked up from his shoes as a slow, foetid smile grew on his face. The rage of months, possibly of years, began to grow in me. I stood up slowly from my chair and it must have seemed to him that I kept growing and growing. As I said, Darren Whiteside was tall, but at six feet seven I generally expect to be the tallest man in a room. I was certainly the tallest man in that office. I motioned for him to follow me. As we left the office he stopped by the wastebasket and let the pupa-like piece of chewed gum drop from his mouth.

I drove to Archfield Road and as we inched up Park Street in heavy traffic Darren took a Walkman from his jeans pocket, slipped on headphones, began to slap his spindly thigh to the rhythm. When we got to the job I motioned Jimmy over, the boss of the team I had there, the men who dig out and lay the foundations and pilings. Jimmy was a monkey of a man, short and wiry, darkened by summers and winters spent outside. Hard as nails. Firm but firm.

'Jimmy, Darren. Darren's new. He slept in late, so he's got plenty of energy.'

Darren stood watching the gang working the earth with a sneer wrapped round his thin, pinched face.

Jimmy grinned. 'Fair enough, Mr Player. We could use some of that.'

I spent the day driving round the various jobs we had going, picked timber up from Robbins, did some paperwork, hauled cement and sharp sand over to Clifton, and then went back to Archfield Road to collect some of the team and take them back to the office. They were waiting by the wall outside, some smoking, their cigarettes flashing in the dark winter afternoon, some reading newspapers, some wandering off to the Cotham Porter Stores. They would find their own way home. Darren sat apart from them all, mouth slack, staring at his feet. I pulled up and hooted the horn. Jimmy waved and three of the men got into the truck, with Darren straggling behind. Jimmy came over and twitched an eyebrow in Darren's direction. 'Lazy sod,' he said.

'You'll have him again tomorrow, I'm afraid.'

'Shit,' said Jimmy. 'Sorry, Mr Player. But he can't do anything. Asked him to mix cement on a spot, even showed him how to, and he still couldn't do it. Kept complaining about his shoes.'

'His shoes?'

'Yeah.'

Darren's face loomed in the window, inches away from me, so close I could see each pustule on his forehead, see the pus gathering. 'Look at my fuckin' trainers. Ninety-five quid they cost and they're knackered.' His face was vicious with outrage. 'You owe me a new pair.'

I laughed. 'Get in, Darren.'

'You owe me a new pair. Ninety-five quid.'

'Get in the truck, Darren.'

He said something and I got out of the truck and stood right by him, so close I could smell his malnourished breath. 'What did you say?'

'Nuffin'.'

'What did you say?'

Jimmy didn't move, stayed so still you couldn't see him breathing. He'd never seen me like this.

'*What did you say?*' Sorry, Harry, but I wasn't bothering right then about modulating my voice. Darren sneered, moved away. 'I can read lips, Darren. I can practically read your pitiful fucking mind.' He moved again, bumped into the truck. 'What did you say?' His eyes began to flicker, side to side, but there wasn't any skinny-arsed rat-pack running with him that day. 'I'll tell you what you said. You said, to me, "Fucking deaf-aid." That's what you said, isn't it, Darren? You said to me, "Fucking deaf-aid."' His eyes were darting now, looking at the men in the truck, who stared back impassively. I bent down until my face was level with his. 'Don't say that. Don't *ever* say that.'

I straightened, walked back to the truck, and in the wing mirror I saw Darren give me the finger as he sauntered away. I wheeled round and Jimmy snatched at my arm with his hawser-like fingers, shaking his head. I shrugged him off and began to run, my boots slipping on the frosty tarmac as Darren glanced over his shoulder and saw me barrelling towards him. Jimmy and five other men sprinted after me, pulling my coat, my arms, my anything, as Darren flew down the hill, spindly legs pumping. My jacket was torn by someone holding on to the sleeve, trying to slow me, and Jimmy locked his arms round my neck, his feet off the ground. Pedestrians stopped and stared, dogs pulled on their leads, mouths flapping as they barked. Mothers on the school run, MPVs packed with children, slowed and stopped uncertainly, centrally locking their cars as six men whirled like a troupe of ungainly, stumbling dancers in the middle of the road. I lashed out, trying to free myself so I could thunder after Darren Whiteside and catch him. I knew there would be the sounds of shouting, of skittering hobnails on tarmac, of laboured, uneven breathing as the pack of them eventually tussled me to a standstill. At the bottom of the hill Darren stopped running and looked back as I was dragged to my pick-up truck, hands pushing my chest, pushing at my heart. Even from that distance I could see Darren Whiteside's acned face in the street-light – and suddenly I heard a question I'd forgotten for years: 'Who's yer mother been fucking today, then?' Martin Sawyer's voice. And I was standing, panting, on a road in Noss Mayo, watching Martin Sawyer's blood trickle on to asphalt. He'd returned to haunt me, the boy who'd messed with Merboy.

I was pinned against the cold metal of the truck, Jimmy mouthing words I couldn't be bothered to watch, and I threw back my head and roared as I finally came face to face with the civilising of Merboy. First they took away his hearing and then, over years, his voice and finally they took his anger.

'I mean, can you believe that?' I asked Sonja later, as we sat in the living room, drinking wine. 'And he wants me to buy him new trainers? What's he doing with ninety-five quid trainers in the first bloody place if he's on the dole?'

'You shouldn't have lost your temper.' She ran a finger round the rim of her glass, staring at the flames of the fire. 'You shouldn't have.'

'I was sorely provoked.' By so many things.

'I agree. But – and, John, we've been through this before, it's really simple – you're too damn *big* to lose your temper. People don't listen to what you say. They just look at the size of you and pretend to agree, pretend to apologise, so they can get away.'

I shifted on the settee, my feet dangling over its arms, my neck bruised by Jimmy's fingers. 'I know, I know. He's such a shit, though.'

'Maybe he's scared and unsure of himself. It's the first time he's had a job. Maybe it's just fear coming through.'

'Fucking idiocy coming through, more like. You should see him and then you'd know what I mean. Well, I guess it doesn't matter. Can't see him coming back tomorrow, and anyway—'

Sonja motioned me to be quiet. 'It's the phone.' She gathered herself and stood up in one easy motion, her skirt wrapping round her hips and thighs. I watched her speaking into the receiver, hand on hip, rocking back and forth, her toes turned up slightly, examining her bare, olive feet. At one point she laid the back of her hand on her forehead as if feeling for her own fever. An odd, touching gesture. I felt my groin spark, felt my hands grow heavy. It had been months. It had been months since she met her Blind Man. I stared at the ceiling, trying to ignore my hard-on, distracting myself by imagining Darren Whiteside's home life.

Sonja put the phone down and rather than sitting on the floor where she had been came over to the settee, nudged me over, lay down next to me. 'That was Dr Laws. He wanted to know if you'd made up your mind.'

'What did you say?'

'I said you had. I said yes.'

'Did you ask him how long before they can do it?'

'Yes. It's usually a few months but he says he's going to bring it forward. He thinks you've waited long enough. Probably about six weeks, with about six weeks to recover.' She looked at my mouth. 'Six weeks, John. January.'

We stared at each other then, blue and grey eyes locked, for a long, long time, acknowledging, both of us, what that meant.

A fortnight before I was due to leave St Thomas' my mother told me she was going away for a week. I was in bed, resting my reset legs, when she told me. She hadn't left my side for over a year. I scrabbled for my pad and pencil – a reflex when I was frightened, when my world was rocked. I had become so institutionalised my world fell apart if my breakfast was late.

Why?

'Because you're leaving here soon and I have to get things ready for us.'

What things?

'A hundred things, John. I want everything to be the best for you when you come out.' She took the pencil and paper from me gently. 'I'll only be gone a week. It will pass without you even noticing.' Her face was even more severe than usual, the lines round her mouth hacked by a careless butcher. She had drawn herself in, into herself, preparing to tell me this. 'And when I get back, you'll be getting ready to leave and all this will be over.' She leaned over and kissed my forehead and I began to scream. I knew I was screaming as she walked

out and Hyacinth and Harry walked in. The whole episode
had been orchestrated so that I wouldn't be left alone for a
moment.

The two of them stayed with me all day as I screamed.
Neither of them was working, they'd come in because my
mother had asked them to, and they listened to me screaming
for hours. One of them went home to eat and change and the
other sat by my bed, trying to hold my hands, trying to calm
me, and then they would switch. Hours passed and, exhausted,
I slept. I woke up screaming. A doctor came in and gave me
an injection and I slept. I woke up screaming. Hyacinth lasted
a day and half, Harry three. And I screamed. I could feel in
my throat that I was making no sound by the third day.

It is hard to understand this if you haven't spent a long,
long time in hospital. At first it is a blur, it doesn't matter
where you are because of the pain. And then it's a prison,
boring and endless, punctuated by the mundane. Gradually it
becomes a comfort, the mundane becomes the anticipated,
the manageable. It encompasses the patient and the patient
embraces it. Finally it becomes a prison of a different kind –
the bars on the windows, over the door, are of the patient's
making. Food, comfort, routine, warmth, baths, companionship – all are to be found there. But outside the hospital
doors? Who knows? The bomb? The big bad wolf? The
Father?

I screamed because the routine of my days had been
shattered. I screamed because my wish – that my mother not
leave me – had been ignored. I screamed because I couldn't
stop the world changing.

The night that Dr Laws phoned and Sonja told him that I
wanted to have the operation, we lay on the settee and both

silently acknowledged exactly what *that* meant. It wasn't a pardon but it was a reprieve. And that night, for the first time in months, Sonja and I made what she describes as smoky love, as opposed to pistachio love. I can't explain it but I know what she means. Twenty years is a long time to share in someone.

I woke the next morning, early as ever, watching my face turn red, but instead of hauling my body from the iron bed to escape that image I lay there staring at the ceiling. Sonja was asleep, smelling, as always, of sweet toffee. My mind drifted and, unleashed, it recalled a night many years before when we had gone to a gig in London.

I can't remember how she persuaded me to go but I did. Four of us in a car, an old VW Beetle, driving to the 100 Club on Oxford Street to see the Darts. Literally, in my case. I'd never been to a gig – why would I? – and I couldn't believe the energy of the club, how crowded it was, how smoky, how mobile. People moved all the time, swaying, touching, grabbing each other, hugging, drinking, waving, smooching, whatever. They were dancing even before the gig began. The Darts came on stage – ironic, retro swing-band apparently, silver suits and leopardskin shoes, a beautiful black woman fronting in an hourglass vermilion dress – and the crowd moved as one around me. The woman could sing – or, at least, I knew she could enunciate. I swayed with the crowd as Sonja held my hand in a blood-stopping grip, constantly darting looks at me. But I was happy. I watched the woman's hips and lips, and picked up some phrases: '. . . the boy from New York City', 'Zing went the strings of my heart'. 'Life', apparently, 'could be a dream . . .' I was enchanted. I was also drunk as a skunk and the beautiful black woman's lips were at the centre of my universe. I swayed with the rest of the crowd, sweating and yelling and somehow knew that it didn't matter what I yelled, no one could hear, except Sonja but she managed to laugh and look appalled at the same time. The people around me were clicking their fingers and I watched them for a while, then picked up the rhythm and joined in. I joined in. When it had finished, when we were standing outside on the crowded, traffic-jammed street, I grabbed Sonja, lifted her off her feet and kissed her, tasting martini and fresh lemon. And lust.

I turned to look at Sonja, sleeping still, her arms thrown back, her hair on the pillow, and thought, I love you, thought, Is six weeks long enough? Thought, Come here.

I walked into the office at half past seven, happy for the first time in months, made slow by rekindled desire. Ian was already there. He turned away from a folder of invoices, looked at me and smiled, raising an eyebrow.

'Life,' I said, falling into my chair, 'could be a dream.'

The door flew open and Darren Whiteside walked in, chewing gum, and said something about 'fucking buses'.

After many months, when my grafts had healed, I was taken swimming. Or, rather, the physiotherapists called it swimming; I thought of it as floating in a piss-pool. As part of my treatment I was wheeled from my room and taken down in the beige lift by one of the porters to the basement of the hospital where there was a small, pale blue cube of chlorinated water. The room had no windows and a wheezing pump laboured to change the air in there, inevitably failing. It smelled of mould and heat, of sweat and wet wool. It smelled of despair.

I would sit in my wheelchair as Miss Handel stuffed a flabby, plastic, flesh-coloured earplug in each ear, smiling cheerfully and chattering. Then I was hoisted out of the chair, a strong

hand under each armpit, and an inflated ring was threaded
over my feet up to my waist. The same strong arms would lift
me like a baby to carry me and my head would fall back, my
eyes open staring at the tiled white ceiling. I *was* a baby, floppy
and useless, my legs and arms hanging, useless. I regressed
in moments. The arms carried me down a short flight of
steps and lowered me into the water, making sure my head
stayed above water because my ears were *never* to get wet.
Miss Handel, small and blonde, pert in her swimming-suit,
would climb into the water and begin to knead my legs, my
arms. My head rested against the barrel chest of the man with
the strong arms as Miss Handel talked and smiled, bent my
knees, flexed my elbows. And I floated in the dead, lifeless
water, staring at the tiled white ceiling.

I couldn't forgive them this travesty, this thing called
swimming. They tried to describe it as a treat and even
my mother was fooled into thinking it might be, as she sat
on a plastic chair at the pool's edge. But I lay there, my head
resting on a stranger's heart, my eyes scanning the white tiles,
and thought of the thundering surf at Crackington Haven,
thought of the jagged, shark's-tooth rocks at the end of
Thurlestone, which created lanes of swirling water. Imagined
the rollers at Newquay, the endless sands of Whitsand Bay.
Imagined climbing the ragged, seaweed-slippery pilings in
front of the cottage and leaping from them. Diving from
the decks of yachts, falling out of dinghies, oars waving, boat
dipping. Remembered the Lido on the Hoe in Plymouth –
one summer's day jumping from the highest point of the
fountain in the big pool and being thrown out by the
lifeguards, watched by timid, admiring boys.

Remembered swimming naked at Constantine Bay one
Boxing Day in response to a dare from my mother. I waded

in, hopping from foot to foot, my shell-like penis disappearing, teeth clacking, stomach freezing. I held up my arms, jumped up and chattered with each swell, trying to save my chest, my heart, from this icy water. I remembered turning and seeing my mother, bent over, laughing, my clothes bundled in her arms, her hair shining in the low-slanting sunlight. She waved, the only person on that infinite beach, and shouted something to me, words that were caught and carried over the Atlantic. (I wonder whether a sleepy sunbather lying on the sands of Mexico was wakened hours later by Mother's voice in their ears, shouting, 'It doesn't count unless you go right in!') I counted to three and ducked under the winter waters, thinking it was a fine way to die.

Worse than all these memories was the thought that only a few months before I had spent weeks falling in and out of a turquoise lake in France.

And they called *this* 'swimming'? Floating, supported by a ring, by someone else's arms, in a pool the size of a kitchen? Miss Handel tapped my arm one morning and I looked at her. 'Try to kick,' she mouthed, and I breathed deeply and churned the tiny pool into a storm of synthetic water, feeling the strong arms slip a little, surprised by the motion.

Any patient considering cochlear implants has to be assessed to evaluate their suitability for the operation. And so one December morning I dress with shaking hands, kiss a sleepy Sonja, and walk dry-mouthed to St Michael's. The doctor – having established that I have a profound bilateral sensorineural hearing loss and having decided I was a healthy enough post-lingually deafened adult – tells me that I'm indeed a suitable candidate. My heart performs a jig and it is then that he tells me of the risks.

The surgery can traumatise the cochlear endosteum, prompting new bone growth, which might further damage the nerves in my ears. There is also a risk of infection at the site of the skin flap behind the ear and of a failure of the flap to heal normally. The operation can also damage facial nerves. Moreover, although there exist encouraging data suggesting that the corrosion of platinum electrodes used for three years was minimal, the effect of current passage has the potential for deleterious effects on surviving neural elements. In short, I might be left irreparably deafened by burgeoning bone, skin oozing and flapping from my skull, my face paralysed in a rictus of incomprehension, as electrodes melted in my ear affecting other nerve centres. I stare blankly at the doctor as if he has taken leave of his senses for it seems that I will surely take leave of most of mine under the knife.

In reply he smiles broadly, rubs his hands briskly. 'However, such problems as tympanic malfunctions must be dealt with first. So we need to sort out those eardrums with a spot of myringoplasty and then we can get down to the serious business.' Serious business? I'd already been told the risks of *that* spot of knifework – post-surgical infection and facial nerve paralysis. Ultimately the decision whether to operate is left to the patient once he has been told of the risks.

I walk for hours after the consultation, down the hill from the hospital, past St Michael on the Mount Without, knowing just how he felt. Down Christmas Steps and along to the docks, where I stop at Brunel's Buttery for a mug of tea.

These operations could kill me, or leave me paralysed. That much I know now. But there is more than that. There is the thought of undressing and putting on a gown, of being shaved, wheeled down to theatre. I can remember the last moments before anaesthetics are administered – my heart pumping, mouth dry, as a nurse strokes my hand. Wanting to roll off the table and run. Special was lifted on to an operating table more times than even I can remember and he lay there dreading waking up to more pain, to re-broken legs, to tight stitches, raw grafted skin, oozing ears. Even now, twenty-eight years later, I can feel his panic, how he cried every time they came with the trolley to wheel him down to theatre and no one could whisper words to calm him, reassure him. Of course, I've been in hospital since then, when I had my heart trouble. But I didn't *choose* that, didn't plan it. Didn't walk into the hospital with my arms outstretched, waiting to be handcuffed to chance.

I finish my tea, stand up and stretch my tight, grafted back, as the steam train trundles along its tracks, billowing pungent, sooty smoke and a woman walks past, wearing headphones, just as Darren Whiteside does, her hips sashaying to the rhythm. Behind her, on the deck of a houseboat, a man is playing a clarinet. I look down and at my table a little girl, maybe three, four, I don't know, is watching me stretch and is pointing, saying something. She is smiling, with a thumb in her mouth, so I can't read her lips. I know it's something about giants but I can't read her. All I can do is smile in return and walk away along the river towards the Arnolfini. And I think about how much I want to hear it all – the ferries, the cars, the buskers, the buses, the smiling child saying something about a giant, the steam train, the planes flying overhead. Most of all I want to hear the man play the clarinet, because I've never heard its music, I only know its name. I stop and look at the river running and I can see Dr Laws' face smiling wolfishly, saying, 'You'll be able to swim.'

I had sat, not long before, with Sonja in the Port of Call watching her realise that she would have to rearrange her calendar, waiting until I was whole to do whatever she wanted to do. Leave me or stay. I'd watched her and thought I would do it, have the operations, in order to keep her. What foolishness, as my mother would say. It was me who would clamber on to the trolley to be taken to theatre. I was the one who'd lie there, watching scalpels being arranged on a steel tray, knowing one of them would be used to slice the skin behind my ears, not knowing if I would wake up with a frozen face or if I would even wake up at all. I look back at the man playing the clarinet and a wave of anger pushes my tongue against the roof of my mouth.

The memory of the smoky love Sonja and I had made stayed with me for days. I took the memory out and examined it, turning it over in my fingers, many times each day. The days themselves turned crisp and sharp as we moved towards December, the freezing rain and grey clouds of November forgotten.

Many builders lie fallow in winter, perhaps turning their hands to interior work, to knocking down walls, replastering, plumbing new bathrooms, sanding floors. Elemental worked right through the seasons. I made sure that each job had been started, the foundations literally laid, before the weather turned foul. Hard wood has an open heart, it is easy and malleable, it can stand the cold and the rain, can be left, once seasoned, in all weathers. Wood withstands all this with a tad of shrinkage and the occasional crack, but human flesh is not as sturdy.

Years ago I had various steel frames made over which tarpaulin could be draped with ventilation flaps so heaters could be used. My men – and a few women – worked in the dry, with heat available no matter the weather. To be sure, they worked in jackets and padded shirts, thermal socks and steel-capped DMs – but they worked, they earned money. They developed an easy rhythm to their days, a camaraderie born of working and living in a small city, a shared work experience, a shared circle of friends. They passed packets of shag to each other during their breaks, reached over with mugs of whisky-laced coffee, lent each other money and stood each other rounds in pubs. They read aloud laughable passages from newspapers to each other as they leaned against columns, walls, bags of cement, under the snug canopy of the tarpaulin. They could break from work when they wanted, there was no routine. I knew them all well, respected most of them and valued the rest, knew them well enough to know that they were working as hard, as proficiently, as they were able. Occasionally I'd duck under a canvas doorway and look around, to see them planing, chiselling, sawing, chamfering, routering, drilling, clamping. And they would glance up at me with the glazed eyes of people who are focused on other things. All of them, that is, except Darren Whiteside, who stood alone, headset pressed to his ears, staring at the floor, twitching to an unheard beat.

Eventually I had no choice but to send him to Cotham Grove, to the home of Psychobitch. The team there needed a gofer, someone to cut lengths of pine, someone to hold a donkey as they sawed. No one else had the lack of skills, so I sent him.

'I don't know how he'll get on,' I said to Sonja that night, as I stacked logs on the fire. 'I just don't see the point of him. He doesn't do anything, he *can't* do anything. He doesn't seem to contribute anything to the world. Why on earth did he come back?'

'He didn't really have a choice. If he doesn't turn up he

doesn't get the money.' She was lying on the settee, crumpled newspaper in her hands.

'Jesus. I feel like giving him fifty quid a week to stay away.'

She smiled and turned back to her paper as I sat, my back against the coffee table, a glass of whisky in my hand. I watched her turning the pages, tried to imagine the rustle they made but it was too faint a memory to recall clearly. I watched her focus on a story, pulling the pages closer, frowning slightly.

'I still love you,' I said, not hearing the declaration.

She lowered the paper slowly and turned her face to me. I had known her face for more than twenty years and yet I didn't recognise her expression, lit by the flames. It was a mingling of sadness, gratitude and exasperation, with a dash of wearied adoration thrown in. I didn't know what to do with it. So I apologised.

'Sorry.'

And within that apology was the acknowledgement of all that had happened, all that was happening.

'I know,' she said.

The next day, I was pondering this exchange, picking it clean, searching for encouragement and finding precious little, when my pager vibrated against my stomach as I drove along Alma Vale East. As usual, there was nowhere to park on the narrow Victorian street, so I dropped down towards Hotwells and stopped in the curve of a driveway. I unclipped the pager and looked at the scrolling LED: *get to cotham grove NOW – Ian.*

I slipped the 4×4 into gear and skittered into Hotwells, along the docks, up Jacob's Wells and on to Whiteladies, dithered and turned up Ashgrove, swivelling the steering-wheel, constantly having to pull over in the narrow, double-parked streets to let other cars pass. When I yanked up the hand-brake as I parked outside the Harpys' house I was already half-way out of the truck door. Jimmy was sitting on the wall outside, smoking a rollie. His dark eyes flicked to me and he shook his head slightly. I jogged down the side of the house, pushed open the side door and there she was. Psychobitch, standing on the pale, unfinished deck. Darren was squatting, resting his back against a wall of the house, earphones clamped to his skull, his pustule-ravaged face swinging from side to side. Around the edge of the garden the rest of the team were evenly spread along the verges. Jimmy and a couple of others outside. Darren couldn't get away – they had him covered. I noticed some of the men looking at me and I knew they were remembering my rage, my savage fight to be free of them. They were nervous.

Psychobitch stepped back across the raw deck, drawing her robe round her as I slammed the side door. I remembered myself, remembered what Sonja had said only days before: 'You're too damn *big* to lose your temper.'

'Good morning, Mrs Harpy. I've been told there's a problem here.'

She glanced at Darren. 'That . . .'

'Excuse me,' I said, and walked across the deck, dragged the earphones away and pulled him to his feet. He struggled a little. 'Sorry, Mrs Harpy, carry on.'

'I came out of my bathroom and there he was, in my bedroom, going through the drawers. He didn't hear me because he was wearing those.' She pointed to the earphones. 'I've noticed a few things going missing. Thought maybe I should have had twenty pounds more than I had. You know. A key-ring, a glass, a bit of money. I thought it was me mislaying things until I saw him.'

Darren stood, chewing gum and I knew he wasn't listening. He was off somewhere.

Psychobitch wrapped her silk gown even tighter, sidled up to me, her lips working furiously. 'Do you have any idea, Mr Player, of the sacrifices Brian and I have made to have this done? We've worked hard, we've burned the midnight oil. And what do we get? A bunch of thieves. You may not know the meaning of sacrifice but I can tell you, we've made sacrifices for this deck and look at it!' She turned with a swirl of her gown and pointed to the bare planks on which Darren Whiteside was slouching. 'We were going to go to the Caribbean this summer and decided to have this built instead. We've given up a lot – and for what?'

'Right.' I looked at Darren Whiteside and he was sneering, chewing his gum. I walked over and looked down at his imbecilic face. 'Empty your pockets.'

'Fuck you.'

'Darren, empty your pockets.'

'Fuck you!' He retreated to a corner of the deck and began to gabble. I couldn't catch all of it. 'Like she'd miss it? Look at her – got so fuckin' much she don' even know when it ain't there. What've I got? Eh? I got a girlfriend 'n' a kid tellin' me how 'ard it is – like I don' fuckin' know! She gives the kid to me and says I should look after 'im and off she goes. An' you, fuckin' deaf-aid, you fink you're somethin', doncha? Just cos you're big and deaf you fink everyone loves ya. Well, you can fuck off!'

'I've called the police, of course,' said Psychobitch.

'You don' know what it's fuckin' like.' Darren's spittle spotted the untreated deck. 'Sittin' up there in your fuck-off

house in Clifton. You always 'ad it so easy. Fuckin' deaf-aid.'
He spat at me, his thin cheeks blowing, and he missed, of
course, the globule of sputum landing near Harpy's foot,
staining the wood. 'You've always had it so fuckin' easy.'

I watched the two of them as they ranted, each complaining
about how their lives had worked out, commenting on the
ease of my life, commenting on my ignorance of sacrifice.
I thought about Darren Whiteside's child – how was it that
he had a child? What had he been thinking of? Come to
that, what had my father been thinking of? When he left my
mother, when he left the flat they lived in while my mother
gave birth – what had *he* been thinking of? What had gone
through his mind?

Darren and Psychobitch ground to a halt and I shook
myself.

'Martin – uh, Darren,' I said, 'empty your pockets.' And
he did, knowing that at the end of it all, when everything was
wrapped up and sealed away, he would still be a pitiful spike
with a kid and girlfriend who wore her hair in ringlets, bunched
on her head, dressed in the same uniform of Umbro shell-suit.
The haul in his pocket was a strange collection: some jewellery,
a small porcelain egg, a silver-framed picture of Psychobitch
on a beach and an unwrapped cake of Elizabeth Arden soap.
Looking at this pile of objects I realised that he'd taken them
simply because they were there. Unless he thought the soap
would work miracles on his acne. Ian arrived as I turned the
soap in my hand.

I turned to Psychobitch and handed her the sad pile of
swag. 'Mrs Harpy, I can't apologise enough. This has never
happened before. I'll replace any money stolen and reimburse
you for any other losses.'

'Of course you will,' she said, and went into the house.

Jimmy tapped my shoulder. 'Police are here.'

Two constables walked on to the deck, one speaking into the walkie-talkie pinned to his lapel. The other looked at Darren and sighed, crossing his arms. 'Well, hello, Darren. What you been doing this time?'

It took half an hour for various statements to be made, for Psychobitch to list the missing goods, for Darren to mumble a few words. When he'd gone, escorted by the policemen, I wrote a cheque for Mrs Harpy – 'Let's say five hundred, shall we?' – and how could I argue? She took it from me, delicately, gently, and in her eyes her small triumph registered. Jimmy was getting the team back on-task and I could see their arms swinging, backs bent as they returned to their sawing and planing. I'd restored order, re-established the routines that enabled others to live their lives as my own life de-railed.

What *had* my father thought as he packed his cases and left? What had he thought when he saw my picture in the papers after the bomb? They chose a photograph from my first year in grammar school – tie crooked, my blazer bunched on my shoulders, grinning at Nicky Tate, who was gurning behind the photographer. Merboy's only formal portrait. Of course, the newspaper pictures were black-and-white but he would have known that my eyes were bright blue and my hair jet-black. At least Darren Whiteside knew his own son.

'You OK?' Ian signed, coming up the steps from the garden.

I shrugged. 'Not really. I don't want to do any more today.'

'Don't blame you.'

'I'm hungry – d'you want to go for something to eat?'

'Sure.'

'Let's pick up Sonja and go out somewhere.'

Ian looked at me and frowned. 'Have you talked to her yet?'

'No, but I'm going to. I promise you, I'm going to. This is all driving me fucking crazy.'

'OK, but don't bring it up now, while I'm there. I've had enough for one day.'

As Ian drove the truck to the deli I thought of the one-breasted bowsprit maiden looking out over sluggish river water, hoping she was faring better than I seemed to be. It appeared I was destined to stand on dry decks for ever, designing and building other people's dreams. And yet ... and yet, soon I might be able to hear, distinguish sound from silence. I might even be able to swim. And would that make me Special again? Or would it make me Merboy? All I knew was that I didn't want to be what I was, I didn't want to live as I was. I wanted to surf Big Wednesday and yell and *hear* it. I wanted to pick up my father by the lapels and slam him against a wall and say, 'I'm OK. See? I'm OK. I may not be special but, then, neither are you.' I wanted to sprawl on hot grass in the garden at Noss Mayo, look up and see my mother's lazy, perfect smile. I wanted to snatch Sonja from her other life. I wanted to be burgundy wine again.

Ian double-parked the truck at a bus stop and I clambered out as the omnipresent, peripatetic traffic warden walked towards us. Behind him I could see Sonja standing in the doorway of the deli, her arms crossed, her face smiling easily as she talked to a blond man holding a dog's harness. For the second time in days I broke into a run, roaring, and Sonja – 'You're too damn *big* to lose your temper' – looked over and paled. The Blind Man was moving his head, trying to tune into the source of what must have been a surprising sound, as Sonja grabbed him and bundled him into the shop.

*   *   *

When I left St Thomas' Hospital, early one freezing morning in December 1972, I was fourteen. My limp was noticeable but improving and I could nearly straighten my right arm. The scars on my scalp were covered by a shock of jet-black hair but the weals on my face were bare. The maze of cuts and stitches, the patches of borrowed skin on my legs were covered by jeans, those on my back by a jumper and duffel coat. It was a tin-cup of a day, hard and hollow, frost still on the ground. Harry came with my mother and me to the car – not a Morris Minor but a brand-new, emeraldgreen Triumph 2000. Harry fielded the few photographers there, come out of curiosity to see the wreck of the boy who had been hidden for thirteen months. They must have been disappointed, for apart from the madness in my eyes and the mashing of my jaw, there was nothing to see. The deepest and most damaging scars were invisible.

At the car I turned to Harry and hugged him, speechless. I couldn't even begin to imagine what I would do without him. It was then that I noticed I was taller than he was, by many inches. I looked at his thinning crown of hair and wondered what I was going to do, what was going to happen to me. What was I going to *do* now? I drew away, got into the car and sat staring straight ahead as my mother and Harry hugged, exchanged goodbyes. In my hands were the two things I took from my Aladdin's cave – the picture of the dwarfed surfing men and the black and gold poster, 'John Player Special – for when you want the best'. I unrolled them and looked at them in my lap.

As my mother started the car and pulled away, the automatic doors of the hospital lobby flew open and Hyacinth came tumbling down the steps. I wound down the window and waved as she jumped up and down, flesh jiggling, blowing me kisses with both hands.

My mother touched my arm. 'Do you want to go back?' she mouthed.

I shook my head. I never wanted to go back there again.

JOAN

11 April 1999

If I was asked which sound rings undimmed, unchanging in my ears over years, I would have to sit for a while and sift through my memories before deciding. The sea has always whispered to me, all down my life it's been there. And with that endless restlessness come other sounds – seagulls shrieking and mast wires clinking as boats shift; pebbles turning and waves tapping sea-worn rocks. Or there's the creaking wrought-iron gate outside my grandmother's house in Southdown Road in Plymouth, which rang out a three-note chord of rust and neglect whenever it was opened; she refused to oil it, saying that the sound had become a friend, and I can hear that iron shriek now. Nearly sixty years ago that gate was blasted from its hinges and thrown hundreds of feet but I can still hear it. I remember, too, the sound of the sirens, whooping and blatting across miles, and the memory makes my heart race, makes my limbs jump and think of death. And, of course, there is the dripping of buildings. But I know that if someone were to ask me to name a sound that rings undimmed, unchanging in my ears over years, I would say – having considered oceans, bombs and sirens – it is the sound of John screaming when I left him in hospital.

I walked out of his room, nodded to Harry and Hyacinth, and moved away from him. His screams filled the space around me, filled the ward, filled the world. I heard the door close behind Harry but the sound was not diminished. I walked stiff-legged down the corridor to the lifts, my handbag crushed under my arm. I saw nurses and patients, orderlies and visitors all turning, amazed, towards the sound and yet I walked on. A matron who knew me, knew John, who realised the source of the screams, moved towards me and I looked at her, shook my head slightly and kept walking. I'll never know how I did that. How I walked away from the sound of John shattering his voice like glass, so bereft that I knew his throat was tearing, bleeding. I knew that he was locked in a silent world and I had left him alone in it. The lift came and I dropped down, bag still clenched. I walked out of the building to my car, turned on the engine and began to drive out of London. I made it as far as Battersea before I stopped the car by a phone box and called Tommy's, called the ward to speak to Harry, and I knew, even as they went to fetch Harry to the phone, that John was screaming still. I could hear him five miles away down the phone line.

I'm sixty-five years old. I was thirty-six when the bomb blew and yet I still think of John's high-pitched baying in the hospital, still think of him screaming and twisting as his flesh was seared and melted like wax, lying under the rubble. People say that enough time has passed, that I should forget. But they don't realise that sound can play endlessly; I know that there is always a part of me listening for that scream, imagining it almost. Others say that only a scent, a smell, could transport me back to the memory of that day; that the olfactory is more immediate, somehow magically adept at peeling back the years. To those people I might reply that if you have smelled your son's arm burning, the odours of life lose their appeal. Not only that – I am, shall we say? unlikely to encounter the smell again.

Another sound I can conjure up is the soft, almost inaudible groan that escaped John as he turned his back on me when he first saw my face. My face – a slopping of whisky in the glass. My face. Twenty-eight years it's been and it still looks back at me from the mirror.

Will it get better?

Maybe.

I know why John turned his back to me when I was first allowed to visit him. It wasn't because I was in a wheelchair, it wasn't because he was tired, nor was it because he was in pain and couldn't be bothered to talk. He turned away from me because he was horrified.

When we left the cottage in Noss Mayo that morning I was beautiful. I had always been beautiful, I was used to it. Some people are good at bridge, some good at painting, writing, playing football, sailing, teaching. I was good at being beautiful. It was effortless, it was what was the case, morning, noon and night. I never had to try. I looked in the mirror and there was my face, clear and seductive. I knew that. I knew it when I was twelve. My beauty wasn't dependent on other conditions, it was a given, something that worked to my advantage. When that speck of Semtex blew I was looking in the mirror of a compact, checking the line of my lipstick and the world shattered. So did the mirror and every piece of glass in a two-mile radius. As the glass blew in, I felt nothing (of course, you don't feel much when glass cuts). Then my eyes filled with blood.

But that was a long time ago. It all happened so long ago. I've written about this so often. I sit here on this deck, writing, whisky burbling down my throat, because I can't think of what else to do. I remember pointing, more than thirty years ago, to this house whenever John and I went for a day trip and saying, 'I'd give anything to have that house.' Remembering that reminds me of the story 'The Monkey's Paw'. My mother must have told me that story decades ago. I didn't realise then what I would have to give up to get this house. 'I'd give anything to have . . .'

Be very, very careful what you wish for.

I don't know, I don't know. I've tried hard, so very hard, to do all the right things and yet I know I've achieved little. It's difficult to live a life of two halves – first the sparkling, stunning social *ingénue* and then the solitary, pitied, pitted, maimed drunk. It's a major shift of roles.

The government paid our compensation quickly, and it would have been hard for it to do otherwise given the public outrage. The papers printed picture after picture of John and me. Editorials raged about the damage done, ran old, close-up photographs of me smiling, holding a glass of wine at a party, laughing in a swimming-suit, grinning at my graduation. All with my permission. When I'd recovered enough, some journalists came to the hospital with photographers and they interviewed me and took photographs of my ruined face. For them it was meat and drink; for me it was a small, sad revenge. I hoped that the men who had placed the Semtex would see these images. I wasn't foolish enough to imagine that they'd be filled with remorse but I hoped they would, if only for a moment, be shamed. Above all I did it for John. I would have done anything to enable him to be again that wild, almost dangerous boy. I missed him, that boy. I still do.

The compensation was enough to pay for John to go to the school for the deaf outside Exeter, to pay for his university education, to buy him equipment that would help him, to pay for private physiotherapy. It was also enough for me to buy this rambling house on the sea. I know that people whispered behind their hands that I had served myself before John, that I was a grasping, covetous woman. I know that I was described as bitter and twisted. And I agree with this last description, because I am bitter and my face is indeed twisted. I knew the first time I looked in a mirror in the hospital that the second half of my life had begun and that nothing I had learned, nothing I had ever known, would help me live it. For thirty-six years the lessons I had learned were predicated on the fact, the substantial, corporeal fact, of my gender and the beauty I owned. It dictated my relationships with my parents, my teachers, my boyfriends, my husband, my lovers. If I walked into a party, a lecture room, a conference room, a school, a shop, if I stepped on to a beach or a bus or a train, the reaction of others to my arrival was governed by the way I looked. And that's still the case though for entirely different reasons. I know this is the same for everyone – that the way they look, the way they present themselves, is their calling card. All I'm saying is that most people only need one calling card for life.

I don't go out often during the day. I prefer nights, dim lights and open, empty spaces. It was because of this desire for solitude and space that I bought this house, knowing I had years of my life yet to fill and that I could spend most of them sitting alone on this deck, drinking, my thoughts leaping back and forth. And that's what I have done.

19 April 1999

It was Harry who brought me the first mirror. He came into the ward, bow-tie askew, red braces snug on his belly, and began to talk to me. There was something about Harry that made me trust him, that made me feel almost child-like, although I was older.

'Joan,' he asked, holding my hand, 'have you looked in a mirror yet?'

'No.'

'Would you like to?'

I looked away from him, staring at the blue square of sky in the window. I was feeling inside myself, trying to find out if I had hardened enough to face my face. I knew I had become hard but was I hard enough? I probed again. 'I don't know.'

'There's no good time to do this, Joan. I have to say that. There's no good time. But you can't go through your life avoiding windows, reflections, mirrors, stainless steel. It will catch up with you.'

'I know.' I had indeed been ducking away from shiny surfaces, closing my eyes, turning my head.

'I know that you were very beautiful.' He squeezed my hand.

'But I'm not now.' It wasn't a question.

'No. Not like you were.'

'Give me the mirror.'

He held it out to me and I took it.

7 May 1973

When I was first wheeled down to John's hospital room, I didn't know what to expect. I'd been told what his injuries were but I couldn't picture them. I was shocked by how thin he was, how long-drawn-out and pale. It wasn't his scars that shocked me, it was his eyes – they seemed larger, deeper and endlessly restless. I watched his eyes scanning my face and tried not to flinch, managed not to look away. And then he groaned – I'm not sure whether he knew he had – and turned his back on me. I looked at the shiny pink scar tissue heaving along his spine as he cried and I ceased to care about myself – what I looked like, what others thought of me, what my future would be. I probed myself once more and discovered that I had finally hardened to stone.

18 December 1972

I went into Plymouth today to buy sheets for the new beds and I saw this notebook, with its black cardboard cover and spiral binding, and thought I must have it. I'm not sure why I bought it but I'm sitting in what will one day be the library, a fire burning in the grate, and I've opened it and begun to write. I can only think that because of the months in hospital spent writing thousands of notes to John I have become used to writing rather than speaking.

So – I went into Plymouth today for the first time since I left John in the hospital. It was the first time I've been in a city since the bomb. I know I've lived in London for a year but for some reason that doesn't count. I never minded people seeing my face there, because the whole city seemed like a large hospital ward. Difficult to explain this. But going to Plymouth, to a place where people knew me before, was different. I was so aware of my scars, of passers-by looking at me and looking away only to glance again, slyly, eyes sliding. What can I do? Wear a veil? Take me to a nunnery?

My journal is christened.

19 December 1972

Today I had to go to Noss Mayo, to the old cottage, to hand
over the keys. It's the first time I've been back there since
that morning more than year ago when we left for London.
I opened the front door, which was speckled with the dry
dust of winter storms, and stepped into the hall where I had
stood so many times as policemen tried to ask me out. There
were papers and envelopes stacked on the hall table, yellowed
with age. Everything was dulled by dust and spiders' webs. I
climbed the stairs to John's room and sat on his bed. As he
had told Harry, his room is full of shells, covering every shelf
and table top. Cowries, conches, limpets and scorpion shells,
and stiff, pale red, weightless starfish. Driftwood covered in
barnacles, smooth grey pebbles and dull cubes of ivory quartz
with rusty veins running through them. Hanging on the wall is
the weathered plank of a long-forgotten dinghy, with its name,
Merboy, faded but still visible.

John's room, this afternoon, still smelled of the sea, even
after all that time, smelled of hope and careless youth and life
yet to come. I sat on the bed holding a tiger cowrie shell and
thought of my wild Merboy and I wondered what I can do to
get him back. Does he even exist any more? As I write this
he's lying with his twice-broken legs in a ward in Tommy's.
He may be screaming still.

I'm selling all the furniture with the cottage – every single
thing in it – the kitchen stuff, the garden bench, the beds,
the wardrobes, everything. The new owners don't want the
dining table and chairs so I've had them taken away. It was
so strange being there – in that house where we lived for

twelve years. Where I watched John learn to stand on podgy, bowed legs, where I taught him to swim, to dive, where he used to sit in his crumpled school uniform, one hand tangled in his hair, frowning and sighing and fidgeting as he did his homework. Where, when he was four, he picked every flower in the garden to make a bouquet to celebrate my getting tenure at Exeter University. The bouquet was full of dirt and slugs and it wasn't until a few days later that I realised he thought I'd got manure. Why he felt that was cause for celebration I never found out. Where, I realise now, we had such a safe life. I walked round the cottage and realised how much I loved the small windows buried in thick walls, the rough rendering, whitewashed and marked by cases and surfboards and satchels. The stable door in the kitchen, looking out on the garden, where John's face would appear, announcing it was hungry. But I've had to do this. I've had to sell it. I can't let him come back to a bedroom that looks out over the pilings he used to climb, the dinghies he used to sabotage, the jetty he used to run along to throw himself into the river. I mean, right now he's learning to walk for the third time. As I forget how to talk.

There is another reason for selling: it's my last link with Dai Davies and I've now severed it. I thought it polite to phone Dai Davies' father who, after all, gave me the cottage, to tell him I was selling. An awkward conversation: we hadn't spoken for fourteen years. His voice was hesitant, embarrassed. He cleared his throat often and coughed occasionally. Eventually, given he could hardly avoid the matter, he asked, 'And how is John?'

'How the fuck do you think he is?' I replied, and I put down the phone. But I managed, somehow, to say it gently.

21 December 1972

So it's done. On Wednesday, the new furniture arrived here
in Thurlestone and a swarm of men distributed it through
the house but it seems to have disappeared. This house is so
big that it's swallowed the tables, chairs, beds, sofas and still
looks unoccupied. I've given John the bedroom at the back,
a huge room with a bay window and a window-seat looking
out over the golf course and the sea. It has a wash-basin in
the corner so he won't have to walk too far. And I've had a
carpenter build him a bed, seven feet long and four feet wide,
so he'll be comfortable. I can't bear the thought of his scarred
white ankles hanging over the end. But is it the right thing to
do? A room where he can see the sea? I don't know. I could
ask him.

22 December 1972

I drove up to London last night and went to collect John from
the hospital this morning. I don't yet know if he's forgiven me
for leaving him to his screaming. As we left Tommy's Hyacinth
came running down the steps, waving and blowing kisses, and
I thought John would want to go back to say goodbye but he
didn't. He's so tall and pale and uninterested. I don't know
what to do with him.

I thought I'd tell him about the new house as we drove
down, explain to him why he wasn't going back to his old
room. Prepare him for the difference. I didn't even think
about it, I was just going to do it. Set him up, ready for change,

prepared for difference. But he can't talk in the car, can he? He can't lip-read because I'm looking out of the windscreen and I can't write messages. So now he's upstairs in a room he has never seen before, his mad eyes flitting, and I'm down here refilling my glass with whisky. How is the money I have in the bank going to help me make my son laugh again? What am I supposed to do?

20 May 1999

I look back over those journals that I wrote when John first came home from the hospital, yellowed now, and torn, stained by slopped booze, and I think I can see that the pattern of my drinking started then, that night, 22 December 1972, when I realised what an inadequate mother I was. What a shit mother I was. There is a problem here, and I know it. As I have said, my life has been lived in two halves: the beauty and the beast. When I was a beauty, I allowed John to thrive, to run wild, to be what he wanted to be, and what he wanted to be was a Merboy. And that allowed me to be what I wanted to be – the most envied, the most desirable woman in a tiny village in Devon. What a pitiful ambition. To be sure, the influence, the *fact*, of my attractions spread far beyond Noss Mayo but that's hardly the point, really, is it?

The reason I got drunk that night, the night I brought him back here, was because I realised then that I'd done everything wrong. I was a terrible daughter, haughty and elusive, judgemental and unforgiving. I was a worse wife – otherwise why would I have been left? And a shit mother. This is not a curriculum vitae of which I am proud.

People talk about me when I walk to the village shop,

whispering and pointing, even now, after all these years. Do they imagine that they say anything about me that I have not already thought myself? Things that I have not already mulled over in my whisky-sodden mind during my hours on the deck? I don't fucking think so, as they say these days. Strange: I don't mind them thinking I'm a drunk, thinking I'm an ugly witch. But I do mind that they think I'm a stupid, ill-educated witch. If I'm to be the Thurlestone Frankenstein, I wish to be thought of as the refined, diffident, erudite local monster. Do they really imagine they can make me hurt more than I can make myself hurt?

I worry about John now. There's something wrong between him and Sonja. I know that. But I don't know what it is. I'm old, I'm sixty-five. I know that's not considered old these days but there are many ways of being old. And there are many ways of being wise, just as there are many ways of being foolish. It's 2.30 a.m. I want to call John and tell him that I love him but it's too late. I want to be able to tell Merboy that I loved him.

25 December 1972

Four days we've been here and now it's Christmas Day and we're still living in the shell of a house. We need more furniture, more books, more *things* to make us feel that we belong. God knows, I should have bought a Christmas tree, decorations, presents. I should have had mulled wine steaming on the cooker, should have piled a glittering mound of parcels under the tree, as the smells of chestnuts, turkey and parsnips roasting floated and tantalised. Of course, there were none of these because I forgot about Christmas.

I can't believe that I forgot Christmas.

This morning I went to John's room to wake him up but he was already awake, sitting on the window-seat, his head resting on his arms, staring at the distant swell. You know what I did? I stood by the door and said, 'Hello.' Can you believe that? I had forgotten that he wouldn't hear me. I heard myself and wanted to run down the stairs to throw myself into the sea and drift away until I slipped away. But then who would care for John?

So I stood and watched him for a while. Of course, he didn't know I was in the room and I could see his lips moving. He is still so handsome and so tall. The doctors marvelled at how he grew, despite the damage to his body. They would measure him and whistle, their brows knitting. One doctor, Dr Webster, a shy, blond man with a stutter, came to me one day as John slept and beckoned me to the door.

'Mrs Player,' he whispered (why? he wasn't going to wake John up), 'I've b- b- b-'

Burned? Burdened? Bombed?

'-been looking at John's r- r- r-'

Right leg? Rectum?

'-records. I've c- c- c-'

Clinched? Climaxed?

'-come to the conclusion that John, when he is f- f- f-'

Forty? Finished? Fucked?

'-fully grown, he'll be six feet seven inches.'

'Jesus Christ!' I cried, and stepped back, knocking John's bedpan from a table.

This morning I looked at him sitting at the window in his pyjamas and he's six feet two at fourteen, so maybe the blond stutterer will be right. I don't want him to be right: John stands out in a crowd enough as it is, with his mashed skin and his limp. I know he simply wants to efface himself, to melt away.

How will he do that if he is scarred head and shoulders above
the rest of the world?

I went up to him and touched his shoulder, his restless
eyes fixed on me and he smiled. The first time he has smiled
in this house.

'I've been up for ages,' he yelled. I twisted three fingers of
my left hand, as if turning a dial – something Harry said I must
do every time John shouts, so that he can learn to temper his
volume.

'Sorry,' I said, 'I must have slept too well.'

I reached out to tousle his hair but he slipped off the seat,
limped to his wardrobe and pulled out three cards and three
presents.

'Happy Christmas, Mum.'

I stood by the window and stared at him. *Christmas?*

'Mum?'

I stared at my gangling son standing in front of me, holding
his presents.

'Mum?' He shifted his feet, his legs obviously hurting.

I sat on the bed and cried. I could feel the mattress dip as
he sat next to me.

'Mum?'

I shook my head, unable to speak. He collected the pad
and pencil from his bedside cabinet, held them out to me. My
nose was running and my vision was splintered. I picked up a
corner of the candlewick bedspread and wiped my face, took
the paper and wrote:

I forgot it's Christmas.

Is that why you're crying?

Yes.

It doesn't matter.

Yes it does. It does matter.

Not to me.

Then it should.

I don't mind.

I looked into his clear, sapphire eyes, momentarily still.

You must always mind, John. Always.

He shrugged.

OK.

Who gave you the presents?

'Harry and Hyacinth.' He spoke to me then, because he felt the storm had passed. 'And there's one for you.'

'For me?'

He smiled, hesitantly, again. 'To you from me.' And he handed over a small, creased and crumpled parcel. 'Sorry, I wrapped it, so it's not very good.'

I tried to smile as I tore the paper, snot running from my nose. In the mound of wrinkled paper I unearthed an engraved, sterling silver compact of powder, a small mirror on a hinge attached to it. 'When did you get this?' My voice was sharp but that didn't matter because John couldn't hear its knife-edge.

'Harry bought it for you. To give from me. Do you like it?' He was troubled, frowning.

I wiped my nose with the bedspread once more and summoned a smile. 'It's lovely. Thank you.' I kissed John on his scarred cheek. 'And what are these?' My voice wavered as I picked up the other presents but again John couldn't hear its fluting.

He held up one, 'Hyacinth,' and the other, 'Harry.'

'Well, go on, open them, then.'

He sat for a moment, rubbing the paper. 'When you said you forgot that it's Christmas, does that mean you haven't got any presents?'

'Yes. I'm so, so sorry. I know what I'm going to get you, I just forgot that I needed to buy it.'

'No – I meant we could share one of these. I've got two and you've only got one. We could share.'

I looked out of the window, chewing my already chewed lip. My wild boy, my salt-pickled Merboy, was sitting on his bed on Christmas Day with his selfish mother, offering to share his presents, his fingers working the paper. 'No, I think you should open yours and we'll have our own different Christmas Day that no one knows about. What do you think?'

His face cleared and he nodded.

'Go on then, open them.'

Hyacinth had given him a white T-shirt with the words 'John Player Special – for when you want the best' printed on it. John laughed – *laughed* – and put it on over his pyjamas. Then he tore the paper from Harry's present – a gull-winged cerise and black kite. Functioning ears are not required for either of these things.

'Can we try it today? This morning?' John's face was open and thoughtless, his eyes fixed on the kite.

'I think that's an excellent idea.' Merboy would have run from the room and clattered down the stairs, his mind filled with wind and tangled string. This boy asked if 'we' could try it. He won't be going anywhere without his damaged mama.

'What about your cards? Don't you want to open them?'

HAPPY CRISTMAS SPECIAL!! GO BOY GO! I HOPE THAT THIS YEER IS GOOD FOR YOU!! WE MISS YOU ALREADY! LOTS OF LOVE, HYACINTH!

John sat and stared at the card, turning it in his hands. It had been signed by all the nurses and doctors on the ward. He put it gently on the bed and opened Harry's card.

Merry Christmas, Special!

Tommy's won't be the same without you. I've been thinking of what to write to you for ages and I still haven't managed to work out what I want to say. So I'm just going to write whatever comes into my head. I want you to know, Special, that you are precisely that. Special. You're an amazing boy, a wonderful boy. A surprising boy. Miss Handel told me about the time in the pool when you kicked and kicked. You were angry and that's fine, because you have every right to be. Stay angry, stay strong and stay on course. Love your mother because she deserves it. Love yourself because you deserve it. Dr W- W- W- Webster told me the other day that he thinks you're going to be 6' 7". That's BIG, Special. Make sure you're big enough a man to fill your body. You can write to me or call me at the hospital, any time, if you ever think you might not be that big. Running out of space – enjoy your life, Special. All this will pass.

Love, Harry xxx

PS. Please give your mother the letter that's in with the card.

John read the card over and over, his lips moving as he read, his eyes focused. Then he gave me Harry's letter.

Dear Joan,

You'll have been in your new house for a few days now and I hope that it's working out. I think you made the right decision to move away from the old cottage – too many memories for John there.

If you're reading this, that means it's Christmas Day and John's had his present – I hope he enjoys it. I'm sure he will. It also means that you've got your present. I know you will have been angry when you opened it – but that wasn't my intention. Do you remember when I brought you the mirror in the hospital? And I said something like 'I know you were very beautiful.'

And you said, 'But I'm not now.'

And I said, 'No. Not like you were.'

And you held out your hand and said, 'Give me the mirror.'

Joan — the conversation was <u>unfinished</u>. I don't think you realised that. When I said, 'Not like you were', I meant that now you're beautiful in a different <u>way</u>.

You've spent more than a year watching your son suffer, watching him learning to speak, to write, to <u>walk</u> all over again. And not only have you done this — been there for him every day, been there for the months that John wouldn't speak to you, been there when he screamed and wet himself in his sleep, when his skin was grafted — you have done this <u>alone</u>.

I can't even begin to tell you how much I admire you. When you invited the journalists into your room to record the damage done to your face, I knew why you did that. When you allowed me to take John outside for the first time, you were generous enough to indulge my selfish whim. When John saw you for the first time and turned his back, you didn't flinch, walk away. You stayed. And that's why John will survive, why he'll live up to his name — Special. Because you've made him so.

We never really had the opportunity to talk, to simply sit and talk about you and John, about my wife and children. About life outside the hospital. But believe me, I know what you've done. I watched as you looked in the mirror that day and I saw your face change. I watched you when I pulled the curtain back on Guy Fawkes Night, and saw your face change. I know that you have given up your life for John.

And I can't tell you not to do that. I'd do the same. But all I'm saying, Joan, is that you are beautiful in a different way. I pity the man, the husband, John's father, who left you. What he has lost. Not many people find more than one form of beauty in their lives. And that's why you have the compact. So that you

can take it out with you and check, every now and then, on your
new beauty.
   Thinking of you,
   Harry

John and I sat for a while in his bedroom, both of us
holding the cards and letters from the people we had known
at Tommy's. Neither of us said – or heard – anything. We
sat in silence and reread the words written by people who
had lives, who were at that moment laughing, drinking,
preparing the table, opening presents, answering phone calls
from far-flung relations. People who were planning afternoon
walks, games of Monopoly and Scrabble, the opening of
huge tubs of Quality Street. As John sat on his bed, in an
undecorated house, next to a mother who had forgotten it
was Christmas.

I picked up the compact and read the tiny engraving for
the first time: 'amor vincit omnia'. Maybe it does. Maybe
it does. How do I know whether it's true? I opened the
compact, looked at my snotty, red-eyed face. My new beauty?
Ah, well.

'Pumpkin, howsabout scrambled eggs on toast? Followed
by a kite session on the beach? And then we can make plans
for our secret, private, personal Christmas Day?'

And that's what we did. I made a huge breakfast of
everything in the fridge and then we walked down to the
beach, both of us howling and laughing as the kite lifted,
skittered, bowled along the sand and finally flew. Of course,
I had to run with the kite because John's legs aren't strong
enough yet. The exercise nearly did me in. John still had his
pyjamas on with Hyacinth's T-shirt flapping under his duffel
coat. We checked the rock pools, then we built a sandcastle,

complete with castellations and parapets. We made flags of seaweed and small, shiny whelk shells. As we watched the sun fall I took out the compact and again I tried to find my new beauty. Still can't find it, Harry. Still can't quite locate it.

I had to help my boy back home across the Christmas Day sands because his legs were hurting. He was draped over me like a long-loved, well-worn coat, because his legs hurt. I half carried him to bed – but for how much longer? He's six two and growing. I pulled the blankets and sheet over him and he looked at me – I love him so much – and he said, 'That's the best Christmas, Mum. Best one I've had.'

I kissed him and turned to leave. Then I remembered something. 'John, this morning, when I came in, you were saying something to yourself, over and over. What was it? You don't have to tell me if you don't want to.'

He blinked sleepily. 'It's the song. The song that was playing on the radio when we went to London. I can still hear it if I think hard.'

'Which song is it?'

His voice was off-key as he sang, '"Is that all there is? Is that all there is?" . . . I can't remember the rest of it.'

I turned the light off before he could see my face change.

'G'night, Mum,' he said into the darkness.

Now here I am, in the kitchen, writing this, whisky in my hand. So – that was Christmas. Is that all there is?

12 June 1999

John came down for the weekend. An all-too-rare occurrence, which makes me feel that it is a duty rather than a pleasure. He came alone, as he always does, and we spent quiet time together. Perhaps it's because I don't see him often enough that I'm still amazed by his size? I often wonder how the stuttering Dr Webster knew that John would grow to six feet seven – is there a formula he used?

Friday evening we sat out in the garden and he cooked a barbecue, something he's always excelled at – it would seem that, if nothing else, he inherited ambidexterity from his father and the cool management of fire from me. He told me about his work, how well he and Ian are doing, about his plans to expand, to move to a bigger office. He described the decks Elemental have built and showed me the latest catalogue. I sat there in the evening sun, flicking through the shiny pages, wondering if he was destined to spend all his life launching these dry decks; a barren naval flotilla, floating across cityscapes.

Once he'd told me about Elemental he fell silent, as if he had nothing else to say. I watched him watching the sea and he looked as he did when he was a student at the school in Exeter, when he'd come home at the weekends exhausted by learning. He'd sit and stare unblinking at a wall, a table, a book, for hours. I never asked him then what he was thinking. I knew – maybe more than most people – that some thoughts are too personal to disclose. But this weekend I did reach out and touch his arm to bring him back. I asked him what he and Sonja were doing for the summer and he was evasive, vague. There's something wrong there, I'm sure of it, the way he shied away from the question, clambered out of his chair to collect the plates, bowls and tongs and carry them to the kitchen. When he came back we sat in the late sun, reading papers until the light failed. This is England is at its best – June, when the heat's rising and the evenings last for ever.

Saturday we drove to Daymer Bay – John's suggestion –

and walked round to Rock. When we got to the end of the beach and rounded the corner, an old wooden yacht, with heavy ivory spritsail and blue and white trim, was negotiating the narrow, sandy channel. John stopped and shaded his eyes to watch it glide past. Someone on the deck waved but John didn't wave back. As we walked on he did an extraordinary thing: he took my hand and held it as we headed for the ferry to Padstow. He hasn't held my hand for years – I can't remember the last time. Even after he'd helped me into the ferry, he sat next to me and took my hand again. We wandered round the town, had lunch, and then caught the ferry back. The tide was running so we walked back over St Enodoc's down to Daymer beach and sat for a while, watching children playing at the water's edge, and I knew that both of us were thinking about when we used to do the same. When I'd watch John swim too far out and try to still my thumping heart by persuading myself he'd be all right. When he finally came in I'd towel him down and he'd complain that there was sand on the towel, which of course there was because every English picnic trip has sand in it. Then I'd pour tea from a flask and unwrap the newspapers parcelled round Ivor Dewdney dozoggie pasties we'd bought in Plymouth. We'd have sugary jam doughnuts and play the game not-licking-your-lips and I always lost.

This weekend I looked at John sitting on the sand, tall and tanned, his muscles made huge by manual work, and noticed grey hairs flecking his hair and beard.

When he left, after Sunday lunch in the Village Inn, I offered to buy him and Sonja a holiday somewhere, anywhere, this summer, thinking that perhaps they need time together. But all John did was shrug and say he had money but no time and I can't give him that.

31 December 1972

It's late now. Too late to be sitting here trying to write. I'm drunk again, sitting drunk again on the deck. Getting to be a habit. Is it next year yet? I don't know. Must be. It's gone midnight.

We've had our special, private Christmas Day. Oh, yes. John and I had our day. We have been in this house a mere eleven days and already we've had two Christmases and another year. I woke him this morning and showered him with presents as he lay on his bed. Literally tipped a sack of presents over him as he was waking. At first his eyes widened to screaming when he saw things falling on him – yet again, I forgot to think – but then he laughed, sat up and tried to catch them. He caught books and jumpers, chocolate bars and Turkish Delight, a football and a tennis racquet, Brazil nuts, satsumas, Meccano sets and water colours, Ben Sherman shirts, a Spirograph and a bowling ball. I poured out the horn of plenty, a cornucopia of boyish delights, and if just one of them sticks I shall be happy. I'm in competition here with a formidable adversary. I have to muster all my resources, because he remembers me buying fins and snorkels, rubber tyre rings and surfboards, even water skis. My adversary is the ocean and I can't really see me winning this one.

We ate Marmite and cheese on toast for breakfast, followed by chocolate mousse, which John claims is his favourite meal but I don't think he's ever eaten it before, and then we went to the beach with ham and mustard sandwiches and a flask of tannin-loaded tea. The sun was white-gold and cold, the sand hard, shallow-pitted by the rain of the night. I watched him wheeling down the beach, awkward and stuttering because of his limp, unable to run like the wind. Unable to throw his pale body into the surf. I could hear echoes of the riotous Merboy's yells as I watched John walk the water's edge, delicate and tentative. He walked with his hands in his pockets, his head lowered, avoiding the rills of foaming water at the wave's end. Twice he walked the length of the beach and I sat and smoked, a blanket over me, smoking and drinking tea, fighting the hangover from last night. I thought of nothing, I simply watched my boy walking. And maybe he listed a little, turned his hip to the left with every step, but he was walking. Not so long ago, as I watched blood pulse from the cuts in my hands and wrists, I thought he had stopped breathing. Yet there he was, a year later, walking on the edge of the world.

He came to sit next to me and I offered him tea. He shook his head and pulled a half-eaten bar of chocolate from his pocket. We sat for a while, hip to damaged hip, in the sand, watching the volcanic arch trying to snare the falling sun.

'What happened to my father?' John asked, his teeth brown.

And I thought I should have known from the curve of his spine, the dip of his neck, that he was burdened with a loaded question. Should have guessed that this was the question.

'Well.' I pushed at the sand with the toe of my shoe, watched the silvery grains cascade down my instep. 'Well. He left. You have chocolate on your teeth. It's bad for them.'

'I know that. I want to know *why* he left.'

Oh, so do I, John, so do I. 'Look, it's getting cold. Why don't we go back to the house and try roasting those marshmallows?'

'Why did he leave?' John was tugging at the grass, pulling it up in unyielding clumps, his back bent in the wind.

'John, it's late and it *is* cold.'

'You're changing the subject.'

'No, I'm simply changing the location.' I creaked to my feet and brushed the blanket free of sand before folding it.

He crouched on the sand and looked up at me – a rare occurrence – and said, 'I'll come with you if you promise to tell me about my father. I'll come if you don't change the subject.' He was squinting as the sun slipped below the low-slung, grey clouds on the ocean's horizon and flashed its last blinding, pale light across the beach. His eyes were chips of abalone shell in the late-winter air.

The prospect of an ice-sweating whisky was, I have to say, a more attractive proposition than explaining in detail to my son the perfidy of his father. More desirable than the prospect of describing yet another chapter of failure in my life. But . . . I'd always known he would ask this question one day. I'd had fourteen years to prepare an answer and was disconcerted to find myself still unready. I fingered the cicatrix over my eyebrow, where skin and worries meet and knit, and nodded. I held my hand out to him to help him haul his many-times-broken bones upright but he shook his head and grunted as he stood unassisted. I suppose he felt that if he was old enough to deal with perfidy, he was old enough to stand on his own two feet.

We walked the slow curve of the beach, our footprints crunching, feet apart from each other. I kept ducking my head, although the golf course was closed, imagining misdirected cannonballs flying past. We passed the point where a sandy path slides on to the beach, where I had stood years before wondering where John was as he lay near-mortally wounded by a bottle of lemonade which fell from the sky. I found myself smiling and I glanced at my boy and he smiled shyly back at me and I thought, We have a life, we have a history, but then I remembered that I was about to describe some of that history and I speeded up, heading towards the bottle of whisky in the kitchen cabinet.

So . . . he had his bath as I sat and sipped whisky by the fire. (I'm not a total failure – I can make a fire in minutes in a centuries-damp cellar, in a swamp, in a swimming pool.) I thought of what I might say to him. In how much detail? With what language? He is, after all, only fourteen years old. John came in and sat on the floor, resting his back against a chair, his startling eyes closed. I leaned over and touched his cheek and his eyes drifted open. 'Are you tired, pumpkin?' I signed.

He nodded.

'Why don't you go to bed and we can talk tomorrow?'

He shook his head wearily. 'I'll be OK. You just talk. Answer the question I asked. I'll watch you.'

I sighed. 'He just left, John. When you were being born he left. I was in hospital so I didn't see him go. He met another woman he wanted to be with rather than me. That's all.'

'That can't be all. It can't be.'

No, you're right, pumpkin, it's not. But how much do I say? 'Well, in a way it is. One day he was there and then he wasn't.' I really didn't want to think about this.

'Have you seen him? Since then, I mean. Since you were in hospital. Since I was born.'

'No.'

John stared at the squat orange-blue flames jigging in the down-draught, drew his dressing-gown closer. Touched the lemonade scar in his black hair. 'Do you miss him?'

'Yes. All the time.'

'But ... but that's fourteen years. Can you keep on missing?'

'Yes.'

'I miss him too. I didn't even know him and I miss him. When we were in Tommy's I thought,' and he tugged the tasselled cord of his dressing-gown, 'I thought he might, maybe, he might visit or write or something.' He looked at me with shadowed, exhausted eyes, which had already seen too much. 'Did he write?' His voice had cracked and squeaked.

'No, he didn't. John – your voice is breaking.'

1 January 1973

When I told John last night that his voice was breaking he looked at me as if I'd wounded him. He shut his eyes and curled into a ball. I lay next to him by the fire and held him until eventually he slept, then I fetched some blankets and we both slept in front of the fire. I couldn't carry him upstairs. I can support him when he hurts but I can't carry him. I don't think his withdrawal was about his father. It was about something else and I don't know what it is. Soon he'll leave me. In a few weeks he goes to the special school where they will help him communicate with the world. There he will be like the other deaf. But of course he won't be, will he? He's six feet two and has a body like St Sebastian's, but without the celestial following.

I *have* to tell him about his father. What to tell? It's been years now and I can no longer muster enough emotion to retell the events as they should be told. And what do I mean by that? As they should be told? There are many versions of

any event. The left, the leaver, the deserter, the bereft. The
indifferent.

21 June 1999

I drove to Bristol today. I hadn't planned to. I woke early, at
four o'clock, head singing, near-bursting with an equinoctial
hangover, and went down to the beach with a flask of coffee.
Watched the colours seep through the dawn, really watched
them, trying to catch them out, the way you watch heliotropes
and the flowers that close each evening. A kind of botanical
Grandmother's footsteps. Glance away for a moment, to light
a cigarette, to pour a coffee, and when you look back there is
purple where there was grey, yellow where there was ivory, red
where there was black. I sat watching the world light up and
thought of the tower of the Wills Building at the top of Park
Street in Bristol, lit by strong, still-warm honey light. Thought
of John stooping silently through his days and I decided to go
to see him.

I was in Bristol by nine, having coffee on the terrace of
the Avon Gorge Hotel, overlooking the bridge, watching the
sun slide across the high summer sky. Tracking. Moving fast.
I thought I'd take John to the Dog at Old Sodbury – eat
mussels in wine and garlic and pints of prawns – and then
maybe walk through Westonbirt Arboretum. Maybe even ask
if Sonja could come too? Leave the shop for an afternoon?
If I saw them both together, perhaps I'd work out what was
wrong. I could look in her eyes and see. Maybe. Maybe not.

I left the coffee untouched and drove to their house, but
John wasn't there. So I went to Whiteladies Road, to the deli,
and I was parking my car when I saw John's truck slew past me

and stop suddenly, askew, on a double yellow line. I watched my son climb out of his truck to stand and stare at the deli's window. I could see Sonja, framed by the pillars of the portico. She handed a package to a customer and then laughed, turned to look out of the window and saw John. I watched her expression change. A traffic warden tapped John's shoulder. John, his face pale, his eyes working, looked at the man and brushed him away. As the warden wrote a ticket John turned back to Sonja and stared, unblinking. Tracking prey.

I left. I just drove home. Because I knew that if I'd moved towards my son, perhaps to stand in front of him, if I'd reached up to touch his face to bring him back, he would have glanced at me and brushed me aside as he had the traffic warden. He would have looked back to the deli. Tracking prey.

2 January 1973

John has stayed in bed for two days now, his eyes closed, breathing deeply. I don't know whether he's tired – well, of course he's tired. The doctors said he should sleep and recover as much as possible and we've been running around the beaches having New Years and Christmases one after another. I've spent the time of his sleeping writing a letter to him. It's a long letter. It's a letter I should have started fourteen years ago. A letter I should, perhaps, have finished fourteen years ago, when my dander was up, when my fury was not spent, when I gave a damn.

Earlier tonight I looked through a mahogany sea-chest left to me by a long-dead great-uncle, searching for a photograph of John's father. I found many things in there I thought I'd

lost, many things I wish I had lost. I found the shoe-bag my
mother sewed for me, which had hung among those of the
girls and boys who didn't make it to the shelters. In it I found a
pencil – a two-inch stub of a red and black Staedtler HB – and
a rubber petrified by the passing years. There were swimming
medals; certificates of scholastic endeavour; postcards from
friends who had ventured to Normandy in the early fifties;
bus tickets kept to stir memories long forgotten; long-dead,
ineptly pressed corsages; the names and addresses of various
sailors who passed through Plymouth on their way to where?
I no longer remember. What, I wondered, happened to all
those boys? All lean and shaved and hopelessly hopeful.

In that chest I found photographs of me sitting with my
parents on bleached Welsh beaches, distant, unnamed relatives
in tow, looking at the camera with smiles like driftwood,
bleached and beached. I discovered a picture of me hanging
over the mangy mane of a long-dead, inexpertly stuffed lion
on the promenade at Torquay. I was sixteen and gorgeous,
the wind-blown skirt outlining my thighs as I bent forward,
laughing. I found ticket stubs of concerts and jazz sessions
– all forgotten now.

At the bottom of the chest, lined still by the front pages
of a 1912 *Times* newspaper, I found the pictures of John's
father. I found more pictures of John's father in my memory
chest than I found of myself and I fanned them out in front
of me, representing the span of a few years. Dai Davies.
John's father. I'd forgotten how handsome he was. I found
our wedding photographs – what teeth, what hope, what
foolishness. And there were my parents, stout and fine, in the
background. Dressed up to the nines, smiling and blessing all
this foolishness. Dai Davies never missed the closing shutter
of a camera, an opportunity, an opening, the possibility for

self-publicity, even at his own wedding, so there are many photographs of John's father and very few of his mother. Of course, the photographs are small, black-and-white and only two of them were blown up into ten-by-eights. In one of these Dai Davies and I smile for the world, teeth flashing, hair flying, his hand on my elbow. In the other, I suspect later, photograph, Dai is looking at the camera as I look at him. And on my face is a puzzled expression, as if I had felt the stab of a pin in the elbow he had held.

And what of the bundles of certificates rewarding scholastic endeavour? I love those certificates, with the embossed crest of the school raised thickly across the paper. Endeavouring to do *what*, precisely? Endeavouring in the absence of anything else? To endeavour. That was the remit of my generation – to endeavour. To serve and to endeavour. I went to Plymouth High School with an IQ of 157 and had completed my A levels by sixteen. It was 1950 – what was I going to do? I was an embarrassment, sitting at home, a healthy, breeding female with nothing to do. So I went back to study and I endeavoured. I went to Bristol University and in three years I had my Master's. When I was twenty I remembered that I was beautiful and that I wanted a life, not an existence marked at intervals by certificates of scholastic endeavour, and I finally lifted my gaze from my books to look around me. And what was the first thing I saw? Dai bloody Davies.

3 January 1973

This is the letter I have written John. The postmark should read 12 November 1958, but instead it is being delivered, by hand, fourteen years late.

Dear John,

You're upstairs sleeping now, as you have been since you asked me two nights ago about your father. It's not that I don't want to tell you, rather that it is difficult for me and I've been putting it off. The problem is mine, not yours. I think it would be better if I wrote to you about what happened. And I'll write to you as an adult because in so many ways that's what you are.

I met your father, Dai Davies, when I was at university. I know you'll find this hard to believe, but when I was young, I was considered a prodigy. I could have gone to Cambridge or Oxford, but my parents said they were too far away and so I went to Bristol University when I was seventeen and got my degree in a year, which is very unusual. Then I did a Master's. But to do that meant that I had to work really, really hard, all day and every evening, so I didn't have many friends and didn't go out to parties or anything like that. And you have to remember that I was young, younger than the students around me, so I must have been nervous, and they wouldn't have wanted to know me, wouldn't have wanted me around because I was so young. But I wasn't lonely because I had my books, my studies. Or maybe I was lonely – I can't really remember, but I don't think so.

I lived with a widow called Mrs Protheroe, as a boarder. The war hadn't been over for long and the world was a very different place from the one you know. Mrs Protheroe – Prothey, as I thought of her – was a timid woman who jumped at the slightest noise. Her husband was killed in the war and, looking back, I think she had a nervous breakdown. I had a small, sad breakfast with Prothey every morning. So many things were still hard to get, you had to exchange tickets for food so that everyone could have some and the rich didn't get everything (as I say, the world was a very different place then). After breakfast I'd walk down Whiteladies Road to the Philosophy Department and stay there all day, even at weekends. When I'd finished, I walked back to Prothey's and we ate an evening meal together. She couldn't cook but the food was terrible anyway. I lost more than a stone when I lived with her. We never really talked and I'd read at the table as we ate. I think she was relieved that we didn't talk.

So as you can see I didn't do very much except study because that was what I knew how to do best. I got my Master's degree when I was twenty, and that was when I thought maybe it was time to have some fun. My parents came up to Bristol to see me graduate and I still have a picture that they took of me, on the grass outside the Wills Building, wearing my gown and mortar board. I've put it in with this.

When your grandparents had left, I went out and walked around the city. It was the beginning of June and I was free for the first time. Or that's how it felt anyway. I wasn't beginning my Ph.D. until September. I just walked and walked, went into shops and looked at clothes, watched other women walking around, sat drinking espresso in the coffee bars. And on Saturday afternoon, when I knew what I wanted to buy, I went to Dingle's and bought a black pencil skirt, a black polo-neck jersey, black stilettos, black stockings, a scarlet scarf, some big gold earrings and my first make-up. I went to a hairdresser and had my hair bobbed and feathered. And then I went back to Prothey's with all my bags.

The reason I did all this was because that Saturday night it was the graduation ball. So I'd done my research (I was a good student, even about having fun) and worked out what all the really glamorous women were wearing. And that was what I bought myself. When I got back to Prothey's I had a bath and put on my make-up. I had to follow the instructions in a magazine — I'd never done it before, which seems funny now. Anyway, then I put on the clothes and sneaked into Prothey's room to look in the long mirror that she had in her wardrobe. I wish you'd been there. I looked in the mirror and my jaw dropped. I looked gorgeous. I remember standing alone in Prothey's room and laughing.

I know that you'll be sitting somewhere reading this and thinking, I don't want to know about what clothes Mum wore when she was young – I want to know about my _father_. The point is, I went to the ball looking like a dream, and the moment I arrived I had men all over me like a rash. There was one unfortunate-looking man who wouldn't leave me alone, kept bothering me for a dance, to buy me a drink, to take me out for a meal. He grabbed me as I stood by the bar even though I tried to stop him. And then, suddenly, there was your father. He took the man's arm and pulled him away, saying, 'She's with me.'

Can you imagine anything as corny as that? 'She's with me.'

I'd never seen him before but the minute I looked at his handsome face I began to have fun. We _did_ have fun, John, your father and I. Remember that as you read the rest of this letter. We went to bars and cafés, went to other people's houses for meals, went to all the jazz sessions in the Old Duke and the Green Room. Your father sometimes borrowed a friend's car and we would drive out into the country and go for walks, go to country pubs. We had a lot of fun that summer and then your father asked me to marry him and I said yes.

He was twenty-seven and I was twenty-one when we got married. That probably seems ancient to you but it's young, much too young. Dai Davies was my first real boyfriend. I'd known a few boys in Plymouth, but they were just boys. And the first three years I'd been in Bristol I'd locked myself away with my books. So what did I know about the world? I knew a lot about time and change and ethics and beauty – because that's what *philosophy is about – but I didn't really know the* <u>*world*</u>*. I didn't know about growing up and taking responsibility, about working and managing a home. I'd been a student all my life because that was what I was good at and people try always to do the things they're good at. I've put some photos of the wedding in this letter.*

Your father was an artist – a painter and a sculptor – and I suppose <u>*he*</u> *was trying to do the things he was good at. So he didn't know much about life either. I realise that now but I didn't realise it then. What must we have looked like? He had a flat in Clifton, off Pembroke Road. It was a beautiful flat, two bedrooms, with skylights and long sash windows. He needed light for his work and one of the bedrooms was his studio. I thought that the flat was his and he didn't tell me that it belonged to a friend of his who had gone abroad. Just as he didn't tell me that the car wasn't his until his friend sold it. These things may not mean much to you now but maybe when you're older you'll understand. Basically, he let me think he was different from the way he really was for so long that by the time I knew what he was like I didn't care because I loved him. Do you understand? By the time I'd worked out that he wasn't who I thought he was, or, rather, that he wasn't the kind of person I thought he was, it didn't matter because I loved him. I* <u>*did*</u> *love him. Never think that your parents didn't love each other because they did.*

Once we were married Dai had to move out of the Clifton flat and we rented a place in Redland. But it was a basement flat, small and damp. Because it was a basement there was hardly any light, it was dark and dingy. I was still a student, working towards my Ph.D., which I thought I could manage in three years. But I had to get an evening job to pay the rent and bills, to buy food. Dai worked during the day in a shop and

I worked in the evenings in a family restaurant at the top of Blackboy Hill. So, of course, we didn't see much of each other and when you don't see much of someone you can drift apart. I tried to study during the day and went to work at six o'clock. We had money problems – the problem being we didn't have any – so I stopped studying hard and worked days as well as evenings. By the time I got home, at eleven, Dai was out with friends. I was so tired that I was asleep when he got home.

Then one day at university I bumped into someone who knew your father. Turned out he hadn't been working for months and that was why we had money problems. He'd been doing a bit of decorating at other people's houses and occasionally selling a design to companies that printed advertisements. But the point is that he didn't tell me. He just said we didn't have enough money and the reason we didn't was because he went out to pubs and coffee houses all the time when I was at work, spending what little money we did have. I wouldn't have minded so much if he'd told me. Maybe we could have talked about it and sorted something out. But instead he lied to me. When I told him I knew what was going on he was furious and told me that I shouldn't interfere.

You have to understand, John, what kind of a man your father was. I've said he was handsome and he was. He was tall, with black hair and blue eyes – and obviously that's who you take after, although I think you'll be taller than he was. He was funny and charming, he was Bohemian, in that he didn't live like other people, he didn't follow the same rules as other people. It was 1957 and people were very conventional. But your father wasn't. He smoked, he drank a lot, he was a painter. He wore baggy trousers and shirts with paint all over them. He wasn't like most people. He was the man everyone wanted to know, the man everyone wanted at their parties – not just because he was different but because he was fun. Even then, I could still have fun with him, when I had time. But the thing is that in the end he went out and had fun on his own because I was too tired to go with him.

I stopped studying altogether and all I did was keep the house clean, work and make food for whenever he came in. I write this now and I am ashamed because I never asked him to do it, because I never said to him, 'Why don't we do this together?' But it was the 1950s and the world was a different place. I was twenty-three and I didn't know that things could be any other way. So perhaps some of it was my fault, my fault because I didn't do something, because I didn't ask for help. I just carried on. You must think about this, John. I want to be fair. Think about it. When your father first saw me I looked like every man's dream woman, I was beautiful and very, very clever. (I was also very naïve – but if you've read this far, that won't come as any surprise.) But after a couple of years I wasn't like that any more. I was tired, I never went out with your father, I never dressed up for him. We stopped talking. Maybe it isn't surprising that he stopped loving me? All because I was too proud to ask for help.

I'm going to go off the subject of Dai Davies for a minute here. Look at that last bit again – I was too proud to ask for help. That was the part Dai Davies couldn't be blamed for, that wasn't his fault. It was mine. I should have asked for help. Should have talked to other women, should have talked to your father, should maybe have talked to my father and mother. But I didn't. I thought it was all my fault. Maybe if I'd asked for help I would have had some. I really want you to remember that, John – if you don't ask for help, you don't get it. And there may be times when you need it. You in particular, because, to be honest, your life will be much harder than it should have been. Perhaps not in terms of money but, in terms of other things. If *you need help at any time <u>ask for it</u>. Pride can trip you up any time. Remember that.*

Anyway, I know now that Dai Davies had already decided to leave me when I told him that I was pregnant with you. I think that to understand the next bit you have to know a little bit more about your father. He was the vainest person I have ever met. To be fair, he did have a lot to be vain about. In our tiny basement flat, which was always untidy no matter how hard I worked at it, there was only one mirror, in the bathroom. I hardly ever got the chance to look in it because your father was always there first, preening himself. Brushing his hair, clipping his moustache, cleaning his teeth. But usually just looking at himself, just standing there and staring at his reflection. As I said, he had a lot to be vain about. But I now realise he also had a lot to be modest about.

Just as I have a lot to be honest about. It hurts me to tell you the rest. It won't take long. Some of these things I found out after your father left and I often think that if I'd known them then, when I needed to know them, everything would have been different.

When I told your father I was pregnant, he'd already met someone else, another woman he loved more than me. Like I say, he did love me, he just didn't love me enough. And maybe I wasn't very lovable. He didn't leave me straight away — he did stay with me while I was pregnant. But then a terrible thing happened — I got German measles when I was three months pregnant. It's a common disease and it's not that dangerous, unless you're pregnant. Because it means the foetus might be damaged. It can be damaged in many ways — it might be deaf or blind, it might be spastic, it might even have webbed feet. (And that makes me smile because I think you'd have liked webbed feet.) Thing is, your father was, as I said, very vain. He wasn't happy with the thought that his child might not be as handsome as he was, might not be as perfect as he

*thought he was. He certainly wasn't very happy with the thought
that his child might be damaged. It was illegal to have an abortion
then but my doctors suggested that I had one on medical grounds.
You have to remember that this was before the days of X-rays
and scans so no one could check what was going on. You were
a mystery locked inside me.*

*But — and this really is the last part of the jigsaw that answers
your questions about what happened to your father and why he left
— when I was in hospital they discovered that my blood was rhesus
negative D minus 7. I can't explain it now — you'll learn all about
blood at school — but it's a very, very rare type; nearly everyone
in the* world *has rhesus positive blood. Blood may all look the
same but we all have different types and they kill each other if
they're mixed. But once they've done battle, once they've been in a
fight, they learn enough about each other to have weapons already
prepared if they ever meet again. Your blood is rhesus positive, so
our bloods* really *don't like each other but you survived because
my blood hadn't yet prepared its weapons. But while you were in
my body my blood did build and prepare weapons for future use. If
I'd had another baby my blood would have killed it. Isn't nature
a wonderful thing? The reason I tell you this is because it helped
me make up my mind not to have an abortion. If I didn't have
you I wasn't going to have anyone else.*

*You were due on 4 November but didn't see light of day until
the eleventh. Always late — even then. What I said the other night
is true: when I went to the hospital Dai Davies was at home in
the basement flat. When, a week later, I went back home, he'd
gone. He'd gone to the woman he loved more than me. It's also
true that I haven't spoken to him since, nor has he ever explained
to me why he left.*

*OK, so now you know the facts. I'm going to tell you what
I think happened. I think your father wasn't ready to marry.*

I think he married someone who didn't really exist, who maybe existed for an evening, like a ghost – the beautiful woman at the graduation ball. I think he wanted to be single, so he could have lots of girlfriends and other friends. I don't think he wanted to be a father. I think he met someone he loved more than me. I don't think he could tolerate the idea that you might not be the best, which had something to do with his vanity.

But, of course, you are the best. You're Special.

I'm tired now, I've been writing for hours.

Read this and think about it for a while. I've tried to be fair, I've tried to be honest. One day I'll teach you moral philosophy and then you can pick holes in everything I've written.

I love you.

This is the letter I've written to John. Of it I have two caveats. The first is that I'm not being entirely truthful: I *did* see Dai Davies again after he left. When I went back to Bristol from my parents' house and begged him to come back. But I can't tell John that now because I still can't come to terms with having begged and been denied. The second is that I haven't mentioned the hairgrip and I am not sure that I ever shall. It wasn't a friend who told me of Dai's affair, it wasn't that I spotted them walking hand in hand, and it certainly wasn't the case that Dai Davies told me what he was doing. I came home one night from work, seven months pregnant, and I found a hairgrip in our rumpled bed. One of those pins that look like an arcane punctuation point, or a musical notation. I pulled back the sheets and blankets and there it was on the pillow, black and stark, a fine exemplar of production-line engineering, with its ripples and in-built torque. It was functional. It was black, shiny, almost new. It was also not mine.

8 February 1973

It seems so reasonable now; the way I told it, the way I explained Dai Davies' leaving to John in that letter, made it seem so reasonable. I've always tried to be even-handed whenever John's asked about his father. Tried to be fair. I promised myself that I would never encourage John to hate his father, that I would always try to be fair about him. But really, when you think about it, what was there to be fair about?

Looking back – and how many times have I done that? – I didn't know anything. I'd studied ethics, I'd torn the words 'ought', 'right', 'good' and 'duty' to pieces and put them back together again. So I thought I knew about people. And maybe I did? Because Dai Davies must have known that he ought to stay with me and John; known that it was his duty to stay, whether he wanted to or not. He must have known that. Everyone else did. Including, no doubt, the woman who left her hairgrip in my bed. I would even conjecture that she thought of the seven-months-pregnant wife as she lay there.

Instead, he chose to slink away while I was in hospital. Did he think I wouldn't notice? That I'd get home and look around thinking, 'Hmm, now what was I looking for? I know I put it somewhere . . . ?' Or did he imagine that I'd think, 'Well, OK, all's fair in love and war. May the best woman win'? I mean, what did he think? It was 1958, I was twenty-four, I didn't have a job and I didn't have a husband. People assumed I was a whore, a single parent, a fool, when I was none of those things. Well, maybe a fool.

What really gets me – ah, there are so many things. His

face when I turned up in Bristol, when John was six months old, dressed to kill and feeling like it. I asked him, standing in the middle of Park Street, people brushing against me, between us, around us, scurrying to their lunch, I asked him with tears streaming down my face as his colleagues looked away, to come home, to come back to me and his son. He closed his eyes and sighed, looked down at the pavement, at the sky, at a passing bus, anywhere but at me and said – very quietly – 'No.' As he walked away, up the hill towards the Wills Building (where I had stood only a few years before, smiling, at my graduation) I grabbed his arm and he stopped, turned round and gently moved my hand away. 'No,' he said again. I walked to Temple Meads and caught a train. His face when he saw me standing outside the building on Park Street – he was amazed. As if I were a ghost, a being who belonged to a different world, as I suppose I was. But he'd obviously thought that I would leave him alone. That I'd never trouble him again. He'd managed to erase me.

As I sat on the train back to Plymouth, surrounded by men trying to chat me up, my milk began leaking on my *faux*-silk blouse, scaring them all away. I watched the countryside pass – beautiful at the end of spring – and I began on that journey to love Dai less. For months I'd been drifting, crying, lying on my bed in my parents' house. I didn't see anyone, I didn't read, I just lay there staring at the ceiling. As the train rumbled along the banks of the Exe I decided to finish my Ph.D., decided to bring John up alone, to get a job teaching. I made my mind up about many things.

When I got back to my parents' house I threw away the stained blouse, fed John, phoned Dai Davies' father and shamed him into giving me the cottage in Noss Mayo. Then I called Exeter University and arranged an appointment for an interview. I told my parents I was leaving and arranged a loan from the bank so I could buy the Morris Minor. A week later I pushed open the stiff stable door of the cottage, with John bawling at my shoulder, and dropped my suitcase in the hall. I had to bring all my belongings from the car one handful at a time, until I found the cradle at the bottom of the boot. It took hours longer than it should have done because it was so difficult to do it alone. Every small task was difficult. When John was asleep that night I had a long bath, the door open in case he woke up. As I brushed my hair, I wiped steam from the mirror over the sink and was shocked by the face that stared back. It was beautiful but so set, so hard. 'Fuck you,' the face said, as it thought of Dai Davies.

As I said, every small task was difficult. The larger tasks — finishing my Ph.D., securing a job, getting tenure, publishing — were easier than finding a baby-sitter, shopping, collecting John from school. But I managed it all somehow, my determination fuelled, literally, by the fire of my fury, which burned more fiercely year after year. Every time I had a paper, a text published, I imagined Dai Davies finding out about it, imagined him reading every favourable review. When I was promoted, I thought of him hearing about it. And every time I had sex with another man I imagined his jealousy. Because I knew he would be jealous, in that primal, irrational way we all are. The day I brought Miles back to the cottage and had him in my bedroom I actually smiled at the thought of Dai Davies watching. I felt, in some obscure way, that I had beaten him, as if it were a fight and I had won.

Then came the bomb. As I knew John did, I lay in my hospital bed during those awful, lifeless hours of the early morning, surrounded by people fighting to live, thinking that Dai Davies should come. If not for me, at least for John.

Then I looked in another mirror, watched John turn away from me with a groan and I realised that the fight hadn't even begun.

Ah, well. God, I'm pissed. I can hardly write. But thinking of being reasonable, as I was – perhaps it was? Perhaps it was logical and reasoned behaviour on everyone's part but my own? I don't know and the point is I no longer care. I've become one of the indifferent, having graduated from the ranks of the left. And not before time.

9 August 1999

This afternoon I went for a long walk on the beach, past families sunning themselves, lying on rumpled, sandy towels, surrounded by the detritus of summer holidays, looking disgruntled. I watched the young boys playing, building elaborate castles, running in and out of the water shrieking. Their yells remind me of my Merboy. He still hasn't come back. Sometimes when I'm drunk, sitting on the deck at night, I imagine I hear his bare feet on the planks, dragging the splintered plank behind him. I turn to greet him but there's nothing there except darkness.

15 January 1973

I took John into Plymouth today – the first time he's been out into a city since he left Tommy's. Come to think of it, for the first time since he went into Tommy's. We walked around Royal Parade and Mayflower Street, lined with boxy grey granite buildings. The covered market with its pitiful tiled murals looks dirty and unloved. It's all so ugly. The crowds were out for the January sales, mad scrums of stout women fingering piles of cotton underwear and sad, unwanted crockery. I've always hated that city, even when I was growing up there. The only place I ever liked was the Hoe, with its red and white lighthouse. I used to cycle the promenade when I was a child, looking out to Drake's Island and Jennycliff, Cawsand flashing at the foot of Mount Edgcombe. I thought the lighthouse was huge but of course it's not. We bought new clothes for John, clothes that will fit his thin frame. He held my hand the whole day, so tightly it hurt. He never left my side. We went to a coffee shop at lunch and sat close, watching people watching us. John watches everything, his eyes unblinking. I can't imagine what this must be like for him. Children stare at the scars on his face, and he notices each look. I'm frankly past caring. Soon he will go to Exeter and I don't know what I shall do then.

16 January 1973

Ellen phoned tonight to ask how we were getting on. I didn't lie to her because I don't have to. She called late and already I was floating in whisky. She said, 'Are you all right?' and I began to cry. I've managed not to cry in front of John since Christmas, and then someone asks if I'm all right. I must have bawled my eyes out for an age, knowing John was asleep and wouldn't see me. I couldn't work out what it was I was crying for, I had so many choices. Ellen held the phone and waited in silence, waited for me to stop. She said, 'I'm coming right now,' and put the phone down. As I write this she'll be driving across England to come to me.

Ellen. I met her one day as I sat on a wall outside Tommy's, smoking. She came outside dressed in a flimsy green gown, her face drawn, walking unsteadily, but about her there was an air of something like dignity. She sat next to me in the pale afternoon sun.

'I've heard about you,' she said, her voice ringing with an American accent. 'I heard about the bomb and what happened to you and your son. I can't say anything that will make it better but I'm so sorry. That's a terrible thing to happen. So pointless.'

'Yes.'

'How is he?' She looked at my face without flinching, able to see every scission in the relentless light.

'He won't speak to me.'

'He's deaf now – that right?'

'Yes.'

'Give him time. Maybe he's just trying to work out the new world in his head.'

'The first time he saw me he looked at my face and turned away. That was a couple of months ago and he hasn't looked at me since.'

'Jesus – well, it must have been a shock. Your face, I mean. I saw the pictures in the papers, of when you were younger. You were very beautiful.'

I looked at her, stared into her unwavering gaze, and realised that dignity wasn't what she had, exactly. Something more than that. I held out my hand. 'Joan Player.'

'Ellen Matthiesen.'

Every day after that, while Ellen was in Tommy's, we met for coffee in the canteen or a slow walk around the hospital. Friendships forged in hospitals are unlike those forged anywhere else, they exist outside time, outside the run of days of normal lives. Everything is suspended as if there is somewhere the person you used to be, frozen at a moment in time (11.03 a.m. on the 11 November 1971?), waiting to resume her life while the other self walks through months, trying to sift what is important from life already lived. Money, careers, parties, sex, houses, cars – all of these are frozen in the other life too. The only thing to focus on is what might be left when – if – you return to yourself. Ellen had breast cancer and the most she could hope for was remission, the borrowing of time. Her right breast had been removed and I knew she wondered, when she was alone, where it had gone.

We sketched out our lives for each other during those slow walks – the husbands, the houses, the jobs – in faint, fine lines, spare and careful. We talked about literature, education, art, talked about anything but the idea that time might only be borrowed. We did talk about John, about what he might expect. Looking back I realise that we had both forfeited something; I think it was the future.

She was – she is – the least sentimental and most caring person I have ever met. And now she's driving through the night to come to me because I couldn't answer the question 'Are you all right?'

10 August 1999

The weather doesn't break, still it's baking and the trees begin to creak. The grass is dry, brown, and the earth is cracking. I have a tan without intending it, the scars always whiter than the pigmented skin. I've been gardening today, the growing delight of old age. When I lived in the cottage in Noss Mayo all those years ago, I left the garden to fend for itself – just as I did – and the trees grew gnarled, the roses whippy. Looking back I could have done so much with it but I was too busy being what I was.

Hard, now, to remember the phone calls, the soft knocks at my office door, as one man after another came to visit me. Colleagues, husbands, students, men from the village. All wanting the same thing: me. Wanting to pin me down, figuratively and literally. Funny to think of that now: I haven't been touched with passion – or compassion – for twenty-eight years. The luxury, then, of being able to choose. Of being able to lie in a dark room with a stranger and imagine Dai Davies watching. I remember that I never felt shame because I chose, because I had nothing else, because I never kept them. Any of them. They would write and call, beg me to go with them, go to them. And I laughed. I'm proud of that, proud of that laughter, because it helped them realise how ridiculous they were, to what degree they had misunderstood. Small, Pyrrhic victories, for I realise now that my losses were as great as theirs.

So, the garden is tended, the grass watered, the bushes contained. Thousands of people are flooding into the towns around, awaiting the eclipse. There's a fever in the air as if something special will happen, maybe something that will change them all. Lord, what fools these mortals be.

11 August 1999

Ellen arrived early this morning, waving newspapers and hooting with laughter. We sat on the deck for hours with coffee and read the breathless accounts of things yet to happen, of impending doom, of small sects burrowing into the earth, of the end of the world as we know it, and we sniggered, reading extracts of the purple prose aloud to each other.

Ellen brought with her the ingredients of brunch and I laid a table on the deck while she cooked. We ate soft scrambled eggs with smoked salmon as we watched the crowds pouring on to the beach and golf course. Hundreds, maybe thousands of them, settling on chairs, preparing tripods and hand-held camcorders, binoculars slung round pink necks. We agreed we could hear, or perhaps imagined we heard, a low rumble. Or, rather, grumble. They looked like sheep down there, penned in by land and sea. The clouds bowled in, as grey and rippled as the sea, and the grumble grew louder.

We finished eating and I lit a cigarette, noticed the flame was unnaturally bright. The light began to fade, the golf course grow dark, the sea retreat, and silence fell as sunlight diminished, then disappeared. Sun and moon passed overhead, unseen behind clouds, waltzing their way from the Isles of Scilly to India. I flicked my lighter again and caught Ellen's expression of blank awe as she looked around. The darkness and silence seemed to last for ever but then the daylight began to inch back across the sea, shadowing the arch. The sounds of clapping, whistles and cheering came from the beach as if this had been a stellar performance put on for their benefit, a football match of the planets.

Ellen looked at me and raised her eyebrows. 'Good God,' she said and held up her arm. I could see the hairs on it standing to attention.

'Scary roads,' I agreed. (Now where did that come from? John, some thirty years ago, picked up the phrase when he was at school and, shall we say? overused it for a while. I haven't heard it since then. I asked him what it meant and he

couldn't explain: 'It means something's different, dangerous
or something. I don't know.')

Ellen and I went back to reading the papers as others
packed away their sandwich boards.

20 January 1973

There's been peace of a sort having Ellen here. When she
arrived a few nights ago she found me with my head on the
kitchen table, asleep, a damp, ragged ball of tissue clenched in
my hand. I'd knocked over a glass of whisky and it had spilled
across the table, making the kitchen smell like a brewery. She
woke me gently, helped me up the stairs to bed, tucked me
in and told me to sleep for as long as I wanted. She'd see to
John in the morning.

I slept for fourteen hours and missed the next day
altogether, waking in the late afternoon when it was already
dark. John came into my room and smiled, bringing a cup of
tea. He sat on the bed and told me he and Ellen had been on
the beach and then prepared a meal. Was I coming downstairs?
So I dressed and ate the roast beef they had cooked, and then
went back to bed and slept again. I felt as if I hadn't slept for
years. I didn't drink, I didn't sit with them, I ate and slept for
three days.

I think I need to retreat for a while, need to withdraw.
Today's the first time I've been up and about, watching John
and Ellen together, but I didn't join in. They sat and played
cards this evening. She makes him laugh, makes him talk. I
know that he needs more than me, conversation other than
mine. She takes him to the beach, she's bought him books,
which they read aloud together. Apparently she's even taken

him into Plymouth – must have nerves of steel. I watched him
with her tonight, sitting on the sofa, learning sign language,
and thought how much he needs other people. Soon he'll
go to Exeter, to the School for the Deaf, where I guess he'll
have all the people he could ever want. Ellen told me that
he's said he wants to go but he's worried about leaving me.
That is, about leaving me alone. Ellen says this cycle must be
broken and I know she's right. I've spent nearly every day of
fourteen months with John and now the time has come to
let each other go.

24 November 1973

I can't go back. Now that John's settled in the school I thought
it would be OK but I was wrong. My colleagues have tried so
hard to help me, tried to carry me through the days but they
can't do it. I can't do it. I've tried for months, tried to stand
in a lecture room and speak for an hour. But all those young,
fresh, staring faces have undone me. I gave in my notice today.
What am I going to do? Drown in whisky?

15 August 1999

Last night I went into the attic and got some of my journals
and sat out in the late evening sun reading them. Curious, now,
to think of how long it took Ellen and me to get personal, to
tell each other about our losses. And even when we did, when
Ellen spoke of her dead child slipping away and I spoke of
the smell of John's skin burning, there was sorrow but it was
muted – not dulled, never dulled, but muted. We both deal

with these things in the same way and that's why we spend
so much time together.

I remember her telling me that John and I had to move away
from each other's concern, because that's what she meant.
Now I worry that we've moved too far apart. We don't see
each other often enough and I feel I'm powerless to help him
now that he's hurting. I drove to Bristol and saw him outside
the deli and left. I call him on the text phone and he replies
with bland statements about work and the weather. Sonja
is the same – comments about the shop, about the house.
Asking how I am, not, I suspect, meaning it. I was always
prepared to let John go, to let him be with someone else,
but I'm not prepared for him to be damaged again. What can
I do? Ellen says leave it. I don't know.

When I drove John to school in Exeter that first day, it
cost me so much to walk back to the car and leave him there,
towering above the other children, his blue eyes working,
flitting everywhere. I felt the same as when I left him to his
screaming in the hospital. But I wanted John to have a life,
to want things, to aspire. I wanted him to be able to talk, to
be able to read and laugh and learn. I wanted him to have a
wife, children, sex. To be as normal as he could be. But we'd
been together all our lives – in the cottage as easy friends, in
the hospital as the equally desperate, and in this house as the
recovering. To leave him there and drive away – it was the
first time in his life he'd been on his own, apart from that
week in hospital and even then he had Hyacinth and Harry.
So I drove to Ellen's and slipped through the house in the
night and drank a bottle of Crown Royal.

Now he's a carpenter. I wished many things for him yet that
wasn't one of them. I suppose I wanted him to be an academic,
a barrister, whatever. But perhaps it's right – a silent world,

where he can touch and chisel, plane and measure in silence? It turns out that all he wants is security and the predictable. And, of course, he wants Sonja. But I'm not sure that he has her any more. I know John won't fight for these things, just as Dai Davies didn't. Merboy went to London and he never came back. Someone else did.

3 November 1999

There was one thing that even Ellen could not persuade me to do: to go back to Exeter University and resume my teaching. She said I should, that I had a duty to do it, that if I didn't I'd wither, collapse in on myself. I couldn't explain to her about my essential hardness, or how I had tested that hardness before looking in a mirror for the first time. I tried to but she couldn't understand – she said that what she spent time doing was learning to forgive herself for suggesting a fishing trip, trying to become softer, gentler, and maybe I should do the same? And I did try. I went back to lecture at Exeter for six months and my colleagues tried to help me but what could they do? Because when all was said and done, when the vice-principal had welcomed me back, when they'd all become used to looking at my changed face – then I had to push open the doors to a lecture theatre and stand in front of a hundred students and speak. I could hear the whispers running round the curved benches, could see the shock on familiar faces, the gawping on unknown faces. They stared, they didn't listen. As my voice echoed their hands remained still; they took no notes as my fingers rubbed Harry's silver compact in my pocket. I stumbled through the days, aching to be alone in my office, dreading the clock hand as it moved to the time when I'd have to stand in front of row upon row of young, undamaged faces to speak of aesthetics. Ellen said it would get better, that I would become used to it, inured. But I knew that every year it would happen again, every semester the timetable changed and I would meet hundreds of unknown faces and their eyes would be riveted on mine. So I stayed for a few months because I knew that would silence people who said I hadn't tried, hadn't persevered Then I wrote my letter of resignation and gave it to the vice-principal who had welcomed me back. I think he was relieved.

That was when I finally retreated from the world. I wrote occasional papers, contributed to academic works, read the current theories, talked with ex-colleagues. Eventually my interest faded, grew cold, and Ellen stopped trying to persuade me to return to academic life, allowed me to live my own. I started to do up the house but soon got bored. Once I'd put down the paintbrushes, I did make one decision which, as it turned out, was visionary. Possibly the only decision of that sort that I've ever made. When I stopped reading texts and poetry and began reading newspapers instead, I turned to the financial pages first, began to understand the world of finance, and in the late seventies I invested in a new company. The company was called Microsoft. The amount of money that snap decision generated has been astounding; quite, quite stupid. I give most of it to charities but set aside enough to keep myself in good single malt and to see the world with Ellen. John, too, has this Midas touch. I know that others must look at us and feel envy, but if they do they're fools. It's been suggested to me that I could use this money to rebuild my face – but, really, what's the point? The surgeons say they could smooth out some of the scars, straighten my eyebrows. But the thing is, I've grown indifferent to many things and my face is one of them. Anyway, I shall never again look like I did – time has seen to that.

4 November 1999

I drove into Modbury today to go to the deli and when I was there the heavens opened. A river of water ran down the high street, spewing like fountains round the tyres of parked cars. It was like the eclipse all over again, the sky was so dark. I inched the car back along the lanes and I could hardly see the road. I spent the afternoon walking round the house, going into rooms I don't visit from year to year. It's so shabby. There's the bathroom with the orange paper – half-finished, bare walls still visible. The carpet in the drawing room is threadbare, the ceiling in the library has damp patches. I should do something about it. Even the deck is collapsing. I went out with a coffee this afternoon and leaned on the railing, which snapped, leaving me lying on my back, stunned, in the flower-bed below, among rotting leaves.

I remember the time and money I spent on this house years ago, when I changed some colours, knocked down some walls but then stopped. I retreated to the deck with my bottle and lamp, waiting for John to come home from school at weekends. Eventually waiting for him to come home at all.

11 November 1999

I'm sitting on John and Sonja's deck, wrapped in borrowed jumpers and a fleece jacket, and they're upstairs in bed, probably both lying awake, feigning sleep. John's birthday present this year is a marble bust of Hercules and a column embellished with volutes on an Ionic capital, as I wasted no time in telling him. I've never been able to shake off my compulsion to teach him words. Hercules and plinth were delivered this afternoon, wrapped in gold paper with a drooping red satin bow tied round the column. John loved it but I have to say I'm running out of statues to give him. I scour the country for a different god each year but the pickings are getting thin.

John also loved my new car, my new toy – a customised dark blue AK Cobra 470 turbo, which I collected last week. I gave him the keys, told him to take it, take Sonja out for lunch or something, and whilst they were gone I walked around their house. It is beautiful but it's also dead. Everywhere there's a feeling of two people living separate lives. Nothing I can put my finger on but an air of absence everywhere. Even my own house has a life of its own: it's shabby and run-down but at least there's evidence of life – newspapers, half-read books, coats thrown down in the hall, muddy, sandy boots left lying around, and piles of empty bottles. But in this house everything is tidied away, hidden, as if John and Sonja avoid spilling into each other's lives.

This evening I took them out for a meal to celebrate, if celebration it was (John's birthday is, after all, the anniversary of many things). It's five months since I drove to Bristol and saw John parked outside the deli, staring at Sonja. I know now that he's walking a knife edge. I also know that he won't talk to me about Sonja, about his marriage, because, as always, he's trying to save me from sadness. I'd really rather know what's going on. As we ate and exchanged talk about nothing very much, I watched Sonja. She's distracted by something and I fear it's love, or something like it.

I've always worried that she pities John and now I'm sure she does.

Over coffee and liqueurs, John told me that he's had the assessments and he's decided to have the operations – the myringoplasty and implants. 'The doctor said that even if I can't hear, I can swim,' he told me and smiled. 'But I should be able to hear *something*. If it works, I'll hear something.' And his face was child-like in its amazement. 'I keep trying to imagine it but I can't.'

'When are they going to do it? Do you have a date?'

'January.'

'Not long.'

'No,' said Sonja, 'not long.' I couldn't work out the expression on her face – but, then, I've never been able to. If I had to describe it I would say it was the picture of abjection.

John and Ian wrestled Hercules and his column to the end of the garden this afternoon and now he's brooding on his column among the ivy, watching me. I can't begin to explain how much I want the operations to work, how much I want my son to hear again. It's been twenty-nine years – exactly – which is penance enough. Penance for what I've never been sure.

13 November 1999

Ellen's just phoned, very late. She's asked me to house-sit for her because she has to begin a round of chemotherapy, and of course I'll go. Lock up my house and leave. I know that she could do the same but if I'm in her house I can visit her in the Radcliffe, look after her dogs. It's difficult to tell with

Ellen how she's feeling but her voice was tight, closed. This is the first time there's been no warning, the first time she has called me and told me that she's being admitted the next day. What would I do without her? Face facts: what will I do without her?

JOHN

Only Ian could have single-handedly stopped my savage rush towards the deli. He must have sprinted after me to grab me from behind, throwing me off balance. I stumbled and landed on hands and face on the wet tarmac of the road. He slammed on top of me as traffic braked inches away from us. I could taste petrol, see the tread of tyres inches away, knew the tarmac had grazed my cheek. I heaved, reared upwards, spilling Ian off my back and nearly managed to get to my feet when he hit my knees from behind. I crumpled and he grabbed my neck – still bruised from Jimmy's fingers – and held me in a relentless arm-lock, dragging me back on my feet. I pushed backwards, slammed him into the side of a white van but he still held on. We reeled across the road, me yanking at his arm trying to shake him off so I could race over to the deli and do untold damage. I could see that drivers were shouting and shaking fists at us as we careered across the pavement, feet slipping on paving slabs made greasy by drizzle, and shoppers dropped their bags and scattered. No one intervened, no one tried to stop us – and I can't say I blame them. I grabbed Ian's wrist with both hands and dragged his arm away, spun round and his massive fist flew into my shoulder. I staggered backwards, crashed into the tables outside a café, shattering cups and plates, reaching to grab something, anything, to break my fall. Ian barrelled in, throwing me against the plate-glass window, which shuddered but didn't break. The people inside, frozen in mid-swallow, darted away like a shoal of fish. As my head smacked against the paving, Ian sat on my chest, pinned my arms as my legs thrashed and I tried again to spill him. Throughout this, the whole time we'd been wrestling, I'd been roaring.

Ian's face above me was bloodied from a badly split lip, the sleeve of his sweatshirt torn away at the seam, hanging uselessly round his wrist. I could tell he was panting violently. I looked into his eyes and I stopped shouting, stopped thrashing my legs. Lay still, waiting for my own breathing to subside. Still Ian sat on me, crushing my ribs. Stunned, I swivelled my head, tried to orient myself, but Ian's bulk was in the way. All I could see was a small girl, wearing a bright red Christmas hat with a silver bell at its end. She was terrified, bawling her eyes out, her arms wrapped round her mother's neck. The mother, who was kneeling on the pavement, muddying her jeans, shot me a furious look. I recognised the girl – she had smiled at me by the Buttery Bar and said something about a giant. I went limp and Ian loosened his hold.

'I'm going to get up now,' he said, and stood stiffly.

I lay on the wet paving for a moment, wondering what on earth I could do next. Ian leaned down and pulled at my lapels.

'Come on, get up. Get up.'

I crawled to my feet, rubbing my neck. I pulled my jacket round me, picked up the damaged chairs and set them straight, as a crowd stood and watched me. Head down, I followed Ian back to the truck. He opened the door to shove me in and I looked back for the little girl in her Christmas hat. I wanted to say sorry but she'd gone, melted away. I sat in the passenger seat, head bowed, as Ian tore a parking ticket from the windscreen, cursing. He started the truck and pulled away.

I looked up and in the window of the deli I could see two pale, twin-like blond heads.

Ian said nothing until we were in the York Café, windows streaming with condensation, tinny Christmas decorations spinning in the fan's draught, the red benches filled with builders, scaffolders and students. He motioned for me to sit down in the only empty booth and went to get two mugs of tea, a glass of water and a handful of paper napkins. How did he know that I couldn't do anything? He dipped a napkin in the water, pulled my hand across the formica table and gently wiped away the blood and gravel. Then he took the other hand, as burly men looked over at us and whispered to each other. With a clean, damp napkin, Ian leaned across the table and wiped the blood from my grazed cheek. I sat there thinking I should do the same for him but I couldn't. He sat back and looked at me trying to light a cigarette with hands that trembled too much. I threw down the matchbox and he signed, 'What the fuck was all that about?'

'I don't know,' I signed back.

'Well, I think you'd better work it out.' He leaned forward and began to speak, reinforcing the words with gestures. 'Jimmy told me about when you went after Darren – Darren, for Chrissake, he's half your size. And what were you planning on just then? Were you going for him or her?'

'Him, of course.'

'Great, oh, great – a blind man. Has it occurred to you that he may not even know about you? That Sonja may not have told him she's married?' It hadn't. 'What's got into you? A week ago I would have said you were the mildest of men. Positively timid. You'd better shape up.'

'It's just—' I stopped. What was it? 'It's just that nothing's right. Nothing works. I can't explain.'

He took the cigarette from my fingers and lit it, blowing smoke, gave it back to me. 'Is it this Sonja business? Is that it? I don't get it – why don't you ask her about it? Get it out in the open? It's obvious something's going on. You can't just go around hitting people. There are other ways of dealing with it.'

I smiled, because I remembered Merboy sitting on a kitchen stool looking sceptical as a policeman told him the same thing.

'It's not funny,' said Ian.

'Right. Sorry. It's not just Sonja. It's lots of things. I keep thinking about my father. I don't know why. And my mother and what she used to be like. What *I* used to be like. When I was a boy. I can't explain. There's a word . . . like I'm undoing?'

'Unravelling?'

'That's it. When I was a boy I wasn't like this, I was different. Different from the way I am now. But I think it would be OK, I think it would all be OK if me and Sonja were OK.'

'Look, I know you've been unhappy, I know you're angry but I can't see what you're doing to change things. I mean, this just sounds like a bloody mid-life crisis or something. Of course you're not the same as when you were a boy. Why would you want to be? Look at it this way: you've been told that you might be able to hear again, that you might be able to swim again. This should be a great time for you. You should be ecstatic, jubilant, exhilarated. You should be bloody radiant. Instead of which you're a miserable git. '

I looked at his grave, dark face. 'Do you like Sonja?'

He frowned. 'Do I like her?' He shrugged. 'I suppose I like what I know. I've known her for a long time but I don't feel I really know her.'

'I'm beginning to think I don't either.'

I dabbed the graze on my cheek, thinking that I didn't talk to Sonja like this. Wished I knew what Ian's voice was like.

I always imagined it would sound like the blackened butter Sonja's mother swilled in her saucepans.

On the New Year's Eve after we left Tommy's, when we were sitting in our new, empty home, my mother told me that my voice was breaking and I thought I'd misread her lips.

'What?'

'Your voice is breaking.'

My *voice* was breaking? Was it in fragments in my mouth? Could she see the fragments rolling against my teeth? If she could, what did they look like?

'What do you mean?'

She stroked my hair, touched my scarred cheek. 'You don't sound like a boy any more. Well, you do. But you're beginning to sound like a man. It just means that your voice is changing, getting deeper. It sounds lovely.' She smiled her crazy smile.

But my mother wasn't newly deaf: she didn't know how important aural memories were. What could I hear? Nothing. But I could remember sound; or, rather, beyond that, I could remember noise. If I closed my eyes, held my hands still, my tongue flat against the roof of my mouth, I could recall the song that played in my head; I always had the sound of the sea lapping or roaring when I went to sleep. I lived in a world of hisses and thumps, all of them lodged for ever in my mind. I heard no sounds generated by the world outside my head. I also had a memory of my mother's voice and a fading memory of my own. Now that memory was redundant. The only person who'd ever hear my unbroken voice again was me if I replayed it in my head. I knew, even then, that I'd forget the sound of my voice over time, that the memory would shrink and disappear. It would never be replaced by another sound for me. Others listen to me speak and hear something I can never hear: myself.

*   *   *

Ian drives me back to Cotham Grove from the York café to
collect my Jeep and there's Psychobitch, sliding on to the leather
seat of her BMW. We sit and wait until she's gone and then Ian
asks, 'What are you going to do?'

'I don't want to see Sonja. I don't trust myself.'

'So what are you going to do?'

'I'm leaving.'

'Where will you go?'

'My mother's house, I guess. She's not there so I can have
some time alone. That's something I never seem to have.'

'Good – go, then.'

'What about you? Can you manage OK?'

Ian nods. 'We start the Christmas break in two days. I can
manage.'

I look at the dried blood on his face. 'I'm sorry. You're right
– I shouldn't have done that. Christ.'

Ian shrugs. 'Look after yourself. E-mail me sometime.'

'You remember when I said that you had it easy? That you
didn't know what it was like to be with someone, so you didn't
understand?'

'Yes.'

'I feel the same way. I don't feel like I'm with anyone.'

I get into my Jeep and drive home wondering what I shall do
if Sonja is there. The house is empty. I go upstairs and begin
to pack my stuff but I can't work out what I need. Clothes,
boots, razor, the pairs of bright-red plastic ear plugs, jacket. I
can't think. Twenty years. Is this what I should be doing? This
thing that I'm doing – can it be undone? I think I'll want to come
back, but will I be able to? My hands are trembling, jumping
among my clothes. I carry the hold-all to the front door and set
it down on the tiled floor. I unplug the mobile text-phone and

cram it into the bag. I look around, at the paintings and mirrors, statues and majestic deck, as if at objects unfamiliar, as if saying goodbye, then grab the hold-all and leave, double-locking the door behind me. Twenty years I've lived with Sonja – half a lifetime. Ten years I've lived in this house. I throw the bag into the Jeep and drive off without looking back.

As I speed over the suspension bridge – too fast, too fast – towards the M5, panic grabs my bowels. The enclosure of a car always makes me more aware of silence. Trucks and lorries thunder past as I join the motorway, throwing up slush-spray from the drizzle that has become snow, and I can't hear them. If only I could sing to myself, shout my disapproval of the Blind Man, if I could whistle, or mutter and hear the self-righteous cant of my own voice. Instead I put the Jeep in fifth and hit ninety-five and what is left of my heart rises into my mouth. I'm alone and the silence defeats me, because no matter what I say it will pass unheard.

Snow begins to pile on the grass verges of narrow, mud-runnelled Devon roads off the motorway. I recognise nothing and I stop on a night-dark road and watch the flakes fall in the funnel of my headlights. How can I be lost? A man with two dogs walks towards me, snow dusting his shoulders and I lower the window and call out to him. He ignores me and turns away, hurrying down a lane. My heart begins to pump with anxiety. I sit in the driver's seat as snow gathers on the lip of the windscreen, piling up on the wipers, and wonder how I have arrived here, on an empty road in Devon, alone. This is not what I wanted. I look over to the passenger seat, where Sonja should be, and see a pair of her gloves stuffed carelessly on the shelf. I pick them up and smell the leather but there's nothing of Sonja in them. I feel as alone as I did

when my mother left me at the gates of the school in Exeter
and walked away.

Often, when I think of my mother, I think of how she was that
day we watched the World Cup Final in a flat in Earl's Court,
a Dusty Springfield record playing in the hallway, her cracked,
soaring voice being drowned out by shouts. My mother wore a
dark blue sleeveless dress, her hair short and dyed black. Men
and women drifted towards her, not knowing why. She spent
the day drinking and flirting, touching people's arms and hands.
I remember her laughing, throwing back her head so that her
neck stretched for ever and laughing. She came over to me often
that day, stroked my hair, asked if I was all right, and I always
smiled and said yes, because I was so proud of her, so proud
of the fact that everyone wanted her, wanted to be near her.
When the match was over, when Bobby Moore held the trophy
aloft as if it was the head of the German nation, I leaned out of
the window and watched the crowds weaving between cars and
waving scarves, the drivers hooting their horns creating wave
on wave of noise. (That's another loop I play in my mind: the
sound of celebration.) Then the TV was turned off and the party
began. Still Dusty crooned and my mother slipped off her shoes
and danced, gin and tonic in one hand, black and gold Sobranie
in the other, as men moved towards her and tried to join her in
her orbit but somehow she always managed to slip away. When
that summer's night finally came – the sounds from the street
still falling in the open windows – people were sprawled on the
carpet, on sofas, and my mother pulled me on to her lap to hug
me. I was eight years old and I wanted to squirm away and to
stay with her for ever. She smelt of smoke and perfume, her
breath sweet with quinine. She held me and rocked me, singing
'How Can I Be Sure' along with Dusty, her voice small, pure

and sure in my ear. When the song finished she looked at me and smiled. 'All right, pumpkin?'

Of course in the end I do find the house, slither down the icy lanes running like drips to the edge of the sea, and pull into the driveway. It is in darkness. I fumble for the light switch and see that the hallway is dusty, unused. There are no muddied boots, no umbrellas, no worn Barbours hanging off the back of a chair; in fact, no sign of life apart from the pile of mail put on the hall table by a neighbour. The light throws pale rectangles beyond the doors off the hall and behind them are rooms I lived in as a teenager. I've never been here alone before – always my mother has been waiting, smiling her twisted smile, reaching for a bottle and two glasses. I drop the bag and walk into the kitchen – so familiar. It's never been changed since we moved in and now it's a museum piece – a tribute to enamel and Bakelite, the pantry with tin-mesh eyes staring at me as I look around. I open it and find the expected cases of whisky and gin, pour myself a drink and walk through the house.

Being alone I see the house as if for the first time; the unfinished bathrooms with their swirling orange seventies' wallpaper. My mother's bedroom, furnished as a cell, with white walls and single bed, the teapot from Southdown Road its only ornament, the slashed brown velvet curtains hanging over the window. The guest rooms with their dimpled headboards and chrome towel rails, bulky gas fires squatting in the fireplaces – never used. I wander through the rooms wondering why my mother bought such a mansion, such a huge, always empty house. But I know why – she expected me to fill it with friends, to bring them every weekend to play with the basketball hoop screwed above the garage door, the footballs, the board games. Expected me to go down to the beach running with a pack of boys to play cricket, to mess about in the sand, to fly Harry's kite. When I was young, when I lived in Noss Mayo, I'd appear in the summer evenings trailing a band of children, disturbing my mother's reading, demanding a party, a picnic. And she would smile her lazy smile and stretch, before inviting them in and telling me to take them through to the garden, where we ran around yelling, pulling branches and hurling leathery quince apples at each other as she made sandwiches. Friends for a summer, for a day.

I never did bring anyone home from the school at Exeter.

My mother watched me until she saw me go through the doors of the school. I couldn't see her but I knew she was watching, in the same way as she watched my back puckering and closing as I lay in the hospital bed in Tommy's. I pulled at my uniform, unused to the feel of shirt collar, laced shoes, rough, heavy blazer. Around me there were other boys and girls, all with the same bright, mad eyes checking for every movement in the world. Fingers flew as they signed to each other, talking (we were to call it talking) about their holidays, their parents, their pets. I walked alone, trying to shrink, wishing I could be like other children. Some stared at me, at my scars, with the blank vacant face of the deaf, which animates suddenly when a friend or an idea approaches. I touched the Corona scar again and again, wishing I was back on that sunny, sandy lane with my whole mother walking ahead of me, hearing the cries of 'Fore!' and smelling heather.

I followed the crowd of children, watching elastic lips move as they lip-read each other's words. We were ushered in to sit before a small stage in the main hall, row after row, until the teachers came in and sat round the edge, smiling crazily. The headmistress stood and began to speak, and another teacher beside her signed. They talked of timetables and lessons, of changes to PE, of the rules about uniform. The headmistress smiled and pointed to me, welcoming me to the school and every face turned. I touched my scar tissue and they turned away. Later I was taken to my dormitory and I found my cases already on my bed. They gave me sheets of paper with the timetable, with meal times, rules about leaving the school during term time (so much *time*) and left me to unpack. I sat on the bed and realised that I wouldn't be alone again. I wouldn't even sleep alone.

My legs hurt so I lay down on the bed, feet dangling over the end. I thought of Hyacinth. I wanted her to come through the door, majestic in her girth, huge hips swinging, gold tooth glinting, singing 'Mary Bring the Cattle Home Across the Sands of Dee' even if I couldn't hear her. I thought of Harry and began to cry. And that was how they found me hours later. I was fussed over, told that every child was homesick at first. I didn't know how to tell them I was people-sick.

Sonja once found a picture taken during my first term at school. All of us lined up on benches, squinting, white shirts dazzling in unexpected sun. I was standing in the middle of the back row, towering above everyone, shoulders hunched. I felt the elbow of a boy – Andrew Mortimer – hit my back as he ran from left to right to appear at both ends of the photograph. I don't remember the names of any of the other children; strange I should remember his. I do remember Miss Cottee, a plump, small woman, who smelled of talc and always wore a high-necked blouse with a brooch dead centre on the collar. She was the one who found me crying on my bed. The one who thought I was crying for a home. She took me down to dinner and sat next to me as I tried to eat. I caught her looking at my scars and she looked away, embarrassed. Miss Cottee taught RE.

Sonja looked at the picture and laughed: I was so thin, so gangly, clean-shaven, so aloof. She said she thought I was looking over everyone's heads, as if I was above them. Which, in a way, I was. She said I seemed to be searching for something. Which, in a way, I was. I was watching the school gates, searching for my father. Something I often did then.

I go back downstairs to the kitchen and see my mother leaning against the cooker, spitting, lime juice flying, telling me not to marry Sonja. Had she been right? It occurs to me: perhaps it was Sonja who left me heartless? As I pour another drink I remember my mother so clearly, how she was that night, how she was dressed, that she was drunk. I can see the ghosts that move in darkened windows, just as her ghost moved, following her clattering around the kitchen. I see her dancing in her sleeveless dress, black Sobranie burning; I see her face when she asked me what they did with all the bags of the children who didn't make it to the shelter; I see her looking up and smiling lazily, a quince bush waving in the wind behind her; I see her looking up from a hand of cards, bottle of The Macallan at her elbow, grinning at Ellen; I see her smiling and saying, 'Oh, well spotted, pumpkin.' The ghosts begin to blur, fading one into another.

I climb the stairs to my bedroom, the room I came back to from the hospital. An unknown, unloved room, with a bespoke seven-foot bed in the corner. I sit on the window-seat and look out over the sea. By the moon's light I can see the snow on the hills, can see that it's settled on the beach, covering sand. I reach for my worrystone.

What am I going to do?

* * *

My father never came. I stayed at the school, learning about pitch and stress, labial, velar and fricative production of sound, about reading the non-verbal indicators of others. I stayed at the school and grew, each year an inch taller until I was six feet seven and a giant among boys. I had physiotherapy to strengthen my legs and to ease the skin on my hand, arm and back. Learned to hold a pen and write quickly and legibly, learned about language, about discourse, grammar and lexis, for the deaf must know all about what they cannot hear so they may guess correctly. I learned new words, tried to say them, tried to write them, use them. (I didn't know then that I would one day marry a woman for whom the word 'rapture' would bring to mind an arching portico, the word 'miasma' the sound of sorrow. Perhaps it was a good thing, that ignorance?) And all the time while I was doing these things I waited and I watched for my father.

When I first came out of the hospital and came here to this bedroom, I slept for days. My mother and I had our strange, empty Christmas and then I fell asleep again. When I woke up there was the letter by my bed, a handwritten letter from my mother. I'd asked her to tell me about my father and she did. I lay in my bed and read the letter again and again. (There was so much I didn't understand – and how could I? I hadn't loved anyone the way my mother loved my father. I hope I never do.) I read it once more. Like my mother said, I didn't want to read about how she dressed, what she wore – I wanted to know about the Father. I was fourteen and I was lonely; I wanted my father, or rather I wanted the person I imagined he might be, to walk in and make me forget, make me whole. But as I lay there in that bed, having woken from a long sleep, I realised that he didn't exist, that the saviour I'd had in my mind didn't exist. Instead there was this strange, untidy, vain man. A man who had left me because my mother's blood had prepared its weapons. I didn't understand it – why had he left my mother? Because she worked too hard? Because she didn't look nice? Was that all? My mother kept saying that they'd had fun – so why did he go? Because of me? Because I wasn't special? I lay for hours, the letter in my hand, trying to comprehend naïveté, charm and vanity. If the man I'd been waiting for didn't exist and if the woman my father married didn't really exist either, then what was I?

It took a long time for me to decide to tip the photos out of the envelope and look at them. I'd never seen a picture of him before and I knew him immediately. He *was* tall and he *was* handsome. He did stare at the camera and not at my mother. I eased myself out of bed and limped to the mirror over the wash-basin in the corner. I looked at my father's picture and then at my own reflection. My face was gaunt, the scars on my jaw livid; my hair cropped unevenly. My father had left me because he thought I might be damaged, blind or crippled. Well, now I was – deaf and damaged and limping. But – and this is what made me howl with rage – he didn't meet Merboy. The Father never met brown, slippery, dangerous Merboy. And if he came now he would think he had always been right.

I sit on the window-seat in my bedroom looking out over the beach, my mouth moving as I sing my song just as I did that morning my mother forgot it was Christmas, thinking of the boy who looked in the mirror and lost something for ever. 'Is that all there is?' But the odd thing is I've never stopped waiting for the Father, waiting for him to appear in the corner of my hawk-like eyes. Even though I know that he isn't who I'd thought he was, I still wait and watch. Forty-one years I've been waiting.

I go to the virulently orange, unfinished bathroom and draw a deep, boiling-hot bath – my mother, careless with her money, has left the water on. I slip the plugs into my ears – an action I perform without thought: in nearly thirty years I've never once forgotten – and sip the whisky, sluicing the water over my body. I think of Ellen, who showers every early evening, 'washing the day away', she calls it. I raise and lower my knees, making waves, hoping to wash away years.

There were two things I excelled at in school: football and woodwork. If we'd played basketball then, I'd have been on to a winner. What must it have been like for spectators? To watch a team of deaf children playing football – eyes flitting, fingers flying, grunting unheard by each other as they ran, hearts pumping. The woodwork classes were an oasis of calm in the middle of the week, on Wednesday afternoons, in the sweet-smelling, sunlit room off the art room. The smell came from the 3-in-1 oil and the shavings of fresh pine. I loved to stand by the bench, looking out at the garden, a whetstone encased in a maple box clamped in front of me, sharpening chisels. Loved the feel of oil on the whetstone, the rhythm of the blade gliding over oil and stone, angled just so beneath my fingers, becoming sharp. I would plane pieces of wood to right-angled perfection, running my thumb along the edge until it was without flaw. The feel of a tenon slipping snug into a mortise to complete a joint calmed me, and the sight of the nubs of dove joints sitting proud, needing only planing, was deeply satisfying. Mr Tompkins, the woodwork teacher, would stop by my bench and touch my elbow, smiling in a way that made me know I was special, although he never called me that. No one at school called me Special and maybe that's why I forgot to feel it.

I never made any friends in my four years at the school. I was a good student, a quiet student. I made no demands of anyone except that I could go home every weekend to be with my mother. I would lie on my bed in the dorm at night and think of my younger self, the young boy who would gather people around him by simply being. I wondered what happened to him – did he disappear when my eardrums did? Did he blow apart when the bomb blew? I could picture him, remember him falling into water, climbing trees, throwing stones at gulls circling above the beach, chasing dogs, his arms outstretched, yodelling. He'd had about him an aura of danger. I knew that I'd been him but was no longer. Many nights I'd lie there crying, mourning him, and no one could hear me. That is the one privilege of the deaf – there is privacy in the dark, when we are sightless. Often I wondered if all the boys were lying there crying, wailing even, and no one knew it.

I sit up late, drinking alone on the deck, watching a distant bonfire flicker on the beach and wondering what I'm going to do. As I drink I think of Sonja, wonder what she's doing. Is she at home? Is she with the Blind Man? Just what did she think when she saw me thundering towards them? She dragged him into the deli, protected him against me. But can I blame her? I drink my way down the bottle and my last thought, before I stagger upstairs and fall fully dressed, starfish-style, on my bed, is that I've left my wife.

When I wake late the next morning I'm parched and I gulp water straight from the bathroom taps, then stand – head thundering – under a cold shower, wondering how my mother can bear to feel like this every day. It's cold on the deck, when I go out there with my coffee. The snow hasn't melted and I can see the black smear at the end of the beach where the bonfire burned. The beach is beautiful and I'd like to walk its length, smell the ozone, taste salt, but there's something else I have to do. I climb the stairs and open the hatch to the attic.

I pull a sheet from the tall object leaning against the rafters and it slips away from Merboy's surfboard – made of plywood, painted pale blue, scratched where it was dragged over pebbles. There are my old rubber fins and the water-skis my mother bought Merboy that last summer – an unused extravagance because then I had my thirteenth birthday. In a suitcase I find my old clothes: the Levi's I wore the first night I went out in London, the T-shirt Hyacinth gave me, faded to grey and ivory by too many washes, thin as paper. A bundle of reports from the school at Exeter. Tub the Ted. The tennis racquet and bowling ball my mother bought me when she forgot Christmas. Both unused, because I thought they were dangerous, because I knew I couldn't use them alone.

Why has my mother kept all of this? What good does it do? But I think I know why – because she knew that one day I'd come here and climb into the attic. It seems to me, as I sit here looking at the debris I've left in my wake, that perhaps I've lived too much in the present. I haven't thought of any of these things for years and yet once they were life itself. I painted my surfboard, washed my fins (and, yes, I would have liked webbed feet) and collected stones and shells. I slept each night with Tub in my arms until I threw him on the floor worrying about my heart breaking.

I pick up the bundle of reports and the near-perished fins, and weigh them in my hands and think, That boy is me. Both boys are me. Merboy and Special are *both* me. When I left this house I turned my scarred back on Merboy and erased Special, the crazy-eyed, quiet boy who went to school in Exeter. I went to London and became John the carpenter and then all three of us turned our backs on my mother.

Last summer Ian and I worked on a deck in Bath, at the back of a beautiful Georgian mansion on Lansdown Hill, which overlooked the spires and crescents of the city, the round spin of the Circus and sweep of Royal Crescent. They were halcyon days, days of sun and light and easy companionship. Ian and I hadn't worked together on a job for years, just the two of us. We designed a deck of Bath stone and cherry, decorated with scrolls of wood and curls of metal. I'd forgotten what it was like to work with Ian – his strength and vision, his perfectionism. We worked without the need to speak, passing each other planes and chisels, cauls and sash clamps, held awkward joints for each other as we drilled, lifted wood and iron staircases together, weights that would normally take four men to move. Each day we ate lunch, provided by Sonja from the deli, on the growing deck – sandwiches of pastrami and dill gherkins, plates of asparagus wrapped in pancetta with crusty rolls, or bowls of tiny fresh artichoke hearts dipped in mayonnaise. We sprawled in shorts, tanning our bare chests, fingers greasy with food, and each day when we finished we'd stop for a pint in the garden of the Crown Inn in Kelston on the way home.

I was routering the supports of the steps one afternoon, when Ian touched me lightly on the shoulder. I looked at him and his expression was unreadable. He signed as I stood in the hammering heat watching his black fingers moving against the pale, untreated cherry. *They've done it again. They blew up a town in Ireland. Omagh. They blew up the shopping centre. I'm sorry.* He'd heard it on the radio as I was shaving wood. Sweat was running down my back but I began to shiver. Over his shoulder I looked at Bath's extraordinary, timeless skyline, at the cathedral, the

Roman baths, the church spires, and I imagined I could hear the dripping of buildings.

The attic is freezing, snow thick now on the slate roof tiles. In the corner I find the trunk I've been looking for. It's heavy, so I drag it across the rafters, scraping the leather. Opening it I find a photograph album, filled with pictures of Noss Mayo, of my grandparents, of me playing with Toulouse. There's the photograph of my mother staring at Dai Davies with a look of surprise. There are lots of photos of me and my mother when we were younger, at picnics, on the beach, me with the groups of friends I would collect for a day. Both of us paddling on the endless beach we found in France, smiling for the stranger holding the camera. The photograph my mother took as I sat on a log by the lake, staring straight into the sun and I'm so tall, so whole, so sure that everything will be just fine. I notice there are no photos of us after the bomb.

Beneath these are my mother's journals. I've never read them but I think this is the time. I think I must read them now. I pile them into a box and climb awkwardly down the ladder. Then I go back into the attic and when I shroud the surfboard with the sheet I notice the board behind it. The plank from a dinghy, weathered and ragged, the word *Merboy* faded by water and years. I turn off the lights and close the hatch.

My mother collected me from the station in Kingsbridge every Friday evening during term time and drove me back to Exeter every Monday morning. Our weekends had their own rhythm: I would sleep late on Saturday because I found the school so hard. It was hard to keep concentrating, hard to catch everything that was thrown at me. I missed Harry's office with its view over London, missed his easy manner, the fact that he knew me well enough to know when to stop. When I woke up, my mother and I would eat breakfast together in the old-fashioned kitchen, then go for a walk, across the golf course or down to the beach. I'd walk along the water's edge, wanting and not wanting to run in, to swim, to drown. We talked sometimes about the future, about what I was going to do. She wanted me to go to university but I was paralysed by the thought of it, although I said nothing. It seemed to me that it was enough that I had already disappointed one parent. In the evenings we'd read or play cards. She'd sit with a glass of whisky as I drank juice and we worked through every game in Hoyle's. Then, just before I left school, when I was eighteen, she poured us both a whisky and I realised that I must have grown up. I sometimes wondered, as I dipped my way through doorways and smacked my forehead against low rafters, if I'd grown up a little too much.

One Friday night when she collected me from the station her face was drawn, pale. I asked her if she was OK. She pulled the car over and stopped. Turned to look at me. 'I handed in my notice today.'

'What d'you mean?'

'I've stopped teaching.'

'Why?'

'I can't do it.'

'Of course you can do it, you've always done it.' I was scared of this change – change: my enemy.

'I can't any more.'

'Why?'

'Because I can't stand in front of them all and talk any more.'

I looked at the dark road, headlights dazzling me. I thought of her standing in front of rows of people, trying to hide her face with a hand. 'But what will you do?'

She shrugged. 'Grow old.'

The bomb in Omagh that blew apart on a hot August day in the middle of a crowded street killed twenty-nine people and injured more than two hundred. I stood, shaking, in Ian's flat that evening and watched the pictures being beamed in, of shattered windows and faces, broken buildings and hearts. I shivered and I watched until Sonja came to fetch me. It was the Real IRA who claimed responsibility. The *Real* IRA? As opposed to what, exactly? Had the bomb that exploded and turned over the Morris Minor as I thought of a pair of jeans and Merboy disappeared, been virtual? As insubstantial as my eardrums? Had I *imagined* it? They said they planted the bomb because they didn't agree with the peace process – well, talk about stating the fucking obvious.

I've since read about the survivors of Omagh, the ones who made it home – perhaps without the normal number of ears, or the odd missing limb, or a shrivelled scalp which will never again grow hair; perhaps even eyeless or heartless. I also read about the Good Friday Agreement. Good Friday. The commemoration of the crucifixion. Seems appropriate.

I carry the box of my mother's journals into the kitchen and empty it on to the table, the same table that she and I sat at for years, learning canasta and pinochle and five-card poker. I pour more coffee before fanning out the journals on the scarred wood. So many. How did she write them all? Well, I guess she had time enough.

The light on the text-phone flashes and I see that Sonja's calling but I don't answer, so she leaves a message: *Where are you? Come home. Please come home. At least call me. What's wrong?*

Taking my coffee out on to the deck I notice the storm lamp

in the corner. Again I remember my mother asking me what happened to the children's bags. And I couldn't answer. All my life, it seems, people have been asking me questions I can't answer: What happened to your face? Hello, John, I'm Harry – how are you today? What's wrong with you? Have you forgiven the people who did this to you? Do you have any idea of the sacrifices my husband and I have made? Can you hear me? Do you love me? What happened to your father? What's wrong?

The ghost of Merboy stalks the attic, his wet, salty feet leaving prints on the boards, leading me to a decision, as the surfers fly through Big Wednesday and the Blind Man sits in my coffee and wheat house. My mother is watching over Ellen's dying. Ian is packing up for the day, nursing a split lip, wondering what his deaf friend is thinking. His deaf friend is thinking it's time to start answering the questions.

One early spring morning this year when Sonja and I were sitting on the deck over breakfast, wrapped in thick Norwegian sweaters, pretending it was warm, Sonja touched my arm and pointed to an article in the obituary pages. Dusty Springfield had died the day before. There was a black-and-white picture of her, with her blonde, towering hair and thick mascara, standing uneasily in a sleeveless dress in front of a television audience, looking hunted. I read the obit and realised how unhappy she had been and it made me sad. I wish she had known that all my life I had replayed the loop of her voice asking how she could be sure, whenever I thought of my mother dancing on a supreme summer's night in 1966.

I'm not my mother's son for nothing: I build a fire in the library in moments and it catches and flickers as I carry my mother's journals through from the kitchen. Lying down on the rug where I fell asleep with the fragments of my boy's voice rolling in my mouth, I begin to read my mother's life at last.

A cochlear implant involves implanting ten to fourteen electrodes in the cochlea. It is an operation performed when the eardrums and ossicles have been damaged beyond repair. The implant leaves the patient with a limited range of frequencies: one hundred thousand frequencies are reduced to fourteen and so the sound, while purer, is disjointed. The human ear must corrupt sound in order for the brain to interpret Mozart's *Requiem* or Pan-pipes echoing around the Andes because the ratio of decibels to KHz is that which is found not in nature but in science. The titanium implant, a steel button, is buried behind the ear in the skull bone and the bone eventually smothers it. It is possible to remove the sensitive tip, like a press stud, and then the patient may swim. Assuming that the myringoplasty has been successful. Assuming that the patient has the desire. Assuming that the patient has the courage.

Once I had left my mother to go to college, where I took Sonja's warm hand in mine, I slipped away from her. My mother receded and became yet another ghost. I never knew why this happened. I didn't love her less. Now I know that it happened because she launched me and let me go. As I lie in front of the fire, my hand loosening in the heat, I read the letter Harry wrote to my mother that Christmas, the letter that came with the compact – 'you have given up your life for John'. So she did. I roll over on to my unfeeling back and remember the days, the months, the year my mother spent in Tommy's watching my scars heal, willing me to live, willing me to care again. Eventually I cared. 'You stayed . . . that's why John will survive.' And so I have, against all the odds. I turn back to the journals.

*   *   *

When I was in Thurlestone the summer before I left for King's
College, the special school behind me, finished, a letter arrived
for my mother. It was from Hyacinth, saying that she was
suffering from variant angina pectoris. My mother called her
and I remember walking through the hall while she was on the
phone, watching her dented face move and smile. Years later I
found out that she paid for Hyacinth to have surgery and then to
go home, back to Tobago, to be with her family. My mother has
a mute generosity which few people know about, including me.
I often wonder what Hyacinth found when she went back after
all those years, whether she still sang about rivers and Scottish
cows. When my mother finished the phone call she came to
find me in my room, packing away my shells and pebbles. She
took my hand in hers and traced the letters: HYACINTH SAYS
HELLO SPECIAL!

I spent years, first at Tommy's and then at school, waiting for
my father to arrive. I watched and I waited and as I did my heart
hardened. I knew that he was out there, I knew he knew about
the bomb and what happened to us. He was out there, like the
wolf's breath in the cave – something felt and not seen. And I
always knew that I was twice-left because I was not special.

JOAN

16 November 1999

The hospital is depressing – I'd forgotten what days are like
spent in such a place. The buildings have changed – they're
modern and sleek, pastel-painted and clean. There's chrome
everywhere and the floors shine, reflecting the simple white
uniforms the nurses wear now. The buildings may have changed
but the routines of hospital life haven't. I see the same dim,
ruined faces every day, smile at them and they raise a wrist, try
to reply. The drugs arrive on cue, the same young women smile
endlessly down their days, surrounded by death. Of course
they're not the same women – the nurses who looked after John
will be old now. Yet these young women have the same resilient
cheerfulness. But there's no Hyacinth here, there's no Harry.

Ellen's in a room on her own, overlooking the bland
parklands and roads around Oxford. She wears a gown and
cotton cap, and tubes feed her what she needs. Christ, I don't
know what she needs. I read to her every day. She likes poetry
and the tales of Updike's Rabbit. It's the only thing I can think
of doing for her.

17 November 1999

It's strange being up here in the Cotswolds, in Ellen's house,
alone. The house is so much a part of her, or vice versa.

I've always loved it, and if I hadn't bought my house in Thurlestone looking out over the sea, I would have liked to come here. It has no comforting deck but it does have unexpected, drystone-walled enclosures in the gardens, covered in climbing roses, and a summer-house that looks over a rolling valley of ancient oaks. Each evening when I get back from the hospital, I walk round the house checking windows and doors, and I remember stumbling in my dressing-gown through the house, full of rancid whisky, Ellen shouting, as I realised just how spacious it was. I asked her once why she bought such a huge house – eight bedrooms, cellars, minstrel's gallery, library and barn – and she shrugged and said she liked it. Which is no answer. Because when she first visited Thurlestone – having driven through the night to come to me because I was not all right – I saw her look around and smile. 'I like it,' I said, and she raised an eyebrow.

But I didn't buy my house simply because I liked it. I bought it for many reasons – because I thought John deserved it, because I had to move away from the cottage, because I wanted to sit on the deck and grow old looking over the sea. Above all, I bought it because I wanted John to bring home friends to stay. It never occurred to me that he would have none.

I sit here in the kitchen, warming myself by the old ivory Aga, hear it clicking behind me, and pour myself another whisky. The dogs pad over to me and flop by my feet, missing Ellen. As I do. Ellen is dying.

4 *January 1973*

When John began to howl I was in the garden and I dropped everything and ran up the stairs to find him in his bedroom, by the wash-basin, holding my wedding photographs. The noise he made was terrible. Eventually I coaxed him back to his bed and he lay there crying for hours. I stayed with him all afternoon, stroking his forehead. Will this never fucking end? I just want my son to stop hurting and start living.

18 *November 1999*

Ellen was bad today – so tired she couldn't speak, so tired she grimaced when I walked in. I didn't read to her. I sat and looked at her, memorising her face. There is no one except John whom I have loved as I have loved her. Not even Miles – perhaps especially not Miles.

I have seen the world, or as much of it as I wish to, with Ellen. I've looked up from the *Boston Globe*, *Die Zeit*, the *LA Times*, the *South China Morning Post*, *Le Monde*, to see Ellen frowning as she blows the heat from her coffee, pen tapping the table, pondering thirteen across. We've sat on Isola San Giulio in Lago Orta eating pasta, our heads ringing with memories of the Monte Sacro of St Francis. We've sipped coffee on the Lido, argued on the steps of the Met, walked the streets of Paris on Christmas Day in an empty city, wondering at its beauty. We've sat in a beach bar in Zanzibar, watching coachloads of Italians spilling out into the African sun, made angry and garrulous by inconvenience. We've shared beds, shared rooms, shared baths, driven across Death Valley, yelled and shouted at each other, lolled in jacuzzis on the edge of Route 66, swilling Buds and dreaming of Kerouac. We've attempted to camp in Grand Canyon National Park, where the ground was like concrete and the tent pegs curled like Turkish slippers when we hammered them. She threw down the mallet, roared, 'Fuck this!' – causing earnest American parents to cover children's ears and shake their heads – and booked us into a hotel. We left before dawn and drove back to the canyon, where we stood alone, leaning on the steel railing as the sun rolled like pale butter across the horizon. Ellen turned to me and smiled, the light gentling her square, handsome, determined face. That is how I shall remember her.

This year we had planned to float around the Tobago Cays on a wooden three-masted schooner from Bequia as the century changed. Ellen said that I could drink champagne all day and all night, that I could pour whisky into the Caribbean and snorkel in it if I felt so moved. The way she looked at it, the fact that either of us made it that far would preclude any restrictions on levity or abandonment. And as that day approaches, I visit her each day in the oncology unit. It may be that we both do not make it that far.

5 January 1973

John was calmer today. He got up and ate lunch with me and when I was washing up he said, 'I'm sorry.'

I turned to look at him. 'What for?'

'For crying like I did. I could tell it was loud.'

I looked at his thin face, his eyes dazzling me. 'You cry whenever you want, pumpkin.'

'Do you want to know why I cried?' He fiddled with the tassels on his dressing-gown belt as his eyes grew brighter.

'Only if you want to tell me.'

I sat at the table again and lit a cigarette as he talked. He was worried because he thought that if his father came back and saw him as he is now, he'd leave again, because he's as damaged as Dai Davies thought he would be. John blames himself – sweet Jesus – because he's not special.

The storm that blew up last night was still raging, slapping branches against the kitchen window, as I smoked and tried to think of what to say.

'John, he's not coming back. Believe me. He won't come back. He's made another life for himself. I know that seems a strange thing to say – that he's made a life, like he's a god or something. What I mean is that he's forgotten the old one with us – just rubbed it out. He has a new wife.' I drew smoke deep into my lungs, because I had to decide whether to tell John that not only did Dai Davies have a new wife, he also had two children. John has, somewhere, two half-brothers. 'He's not coming back. You don't have to worry about him and you don't have to think about him because you'll never see him.'

'But I want to.' John lowered his head and I knew why he did that – because he thought he was rejecting me.

'Well, maybe when you're older you will. But right now, pumpkin, I think you should just think about sleeping and resting and getting better.' I went back to the sink and my hands trembled so much – hangover? fury? both? – that I broke a glass in the soapy water.

I don't know where Dai Davies and his spawn are, but the thought that even from the distance of years he can make my son feel not special enrages me.

4 February 1973

Ellen went back home today and I know that John's missing
her already. The way she is with him – I'm strangely envi-
ous. She lays a hand on his arm, so easily, so quietly, and
he looks up and smiles. I've watched them sitting out on
the deck as I clear the kitchen and they sit in a circle
of easy companionship, which at the moment I feel with
neither of them. Yet why should John feel that way with
someone like Ellen – she's a forty-one-year-old woman?
He knows nothing about her. But that's Ellen's gift – she
can absorb other people's fear. She hasn't absorbed all of
mine but enough of it to enable me to live from day to
day.

John asked me the other night, as I tucked him into bed
and sat with him for a while (which I always do – let it not be
said that I didn't learn my lessons when my face disappeared),
what is wrong with her. He knows there is something wrong,
as if he has acquired a sixth sense, or in his case shall we say
a different sense to replace the one that was lost? An acuity
that others lack.

'She has cancer. Breast cancer.'

'Is that bad?'

'Yes.' I smoothed his candlewick bedspread so I didn't
have to look in his eyes. I may have learned many lessons
but I'm still not sure when I should lie to my son.

'Will she die?' John's blue-blue eyes were fixed on mine.

'No – well, she will, we all will. But not right now.'

'If we like her enough, maybe love her enough, will that
stop it?'

'It can't hurt, can it?' I heard myself and smiled. Love can't hurt?

'So what happened to her?' John inched himself up and leaned back against the pillows.

'She had to have one of her breasts removed because that's where the disease was. That's when I met her – when you were in hospital and she was there at the same time. But now it's gone and she should be OK.'

John looked out of the window at scudding, pale-moon-lit clouds. 'I like her.'

'Good. So do I.'

He looked back to the clouds, watched them fleece the moon, and then turned back to me. 'When I'm with her I don't care. Y'know, about all this.' He stroked the scars on his jaw. 'It's like she doesn't see them.'

I smiled again. 'I don't think she does.'

John stared at his hands working, flexing, along the edge of the bedspread. 'Does she see yours?'

'No.'

'Can I touch them?' I nodded and he reached out and felt my face, his fingers cool.

There are places on my face where I cannot feel, where the dermis and hypodermis are too damaged to be sensitive, the nerves' fine connection to my brain severed. When I was in London, visiting John in Tommy's, I read as many medical journals and books as I could find, about deafness, about skin damage and repair. I wanted to know why my bones hurt where they mended, why I couldn't feel my face, what had happened to John's hearing, whether he would ever be able to walk without a limp. I asked doctors and specialists to explain to me what had happened to us and what we could expect. At first they brushed me aside, patronised me.

But then they realised my determination to understand, my ability to understand, and they sat with me, drawing diagrams, outlining the extent of the damage and the limited possibilities of repair.

I've written elsewhere that I've always been a good student, conscientious and dedicated. (I smile even now when I remember studying how to be glamorous before I went to the graduation ball.) I'd always thought that once something – a concept, an idea, a theory – had been named and understood, it had been conquered. I was, after all, an academic. So I read the journals, quizzed the doctors, visited the library and studied anatomy. But even though I named everything, understood its function, knew why skin and ears no longer worked, there was no sense of victory. Quite the opposite. Because then I realised that nothing could be done to reverse the effects of a modest cube of Semtex.

19 December 1974

I'm out on the deck, wrapped in a tartan rug, lamp burning as the rain lashes down, trying to wrestle with the memories of an extraordinary night. I went to a faculty party in Exeter yesterday – Bob Deedes invited me. Something must have pricked his conscience. I haven't been in touch with anyone from the university since the day I handed in my resignation. The party . . . I didn't know whether to go. Normally I wouldn't have considered it, but Miriam Fraser, who I shared an office with for years, was back from her sabbatical in Australia and I wanted to see her.

I left my arrival at Bob and Jane's late, went to the Queen Vic first for a couple of gins to fortify myself. I wanted other people to be there when I arrived so I could hide among them if I needed to. Bob opened the door, pecked my cheek and fussed with my coat. He hasn't changed at all and why should he have? He's still ineffectual, stooped and apologetic. I followed him into the front room, aching for a drink, wondering why I was there as Jane came towards me. I'd forgotten that I hadn't seen her for years and she approached in the darkened room and stopped suddenly, her hand reaching for her mouth before she recovered and smiled glassily. Pressing a glass of wine into my hands, she told me to mingle before taking her shock away elsewhere. I stood in the corner and drank and looked around the dim room. There was David, standing by his latest wife, trying to avoid my eye. Ben and Alistair, and over by the door, leaning against the jamb, looking louche, was Miles Brandrin. I'd slept with them all and they didn't know what to do with my presence, whether to pity me, or pretend that nothing had changed, or ignore me – and wouldn't *that* be misunderstood? Quite apart from the fact that none of them would even consider sleeping with me again.

The wives hovered and asked me about John, pressed pineapple and cheese, sausage rolls and vol-au-vents into my hands. Even Miriam was taken aback by me; I'm sure that she had been told but no doubt the description never matches my appearance. Welcome to Reality Challenge. The women tried to smile brightly and ignore the ruin of a face looking back at them. God knows, they probably even forgave me for sleeping with their husbands and lovers. I hope not because I shouldn't be forgiven for that. The men – apart from Bob – didn't come near me and what else did I expect? Dai Davies married a woman who never existed and they had loved a woman who no longer existed. But I kept thinking that I *was* the same woman – still the same woman they'd worked with and slept with. When I left, Miles looked over to me and attempted a smile but I think I shrugged in such a way that he was relieved of the burden.

I picked John up this morning from school to come back home for the Christmas holidays. He was so excited that I'd been to a party. I forget that he's sixteen now and old enough to recognise loneliness when he sees it. Indeed, I fear it's a too-familiar sight for him. He asked me about the party, and I lied and told him that it was great fun and that I'd talked to lots of old friends. At least it seems that now I've finally learned when it's OK to lie to my son.

25 November 1999

The weather here in the Cotswolds was beautiful this morning – cold but clear, with a thin, low-lying mist. When I went down to the kitchen and looked out of the half-glazed door the mist was floating round the mossy mushroom stones and the valley had drowned. Yet I could see the cows looking up from their grazing to peer over the fog in amazement, leaving loops of grassy breath.

I walked the dogs through the fields, cows looming up suddenly around us, and up to the ridge of the valley opposite. The mist burned away as I walked, and I stopped and looked back to the house. I've known it for nearly thirty years yet its beauty still surprises me. Soft, rounded by centuries, the roof covered in a blanket of lumpy moss. After a high wind the paths are covered with blobs of peaty, dark green lumps. By the time I stepped back into the kitchen the sun was dazzling and the drive into Oxford – through Enstone and

Woodstock, along tree-lined roads, past the excrescence that is Blenheim – was, for once, a delight.

But when I got to the ward, I found Ellen's room empty. My mouth went dry, suddenly parched. I stopped a passing nurse, grabbed her arm so hard she nearly dropped a spotless kidney bowl. 'Where is she? Where's Ellen Matthiesen?'

'I'll get the doctor for you.' She swivelled on the heels of her sensible black brogues and was gone.

Ellen?

The doctor came, smiling and avuncular, and told me that Ellen was having some tests, that if they were satisfactory she'd be allowed home for a few days. 'I believe you'll be there?'

'Yes.'

He put his hand on my arm, smiled again. 'It will do her good to be away from here for a while.'

I looked him in the eye, full face, no hiding hand, letting him know that I was, shall we say?, used to the small disappointments that life can throw up. 'Is she dying?'

'She's doing better than any of us expected.'

'Doctor, that's not what I asked. I need to know because then I'll know what to do. How to talk to her. What to say. You see, I haven't said everything that I want to say, I haven't told her things I want her to know.' How much I've always loved her, for instance. That she has made my second life bearable.

The doctor looked closely at my face, at my striated hands. Perhaps he sensed just how deep the silence in the basement flat was when I opened the door, balancing the days-old John on my hip. Perhaps he could sense for how long I scrabbled at the door of the Morris Minor when I thought John was dying and I couldn't reach him. Perhaps he sensed that, for once, I wanted to finish something properly, to feel the end of the circle pass through my hands and feel no regret. He coughed and shifted his weight from one leg to the other. 'Yes, she's dying. I really can't say how long it will take but she is quite weak. The secondary cancer has spread and all we can do is alleviate her suffering. I'm sorry. I've known Ellen for some time and she's a remarkable woman. I wish I could say something else.'

'Thank you.' I walked away, out of the ward, to the lifts, and out into the glorious day. I sat on a wall and smoked a cigarette, trying to prepare myself. I was reminded of the day when we met, sitting on a different wall, outside a different hospital.

Will I be enough for her?

30 August 1979

It's taken me years to tell Ellen about Miles, and even then the admission was prompted by her question this evening. We spent the day clearing John's bedroom, packing and carrying boxes up into the attic. It's been a sweltering summer and all the windows and doors in the house are still open, even now, to try to create some breeze, as Ellen's dogs lie panting on the flagstone floor of the kitchen. John has gone, married, now, to Sonja, and it was Ellen's idea to change his room. She said it would mark a rite of passage. I can't believe that he'll never sleep in that room again, that he'll make his own bed and lie in it with Sonja.

I had a bath in the early evening, while Ellen baked the dough she made this morning and knocked up a chicken salad. We took the meal out on to the deck, and watched the sunbathers straggle across the rough of the golf course, struggling with chairs and ice boxes, dragging exhausted children. The sun was still warm, and as I ate I thought of the pale, blind rectangles left on the walls of John's bedroom where the two posters had been for years.

'Did you ever think of marrying again?' asked Ellen, settling herself against the newel post of the steps that run down to the garden.

'What?' I was shocked back to the present – this was definitely personal.

'After your husband left, did you think of marrying again? I mean, today I saw those photographs of you and John when he was a young boy. Don't tell me that you didn't have offers. Quite a few, I shouldn't wonder.'

I gulped from a glass of chilled white wine. 'No – I didn't want to get married again.'

'Why not? It can't have been easy being a single mother then. God knows, it's not easy now.'

'It wasn't. But it seemed to me that marriage wasn't something I was very good at.'

'OK.' Ellen shifted, shielded her eyes from the sun to look at me. 'So what did you do?'

'What d'you mean?'

'Like I said, I saw the photos. You sure didn't look like an old maid.'

I laughed. 'I wasn't.' I thought of the cottage in Noss Mayo, of the small bedroom I had had there, the ceiling always shot rippling silver by the waters of the creek. Of how often I lay there calculating the time I had before John tumbled in from school, only to tumble straight back out again, even in winter.

'So, come on.'

'What?'

'Tell me about it.' I looked at Ellen and saw she was smiling. 'For crying out loud, we're two middle-aged women sitting in the sun after a day's hard work, with a bottle of wine. What better time for a few racy reminiscences?'

I smiled too, and looked back to the distant beach. 'Maybe you're right.'

'So – go on.'

'Well, when Dai Davies had gone, I moved into the cottage and began working at the university. John stayed with his grandparents in Plymouth a lot when he was a baby. I must have been, what, twenty-four, twenty-five? All my life I'd assumed that I'd get married and that would be that. I'd stay with my husband and have babies. Never occurred to me to do anything else. But by the time I was divorced there was the pill. A bloody miracle. And I really mean that – if I'd ever got pregnant again it would have been a disaster. But if I was on the pill . . . so I went to the doctor and that was it.'

'Well, what? So, you did get lots of offers?'

I guffawed. 'Yes.'

'And? Good Christ, this is like getting blood from a stone.' Ellen was laughing too.

'I accepted most of them.'

'No!' Ellen was scandalised. 'How many?'

'I've no idea. I never kept count.'

'Well, who were they?' Ellen poured herself another glass of wine, never taking her eyes off my face.

'Research students, post-grads, lecturers. A couple of men in the village. There was even one undergrad – God, I'd forgotten about him. He was called Tim and he was very sweet but he was a bit young.'

'But how did you manage it? With John, I mean.'

'I'd go to their houses or bedsits in Exeter, or even,

sometimes, a hotel. Once I allowed someone to come to the cottage. But I never let John meet them, he never knew. I don't know if he's worked it out now or not.'

I fell silent, thinking of all those men, all of them hopelessly infatuated, endlessly grateful when I undressed and lay down for the first time, thinking, perhaps, it *was* the first time, desire rendering them naïve and innocent, ever hopeful. I'd learned my lesson from my time with Dai Davies and I never pretended to be other than I was. I never encouraged any of them to think that they would be anything but a diversion. I enjoyed the sex, I enjoyed lying in bed, talking, drinking. I enjoyed saying goodbye to them and walking out into a cold, sharp autumn afternoon, leaves swirling, knowing that John would run in from school and find me reading by the fire. None of them believed me when I said it was over, that I had never meant anything by it, that it had been a delight but it was finished. I never lied and I never expected anything of them. I soon learned another lesson and refused to tell them where I lived or to give them my phone number. At first they smiled conspiratorially and agreed, giggling nervously with lust. But within weeks they'd be begging me to let them closer, trying to follow me home, asking colleagues for my phone number. It was then that I let them go.

'What?' Ellen had asked me a question.

'Were any of them married?' She wasn't laughing when she asked me that.

'Yes.' I looked away from her unsmiling face. 'I'm not going to apologise for it. I never asked any of them to care about me, I just wanted some fun. I never said I wanted them. I never asked any of them to leave their wives and children. I'm *not* going to apologise.'

'I'm not asking you to.'

The sun began to lose its heat, fall towards the sea and we fell silent. Ellen's dogs came padding out to the deck and slumped against her, panting quietly. She stroked their fur, rubbing the short hair above their eyes the wrong way and then smoothing it, as I thought, not for the first time, about the unexpected blackness of a hairgrip lying on a white pillow.

'*Was* there anyone who mattered more than the others?'

A clamour of rooks clattered out of the plane trees behind the house, cawing raucously.

'Yes.'

'You don't have to tell me.' A dog yawned and toppled sideways, stretching his paws out, hairy toes separating.

'I know.'

Now, while Ellen sleeps, worn out by the efforts of climbing into the attic and keeping scandal at bay, I sit here and write this.

Miles. Miles Brandrin – the one who mattered more than the others. Miles – whom I noticed often as he walked from Devonshire House to the lecture rooms, carrying folders and books, whose easy walk and long blond hair caught my eye. Miles – who sat next to me in the Ram as I marked undergraduate essays on Fichte's being inconveniently stuck on an ought-to-be.

'Hi,' he said.

I looked at him and back to the essay.

He put a tanned hand on my pale, bare arm. 'I'd very much like to take you out for dinner. I realise that I'll have to wait some time for the privilege – your diary is probably full for the foreseeable future. But if you can find a free evening please let me know. My name's Miles Brandrin. You can put a note in my pigeon hole in the office.'

'Are you married?' I asked.

'Yes,' he said, and smiled. 'So you're safe.' And he walked away.

Arrogant bastard, I thought, writing a note to Tim cancelling our drink that evening and writing another to Miles, saying I'd be happy to meet him later that day.

I read what I've written and I'm astonished by the degree of my confidence, by the extent of my own indifference and arrogance. This happened eight years ago and it seems as if it happened in a different lifetime. Which, of course, it did.

1 January 1985

The beginning of a new journal – virgin paper, clean hard covers. One of my many rituals. I went into the attic this afternoon to perform another ritual: putting last year's collection in the trunk. When I gathered them together this morning there were very few for a year, thin pickings indeed. It seems that when a year is easy, when it rolls by without hitches or bolts of the unexpected, I write far less. As I get older I read more and write less. I vowed I would simply climb the ladder, find the trunk and put the journals in but I was, as usual, distracted by what I found up there. John's surfboard always surprises me, rising up, ghost-like, from the corner. Then there are the journals of past years. Always I think I'll ignore them but I end up opening them at random to remind myself of other times.

There's a distinct rhythm to the years – panic and uncertainty when John and I first left the hospital. Looking back, reading those entries, I realise I was unhinged and I think I would have stayed that way if it hadn't been for Ellen. I was so attentive, so attuned to John's moods, so vigilant, that I wasn't a good mother: I was a dangerous one. I spent his adolescence quivering with guilt and fear – poor bugger, when I look back. I spent my life worrying about first his friendless state and then his childlessness. Perhaps if I'd guessed both would be the case I would have quivered a little less and lived a little more? The journals for those years, when he was at school and university, are many, dog-eared, stained by rings of ice melting in whisky glasses, the paper fibres of each page fattened by moisture they soaked up. Each night I'd sit and doggedly write beyond the point of sensibility. Many entries are unreadable, indecipherable and, so, locked in time. I wonder if that is how the practice of conversation is for John. Or, if not conversation, his memories of sound.

Once he married Sonja the tone of the journals changed, the quivering, it seems, died down. The years acquired a rhythm matched by the seasons. Each year Ellen and I travelled, once she'd had her annual check-up, and if it was OK we would go somewhere from April to July. Winters spent driving back and forth to the Cotswolds, and Ellen spending some of the summer here. As I flipped through the journals today I was reminded of so many things, so many times I'd forgotten. Holidays in Scotland with Ellen; weekends spent awkwardly with John and Sonja in Bristol; leaving teaching; taking my first trip into Plymouth. But the later journals are slimmer, the writing more legible, the water rings fewer.

That is the other calibration of my life – how far down the whisky bottle I sink each night. This I wonder about. I fill these notebooks and pack them away so that John can read them one day, if he wants to, and I have the feeling he will want to. And when he does, the writing and the water rings will reveal my life for what it is: the life of a drunk. Will he forgive me?

9 October 1979

The first night I went out with Miles, I slept with him. I'd never done that before – gone out with a man and slept with him within hours. Miles took me to Topsham, to the Bridge Inn, a barn of a pub full of small dark cubby-holes with fires roaring. We huddled over a small round table, which wobbled beneath our elbows, and talked of work and literature, colleagues and their inadequacies. He taught politics and sociology, subjects I knew little about. I became increasingly inarticulate as he stared at me, crept closer. The skin of my face grew warm and I found it difficult to concentrate on what he said, I was so busy looking at his beautiful face. He had the ridiculous sideburns of the time and blond hair which flopped over the collar of his shirt.

After a few pints he became even more animated, kept touching my arm, moving ever closer, as he talked about his specialist subject: Northern Ireland. It was February 1971 and the first British soldier had been killed that day by a gelignite bomb as he moved into riots in the Ardoyne district of Ulster. Miles was outraged. Not by the soldier's death but that he was there at all. He bought another round of beer and whiskies and slipped an arm round me as he sat, his hand encircling my waist. 'The British should just get out, let the Republicans exercise their birthright. We've got no bloody business there.'

As it turned out that was exactly what we had – bloody business. In those early years I worried very little about the Troubles, as the never-ending battle was quaintly named. It was not that I was uncaring as such but the world at the time was frankly overwhelming. American troops were in Cambodia, the American National Guard was shooting students at Kent State University. The PLO took hostages and blew up jumbos on airstrips. A tidal wave killed 150,000 people in East Pakistan, the steel railings buckled at Ibrox and Charles Manson was found guilty of slaughtering the pregnant Sharon Tate. In England the strikes were beginning to take hold. The death of a soldier in Ulster was as nothing compared to all this, as nothing compared to watching Miles' soft lips talking so close to mine.

I'd already arranged for John to spend the weekend with his grandparents in Plymouth since I'd been expecting to see Tim that night. I discovered later that Miles had been so sure of himself, so sure of me, that he had asked me out on the Friday night of a weekend when his wife and children were away. We left the Bridge Inn late that evening, my head swirling with beer and whisky, but even so, as we staggered drunkenly into Topsham heading for the Globe Inn, I knew what would happen. Not all of it, not all that was going to happen, because if I had I would have listened to Miles more closely and then walked away from him.

The next morning when I woke, headache pounding, it occurred to me that Miles must already have booked the room. He was in the bathroom, shaving, when I asked him if he had and he said, 'Yes.' A flash of anger, mingled with a streak of faint shame, splashed over me, soon to pass. We spent the weekend together, most of it in the hotel room, a few hours walking the banks of the Exe and the Turf, and then Miles went back to his family and I drove to Plymouth to collect John.

Miles and I were equals and that, I suppose, is why we were so drawn to each other. Literally drawn. I would be sitting in

my office, the door open, and would look up suddenly to
find Miles watching me. We seemed instinctively to know
where to find each other in the labyrinthine corridors of
the university; at the day's end we would drift to our cars
and, wordlessly, one would follow the other to a pub, to
a hotel, to a park. Eventually to Miles' family home. I
remember following his car – a grey, utilitarian Mini with
sliding windows and cracked red leather seats – in my bul-
bous, much-loved Morris Minor, pulling into the drive and
sitting in the seat. Miles came to my window and I wound
it down.

'What's the problem? Aren't you coming in?'

'No.'

'Why not? There's no one in.'

'That's not the point – it's not right.'

Miles pulled his familiar dark-green corduroy jacket, with its
leather, four-quarter buttons, tighter round him, because the
day was cold and damp. 'Don't be silly.'

Silly? That was a word I would use to describe a child, an
infant. 'Don't be *what*?'

'Look, you know and I know what we're doing. Where we
do it is, surely, irrelevant.'

'Maybe to you,' I said, and I put the car in reverse and left
him, hugging his jacket and blowing on his hands.

The next day he came to my office and apologised. That
afternoon I took a man back to the cottage in Noss Mayo
for the first time. John had a rugby match after school and
wouldn't be back until late. Opening the familiar door, being
followed by Miles, his hand on my back, pushing me towards
the stairs, pushing me down on the bed, was one of the most
erotic moments of my life. I found I liked to have him there,
although I hadn't expected to. I had expected to feel guilt,

to feel invaded, and instead I felt whole, as if the cottage was full, complemented.

As the light died early one grim March afternoon, we lay naked on the bed, eating Marmite sandwiches and drinking coffee, listening to the radio droning, and we heard that Lieutenant William Calley had been found guilty of murdering Vietnamese citizens at My Lai. Looking back I see that my affair with Miles was conducted against a backdrop of global violence and perhaps that's why I burrowed deeper and deeper into him in a way I hadn't with others, not even with Dai Davies.

Miles was beautiful, intelligent, engaging and sensual; the same attributes, I know, that he thought he saw in me. We loved and were indifferent in equal measure. I had John and he had his wife and children and, at first, it never occurred to us for a moment that it would be otherwise. He didn't insult me by saying that he no longer loved his wife – he did, and he slept with her, ate with her, took holidays with her; he was, in short, her husband. I spent every moment that I could with John, never compromising our relationship. Even if Miles had a free weekend, if John was at home and wanted to go out for the day – usually snorkelling around the rocks at Crackington Haven or tramping the sands at Rock – I stayed with John and I never begrudged him a moment.

Miles and I suited each other because we were both predators. We'd sit in bars and I would see his amber and brown eyes flick over to a young blonde woman, or follow a student as she moved around the room. I would sit and watch men as they walked and talked, bayed in their groups, hugging pints of beer close to their chests, covertly glancing at me. Miles and I would smile at each other and leave together; we deserved each other. I knew that he found me utterly desirable, could not stop seeing me, touching me, and the feeling was mutual. Both predators, we had no inhibitions and I never tired of having sex with him. Nor of talking to him and it was this fact – that we revelled in each other's stolen company, that we were good friends, intellectual equals, as well as lovers – that made what happened even more difficult to bear.

29 November 1999

I took Ellen back to the hospital this afternoon. She spent the weekend here, at her own house, and I think she enjoyed it. She's so weak that even enjoyment drains her. I spent Thursday night, once I knew that she was being allowed home, rearranging the house so she could get to her bed easily. I moved her things to the first bedroom upstairs, the one with the huge window that overlooks the valley, with twin beds so I could stay with her. There's a wash-basin in there and a bathroom across the hall, so I thought it suited. Friday, I cleaned everywhere and ran into town to buy chicken and prawns and scallops, sourdough from the bakery and toothsome morsels from the deli. I sprinted back and drove to the farm shop, where I bought beetroot and curly kale, leeks, parsnips and swede, raspberries and small, bitter strawberries. When I got back to Ellen's, I staggered round to the kitchen, plastic bags dragging at the skin of my fingers, welting them, and dropped everything on the table. Swedes and kale rolled and plummeted to the floor, to be joined by chancy Braeburn apples and tomatoes on the vine – just at the moment I remembered that I can't cook. Ellen was coming for two days and I had bought enough food for a battalion of Spanish soldiers. I panicked, found an ancient Katie Stewart cookbook and turned up the Aga, running ineffectually around this shabby old kitchen (neither Ellen nor I have ever felt the need to upgrade). I stuffed a chicken with a lemon, threw some beetroot in a pan and shoved it all in the oven. I had ten minutes to pack away the rest of the food and leave. Ellen had had the foresight to bring with her from America her vast, cumbersome walk-in fridge and drum-like Maytag washing-machine – as I say, she is not sentimental: she knew these would serve her over the years better than photographs of her drowned husband.

I drove too fast all the way to Oxford but, then, I have always driven too fast since I've travelled alone. I've always bought sleek, swift, expensive cars since John married and I drive them as if possessed. Even so I was late – Ellen was waiting in the lobby, in a wheelchair, her now-thin frame swamped by clothes. She was wheeled to the car and a too-young nurse gently helped her into the low-slung seat.

'Shit – I should have brought your car. Sod it, I didn't think.'

The nurse looked at me – astonished that a such a well-groomed, if damaged, older woman would say such a thing.

''Sokay,' murmured Ellen, settling a rug round her legs. 'Just drive like fuck as you always do. I want to get home.'

The nurse reeled back as Ellen and I both smiled and the AK Cobra roared out on to the open road. The fishtailing drive must have exhausted Ellen because when she got home she wanted a nap in bed. I helped her out of the car, held her arm as she walked slowly along the path and up the stairs. She made no mention of the change of rooms, simply lay down with a soft sigh and stared at the ceiling. 'I never wanted this,' she whispered.

'No, I don't suppose you did,' I said, fussing around, getting out towels and soaps, anything to hide my rush of tears at the sight of Ellen – tall, rangy, handsome Ellen – wraith-like on the bed, hardly making an impression on it.

'Where are the dogs?'

'I locked them in the kitchen – I was scared they'd be, y'know, too excited when they saw you.'

'Can you bring them?'

So I went down to the kitchen and lifted the latch of the wooden door and the two half-lurchers ran past me, fur flying – shit! – and I sprinted after them, up the stairs to the bedroom. When I got there, they were at the door, which was open, and they waited for me, tails wagging feebly at half-mast. They waited – they *waited* – until I was there and the three of us went in together and they went to either side of the bed to lick Ellen's hands, resting their heads on the mattress, eyebrows lifting, tails still wagging. How did they know not to jump on her? Then they both slumped on the carpet next to the bed and I said I was going to check on the food so why didn't Ellen get some sleep?

The food, to be honest, was not in good shape but it hardly mattered because Ellen, when I helped her down the stairs a couple of hours later, wasn't that hungry. She only had a few mouthfuls of overcooked chicken and some beetroot and kale. I had built a roaring fire in the music room and I settled her on a settee and then cleared the kitchen. When I went back to her she was dozing, with the dogs lying on the floor next to her. She woke and smiled. 'Sorry – this can't be much fun for you.'

'It's good to have you here.'

'Maybe if I sleep well we can go out tomorrow.'

'Whatever you want to do.' I stood up to go to the drinks cabinet and stopped, suddenly realising that I shouldn't drink – what if something happened in the night and Ellen needed me? I broke into a light, chilly sweat and sat down again, fiddling with my cigarette lighter, not knowing what to do with my hands. This I hadn't thought of. Ellen looked at me and smiled again. 'It's only for a couple of days,' she said.

And so it was but there's no one else on this earth for whom I would have done that, except John. The first night I lay in bed, feet away from Ellen, unable to sleep, pulse jumping as my blood raced round in search of alcohol. I could feel my body working up into a tantrum with each beat of my heart and I thought of my night-time foray of years before, when I had drunk a bottle of Crown Royal. I didn't sleep at all, tried to think of anything but drink and failed dismally.

On Saturday morning, exhausted by my own desire, I took Ellen for a drive, a relatively sedate mosey across the Cotswolds through all her favourite villages, the Slaughters, Chipping Camden, Stow and Woodstock – a looping, rambling journey through a warm late-autumn day. Houses and spires glowed in sunlight, stone mushrooms listed and drystone walls ran on for ever through ghostly brown fields. Pheasants lumbered unexpectedly out into the road, peacock breasts flashing. Ellen remarked that the beauty of the landscape of this part of England lay entirely in its lack of drama, and when I looked over at her I knew that she was committing it to memory, just as I had committed her face to mine. I knew also that she had always felt displaced, a member of the rich American diaspora that settled here, all escaping from something. She had never lost her accent, although it had softened enough to ensure that when she went back to the States to visit, people mistook her for English, while when she was here she was known as the American woman with the big house. She told me that she felt she had lost her citizenship somewhere over the Atlantic, that she belonged to neither place. I think that suited her, for I know that after her husband and child died she wanted nothing but to disappear and that was one way of doing it.

We had a late lunch in Bledington, an agony for me as I watched a table of businessmen ordering and drinking bottles of wine and shots of whisky. Again Ellen had to sleep when we arrived home, irritated with herself and, I know, jealous that I was to take the dogs out for a walk. We spent the evening listening to music and reading. Last night was worse, my sweating more pronounced, a distinct tremble appearing in my fingers as the hours passed. But I wouldn't give in, not if Ellen was there.

This morning we read the Sunday papers by the fire in the library and a rainstorm moved in, dousing the sun and thickening the glass of the windows. I kept looking up to see Ellen scanning the book-stacked shelves, the rows of bound *New Yorker*s, shelf after shelf of poetry and drama, hundreds of hardback works of fiction, some rare, some first editions, many out of print. Or I would glance over to find her staring at the rolling, oak-studded valley with its herd of stark black-and-white cattle, staring at it for hours on end. I find it hard to say nothing, to ignore this long-drawn-out goodbye. But I must – it's her prerogative.

Driving cautiously back into Oxford, to return her to the hospital, easing through the lakes of water across the roads caused by the storm-burst, I thought of what I had said to the doctor and suddenly panicked, thinking Ellen would never again sit in the library, look out over the fields, stroke the dogs' fur the wrong way. I turned to her.

'Ellen . . . um . . . I want . . .'

'Not yet,' she said and smiled with half her mouth, a mirror image of my own smile. 'Soon, maybe, but not yet.' She reset the rug around her legs. 'D'you want to go home? Back to Thurlestone? You've been gone a while.'

Again the panic fluttered. 'No – no, I don't. I want to stay here.'

'Good,' she murmured. 'Thank you.'

The moment I got back here I headed straight for the whisky bottle and poured a large shot, downing it before I even took off my coat. The dogs looked disgusted.

24 August 1979

John was married this weekend, a curious, low-key affair. They married in Chelsea Town Hall, a cavernous, rather gloomy place. Harry provided the only splash of colour – still wearing his red braces over an ever-extending belly. I didn't know John had invited him and when I turned to see him trotting, late, towards us, I was delighted. John was watching, scanning the crowds, and we both saw Harry at the same time, both broke into a run to meet him. I watched John thundering down the steps, jacket flying, a laugh bursting like a snowstorm from his black-black beard, eyes flashing. In his ear he was wearing a small gold ring – the first sign of vanity I have ever seen in him. He was roaring with delight, and suddenly I saw him as a pirate. Swinging from the ropes, scimitar or cutlass between his teeth, bellowing as he leaped from gunwale to gunwale putting the fear of God into his enemies. What must people have thought – a bearded giant, a veiled middle-aged woman and a stout, balding man, dancing a jig of sorts on the pavement? We had to break off when Sonja and Ellen called to us, pointing to their watches.

John was twenty when the five of us stood at the kerb after the ceremony, trying to hail a cab to the restaurant I had booked on Beauchamp Place. Twenty. Even younger than the young woman who had looked into Dai Davies' eyes with surprise while her parents smiled benignly on such foolishness. And now I felt I was doing the same.

We were shown to our table, the waiter literally backing away as John thudded into a low lintel, banging his forehead, looking stunned before laughing. In his fine black suit he looked, frankly, terrifying and the waiter seemed relieved when he finally sat down. I'd ordered a bottle of Krug, and when I took off my hat with its veil to drink a toast, Harry looked at me, scanned my face, and smiled. He leaned over and kissed my cheek as John kissed Sonja's flawless lips.

Harry took my hand. 'Joan, how lovely to see you. You look very well.'

'It's true that I'm blessed with rude health despite my best efforts.'

'And Special – will you just look at him! Dr W- W- Webster was right, then – six feet seven?'

'To the millimetre.' John, in his dark, pressed suit and white shirt, reminded me too much of his father and I reached again for the champagne. 'How did he get in touch with you?'

Harry looked surprised. 'John and I have written to each other for years. It started when he went to school – he wrote to me at Tommy's.'

'What?'

'He wrote to me because he was afraid he wasn't going to be big enough.'

'*Big* enough?'

'Yes,' Harry laughed. 'What he meant was he didn't think he'd be enough. It was about something I wrote to him once.'

I remembered the letter Harry gave John when he left the hospital: *Make sure you're big enough a man to fill your body.* 'So we kept in touch. He didn't tell you?'

'No. But that's fine.'

When the meal was over and we were standing on the pavement outside, Sonja kissed Harry as if she meant it and John nearly broke Harry's ribs with a bear-hug, before turning to me. Then they disappeared in a taxi to their hotel, to leave the next day for a week's honeymoon in Paris – my wedding present. Harry, Ellen and I looked at each other.

'That's it, then,' I said, desolate. Twenty years seemed to have passed without my noticing. 'John's married.' I wanted to claw the day back, begin again. I wanted to claw back so much time and spend it all differently.

'Joan, I have to go in an hour or so. Why don't we have another drink somewhere?' Harry asked.

I nodded, aware of the ridiculously inappropriate hat I held in my hand, like a Christmas bauble in the summer sun. We walked in silence down the King's Road, dodging the crowds. The last time I was on that road I was driving a Morris Minor, looking for the turning into Sydney Street leading eventually to the car park on Gloucester Road. We kept walking because I needed to and after half an hour found ourselves outside the Anglesea Arms in South Kensington, with the tables outside still in sunlight. Harry fetched the drinks, came back out and sat next to me.

'How are you, Joan?'

I grimaced. Harry was the one person I could think of, other than Ellen, with whom I could be honest. I thought of the silver compact in my bag. Should I tell Harry that I still couldn't quite see the beauty he had written of? Ellen excused herself and went to the bathroom. 'Up and down.'

'It's been a long time – nearly seven years. It *is* good to see you – I've often thought of you and John and wondered how you were getting on.'

'We survived.'

'Ah, come on, Joan, you did more than that.' Harry took my hand again and this time he didn't let it go. 'Be gentle with yourself. You did more than survive or manage or get by. I know that because of what John's written to me over the years. You were the best mother he could have had.'

'He didn't have much choice.'

'Well, let's put it this way, he would have chosen you anyway. And now look at him – he can speak and lip-read, he can walk without a limp, he's got a job, he's huge and he's handsome. And he's married. So what are *you* going to do?'

I looked unseeing at the people in the bar, burned by the sun, red-faced and laughing. John was with his wife, he had a tiny flat in Battersea and a life to go to when he returned from Paris. I had my deck and my whisky bottles. I knew Harry had to leave soon – our conversation for ever unfinished. There was not time to tell him how I was and that, despite everything, it was all right, it was enough.

'Y'know, I think I'll buy myself a Porsche,' I said, and Harry roared with laughter, not realising that I meant it.

17 December 1999

The days and weeks have fallen into a pattern now. I'm woken early by the dogs, who whimper and paw at my blankets once their bladders are full and they need to be let out into the gardens. I make myself tea while they pee and then feed them. It's always too early for me. I breakfast on Nurofen, juice and coffee, then drive into Oxford to the hospital and read to Ellen as long as she can bear it. Then she falls asleep and I wander the streets of Oxford for a couple of hours. It's a terrible city now, dirty and over-built, the colleges and whispering bridges lost in crowds of tourists, the covered market dying. If Ellen's awake when I return, I sit with her and she says nothing. I think she's playing old home movies in her head – of her childhood in Boston and Beverley, her days at Harvard, her married life in Connecticut. They must be short films; perhaps she plays them again and again.

This afternoon I was dozing in the chair when the doctor came in and tapped my arm and I followed him outside, suddenly wide awake. He looked at my scars as intently as he had the last time we spoke and I wasn't sure if he was appraising them professionally or gauging how much more I could take.

'I'd like Ellen to go home for Christmas and the New Year,' he said.

'Why?'

'Because I think she'd benefit from being there. You will be there?'

'Yes.'

'I'd like her to go home next Wednesday. We'll be getting her ready in the interim.' His face was drawn, the lines deeper than the last time I spoke to him.

'Getting her ready for what?' But he was staring into the distance, fiddling with a pen in his breast pocket. 'Getting her ready for *what*?'

'Um, well, ready to come home. There'll be some drugs she'll have to take with her but nothing too difficult.'

'That's it?'

'For now, yes.'

So now I have to plan a Christmas, not something I've ever been very good at.

15 October 1979

Miles and I had the luxury of spending that early summer together, since university finished earlier than school. We had days of lying in my small bedroom, watching the light change on the ceiling as the creek filled and emptied with the tide. We would sit outside the Swan or the Ship, eating lunch, knowing that we were far enough from Exeter to be safe, to be unseen. I had ceased to look at other men, for Miles' tanned, beautiful face was now all I wanted to see. And he, I noticed, no longer looked at other women. This worried me – I didn't want to want. I didn't want things to change. I wanted them to remain always as they were in those weeks of endless time when the sun climbed ever higher. Even the world seemed to have slowed, to have calmed – men drove buggies on the moon, England prepared at last to become a part of Europe, French riot police were deployed to force topless women to put on their bikinis. The Troubles rumbled on – Belfast was bombed and people were killed and Miles grew quiet then furious whenever the news came through on the radio whispering in the bedroom.

We would lie in bed and – as all lovers do – fantasise about being able to spend a weekend, even a week, together. We imagined ourselves in Paris, in Venice, knowing it would never happen. Then the summer holidays began and Miles went away with his family and John and I were left alone.

Looking back at those few early summer weeks during which Miles and I tried to pretend that nothing would change, I know

now that the world was simply drawing breath, preparing to blow us all away. It began once Miles had gone back to his wife and the world's eyes focused on Northern Ireland. In the month of August, while he was away camping in Brittany, more than seven thousand homes were burned to the ground, riots broke out and dozens were killed. One afternoon I sat in my garden, half watching John as he jumped again and again from a yacht into the deep waters of the creek, yelling and laughing with a group of friends, and idly read the *Western Morning News*. I saw that the IRA were threatening to bomb the mainland and all I thought was that Miles would argue that they had been forced into the decision by the presence of the British troops. That summer whatever I read, or ate, or heard, reminded me of Miles. Every sensation I felt – sun on my skin, cold wine in my mouth – made me think of Miles.

23 December 1999

John called me late tonight – he's been in Thurlestone for a couple of days and wants to come up here to Ellen's tomorrow. He's been down there on his own. But I've never known him travel without Sonja. What is going on? I asked him about Sonja but he evaded the question. I know he doesn't like to communicate by phone and I don't blame him. It's difficult enough for us to discuss the intimate anyway – on Type-Talk, with an operator translating speech into script, listening in to every word, it becomes impossible. Still, we haven't spent a Christmas together for years. This afternoon I bought and decorated a tree and the dogs have already peed on it twice. I've been here alone for weeks and now I shall be inundated.

20 October 1979

When that long-gone summer was over, when Miles had returned from France with his family and John had gone back to school, I slipped back into my life at the university like a seal slipping through an ice-hole, with barely a splash, in search of something. Even now I remember walking into the department office and there was Miles – even more tanned than usual, his hair bleached by salt and sun. We smiled at each other and said nothing. Within hours we were in Noss Mayo, lying on my bed, tracing for each other the weeks we had been apart. Our talk was oddly stilted, the sense of silences louder than anything we said. Soon we lay there, unspeaking, tracing each other's bodies rather than our histories.

'I missed you,' Miles said. 'I missed you too much.'

I turned away from him because I didn't want him to see my small smile of victory. He had said it first – he had conceded defeat of a sort. The predator unarmed.

'I missed you too.'

'Too much?'

'I'm not sure what that means.' But I was sure and I had.

As Miles turned my face towards him and began to kiss me, the hundredth victim of the Troubles was shot dead on the streets of Ulster.

A month later I broke the promise I had made to myself when I opened the parcel Dai Davies sent back to me: I arranged to go away with Miles – to steal him from his wife for a weekend in Amsterdam in December. My carapace of uninterest had cracked and I'd been revealed for what I was – a lonely woman. I'd been alone for a long time: it was twelve

years since Dai Davies had left me for an unknown woman. I
was thirty-six and aware that my . . . charms shall we say? were
beginning to fade.

Miles phoned me when I was packing the suitcase for the
trip to London for John's birthday and I remember laying out
John's clothes for the next day on my bed as I talked to Miles,
his voice soft so he wouldn't wake his wife, asking if he could
come with John and me. I laughed and said, 'No.' I didn't
know then that it was the last time John would wear those
clothes. Neither did I know that it was the last time I would
speak to Miles.

21 October 1979

Ellen reopened the wounds I have carried about Miles' silence
by asking me whether I ever considered marrying again. Then
again, I have so many wounds that I don't suppose that these
amount, really, to very much. But they hurt. I remember lying
in my hospital bed, unnerved by pain and unable to go to John,
waiting for Miles to come. He never did. No doubt he was back
out on the loose, preying. My eyes were wrapped in bandages
and I was blind for weeks as the skin of my eyelids fused.
In the darkness I played the memories of lying in my room
with the water shadows running across the ceiling, holding
Miles. I wanted to hear his voice; I wanted to feel his hand
take mine and tell me that I would be all right, even if I
knew he'd be lying. I've often wondered what he thought
when he was told about the bomb. Did he remember that
he'd asked if he could come with us? Perhaps he saw our
pictures on the news, in the papers. Wherever. What would
he have said? That the English got what they deserved? That

it was a political war and the IRA terrorists in the prisons were political prisoners? Would he have railed against the British troops while the emergency services walked among the glass and rubble in the car park on Gloucester Road, trying to stop the dripping of buildings? What would Miles have said? I think now that, like Dai Davies, he was beautiful and weak, handsome and empty. Perhaps he was all I thought I deserved because, to be honest, I had thought of marrying him, should he ask.

When Harry gave me the mirror and I paused before I looked at myself, testing myself for hardness, for indifference hardened to near inhumanity, it was Miles I was thinking of. It was two months since I'd seen him and the last time we'd been together he had run his tongue over my lips as he left and smiled, saying, 'You are quite the sexiest woman I've ever known.' I held up the mirror and saw a twisted, grotesque mask, those same lips sliced and torn, healed in white welts. Strangely, I didn't cry. I said nothing. I gave Harry back the mirror and lay down.

Perhaps this is something else that Ellen and I have in common – we have both been relieved of the burden of ageing. Both of us can point to a moment in time and say, 'That's when I ceased to care about the face I present to the world.' When Ellen's husband fell out of a fishing-boat and out of her life, when her womb contracted and stifled her unborn child, she relieved herself of the need, the desire, to be attractive to men because she ceased to care. As I did when I looked in the mirror. I saw Miles at that party in Exeter two and a half years later and he ignored me. I can understand it; I don't blame him. But I relieved him of the burden of smiling and he should have relieved me of something.

JOHN

Do I ever think of that morning when my mother pulled into a parking space on Gloucester Road? Of course I do. I think of it every day. It's my first thought every morning. I must be thinking it even before I wake up because when I do the thought is already there waiting for me. I can't remember exactly what happened; it was too violent an event, too bloody. I was blown apart in seconds; I didn't have time to run and hide, didn't have time to negotiate an escape; didn't even have time to put my hands over my ears, lower my head and protect myself. I was stretching, head thrown back, arms raised, completely vulnerable when concrete collapsed in on itself and the dustcloud began to mushroom. Strange that I always picture myself, Merboy, from a distance. It's him standing there being watched by his older self, an observer. I see him stretching, see his jaw working, mouth open, tall even then, shifting his hips a little from side to side in a yawning shimmy, and I see him being hurled forward into the razor-sharp edges of the car, his face hitting first, splitting open, as he throws out his arms and embraces a red-hot exhaust pipe. I know it's time that has swept me away from him, time that's put that distance between us, time that has made me an observer. But I can't forget him, can't forget Merboy, because every morning when I wake up I am reminded by the silence around and inside me of his face turning red.

*   *   *

'Oh, well spotted, pumpkin.'

It was Harry who introduced me to the language of language.
It was unfortunate that he did this when the only thing I knew
was the language of pain, yet some things broke through that
barrier. He taught me about phonology – accent, stress, pitch,
speed, intonation, register – the sound of language. Which
was laughable, really: he might as well have talked about the
unicorns of language, or the language of unicorns. But because
I was a post-lingual patient he said it would help and perhaps
it did – how could I tell?

At special school the teachers taught me about grammar,
about the features and functions of language, about tenses
and sentences, collectives and agreements. Merboy would
have hated it, would have balked at it, but Special watched
with his mad, moving eyes and learned because it was the
only escape route from his silent world. Those teachers also
taught me about graphology, about the signs of language; the
conventions of writing. With my hawk-like eyes I soon learned
to lip-read and to watch distant flying fingers, moving lips, and
translate their movement to meaning.

The summer I prepared to go to King's College, my mother
tried at last to teach me aspects of philosophy as she had
promised to do all those years before. She sat on the deck
with me and read with me, questioned me, tried to enable
me to understand the lexis and the discourse of language.
'Language,' she signed, one dazzling afternoon as gulls and
rooks fought over the remains of fishermen's bait on the beach,
'has two primary functions – communication and memory.'
She talked and signed and scrawled words on a pad of paper:

etymology, morphology, context, semantics. She segued from lexis to discourse and on to coherence, cohesion, text and subtext. I squinted, shaded my eyes and nodded, over and over. I had absolutely no idea what she was talking about. She was, after all, a prodigy, a woman who had mastered these concepts at seventeen and had never tripped over them again. My mother drew swirling web diagrams, the words 'semantics', 'portmanteaux', 'idiom' floating across the page, and I thought of the thought of university. I think it was late that afternoon, when the ice-cream vans had left and the golfers had altered their cards before they reached the clubhouse, that I first thought of becoming a carpenter.

Later still, Ian and I developed our own language of hands and faces, notes and symbols, unintelligible to others. Ian also took it upon himself to teach me those words found at the outposts of our language – flimflam, rodomontade, gudgeon, smutch, homeostasis. But it was with Sonja that language became something other than my mother had described to me because for Sonja a word often meant something other than it meant for others. For Sonja the word didn't change – it was its sensory equivalent that slithered around her linguistic map. We also shared the non-verbal indicators my teachers at school had mentioned but I don't think our indicators were what they had in mind.

Silence, however, has its own language.

Ellen found me a place to stay when I finally went to King's College, London, to study for a philosophy degree. She had an American friend, Caroline Speekes, who lived in a flat in one of the red-brick mansions behind Harrods, between Brompton Road and Sloane Street. Caroline said that I didn't have to pay rent but my mother insisted. It was a huge flat and I had it to myself, apart from the few nights when Caroline stayed in town. She was a tall, gaunt woman of few words, which suited me. When she was there I'd go out and walk the streets until late, pretending social engagements.

London frankly terrified me – after all my years in Devon it seemed a mad place, fractured by movement. Buses jammed the streets, cars sat in metal ribbons, gridlocked, as black cabs shuddered and lights glared, neon flickered. There were people everywhere, strangers packing the tube, blocking the pavements, spewing out of shops and train stations. Always pushing, always shouldering. Courier bikes and cycles mounted pavements, swerving between pedestrians, always assuming everyone could hear their approach. Litter – foam cups, newspapers, bottles, plastic bags – swirled in the winds and the draughts from speeding trucks. There was always an excess, a true riot of colour – flower stalls spilling out of subways, shopfront displays of statues and spinning wheels, posters and billboards, graffiti sprayed in tags on walls. London moved too much for me – I couldn't read it, I couldn't read people and their lips.

Each morning I'd sit at the kitchen table in the flat, drinking coffee, reading the set texts, dreading the moment when I'd have to leave and walk through the lobby and out into the streets. For the first week I was at King's I used the tube but the smell and motion, the crush of other people, made me nauseous. I could only stand in the middle of the carriages and clusters of Japanese tourists would gather round me, giggling, taking photographs of each other standing next to the English giant. So I began to walk to college. Each morning I stopped to look at the Houses of Parliament as I passed them and sometimes I wondered in which room the decision was made to send the troops into Northern Ireland, in which room the cheque was written to compensate me for my hearing. I knew why there was so much rubbish – all the litter-bins had been removed because bombs might be left in them. I also knew that there were plenty of other places for bombs to hide.

I went to all the lectures and seminars and, as ever, I was a conscientious student, a quiet student. I said nothing and I heard nothing. I'd sit in the cavernous lecture rooms, trying to follow the lecturers' faces, follow their lips, but they'd turn away, write on the board and I'd lose the thread. I couldn't make notes as they spoke so I tried to jot down words and look them up in the library afterwards. I asked the lecturers if they could give me notes to follow; some did, some didn't.

My mother had spent that summer trying to tell me about philosophy as well as language but I never did understand it. When I walked into my first lecture I saw, chalked on the board, 'The aim of metaphysics is to arrive at profound truths about everything.' This struck me as being a little too *ambitious* for me. After all, I wasn't even sure why I was studying it. While other students were out drinking and partying I wrestled with Xeno's four paradoxes and Wittgenstein's pink triangles. I tried to get to grips with Kant's transcendental unity of apperception and the only conclusion I could reach was that he, Kant, was obviously barking mad. However, the intellectual hurdle I could never clear was Quine's truth-functional logic. I decided to agree with him when he threw out his two dogmas with the baby and the bath-water. I even applauded his escape from the entanglements of Plato's beard – but what did he mean by logic?

I spent hours in the flat trying to ignore the flashing of neon across the ceilings, reading Quine's arcane text. I read again and again about quantificational schemata and the extension of equivalence but nothing ever became clearer. Each chapter was followed by exercises that baffled me. 'If Hawkshaw saw me, the jig is up' reduced, apparently, to ~(Hawkshaw saw me. ~the jig is up). I eventually grasped that what I was being asked to do was replace words with symbols, but which symbols and why? ($\exists x$) (x is prior to Sept. 14 1940 . Olaf sees Stromboli at x . ~Stromboli erupts at x). Quine swept through this without remarking on why Olaf was there, watching a volcano erupt, and he certainly never remarked on how Olaf *felt* about this experience. 'Put the following into symbols,' Quine instructed: 'When it rains in Pago Pago it pours.'

Eventually I asked Dr Price, a young lecturer who seemed the least terrifying of all of them, to explain predicates to me. 'The introduction of a predicate or predicate-schemata P,' he explained, 'at a given occurrence of a predicate letter, consists in supplanting that occurrence and the attached string of variables by the expression which we get from P by putting the initial variable of the string for one, the next variable for two, and so on.' He smiled broadly as I stared at him, appalled. 'So . . .'

He stood up and began to write the proofs on the board behind him. Not knowing what else to do, I began to copy them.

1) ($\exists v$) ⑤ owes ② to ④ for v . ~ ① paid ② to ④ for v)
at the second occurrence of 'G' in:
2) ($\exists z$) ($Gxwyzy$. ~($Gywwzx$)

And on and on and on for a further eighteen impenetrable lines. I stopped writing as he filled the board with symbols and instead I watched the buses trundling along the Strand.

'So, do you have any questions?' Dr Price asked when he'd finished.

'Do you think carpentry is an honest profession?'

He frowned. 'Carpentry is an honest profession. A statement. So . . .' He turned back to the board, sketched the proposition '– carpentry is a dishonest profession' $(\exists x)-($

I interrupted him. 'I have to go. Thank you.' Dr Price looked surprised.

The anonymity of the ever-changing lecture rooms and the fact I didn't live in halls meant that my loneliness was undetected by others. A couple of students did ask me if I'd like to join them for a drink but I never went because I didn't know how to. I didn't know what would be expected of me. I was nineteen and for six years I'd been alone. I guess I'd forgotten how to be anything else. So I went to the lectures, read the books, wrote the essays and walked around London. My size made me safe if not invisible, which I would have preferred. Gradually I became used to the movement of the city and on long winter nights I'd walk for miles along unfamiliar streets. It's easy to disappear in London because other people always assume that you have a purpose, a goal you're trying to achieve, that you have a life. I learned the tricks of walking as if running late, carrying newspapers and books, of looking as if I was waiting for someone. Which I was: still I scanned crowds for my father.

At the end of my first year I sat my exams and failed the logic paper quite spectacularly. It was the finest failure the college had ever known – a mark so pitiful the authorities couldn't even bring themselves to tell me what it was. Dr Price asked to see me and I went once again to his office, where he explained, quite gently, that I had to pass the logic module to get my degree, that I'd have to take it again the next year and the year after that if necessary. I looked at him and thought of sitting in the luxury of Caroline's opulent flat, abandoned to the company of Olaf and his volcanoes, stranded in the wetlands of Pago Pago for months and years to come. I thought of my mother sailing effortlessly through her university days. She'd finished her degree, even her Master's, by the age of twenty and here I was, incapable even of putting Hackshaw and his jig in their place. I didn't want to do it. Not because I was afraid of failure but because I was convinced of it.

I stood up, hit my head on the lampshade, shattering the bulb, and said, 'In that case, I don't think there's much point in carrying on,' as I brushed fine glass from my shoulders, picked it out of my hair and beard.

'I'm sure that if you had extra tutorials—'

'No. I don't think so.'

'But what will you do? Switch subjects?'

'I'm going to be a carpenter.'

'An honest profession,' he said, and shook my hand.

I walked back to the flat, smiling at strangers as Olaf receded in my memory. St James's looked beautiful, spotted with green and white deck-chairs, the trees not yet heavy with the lead poisoning of summer. I reached Hyde Park Corner and fell in love with London at last, with the circus of cars wheeling the roundabout, the avenue of Park Lane and the black and gold railings of the park itself. All of it. I sat by the Serpentine watching horses prance down Rotten Row kicking up dark sand and dust, and lay on the grass. I fell asleep in the sun and when I woke up I saw Merboy's face turning red.

Well, Willard van Orman Quine, tell me about logic. Tell me: what is logical about wrapping your arms round an exhaust pipe as your mother's face fills with shards of glass? Tell me:

how was I supposed to make sense of the world when I walked down the steps and left Tommy's behind? Explain to me the logic of never having heard my own broken voice. Tell me: was it a punishment for not having done anything wrong?

I went back to the flat and dressed in clean jeans and T-shirt, clipped my beard, threw *Logic* in the bin and went — nerves jabbering — to the student union. I stood uneasily at the bar trying, at last, to join in, and a beautiful blonde woman with grey eyes came over and held out her hand.

When I wake up on the floor this Christmas Eve morning, the fire's dead, ash drifting from the grate on the draught from the ill-fitting door. My back's aching because I slept on the rug without pillows and my hand is stiff with cold. The snow still hasn't melted, and in the early-morning light the beach looks white and dead, scarred by rocks. I stumble, clumsy as ever, towards the kitchen, knocking the pile of letters from the hall table to the floor, before filling the kettle. I have to pack my few clothes and lock up the house before leaving for Ellen's. I pour a mug of tea and sit at the table where I spent so many evenings with my mother.

My mother. I've read the journals, all of them. Twenty-eight years she has spent writing them and now I know about Dai Davies and what he did, that he left a hair-grip that was not hers in the middle of a pillow while she worked in a nearby restaurant, seven months pregnant. I know, now, the extent of her loneliness. I know that someone called Miles wouldn't smile for her. I know how my back looked when I turned it to her in the hospital. I know that I have, somewhere, two half-brothers. I know that she thinks I married too young. I know how much she loves Ellen. I know, too, how much she loves me.

And I've never really told her anything. I haven't spoken to her about Sonja, about what's going on, about my paralysing fear of being lonely again. I haven't told her about the Blind Man. I never told her that I knew when she sat with me in my room at Tommy's, that even though I couldn't hear her come in I could sense when she was there and it comforted me. I never told her that coming home from school and seeing her reading in the garden made me feel safe. I never apologised for my tantrums, when I blew up and howled because I couldn't hear things, couldn't do things, couldn't swim. I've never tried to do something about her drinking. Never explained why I became a carpenter. I never even told her that I knew it wasn't her fault I wasn't special.

And I never asked her for help.

I look at the pile of letters scattered on the hall floor and bend, stiffly, to pick them up and open them. Last night on the phone my mother asked me to pay any bills before I leave. There are Christmas cards (but so few), circulars and junk mail. There is also a handwritten letter on thick, ivory vellum.

I am aware that for years I have indeed heard the wolf's breath in the cave, because the wolf falls suddenly silent. My father is dead. The Bohemian, handsome, vain father, who married a woman who didn't exist, who never came, who never thought I was special enough, is dead.

Dear Mrs Player,

This is a very difficult letter to write. You don't know me – I am Dai Davies' second wife and I'm writing because I think you should know that Dai died last month. He didn't suffer and it was very sudden, as he had a massive heart-attack. I know that John will want to know and I don't know where he lives. In any case, I think that you should be the one to tell him since you will

find the right words. The funeral was held last month in Oxford.
We are all devastated.
    Yours in sorrow,
    Hilary Davies

My father died on a numberless November day, the day, perhaps, when I first met Darren Whiteside? Or maybe during the night, as Sonja and I made our smoke-flavoured love? I don't know and I'm not being told. I sit and hold the letter, a letter not meant for me, and I can feel the empty space left by the wolf's breath. I've heard it in my dysfunctional cochlea for nearly thirty years and now it's gone.

Ian once asked me what I would say to my father should I ever meet him. 'Would you offer him forgiveness? Would he be shriven?'

'Would he be *what*?'

'Would he be exonerated? Absolved?'

I looked at Ian's soot-smudged face, at his still, calm hands on the table. 'For what?' I asked, unsure myself.

'Indifference. Lovelessness.'

We were sprawled across the benches in the garden of the Highbury, two sweat-stained giants considering the various delinquencies of the lovelessness of men.

'I wouldn't know how to,' I decided finally.

'Then forget about it,' he said, swinging his feet to the ground and going to the bar for a pint of Smiles'.

And now, years later, I can. I gather together the journals, repack them in the box and climb once again into the attic. Before I switch off the light I look at the pale plank from a dinghy that went down years before. Now is not the time to take it, but one day I will. I throw my clothes back into the hold-all. I walk through the house, locking and checking doors and windows, resetting the timing of the heating.

The Jeep is covered with vicious, thin-skinned frost and I scrape at it, breath misting, trying not to think. I put the Jeep in four-wheel drive to climb up out of the valley and soon I'm on a near-empty motorway, heading towards my mother and Ellen, a letter folded into the back pocket of my jeans. The fields of Devon race past, grey with snow, scabbed by black, skeletal trees. I touch the Corona scar and I'm reminded of summer and the sound of my own yell. I remember, as I speed over the Avonmouth Bridge, that I have left my wife. I packed my bags and left our house when she wasn't there, just as Dai Davies did.

The atria of the heart are tiny – small and delicate as silver Turkish thimbles and as intricately decorated with filigree arterioles. They are the Chippendales of human organs, holding a mere three and a half teaspoons of blood – a nosebleed; a careless, sharpened chisel. The ventricles are hardly giant vessels either, holding no more than a quarter of a cup of blood. Yet these thimbles contract and spill more than two thousand gallons of blood a day, filling and emptying more than one hundred thousand times. This is masterminded by the sinoatrial node and if it fails a pacemaker can replace it. No larger than a pocket watch, it nestles in the fat of the chest wall and has a battery that lasts between five and fifteen years. Sometimes I feel as if the battery of my heart is running down but my doctor tells me it isn't.

How would he know?

*   *   *

The day Ian and I had our first order for a deck in Cotham, Sonja cooked up a feast to celebrate. We were living in a small flat in Kingsdown then and the three of us sat at the kitchen table, wolfing down food and laughing about the possibility of riches. Ian drank buckets of wine, became morose and eventually fell silent. Sonja and I were clearing up when he tapped me on the shoulder. 'It's different for you,' he signed.

'Eh? What are you on about?'

'Deafness. You can't see it.'

I put down the plates I was carrying. Faced him. 'So?'

'It's invisible. You can't see it.'

'I know that.'

Ian slumped against a counter, folding his massive arms. 'And you,' he said to Sonja, 'no one can see your problem. Both of you can walk into a room and nobody notices anything. You're lucky.'

Lucky? Sonja and I glanced at each other. This was something neither of us really wanted to think about. I was getting nervous.

Ian held out his hands, turned them over again and again so the pink palms appeared and disappeared. 'I walk into a room and I know the first thing people think is, He's black.'

'No, it's not,' said Sonja. 'The first thing they think is, Bloody hell, he's handsome.' And she smiled, walked over to Ian and wrapped her arms round him, as I picked up the plates again.

I arrive at the gates to Ellen's house as snow begins to fall again, flustered into eddies by a light wind. I climb out of the Jeep and push the gates open, difficult even for me because they grate across gravel, and I see my mother helping Ellen from her car. The outside lights are on, flushing the snow

deep yellow in the dark afternoon, and I stand and watch
them, shocked. They look so old. Ellen staggers and her
blanket falls from her shoulders. Beneath it she is a waif,
a shadow. This is *Ellen*? My mother frowns, reaches for the
blanket, Ellen holding her arm. I run across the gravel and they
both look up in fear. Wordlessly I pick Ellen up – she weighs
nothing – and carry her to the door, my mother following.

'Where?' I motion.

'In the library.' My mother leads me and I lay Ellen down
on the bed that's been put in there. Her eyes are shut and
her mouth is slack. My mother waves me away and I go back
outside to bring in my car and close the gates, then wait in
the kitchen sitting by the Aga, my eyes aching. My mother,
when she comes in twenty minutes later, frowns and shakes
her head.

'Is she OK?' I ask, stupidly.

'Of course she's not fucking OK.' She crosses to the
half-glazed door and looks over the valley, turns back to
me. 'I'm sorry. I just worry, that's all.'

I walk over and hug her, hold her so closely that I can feel
the rhythm of the egg cups of her heart filling and spilling.

When I was young my mother was always trying to hug me,
trying to cuddle me and always I would slip away from her,
twist away from her hand reaching out to ruffle my salt-thick
hair. She'd laugh and pinch me gently instead. But there were
nights when I'd go to her and knock aside her book, to sit in
her lap, for a moment, for an hour, and she'd talk to me about
what she'd done that day, stroking my arms, examining my
hands until I'd had enough. Always and only until *I* had had
enough. The selfishness of the young. Now I know that she
had others who held her, who stroked her, and that makes me

mind less about that selfishness. Once we'd left the hospital we hardly ever hugged, both nervous of touch. Aloof, Sonja had called me, but I know that my mother and I thought we didn't deserve it – we were too disfigured, too mutilated. Too defenceless, too unworthy.

I lead my mother to a chair, sit her down, make coffee, sandwiches. She eats a few mouthfuls, then lights a cigarette. 'I'm sorry,' she says. 'Not much of a home-coming.'

'That's all right – it's not my home.'

She smiles weakly. 'It's lovely to see you.'

'I didn't know Ellen was that bad.'

'She's got worse in the last few days. She'll sleep for a few hours and then she'll be livelier.'

'Where are the dogs?'

My mother twiddles the invisible volume knob and I know that I've been shouting. 'They're in with her – they stay with her.' She glances at the clock. 'They need to be walked – you want to come?'

I nod. My mother collects the leads, puts on wellingtons, and I go into the library. Ellen is sleeping and her face has been cleared of its pain. She looks like the Ellen I remember playing cards with on the deck when I was a boy. Her skin may be thinner, her bones nearer the surface, but her mouth, her eyes, are at rest. I want to do something for her but all I can do is leave her. I search for my worrystone.

We walk down the valley with the dogs running ahead, coats flowing, thin ice shattering when we crack the ruts made by cows wandering backwards and forwards to the troughs and hay bales, and as I walk I think about the language of loss. For all that my mother has ever tried to explain to me about words conveying meaning, I've never felt anything but their essential inadequacy. I couldn't ever really tell anyone – Sonja, my mother, Harry – about what it was like to realise that I couldn't hear, and, worse almost, that I couldn't swim. I know my mother has never been able to describe adequately, completely, what she felt when she looked in the mirror Harry gave her. Words fail us; they have always failed us. So when we're in the dense woods on the ridge, I touch my mother on her shoulder and she turns to me. I pull the letter from my pocket, hand it to her without speaking, without words, and I walk on. I walk slowly, through the woods, past the crumbling byres at their edge. Looking back I see my mother sitting on a felled elm trunk in the distance, the letter in one hand, a cigarette in the other. I call the dogs from a rabbit-hole and head for the house.

I sit in Ellen's kitchen stroking the dogs, pulling the tip of my beard, waiting for my mother. The light in the kitchen changes and I turn to see her opening the door. She's been crying and I can't remember the last time I saw that. Unthinking, I reach up to scrub at the zest of a lime spraying my cheek. She disappears into the music room and returns with a bottle of Crown Royal and two glasses. She pours us each a shot, downs hers and pours herself another. We sit in silence (no change there, then) and stare at the dogs yawning and licking in their old cane chairs. There is a stillness about my mother I've never noticed before, or rather, I think there's a stillness that has never existed before. If I have spent nearly thirty years listening to the wolf's breath, what has she been doing? Whatever it was, it's stopped.

She stretches out both hands to cover one of mine. Her skin is cold. 'How do you feel?'

I shrug. 'It's over,' I say, and I wonder what exactly I'm talking about.

'Are you all right?'

'Yes.' I try words. 'For a long time I could hear – there was a sort of noise in my head . . . It's stopped.'

'Good.' She pours another drink and I see her hands shaking a little.

'What about you? I never knew him but you did.'

'What about me? Well, I haven't been hearing noises in my head but I'm glad it's over.' She smiles weakly. 'It just went on so long.'

That was how Sonja found us, sitting with a bottle of Crown Royal, my mother holding my hand, a letter on the table between us. She opened the latch door and looked at me with grave, grey eyes.

Merboy went out one afternoon to hunt for shells. I remember him tanned at the dusk-end of a summer; barefoot, covered with whole, undamaged skin. He crashed through the bluebell woods lining the creek, on past the boat-house, up the track to the end of the headland, where he paused to look out over Great Mew and Little Mew, towards Plymouth Sound, before running through crisp, fading bracken down to Cellar Beach. The beach was empty at the end of the summer: the yachties had left. He paddled the water's edge, crabbing along, bent double, scooping up handfuls of sand, sifting them through his fingers. He watched his hands change colour each time he dipped them in the sea to rinse away the sand that was left. He did this for ages as the light deepened and stretched the shadows. I remember Merboy reaching the rocks at the far end of the beach and digging deep, feeling coarse sand grate beneath his nails, pulling the reluctant pile through foaming water. I remember him standing and letting dollops of heavy, damp sand fall, until left resting on his palm was a wendletrap, at least three inches long. He stared at it and closed his hands round the shell before rinsing it and lifting it to the falling sun. He counted the pale, fawn ridges to be sure – fifteen whorls. An undamaged, three-inch wendletrap. A dinghy rounded the headland and he looked up, distracted by the buzzing of an outboard. The man waved and Merboy flapped a hand in his direction (and nothing happened). I remember Merboy looking back to his hand and seeing pale flesh emerging tentatively from the shell. He looked at it for a long time. I don't remember what he thought as he looked at the animal and neither do I remember what he felt in his heart but I do remember Merboy drawing back his arm suddenly and throwing the unique, spiralling shell back into the water. He watched its fall and splash, then turned to run back through the bluebell woods, running home to his mother, wanting to knock aside her book and sit on her lap.

Sonja and I are lying in bed in Ellen's house. It's late afternoon and through the sash windows the changing colours of Christmas lights wrapped round a tree in the neighbour's garden are thrown on to the ceiling, and as I watch them I'm reminded of the night when I lay on the settee and thought about Sonja buying her deli, wondering whether she'd be able to do it because every taste, every sound, every touch bleeds one into another for her, and then I went to wake her and my heart stopped and I fell, '*Timber!*' on the carpet and when I came back to life I was running on batteries and Sonja was butchering all the bleeding hearts in the garden, and that reminds me of the tangled, untamed garden where my mother sat and read while she waited for Miles Brandrin, knowing that he would make her smile and feel loved whereas nothing I ever did when I was Merboy made her feel that way, yet I'd arrive home to find my mother waiting for me, making plans for my life, plans that didn't include us being blown apart, forcing us to live different lives, lives that weren't what we wanted, weren't what we anticipated, and so we've become heartless, encouraged to live only by a man wearing bright red braces or so I thought until I met Sonja who fell on to a rumpled bed with me and brought me back to life but now that life is gone because she's chosen a blind man over a deaf one – a decision Dai Davies would no doubt have applauded because I was never special, even before I was born I wasn't special enough for him and I can imagine that somewhere my two half-brothers are living their special fucking lives, mourning Daddy, and I don't want to see them because what would they ask me and how would I hear them and anyway I have a question of my own. I turn to Sonja and ask, 'Who is the Blind Man?'

Once I'd thrown logic into the bin and then met the One, my life changed. Sonja and I spent every evening together, usually in her small chaotic room in halls. I could never find a safe foothold among all the clothes and books on the floor and Sonja would watch me flail around, crashing into the sink, knocking the lampshade, eventually falling on to the bed. For weeks we talked and then one evening Sonja fell on to the bed with me as the light-bulb swung crazily and my hands became burgundy wine. Later she held one of them, looked at it a while.

'We both live on small islands,' she announced, and promptly fell asleep.

Small islands? 'Right,' I said.

I look at Sonja, her face flushing red, green and yellow as the Christmas tree opposite flashes and I can see she's crying.

She's lying on the bed, on her back, and colourful tears are trickling down on to the pillow.

'Who is the Blind Man?' I ask again.

She turns towards me, her hands tucked under her chin, her knees bent, foetal, and she cries without moving. 'His name is Thomas. Thomas Cornwell.'

'I'm not asking about his name. Who is he?'

'He's a friend of mine.'

'I know that, I *know* that. I want to know what sort of friend he is.'

'He's a good friend.'

'How did you meet him?'

'He's a regular customer in the shop. We had coffee and then drinks and then lunch.'

'Is that all?'

'I was scared when you came, with Ian, y'know, running and shouting.' She wipes her streaming nose with the back of her hand. 'I didn't know what to do.'

'Is that all?'

'I never thought that you'd see him.'

Will she never answer? 'Is that all?'

Her reddened eyes scan my face. 'Are you asking if I've had sex with him?'

'Yes.'

'Is that what you're worried about?'

'Yes.'

'Then you're a fool.' She rolls on her back again and speaks and signs, 'No, I haven't slept with him.'

I feel a blanket of relief cover me.

'John, I know you feel relieved but I don't think you're thinking about this properly. Sex isn't everything.'

'What do you mean?'

'Think about it.' Sonja rolls off the bed and leaves the bedroom, wiping her face.

I think about it.

There was a girl at special school who had a crush on me. She had long, dark-red hair and green eyes, and had to wear a brace on her teeth all the time. Her name was Moira. She was profoundly deaf and also had a degree of visual impairment, which meant that she wore thick, National Health tortoiseshell glasses. I knew she had a crush on me because whenever I walked into the common room she'd snatch off her glasses so that I could see her beautiful sea-green eyes. But then she couldn't see and her head would swing around bovinely, trying to track me as I moved around the room. When she stood up to leave she'd bump gracelessly into chairs and door frames. I took pity on her one evening and crossed the room to ask if she wanted help. She wore two hearing-aids, like a smooth pink whelk in each ear, and she reached up to touch them, wanting to hide them, then reached out and took my hand. It must have been an early summer evening, May or June, because it was warm enough to sit out in the gardens. We sat on a bench not speaking or signing because that would have been awkward and I didn't really know what I was doing there, while her hand grew damp in mine. She leaned suddenly against me and her face was on mine, her tongue between my lips, her breath tasting of the cheese we had eaten at dinner. My groin jumped yet I was simultaneously repelled. Somehow I knew it would be rude to pull away. Her hand reached down and touched my erection and I jumped up, appalled and frowning. 'What's wrong?' she mouthed. I shook my head wildly, speechless, signless. Moira put on

her glasses and looked me up and down coolly before
walking off across the lawns, back to the common room.

I haven't thought of Moira for years and I lie on the bed
wondering what happened to her. Does she wear contact
lenses? Has she had a cochlear implant? Did she ever find
a penis that responded as it should? I realise that Sonja is
right – sex isn't everything, it's really not very much at all.
It's not sex I should be worrying about, and at that moment
of revelation the bedroom door opens and my mother signals
that supper is ready.

When I appear in the kitchen, Ellen is dressed, sitting
at the table. She looks up and smiles when she sees me.
She stands for a hug and again I'm shocked by the feel of
her bones. The four of us eat, talk about the weather, the
property market, Sonja's deli, the media's obsession with
the turn of the century. When dinner is done we move to
the library, where my mother has built one of her roaring
fires, and spend a couple of hours playing Scrabble. Four
people whose worlds are out of kilter, who perhaps have
too much to talk about and so elect to say nothing. I
don't know if my mother has told Ellen about my father.
I hope not because I think Ellen already has enough to mull
over during the night hours when I know that she doesn't
sleep. We talk about tomorrow, Christmas Day, and I realise
that I haven't bought any presents. It's my turn to forget
Christmas.

I help Ellen to her bed and as she settles she touches my
hand. 'We'll talk tomorrow, John.'

'Right,' I say, and climb the stairs to the bedroom, where
Sonja and the Blind Man are waiting for me.

*   *   *

Ellen has moved in and out of my second life, appearing unannounced in Thurlestone or inviting my mother and me to the Cotswolds. When I was at special school and I went home for the weekends she helped me to learn sign language, sitting out on the deck with me, moving fingers and thumbs, reading the manuals with me while my mother sat alone on the steps, drinking her whisky. I once told my mother that when I was with Ellen I forgot about how I looked, thought more about how I sounded. It was Ellen who taught me to drive – a thankless task, as I couldn't hear the instructions. Nor could I hear the screams of 'Stop!'

Now I've read my mother's journals I know that Ellen came and looked after me so my mother had time to grieve, had the privacy to grieve. I also know how much my mother loves Ellen, and more than anything I want Ellen to live, knowing she won't.

I strip off my clothes and Sonja watches me from the bed. I climb in next to her, knocking the bedside lamp from a table with my usual clumsiness. Sonja and I face each other once again, not touching.

'I've thought about it,' I say, and Sonja turns down the volume knob. This is not a conversation she wants overheard.

'And?'

'You're right – sex isn't everything. But it means a lot to me. I've missed it, I've missed you.'

'John, I want you to read me very carefully, because I want to say a lot of things. If you miss something, let me know.' Sonja sweeps back her hair and shifts on the pillow, her eyes watching me intently. 'I didn't go looking for Thomas and he could hardly go looking for me. He's been coming to the shop for years and we've always talked because conversation is very important to him.'

'Right.'

'And you know it's always been important to me. When we first met, you and me, you used to talk as much as you could. You always used to tell stories, you used to tell me the jokes the people at Elemental told you, you told me about your days, about Ian's love life, whatever. You used to laugh and bully me into doing things like playing pool, going on the ferry, going up to London for the weekend. But you stopped, very slowly, over years, you stopped. Then after you got your pacemaker you were just silent. At first I thought it was post-operative depression or something but it didn't go away. It was as if you forgot about me, as if you could only think about you and everything that's happened to you. What was I supposed to think? What was I supposed to do?

But what happens when your heart is damaged? What do you favour? I'll tell you: you favour yourself.

'And so when Thomas – who couldn't see me, who had no idea what I looked like – began to talk to me, what was I going to do? I didn't mean to fall for him, that was never my intention. I thought we'd just meet for coffee or something. That's why I didn't hide away with him at first – because we were friends. But things like that aren't static, they keep moving. We listened to music, and sometimes he would play his clarinet for me but only in private because he's lost his confidence. So I began to go to his house and then I knew that we were more than friends.'

'You said you didn't have sex.'

'Think, John, think. *You* said sex isn't everything. Thomas and I were happy in each other's company – we talked, we listened to music, enjoyed each other's company.'

I can feel rage beginning to uncurl. 'But I *can't* listen to music – I'm fucking deaf!'

And Sonja – 'You're too damn *big* to lose your temper' – reaches out and touches my lips, smiling. 'I know that, John. But you can ask me to dance. You can come into a room and ask me to dance. I know you've been walking through life wondering what's happened to us and wishing it was like it used to be. Well, when I touch you I feel blue, your hands are blue where they used to be wine. Make it like it was. Talk to me, ask me about my life, tell me about yours, about Ian, about work. Read things aloud to me. Your voice is changing you use it so little, it's getting loud and flat. Bully me into doing things.'

'I'm sorry.'

'Don't be sorry. Just be like you were.'

I watch her face, her familiar face. 'If I can hear something, after the operations, if I can hear, will that help? Will it make a difference?'

'I don't know. How can I know that? It won't make me love you more. How could it?'

'Will you see him again? The Blind Man?'

'Not if you don't want me to.'

'Right.'

We lie there staring at each other.

'I'm so sorry about your father,' Sonja says, and she holds out her arms and I fall into her and she holds me very, very tightly and it occurs to me that I'm sorry *for* my father.

The four of us make sure that Christmas is full of good food, wine, fires and space. But still it seems to me that we are walking gingerly around each other, walking on eggshells once more. Sonja and I take the dogs out every day, long rambles across bare fields, through frozen meadows, over stiles and kissing gates. Sonja holds on to my arm as if she will never let go and I talk. I talk for hours because I have not talked for so long. I tell her about my mother's journals and everything I found out after thirty years. I tell her about Miles Brandrin; I talk about Ellen and school, tell her about Moira. I make plans to fix my mother's deck. The dogs trot in front of us, sniffing in ditches and chasing elusive birds. When we return to the house there are my mother and Ellen, lying on the sofas in the library, reading, talking. In the evenings Sonja and I walk into town and try different pubs, sitting in snug nooks and completing the day's crosswords. And every night Sonja is waiting for me when I get into bed, reaching out for me before I can pull the blankets round us. But everything seems cautious and frantic at the same time.

Sometimes I sit with Ellen as she sleeps, watching over her, stroking the dogs, who never leave her except for walks. One afternoon I doze, to be woken by Ellen taking my hand. 'It's OK,' I say, without thinking, still half asleep, and she nods, as if to say that indeed it is.

Apparently Ellen announces that she would like an Italian meal on New Year's Eve, *fagiano caldo in carpione*, to be precise, followed by *brustengolo*. My mother, Sonja and I look at each other in horror, me because I haven't understood a word and Sonja and my mother because they haven't either. We find Freson's *Savouring Italy* in Ellen's kitchen and pore over it together, leaning on the kitchen table, elbows brushing. Pheasant with shallot sauce followed by cornflour cake. I send Sonja and my mother out to hunt for fresh herbs and dead birds while I prepare the vegetables. They burst through the door later, carrying bags full of chocolates and cheeses, champagne and sparklers, and they're laughing as the dogs trot behind them, sniffing at the game. Sonja and my mother fill my hands with silver cutlery and shoo me out of the kitchen, gesturing at the table in the dining room – I am to create something fit for a *fin-de-siècle* meal.

When I've finished I go to the library and find Ellen looking at all her books, fingering them as she moves along the shelves.

'I shall miss them,' she says, and she inches around the sofa, to sit down. She motions for me to sit next to her. 'I never did get used to how big you are, Special,' she says, as the cushions sink and she topples into me.

'Sorry.' Her thin, drawn face with its bright eyes – how familiar it still is.

'I want you to know that I've loved having you all here, seeing the house used as it should be. It was a lovely Christmas.'

'Right.'

'I can't believe I spent all those hours in Thurlestone teaching you vocabulary and all you say is "Right" – don't you remember anything I taught you?'

'All of it.'

Sonja throws open the door, covered in flour, hair wild, and says it's time to dress for dinner. Dress for dinner?

An hour later the four of us are in our finery, sitting at the Georgian dining table, candelabra blazing, decanters of wine spilling bloody shadows on the damask cloth, and my mother is telling us how she and Ellen were going to spend this night in the Tobago Cays, on a schooner floating from Bequia, the sea frothing with champagne. My mother is drunk but she does it so well that even a passing policeman wouldn't spot it. She hasn't been drinking at all because of Ellen so I told

her I'll take it easy and she can drink what she wants. I miss
a lot of what she says because her mouth slackens when she's
drunk too much wine but I get the picture (when she drinks
whisky I see every word, every picture). I look at Sonja, and
the candlelight has erased the faint lines round her mouth
and eyes and she looks like the woman who took my hand
twenty years ago and said, 'We both live on small islands,'
and I want her to know, right now, I want her to know that
that's all right as long as we live on the same small island. But
then my mother walks in with a steaming plate of *brustengolo*
and the moment passes. Ellen cuts the cake (she's so weak
I don't know how she manages) and it's magnificent. Sonja
looks at me and signs, 'Like clouds over Nebraska,' pointing
at the rich dessert and I frown because I know she's never
been there but I know exactly what she means (and would
the Blind Man have known what she meant?).

Suddenly it's ten to midnight and I help Ellen wrap herself
in a duvet and carry her outside, to a chair in the garden that
looks over the valley and the town beyond. My mother lit a
bonfire an hour before and Ellen smiles as she feels its heat.
Sonja and my mother come out with a bottle of Krug, a
portable radio and handfuls of sparklers. Fireworks scatter
over the town and I look at my watch and realise that, not
unlike my heart, it's running slow. I yank the cork from the
bottle, my mother lights sparklers and it's here, the new year,
new century. Before I can pour champagne Sonja grabs and
kisses me. Wraps her arms round my neck and pulls my face
to hers and kisses me as if for the last time, her fingers locked
in my hair.

For twenty minutes we stand and watch orange and blue
star-bursts, rockets, red-balls, colossal roman candles loom
over the valley, dwarfing the trees and fields, even the town

itself. What, I wonder, do the cows make of this? I can't hear the bangs and thumps that my mother has described to me, but it hardly matters. Merboy, Special and I have always loved fireworks, because they're beautiful, because you don't need to hear them, because they usually mean it's nearly my birthday.

One night, many years ago, a gangling, nervous, near-bald boy, dressed in a T-shirt and a too-big pair of Levi's, stepped through sliding doors, let go of Harry's hand and stood alone watching colours spray against a sky just like this, as the wolf's breath rasped. I'm not sure how that boy travelled from that shivering night to this silent one but somehow he did. I look at Sonja, lit by fierce firelight, and I see that she's crying.

JOAN

4 January 2000

Ellen and I have returned to our routines now John and Sonja have gone back to Bristol – I clean and cook, walk the dogs and do the shopping; in the evenings I sit with Ellen, read to her – newspapers, novels, poetry, whatever – and she sleeps and wastes away, taking drugs, shifting in her bed. She hasn't been out of her bed since John and Sonja left on New Year's Day. I think Christmas wore her out, sucked out the last vestiges of her life. I also think she chose to do that, chose to use whatever she had left then, rather than eke it out over weeks. She says she won't go back to the hospital, and I've spoken to the doctor and he agrees that there's little point. A nurse comes twice a day and I sit in the kitchen while she deals with Ellen and I wonder how long this can go on. John offered to stay with me but he has a life, he has work to do and his operation is looming, so I told him to go. He says he wants us to meet more often, that he'll visit me at home. He wants to fix up my house, build a new deck, convert the attic. Well, maybe. But let me get this over with first.

The day John and Sonja left he spent an hour with Ellen in the library and when he came out he was crying. He tried not to, kept coughing and clenching his teeth, rubbing his hands, reminding me of Merboy when he was hurt. But the tears came anyway. Sonja drove them home because he couldn't.

I don't know what he and Ellen said to each other but it must have been a goodbye of sorts.

Is John happy with Sonja? I don't know. I don't know. The day she arrived, when they went upstairs to unpack, I heard him shout, 'I *can't* listen to music – I'm fucking deaf!' but then he's always had a penchant for stating the obvious. Later still, as I prowled along the landing, fighting the desire for whisky, I heard John and Sonja making love, heard John's yodels. I suppose Sonja didn't feel the time was right to twist her fingers and turn down the volume.

5 January 2000

John left me the letter from the second Mrs Davies – he said it was mine because it was addressed to me. 'I think you should be the one to tell him since you will find the right words.' What on earth makes her think that? And what would the right words *be*? It's as if she knows them and assumes I do too, but I don't. I can't imagine how I would have told my son that his forever-absent father was dead. I ask myself again – was I a good mother? Always the answer is the same.

Dai Davies – the last time I saw him I was standing in Park Street, dressed to seduce, breasts heavy with milk. 'No,' he said, and my brain – that fine-tuned instrument which could cope with the uncertainties of metaphysics and aesthetics, ethics and semiotics – jammed. I might have been able to grapple with signs and signifiers, teleology and ontology, but the word 'No' undid me.

Do I mourn him? No, I don't. I cried enough for him when he was alive. I have thought about him everything it is possible for me to think. Ultimately, I suppose, he became one of my many 'what ifs'. What if he had stayed? Would I have been content? Or would I have fallen into bed with others as I ended up doing? Would I have driven up to London for John's birthday? How different would our lives have been? What if I had ended up leaving him? Pointless. All these imaginings are pointless. I have nothing left to think about him for myself. I've always worried that John thought of him too often, that John's waiting for his father to appear stopped him doing other things. Now I worry about John's half-brothers – I don't want them to appear, Dai Davies' cubs, because John doesn't need to see them.

Since John and Sonja left I haven't had a drink and it doesn't get any easier – it seems that my blood needs alcohol to move quickly, to make my mind wander. There's not one watermark in this journal and it's five days old.

8 January 2000

At Christmas John told me that he'd been into the attic at Thurlestone and he'd found my journals, read them all. I know that was what I wanted, that it was a conscious decision not to destroy them, so that he could find them if he wanted to. But, but . . . over the past week, as I've tramped through rain with the dogs and the clouds of toxins have dissipated, leaving my memory no hiding place, I've remembered things I wrote that I didn't, really, wish him to know. There have been times when I've been walking through the woods and been suddenly paralysed by an image, by a page I wrote, in the same way that drunken behaviour reveals itself the next day in embarrassing, stuttering, time-lapse montages. Did I want John to know about Miles – that I slept with him at the cottage? That I lied to John? That I kept the truth about the hairgrip from him? Did I really want him to know that I often forgot at first that he couldn't hear? That I didn't tell him about his half-brothers – the biggest lie of all? And what, exactly, did he make of the picture of me crawling on bloodied knees on the path outside Ellen's kitchen, sweeping up the evidence of a drunk's binge? Attractive. I suppose he always knew I was a drunk, that the people of the village whispered behind their hands that I was a witch, a monster, a grotesque. I don't think they think that now but neither do I imagine that they will ever consider me their erudite monster. But the thought that made me stop dead, half over a stile, a boot slipping on thick red mud, was that he now knows how vain, how shallow I was when he was young. That all I wanted was to be desired and I didn't really care by whom. He will think that I deserved Dai Davies.

Another thought: perhaps I did?

14 January 2000

John called via Type-Talk this evening. He sounded sleepy. He had the myringoplasty the day before yesterday. No problems, everything went well. Apparently he spent yesterday waiting for the bandage to be removed, and when it was, both ears were revealed intact. He has to rest now for two weeks and then he goes in to have the gauze removed. I wish I was with him. I know how to look after him – after all, I've had enough practice. But I can't leave Ellen.

The first step is over and I can't wait for him to be able to hear, no matter how much, how little, to hear *something*. I told Ellen when she woke up and she nodded and smiled, which

is all she's capable of. The timing of all this is shit. I wish I
could have a drink.

18 January 2000

It's a beautiful morning, a late, pink-golden dawn over the
valley. I can't remember if I've ever written an entry this
early before. I haven't slept because Ellen and I talked all
night; well, that is, Ellen talked. She woke yesterday evening
and began to ramble, so quietly I could hardly hear her, her
hands stroking the blankets. Occasionally she'd stop and doze
for a few minutes, then wake to begin again. I realised that she
was hallucinating, wandering, sliding over the ice rink of her
life from present to past to future. I threw logs on the fire as
the night went on and simply let her speak.

'I knew,' she said, in a feathery voice, so light I had to lean
near to hear it, 'that Matt was dead, that he'd fallen out of a
boat because I was there with him, not there with him, but
in my head I knew. And that night when he and I went out
in Cambridge and there were protests all over about bussing
and during the Bay of Pigs we hardly dared move, hardly
dared breathe. My mother asked me when I was going to
marry again and I told her never because I loved Matt and
so that was it. The nursery was at the back of the house.
It was pale yellow with orange curtains. Sometimes wonder
what would have happened if it had been different colours,
but what's the point? We had sex before we married and
I lay there afterwards thinking a bolt of lightning would
smash right through the ceiling but it didn't and I'm glad
because we stayed together. I went to Paris with a friend
and we went to the Grand Canyon – that's in America –

and had ice-cream in a truck-stop someplace. My husband and I live in America, which is a good place to live apart from Kennedy was shot yesterday. He was sitting in his car and there was Jackie covered in blood and we couldn't do anything. Then we shot Martin Luther King, which wasn't right but it's OK now.'

She rambled for hours. I can't begin to recall everything she said but I'll try to when all this is over. She said she had a friend who lived by the sea, a friend who everyone thought was ugly but she wasn't. I smiled when she said that.

The next time she woke it was with a small cry just before dawn. 'Where am I? Am I dead yet?'

'Sssh – you're at home, Ellen, it's OK. You're at home. You've been sleeping.' I stroked her arm.

'Joan?'

'Yes.'

Ellen sank back on to the pillow and one of the dogs licked her hand gently. She stared at the fire in the grate. 'Can I tell you something?' Her voice had changed – it wasn't loud but the feathers had flown.

'Anything.'

'It's not very nice. But I never told anyone this and I need to tell you.'

'Then tell me.' And I knew it might be our last chance to get personal.

'We've often talked about that night when Matt didn't come home.'

'Yes.'

'The conversation was never finished.'

Another unfinished conversation? Harry and Ellen could talk into eternity, their conversation for ever unfinished. 'In what way?'

Ellen closed her eyes and her fingers began to pick at the blanket again. 'Y'know I told you about the policeman who came to the hospital and hugged me?'

'Yes.'

'Well, thing is . . .' and her voice faded again '. . . I let him hug me and I cried and cried. But, the thing is, I didn't tell him that I was relieved. I was crying tears of relief. He was hugging me because he thought I was falling apart but I was relieved. Without Matt I didn't want anyone else, I didn't even want his child. Joan, I'm sorry,' she whispered. 'I tried to keep it to myself, promised myself I would. Looks like I didn't manage it.'

'Don't be sorry,' I said, and my voice sounded like mercury dropping down the tube as I wondered how Ellen had lived with that guilt all these years.

She dozed off and I watched her in the firelight. She was wearing the crazy turquoise bejewelled turban that I'd given her for Christmas to cover her near-baldness, and she insisted on wearing it in bed. Where else was she going to wear it? It occurred to me that Hyacinth would love it, would wear it to her Seventh Day Adventist church on Sundays, bumping and grinding her way through the service. Thinking of Hyacinth I reached over and took one of Ellen's almost transparent hands, the blue veins bulging over prominent knucklebones, in mine and traced, 'I have always loved you,' on her palm. I couldn't say it so I wrote it on her skin as she slept.

'I know,' Ellen murmured, and tumbled into a deep morphine hole.

Now I'm sitting here with coffee and a cigarette, watching the nurse walk up the path to the kitchen door as the sky flushes pink, as if it were evening. The dogs pad into the

kitchen and wait by the door, tails wagging slightly, wanting
to go to Ellen. They have always loved her when no one else
has. Except me.

21 January 2000

It's nine o'clock in the morning and I'm in the music room,
drinking a large, a very, very large, glass of whisky and I can't
think what to do. Ellen died last night. I was sitting with
her and I must have napped for a while because her feeble
coughing woke me. I watched her face for hours and then,
one moment, I knew she was dead. I didn't see her die. I
reached out and touched her hand and it was cool, not cold,
but cool. It was four in the morning and I didn't know what to
do then – so I stayed with her in case in some way she needed
me – and now I don't know what to do. The doctor is here in
the library with Ellen. I keep thinking of my conversation at
the hospital – 'You see, I haven't said everything I want to.'
But I think I did, I think I did.

A couple of nights ago, when her mind was flying, Ellen
focused on me for a few minutes, seemed to know who I
was. 'You know what one of my best memories is?' she
asked. 'That afternoon when we were in Zanzibar, in Nungwi
– remember?'

I nodded.

'Sitting in the beach bar, looking out over the beach. We
had crab legs and wine for lunch, sat and watched the tide
come in.'

I remember that afternoon. Heliotrope Ellen, tanned by
equatorial sun, eyes hidden by sunglasses, sprawling, a leg
over one chair arm, a straw hat shading her remarkable face.

When I asked the barman for another bottle of white wine she looked at me and smiled, took off her hat and threw back her head, willing the sun to wash over her.

And now I don't know what to do. I'll never sit with her again as she frowns over thirteen down, as she barks with laughter at ever-mounting evidence of human foolishness, as she rubs absentmindedly at the flat skin covering her ribs. I miss her so much already. What am I going to *do*? I know I'm going to get very, very, very drunk for as long as it takes to stop hurting this much.

A few weeks ago I read Ellen a poem she wanted to hear and I thought when I was reading it that I'd never forget the last lines. Now I know I shan't.

> *She took her need away, I thought her selfish*
> *But stronger than God and more beautiful company.*

Always.

JOHN

It was a black nurse who shook my shoulder and woke me from the mouth-heavy, slack-boned sleep of anaesthesia. I looked up and saw her face as if through grease and thought she was Hyacinth. Thought I'd woken up in my bed at Tommy's waiting for the pickaxe of pain to smash through my bewilderment. I tried to lift my arm to push the pain away but my movement was so drugged that the nurse thought I was reaching for her hand and she took mine in both of hers, mouthing, 'What's your name?'

'Special.'

She frowned. 'What's your name?'

'Um . . . John Player.' My lips and tongue were glued with old spit, and I wanted water.

'Where are you?' Her brown eyes moved over my face. It wasn't Hyacinth.

I reached up to my head and found a mound of crêpe bandage. 'I'm in hospital.' My lifetime with Sonja telescoped to nothing. I'd been lying for ever in a hospital bed, growing older, waiting to be made whole. I looked towards the door, expecting Dr W- W- Webster to appear, tape measure in hand.

The nurse tapped my cheek and I focused on her again. 'Which hospital?'

I thought for a moment. 'St Michael's. In Bristol.'

The nurse stroked my hand and smiled. 'We'll be moving you to the ward soon.'

'Are you from Tobago?' I asked, as she stood up.

'Yes, I am – how you know that?'

I shrugged and fell asleep again.

When I was woken the next time I was on the ward, curtains pulled round the bed. Another nurse was leaning over me. 'Mr Player,' she signed, 'I want you to smile.'

Smile? What was there to smile about? But I pulled my lips back and bared my teeth.

'Good, now frown.' I frowned, which was easier.

'OK, now grimace.' Grimace? What was a grimace? I wasn't sure that I'd ever done it before. I wanted Ian to be there so he could explain it to me. 'The face you'd make if you found something horrible, disgusting,' the nurse prompted me. What was this? The Stanislavsky Method of Care? I thought of raw celery and gurned at her. She nodded, satisfied by something.

'You're doing fine,' she signed and mouthed, 'We ask you to do that so we can see if you've lost any movement in your face. Those three movements use every facial muscle. But you're fine.' She pulled aside the curtains and left me.

I turned on my side, the bulk of the bandage on my head twisting my neck, the bed too short for me to stretch my legs out. I lay there and worried that I hadn't grimaced properly. What if I'd left out a tangle of muscles near my mouth? I closed my eyes and practised grimacing until I fell asleep yet again. It was Ian sitting on the edge of the bed that woke me, his weight dipping the mattress to make me roll towards him.

'What's on earth's the matter with you?' he asked.

I realised my face must have moved as I slept, registering endless disgust. 'Nothing.'

'Here,' he said, and laid a bunch of flowers on my chest. 'I'll get a vase.'

When he returned I could see he was trying not to smile, his chin trembling. I couldn't move my neck it was so sore, so I looked at him out of the corner of my eye. 'What?'

He produced a vase and a mirror. I took the mirror from him and looked. The bandage wasn't a turban — it was a balloon, a wobbling balloon of ivory crêpe, sitting low on my forehead, wads of cotton wool tufting out over my ears. I guffawed and my neck seized. Ian began to laugh, and the two of us giggled as other patients looked over with disgust — not grimacing at us but something like it.

Ian put the flowers in the vase and stood by the bed: 'I'm not going to stay. I spoke to the nurse on the desk and she says you're doing fine. You'll be home tomorrow so I'll come round then. Just wanted to see you were OK.' Looking at his face I could see the hair-thin scar running through his lips where my fist had split them.

It wasn't until Sonja and I came back from our honeymoon, when we moved into our studio flat off Battersea Park, that I realised I was a man — or, at least, according to everyone else I was a man. I'd grown up. I spoke to people about 'my company', 'my career', 'my ambitions'. But all these labels, these names for things, never seemed to belong to me. I bought house insurance, applied for credit cards, started a pension. I filled in forms that asked about my 'wife'. My wife? It had happened too quickly. I wasn't capable of being this thing — this grown man, a husband. I said nothing. I nodded and ticked the 'married' box with one hand and I rubbed my worrystone with the other, waiting to be found out, rumbled. I even learned to be called 'Mr Player' without smiling broadly at the humour of this.

I know now the reason for that feeling of dislocation, why I felt fraudulent: I was never a teenager. I went to London on my thirteenth birthday, then spent the next six years learning how to walk, how to speak, how to listen all over again. There were no girlfriends or parties. I didn't have the opportunity to brush tongues and feel breasts in dark bedrooms, lying on piles of coats. I didn't have my blooding in a pub, getting drunk for the first time. I didn't lie in bed late every weekend morning, listening to music and masturbating. I didn't watch television. I was even robbed of that rite of passage – the first pair of Levi's. I didn't play pool or darts, didn't drive down to Newquay with a group of friends, surfboards and tents lashed to the roof-rack. I didn't have a Walkman, a stereo, a car radio. What I did have was my mother and Ellen and my books. And then I had my wife.

Sonja brought me home from hospital after the bandage had been unwound and the needle in my hand removed. I was tired because I'd been woken every half-hour the night before for my blood pressure to be taken. The skin on my skull was sore and my neck stiff. I changed into pyjamas and lay on the sofa in the living room. Sonja brought me scrambled eggs, bowls of Häagen-Dazs, chocolate mousse and painkillers. She stoked the fire and left me to sleep, which is all I did for the next few days. She came home every lunchtime and left work early every night to come and sit with me, bringing me newspapers and flowers, fresh meringues and the pecan and walnut twists I loved. Every few hours she changed the pillow case because blood seeped through the gauze and left penny-size spots on the fabric.

When Sonja was at work I lay in the gloom of winter days
and imagined I could hear sounds – doors closing, radiators
groaning, pages turning. Of course I couldn't. Even when
they pulled the packed gauze from my ears in two weeks'
time, I'd hear nothing. Only when the electrodes were buried
in my head and the implants slipped under my skin would it
be possible for me to hear. I thought about how once again
I'd stopped talking and I did try to make conversation with
Sonja but what did I have to say? My thoughts were constantly
reflected back to me, back to my hearing. After a few days I
touched the scars. The stitches were rough, scabbed, and the
feel threw me across years, to Tommy's.

For a week I lay in the living room, the skin on my skull
closing as the tissue from my neck nestled deep in my ear
canal, protected by antiseptic gauze. I read, I ate and slept.
When I was awake I thought I could hear and I wondered
what Sonja was doing. Was she still seeing the Blind Man?
She had opportunity enough.

The last summer when I was Merboy I sat one early morning
on the garden wall and watched my mother, her cheeks
flushed, the armpits of her cotton dress stained, climb awkwardly backwards out of the car, pushing at bowls and
suitcases. She brushed back her short black hair, damp with
sweat. 'Come on, John. Get in and then we can get going.'

I swished at pebbles with a long blade of grass, jaw aching
as I chewed a sour quince apple. 'Don't want to go.'

'Frankly, you don't have a choice.' My mother shaded her
eyes against the glare of the July sun. 'You've done nothing
to help me, you haven't carried one bloody box or bag out
here. I've done it all, and now we're ready to move, so let's
move, buddy.'

'Don't want to.'

'I don't care. Get in.'

I scowled and sat in the passenger seat. My mother put a washing-up bowl of flasks and sandwiches and boxes on my lap. I swivelled in the seat and tried to jam it on the back seat but it was already crammed with things.

'You'll have to hold that on your lap,' my mother said, starting the engine.

'*What?* All the way there?'

'Yes. All the way there.'

A tantrum began to build in me as the car wound out of Noss Mayo and we headed into Plymouth to catch a ferry to Roskoff, my mother constantly stabbing at the choke button. Fury built inside me when I thought of spending four weeks – four weeks! – of the summer away from the river and beaches. I wanted to break something, run and scream, but there wasn't enough room in the car to do anything except scowl.

It took the old Morris Minor four days to get down to Ispes, south of Bordeaux. Three days of setting up the tent every evening, rummaging in the boot for clothes and packets of dried soup. My mother had bought a second-hand two-room tent and it took the two of us hours to unfold the heavy canvas and sort out the poles. The tent always looked lop-sided, ungainly. It was an embarrassment – like a third-world shanty. Its sides were never taut and the guy ropes sagged so when it rained, as it did on the third night, water first seeped then flooded in. It was night when we arrived at the campsite in Ispes and a fine drizzle had set in. I got out of the car and sat on a log while my mother pulled at the heavy, wet tarpaulin in the dark. I think she must have realised that I was beyond childish tantrums or unreasonable behaviour because she came and sat on the log next to me and lit a cigarette.

'Well, pumpkin, this isn't quite what I planned.'

'Why did we have to come here? We could have stayed at home.' I kicked at the pine needles at my feet.

'Of course we could. We could stay at home all our lives and never see anything at all. Aren't you remotely interested in seeing another country?'

'No. It's got horrible cheese.'

My mother laughed and as she did a man walked past and shone a torch at us, its beam lingering on my mother's face. The tent was up within half an hour, a group of four Frenchmen showing off their camping expertise in pools of gas-light, snapping poles together with gusto, pulling the canvas snug round the frame. And all the time my mother sat on the log, smoking pungent Gauloises and piping, '*Merci, messieurs, merci.*' I was disgusted and wandered off to find the toilet.

I returned, speechless, to find the tent erected, furniture laid out, mattresses inflated. The men had brought bottles of wine and were clustered round my mother, filling her glass, shrugging and gesturing, interrupting each other. I pushed between them and grabbed her arm.

'What's up, pumpkin?'

'The toilet . . . it's . . .' I couldn't find any words.

'You'll get used to it.'

We were invited to join a family for dinner in a nearby tent. They had a caravan with an awning, a long table laid out beneath it. I sat opposite my mother on a bench, unable to understand a word of what was being said. I was given a plate of food which I looked at for a long time.

'What is it?' I asked my mother, whispering.

'Couscous.'

'What?'

'Eat up and smile.'

Smile? I forked a pile of rice stuff and unmentionables and put it in my mouth. I appeared to have an eyeball resting on my tongue, salty with tears. I looked wide-eyed at my mother, who shook her head slightly, glanced up the table and expertly spat an olive into the sand under the table. She looked at me and winked and I spent the rest of the meal spitting green bullets, the game being to remain unseen doing this. I went to bed as soon as I could but I could still hear my mother and the rest of them laughing, the sound of glass clinking coming clearly through the canvas. I stared at the fabric lit by the gas-lights and wished I was in my bed at home, holding Tub, knowing I'd wake up by the creek.

As it was, I woke up at dawn, unzipped the tent and pushed my way out to pee against a nearby tree. No one else was awake so I stood there, unabashed, yawning and scratching my bed-head hair. I looked up when I'd finished and there was the biggest, pale turquoise lake I had ever seen, a golden, sandy beach running round it as far as I could see. I began to run, snaking through pine trees, heart pumping, and thundered into the water until my momentum slowed and I fell forward, arms akimbo and sank into the first fresh water I'd ever swum in. I bullied my mother into wakefulness half an hour later, dripping cold water all over her as I shook her arm and told her she had to get up and come and see.

Sonja helped me wash the first morning I decided to leave the comfort of the sofa. She ran a bath and helped me to get in, then sat with a coffee on the toilet seat as I swished the soap around. When I was ready to wash my hair she pushed wads of cotton wool smeared with Vaseline into my long-suffering ears and then sat on the edge of the bath and held a plastic cup over each ear while I used the shower to rinse off the suds. I fingered the scabs and the stubbled skin, which itched. She waited until I was dressed and back downstairs before kissing me absently and leaving for work.

I went downstairs and sat in the study looking through my diary, beginning to plan work again, pencilling in dates and times for materials to be delivered, for a team to start work. I reached for the text-phone to contact Ian and saw its light already flashing. The Type-Talk operator spelled out that it was my mother calling to tell me Ellen was dead. I put the phone down and went back into the living room, where I undressed and lay on the sofa again, pulling the duvet tight over my scarred head.

When I sat in the York café with Ian and asked him if he liked Sonja, he said he couldn't answer because he didn't know her. And I realise that in many ways I don't either. Sonja has said, and maintains to this day, that her synaesthesia is not a disability. On this point she is forceful, some might even say aggressive. Is it a disability? I don't know and I can't begin to guess. I have phenomenal vision – and that is how I see the world. My mother has an acute mind, so sharp she could cut herself and she did. And that's how she interprets the world – as mental constructs to be taken apart, examined and reassembled. Sonja? I don't know. I don't know how she sees the world. Are there no constants? Nothing she can accept as a given, *a priori*, as my mother would say? There has to be – otherwise she'd have to relearn everything she knows at every moment of waking. Am I the constant for Sonja? I rather think I must be. Unchanging and unchanged. Did she feel my fear of change when I first touched her breast? And, if so, what did it taste like? How did it sound? I've spent a lifetime trying to touch her heart and I think, now, that the organ that has always responded is her brain.

Merboy spent his last summer diving, bowling, thundering through water. The Étang de Cazeaux was his playground, the campsite his fishing waters. He woke at dawn every day, slipped on T-shirt and shorts and went down to the water. The campsite had no showers, only one tap, so he washed in the lake with every other child there. He learned not to wake his mother until the dented grey 2CV van came to the site, bumping over tree roots, crushing needles and scenting the air with croissants, brioches, baguettes, *grands pains* and pine. Then he'd run back to the tent, unzip the door and shake his mother to wakefulness. She'd yawn, fumble in her bag, then give him some franc notes, which he crumpled in his hand as he ran after the van, yelling, a stream of French children following and he looked back and grinned. Sometimes he smacked a toe on a tree root and fell to the sandy, needle-strewn floor with a yelp, only to pick himself up again to chase his own tail of followers. The bread man recognised Merboy after a few days and gave him a free *baignet* every time he arrived, panting, at the van's open doors.

It took only days for the routine of home, of Noss Mayo, to be re-established. Merboy disappeared in water while his mother drank and men sat with her, slept with her, but he always came back to the tent to find her alone, reading, a glass of wine in one hand, the lazy, perfect smile on her lips. They both knew how life worked. Merboy chanced on a family who had water-skis and a speed-boat, made friends with them for more than a day, more than a week. He gripped the handle on his first run as the skis bobbled beneath him and muttered to himself, glancing at the blond teenage son. Better than him.

I can do better than him. But when the boat sped away, the rope snapped taut and Merboy's legs spread, water slamming into his crotch as he fell. He swam back to the shore and tried again and again and again until he could skip the waves, dog-leg and turn-around.

More than all of this – more than the tiny fish swarming round his ankles, more than the feel of a windsurf flying away from him, more than the smell of fresh sardines caught by one of his mother's admirers, cooking on a fire – were the evening trips to the sea. Late one day his mother packed a bottle of wine and a flask of coffee and told Merboy to get into the car. They drove down the coast as the sky slowly darkened to a blue that would not be dark unless it was the sky. His mother parked the car on sand, pulled the bag from the boot and motioned that Merboy should follow. The two of them shuffled upwards on dry sand, climbing a massive dune. For each step they took a shovelful of dry sand would appear and they slithered backwards. Eventually they crested the dune and slumped on the sand, laughing. And what did they see? They saw a coast that ran for hundreds of miles. They could see the lights of Bordeaux on the right and the orange glow of San Sebastián on their left – they could see across countries, they could see across Europe, across continents. Above them satellites wobbled in their various trajectories. Shooting stars of minute meteorites flashed and fell into the infinite, unquiet sea. They watched and wondered as they kept an eye on the affairs of state of two countries. Then the wine and coffee were poured and they both sank to lie on their backs staring at the wheeling stars and not a word was said because what would you say?

I have told already how Sonja and I slipped into the complacent years once we moved to Clifton. Now, lying on the sofa

waiting for my scars to close, I think about just how deep
that complacency has become for me. I've drowned in it. I
was so sure of myself and of Sonja, so sure of our relationship,
I was never aware of that drowning. Ever since my mother
walked out and left me in my room at Tommy's, twenty-eight
years ago, I've been scared of change. Lying here I realise
for the first time that change can mean difference, it doesn't
have to mean bad. More than this, I realise that I've changed
without even noticing.

Not long ago I thought that if Sonja left me I would lock
myself away because no one could ever stand next to me in
the space she's occupied but I'm now wondering if that space
needs to be filled.

When I was rummaging through the boxes in the attic of my
mother's house, I found the photos of that summer in Ispes.
Found a picture of Merboy sitting on a tree-trunk, his feet
dangling in the lake. He was tanned and relaxed, easy with his
body, which was tall even then. His hair was long, a shock
of black against brown skin. His chest had begun to fill, the
muscles on his arms showed, and the wet black hairs on his
legs were sleek with dripping water. He was looking into the
sun and his eyes were small chips of blue as he squinted. I sat
on the rough joists in the attic and looked at that photograph
for an age. I stared at Merboy across nearly thirty years and it
seemed to me that he was staring back, challenging me. For a
wild moment I thought he was going to speak. He didn't but
that hardly mattered because I knew exactly what he would
have said.

Today was Ellen's funeral. I can't imagine life without her.
I suppose I should be grateful that she lived as long as she

did but I'm not because it wasn't long enough. I can't stop crying. What on earth will my mother do?

Not long ago I packed my bags and left, worrying that I might never come here again, back to this house that I share with Sonja. But I did. I came back. I'm no longer sure why I did. I don't care about the house any more, I don't have a sense of peace when I come home to find Sonja already there. I feel nothing.

I slept alone on the sofa far longer than I needed to, making excuses about having to get up all the time, saying that I moved around too much trying to get comfortable, to sleep with Sonja. Eventually I went back to our bed, on the day they pulled the gauze out of my ears (*feet* of it, a never-ending blood-soaked string), but I don't sleep. I lie there and think of how I arrived here and whether it's where I want to be. I've lost interest in Elemental, I'm bored of dealing with other people, customers and workers alike. Sometimes I think that if I could go back to when we started, Ian and I, if we could work together, do manual work together, maybe I'd feel differently. Now I'm just a manager. I don't do anything. I manage accounts, draw up plans and quotations, struggle with VAT. It's not what I wanted. Sometimes, during what are called the witching hours, I stare into the darkness and feel as if I'm blurred, as if I'm indistinct.

I skipped work today. I got up and dressed, drove to Bedminster, walked towards the office then turned round and left. I got back into the Jeep and drove to Noss Mayo. The sun followed me, made the journey short. I haven't been back there since the morning of my thirteenth birthday and it

has changed but not as much as it might have done. Driving
through the village I could see boxy new houses squeezed
into back gardens, holiday apartments in the huge old barns
and warehouses at the head of the creek, but the river was
still in place, the pilings still weathering. The Swan and the
Ship were unchanged. The village hall and the church looked
the same. The tide was out so I parked on the shale and sand
outside the Ship and walked round the back to the lane. The
tiny cottages were as I remembered them – front gardens
thick with roses, small windows open on a surprisingly hot
day. At the end of the lane, looking over Newton Ferrers,
was the cottage Merboy lived in. I sat on the wall opposite
and lit a cigarette, sat and looked at the window where his
bedroom had been.

A grey-haired old lady, dressed in pleated skirt, cardigan and
Barbour, came out of the cottage next door, pulling a tartan
shopping trolley. She closed the front door, pushed it with
a blue-veined hand and glanced at the sky. I ground out my
cigarette butt and looked back to Merboy's window. I felt a
tap on my shoulder.

'John? Is it John?' The old lady's eyes were rheumy, sagging
under the weight of years.

'Yes, yes, it is.'

'I thought it was. Do you remember me? Mrs Bennet? I
lived next door to you and your mother.' She pointed at her
cottage.

I looked at her face, scored by wrinkles, her wispy hair
blown in the breeze. I thought I could see someone else,
someone younger. 'Mrs Bennet?'

'I knew it was you. Come here.' She held open her
arms and I stood up. She wrapped her skinny arms round
my waist, her grey head resting on my chest, and hugged

me. She looked up. 'How are you, John? Can you understand me?'

'Yes, I can lip-read.'

Her rheumy eyes filled with water, making them pale and
insubstantial. 'When we heard what happened we couldn't
believe it. Awful, just awful. I couldn't believe it. And we
never saw you again.' She loosened her hold and stepped
back, wiping her tears. 'How do you cope with something
like that?'

'I don't know,' I said, and I meant it.

'How's your mother?'

I thought of my mother sitting on her deck drinking, as I
knew she had ever since Ellen died. 'She's OK,' I lied.

'When George and I saw the photos of her – well, what
can you say? I remember her being so pretty, so beautiful.
And she was clever, too, if I remember rightly. Never could
work out why she was alone. And then you both disappeared.'
She wiped her tears again. 'Awful.'

'Yes.'

'Do you remember when you were a boy and your mother
didn't get home till late so you'd come in and have tea with
us? With me and George?'

I did have a vague memory of sitting with a couple I
thought of as old, although they must have been only fifty
or so, eating ham sandwiches and homemade cakes or a pasty
and salad in their tiny living room, waiting for my mother to
come home.

Mrs Bennet smiled at me through her tears. 'You always
wanted to go swimming. I used to have to come and sit here,'
and she slapped the wall, 'and watch you in case anything
happened but it never did. You were like a little seal.'

'Right.'

'Now look at you – you're so tall! You always said you
wanted to be a sailor or a fisherman when you grew up. So
what did you end up doing?'

This woman, I thought, knew Merboy. She was the only
person I had ever met who knew him. 'Did you like him?'
I asked stupidly.

'Who?' Mrs Bennet frowned. 'Sorry, it's my fault. I was
wondering what you do now?'

'I'm a carpenter.' I held out my giant hands, showing her
the scars of my profession, my badges of honour. 'What was
I like, Mrs Bennet? When I was here, what was I like?'

Mrs Bennet leaned against the wall and looked over the
creek, sparking with sun on the shallow water. She turned
back to me. 'You were a wild boy. Always in trouble. Always.
But there was something . . . I don't know. No one could
stay angry with you for long. Do you remember when you
had a fight in the back garden with some friends and you
knocked down our fence? You came round straight away and
apologised. You didn't pretend it wasn't you and then you tried
to fix it.' She smiled again. 'You made a pretty poor fist of it,
I have to say. George spent the next week putting it right but
only when you were at school so you wouldn't know. I hope
you're a better carpenter now.'

'So do I.'

'George, bless his soul, died many years ago.'

'I'm sorry.'

'So am I. He liked you. He was devastated when we found
out about . . . about what happened.' She pushed herself off
the wall and reached for the handle of the trolley. 'Well, I
must make a move while the tide's right.'

I offered to give her a lift into Newton Ferrers but she said
it would be quicker to walk, waving at the concrete walkways

across the creeks revealed at low tide. I kissed her soft, papery cheek and she hugged me again.

'Look after yourself, John. God bless.' She walked away, head bowed, thinking no doubt of other times, when George had walked with her.

I set off along the lane, past the ferry stop, past the few houses half buried by trees on the creek's edge. I knew where I was going, and when I stood on Cellar's Beach, looking out over Great Mew, standing where Merboy had when he threw the wendletrap back into the water, I thought of Mrs Bennet's generosity. How she had sat on that wall, wrapped against the cold, making sure nothing bad happened to him.

The operation to place the implant is, surprisingly, less painful, less intrusive, than the myringoplasty. Again I'm woken by the Tobagonian nurse, again I have cotton wool tufting from my ears, and tender bumps where the tiny transmitters are hidden beneath skin. But there are no scars inches long, no stiff neck. I'm sent home with a course of pills to prevent rejection and once again I lie on the sofa, Sonja appearing and disappearing bearing delicacies. When I have the stitches out the doctor plasters gauze beneath my ears to catch any weeping blood and plasma. For six weeks I will have to walk around with the gauze stuck to my face and then they'll tune in the electrodes floating in my head.

Sonja spends two of these weeks with her family in Estonia and for fourteen nights I lie in our bed alone, thinking. One day when I'm driving down Trenchard Street I see the Blind Man and his dog. I have no desire to stop the car and run towards him, roaring. My ears weep as I drive on.

My mother has seen the world. She has travelled from Alaska to Zanzibar. All I've ever seen is Paris and a lake in the

South of France. I read books that describe Amsterdam, the Serengeti, the temples at Machu Picchu. I see images of the Australian outback, Las Vegas, Florence, the Caribbean islands, moving silently across the television screen. Polar bears charge through Churchill and seals loll on the beaches of New Zealand as I drive around Bristol.

When Sonja comes back from Estonia, she unpacks her bags laden with sharp vodka and the intricately painted ornaments of her homeland, then pours herself a drink and sits at the huge pine table in the kitchen. I sit across from her, watching her face. We sit there for minutes without speaking. Finally I say, heart thumping, ears crusty, 'I'm going to leave.'

Sonja's grey eyes lock on mine. 'I know.'

'I'm sorry.'

'So am I.'

'You're not surprised?'

'No.' She doesn't cry. She just stares at me. 'I've been waiting for this to happen.'

'Why?'

'I always knew it would.'

'Don't be ridiculous. Just because I walked out at Christmas.'

She smiles a twisted smile. 'No, not because of that. I've known for a long time. I've known for years.'

'Why did you stay, then?'

'Maybe because I hoped it wouldn't happen.'

'Are you still seeing him?'

'Yes.' She looks away.

It hurts. It shouldn't because I knew this already but it does. 'I knew you were.'

Sonja frowns. 'How? How could you know?'

Because of so many things. The way she looks at me,

the way she moves, the silences and the gaps that have yawned open in our lives. 'Do you remember when I asked at Christmas if you'd slept with him?'

'Yes.'

'And you said no. I was watching you, Sonja. You know how closely I watch when you speak. I saw you were lying.'

'Why didn't you say something? Why didn't you say something then?' Her hand trembles as she reaches for her glass.

Why didn't I? Because right then I wanted her to hold me and fill the space left by the wolf's breath. I wanted to believe her because I'd felt that I was unravelling. 'What good would it have done?'

'I'm sorry.'

'Don't be. I know I've been a bastard to live with.'

The two of us sit there at the kitchen table, our hands trembling. We don't shout, because ours has always been a quiet relationship and we both know better than most that volume has no meaning.

'When will you go?' she asks, as I stand up to leave.

'As soon as I can get a van arranged. Tomorrow, I guess.'

'Where will you go?'

Twenty years. 'Thurlestone.' Twenty years become nothing as I realise it's none of Sonja's concern.

'John, I'm sorry. I'm sorry it all ends like this. It doesn't seem enough.'

I stop by the door. 'I have to ask – what is it about disabled men that lights your fire?'

Sonja flushes, whether with anger or shame I don't know. 'What do you mean?'

'Well, I'm deaf and he's blind. I mean, there's a definite pattern emerging here.'

'I don't have to answer that.'

'No, you're right, you don't. But it might be worth thinking about. Maybe it's that you need to be needed. Is that it?'

I can see that she's angry rather than shamed. She stands suddenly, knocking over her glass, which spins, fanning red wine over the wood of the table. 'I've never pitied you.'

And now I know she does because I've never mentioned this. 'Pitied me?'

'Never. And you've never asked for my help.' She strides across the room, jabs her finger in my chest. 'I have always given it because I wanted to. When I first met you there was something about you that made me love you. I didn't want to because I knew it would always be harder than it should be and it has been. But don't think, don't ever think, that I didn't love you.'

It's as if I'm hearing the letter my mother wrote me about Dai Davies. I've heard all this already, years before. 'Right.'

I walk away from her, close the door behind me.

Dr Laws puts down the phone and looks appraisingly at me. 'This is not ideal, John. I've managed to arrange for the audio unit at Derriford to take over your care but I'd much rather you stayed and finished the course of treatment here.'

I say nothing.

Dr Laws takes off his glasses and pinches the bridge of his nose. 'It won't help if you're stressed. It might slow your recovery time. It may even affect the outcome of this.'

How can I explain to him that to stay here in Bristol would be worse than leaving?

'We've known each other a long time, John. I have to say I'm really quite shocked about you and Sonja. I always thought that the two of you were very happy.' He plays with his glasses, swinging them by the earpiece as he looks at the view of Bristol from his office window. 'But, then, what do we know about other people's lives? It's all guesswork. I'm sorry, though. It's not come at the best time for you.'

And when would be a good time to leave your wife? I wonder. Are there best times, right words that I don't know about? *I think you should be the one to tell him, since you will find the right words.*

Dr Laws sighs. He looks old and tired, incapable of smiling wolfishly. 'Ah, well. I hope that everything works out for you. The operations have been a success so far, anyway. I wish I was seeing you through to the conclusion but the team in Plymouth is as good as any. Let me know what happens.'

'Right.'

'I mean it – let me know. They'll tune your electrodes in two weeks' time and you'll know then if it's been successful. But don't forget that they retune them after three days, fine-tune them. So if the sound is distorted at first, don't panic. You remember, don't you, that you still won't hear much? You won't be able to hear music properly, you'll just hear the rhythm. You'll be able to hear traffic, clear conversation but not quiet sounds, especially if there's a lot of background noise.'

I nod. The thought of being able to hear a passing lorry.

Dr Laws does smile then, not wolfishly, but it is a smile. 'Anyway, I think you'll be pleased to know that the myringoplasty has been extremely successful. A fine bit of knifework, if I say so myself. Mr Player, you have two stout, impregnable eardrums, impervious to water.'

I swallow, shift in my chair. 'Right.'

'You can go home and throw away your ear plugs.'

'Right.'

'And then I suggest you get to a beach and go swimming. I warn you, though, it'll be bastard freezing.'

To my embarrassment I burst into tears and Dr Laws hands me a box of tissues.

I slam the door of the removal van, leaving Hercules and Achilles to slug it out during the journey, and climb into the cab. Ian signs, 'Ready?' I look at the house for the last time. I nod and we pull away. Automatically I feel for my worrystone, feel the jagged edges of the broken pieces in my pocket.

Travelling the familiar roads down to Thurlestone I think of Sonja. She stayed away for the two days it took me to contact a solicitor, pack my belongings and arrange my leaving. Where did she stay? With the Blind Man, no doubt. I've decided to give her the house. My solicitor is baffled by this because, he says, it is Sonja who is the adulterer. I hadn't thought of it that way, that she is a hussy, a Jezebel, as Ian would say. That I am a cuckold. Because it doesn't feel that way. I tried to explain to the solicitor that it doesn't, really, have anything to do with the Blind Man. That I was as much to blame because I became someone else. I was no longer the man Sonja married. I knew the solicitor was exasperated by my refusal to allocate blame.

Blame. Who is to blame for all this? Who is culpable? Just how far back should I go to lay my charges? To Dr Price, who couldn't teach me logic? To Moira, who put her hand on my cock and shocked me into wakefulness of a sort? To the surgeons at Tommy's who tried to mend my ears and instead left them destroyed? Or perhaps even to Mrs Bennet, who sat on a wall and made me feel safer than I was ever going to be? The most likely suspect for culpability is Dai Davies. The father who never came. But what, in the end, did he do that I'm not doing? He left his wife and I'm leaving mine.

The blame, of course, lies with the men who laid their own charges in the car park on Gloucester Road. I know it wasn't Sonja who made me heartless, nor was it my mother or my father. It was those faceless strangers who made my heart break into the two bloody halves I worried about as I lay in my childhood bed, hugging Tub.

'We both live on small islands,' Sonja said, the first night we slept together, and I thought that was fine as long as we lived on the same small island. Twenty years later we don't.

When Ian and I finish dismantling the last joists of my mother's deck, so rotten, some of them, that they crumble in our hands, we carry them to the skip, dump them, then lie on the grass in the garden, drinking cold beers. It's June and the golf course is virulently green, the trees overloaded with leaves. My mother sits on a nearby stone bench with a newspaper and a bottle of wine, looking put out that her deck has disappeared. When we arrived here a few days ago she was blind drunk, asleep on the sofa, but since then she has steadied herself, reduced the river of alcohol to a constant dribble. I think our being here has helped, has filled some of the emptiness left when Ellen died.

I push myself to my feet and gesture to Ian with a bottle. 'Want another?'

He nods. Signs, 'I found my word for the week this morning. It was in an article in the paper. I think you'll like it.'

'What is it?'

He spells it out: 'Nepenthe.'

'Nepenthe?'

'Look it up.'

When I went into the library all those months ago Ellen was awake, looking through the window at the cows tramping across the valley. I sat by her on the floor and she held out her thin, shiny hand for me to stroke. She was difficult to understand because she was so weak but she tried, shifting on the bed to turn to me, looking me in the face.

'So, Special. This is it.'

I wanted to shout, to pulverise whatever it was that made this it. I tugged at the tip of my beard, fighting the desire to cry.

'You're going home today? With Sonja?'

I nodded, not trusting my voice.

We were silent for minutes as Ellen struggled to speak. 'John, I know you're not happy. I want you to promise me something. I want you to promise me that you'll think long and hard about your life when you get back. I've known you a long time, since you were a boy.' And she stopped, coughed. 'I know you've always thought that as long as nothing bad happens, that's as good as it gets. Well, it's not. It's not enough, John. I want you to think about that.' She smiled weakly. 'I guess I'm saying I want you to be brave. Will you promise me that?'

I nodded again.

'Promise me.'

'Yes.'

'Ah, well, I think I've told you everything I wanted you to know. You're a good man, John. Look after your mother. I think she'll need you.'

Was that it? It couldn't be it. I didn't want words of wisdom. I wanted Ellen to live.

'There is one thing,' and Ellen paused, frowned, pain slamming through her. 'When my husband died I thought I'd never live again. That I'd sleepwalk through life. But I didn't. I've had a good life, a much longer life than I thought possible. Longer than I maybe deserved. Sure, I didn't have Matt but I had you and your mother, other friends. It was enough. I guess all I'm saying is you don't always have to live with people to love them. Lives change and that's OK.'

'Right.'

She smiled and patted the bed. I stood up and gingerly lay down next to her. We lay on our backs, staring at the ceiling, as I stroked her hand, and if there are qualities to silence (and I believe there are and I should know), the quality of that silence was precious. After a while I looked at Ellen and she was asleep. I kissed her cheek and rolled gently off the bed, leaving her behind.

Today Ian, my mother and I went back to the ENT clinic at Derriford so the electrodes could be tuned in. I was taken into a small, dim room, where an unfamiliar doctor was waiting for me, keying words into a computer. My hands wouldn't stop sweating and I had damp patches on my jeans where I kept rubbing them dry. He looked up, smiled distractedly and waved for me to sit down, then told me to expect hisses and screeching sounds. He told me to expect sounds. The doctor turned various knobs on a console and my head filled with noise. As I wondered at the beauty of a hiss, it faded, to be replaced by well-known silence. Still the doctor adjusted frequencies and the hiss reappeared, followed by feedback. Then silence. He looked up from his machine, his face lit by a blue glow and he said, 'Can you hear me?'

And I looked at him, unable for a moment to speak. Then

I said, 'Yes,' and I stood up and hugged the man; I think I hugged him so hard he thought he was going to break. When it was done, when he'd identified the best frequencies and refined the sounds I heard, I walked back out to the waiting area and there was Ian. I sauntered over, hands in pocket, trying not to smile.

Ian stood up, his face grave as ever. 'Well?'

A door slammed behind me and I heard my mother call, 'John?' The first time since I was thirteen that I'd heard my mother's voice, and I turned round to face her.

The day my mother's deck is finished – a plain, Shaker-style affair of clean lines and simple, straightforward angles – Ian and I scrub ourselves clean, dress in red and white shirts and bully my mother, who is merely squiffy rather than plastered, into coming with us to the hotel in the village. The three of us walk down the lane, my mother between Ian and me, a munchkin among giants. The hotel bar is heaving, hot with thundery air, cigarette smoke floating in fields. The screen at the end of the bar is huge and Ian and I stand at the back, lifting my mother to perch on a window-ledge so she can see over the crowd.

In 1966, when I was eight years old, my mother and I watched England beat Germany on a small, black-and-white television in a flat in Earl's Court. They thought it was all over then and it turned out that it was because we haven't beaten them since. Thirty-four years later Alan Shearer stoops in front of a goal line and heads the ball into the net. The crowd in the bar leaps up and roars its approval as the floor shudders. People wave scarves, jump up and down, hug each other. Even my mother is on her feet, clapping and yelling. Passing drivers hoot their horns and the singing begins. For first time in thirty-four years I'm listening to the sounds of celebration again.

I have spent my life with damaged women. I don't believe this changed me. I don't believe, either, that it damaged me. Ian once spoke of the invisibility of some damage – said that Sonja and I could pass muster in a crowd. I think that is what most people do. I've said that I can map out my life by scars; I've also said there are many scars I can't see. I believe this is the case for everyone. We look at others and we see what we can and we judge what we can't. As Dr Laws said, it's all guesswork.

JOAN

26 January 2000

It was Ellen's funeral yesterday. I arranged for her to be buried here. She has no family left in the States so why not? The day began with grey skies but as the cortège left the funeral parlour the sun came out and the village looked stupidly beautiful. I kept looking at the limousine in front, trying to imagine Ellen's body in there, but luckily I couldn't.

John, with his blood-raw, crusty stitches around his ears, black and grey stubble growing through, was inconsolable. He bawled in the church, bowed over and shaking. I rubbed his back and gave him tissues; I even held his hand. But I didn't motion for him to turn the volume down. He had to grieve, even if that grief rose above the priest's oration, even if it filled the church and near-lifted the rafters. I found myself – amazingly – smiling and looked up to see Harry grinning a wobbly grin too. Ellen would have loved it. The cant of centuries drowned out by a deaf boy's sorrow. Because he *was* a boy in that church. I knew he was remembering Ellen teaching him words, teaching him to sign, beating him at five-card poker, bringing him presents, walking with him across the beach with the dogs. They had a relationship that had nothing to do with me. And the way I looked at it, if John needed to become child-like in order to say his goodbyes, that was fine by me.

When the mourners had left, when the last of the sherries

had been drunk and the plates of uncaten food cleared away,
John and I sat in the library. His face looked ravaged, eaten
by misery, but he had stopped crying and I wonder just how
much he cried for. Or, rather, what he cried for. I know
he misses Ellen and he always will, but I think he cried for
many things as the sun blazed through every stained-glass
window in the church. I think he cried for Merboy, for Dai
Davies, for every sound he has never heard, for waving at
an empty parking space. For Hyacinth and her failing heart,
for his own battery-operated heart, for days of silence and
never being special enough. More than all these, I think he
cried for me.

'What will you do?' he asked.

He asked the same question when I left teaching and I gave
him the same answer. 'Grow old.'

And that's what I shall do. I shall retreat to my deck and
sit out there every night, watching the waves, watching the
moon slide, grow small, watching the volcanic arch being
eroded by time.

20 April 2000

Ellen's house sale was completed today – she left everything
to me and I wanted none of it, apart from her books and the
drinks cabinet from which I once filched a bottle of Crown
Royal. I've arranged for the estate to pass to John because I
have no use for the money and I think soon he might have.
I did keep the dogs and now they're used to being here in
Thurlestone, although I suppose they knew it already from
their visits. I'm glad I have them – they sleep in my room
and follow me everywhere, as if I'm their last contact with

Ellen. Sometimes I think they're watching the door, waiting
for Ellen to come in. I know I do. It's been months and I still
can't believe I shall never see her again. As I promised myself,
I did get and stay very, very, very drunk for a long time, but
not long enough, it would seem, for it to stop hurting.

30 May 2000

John and Ian arrived today when I was passed out on the sofa.
They scattered statues through the garden, unpacked their
bags, then woke me with coffee. I felt terrible, still half-cut.
But I had to go with them to the beach, stumbling across
the golf course, Ian practically carrying me. He poured me
more coffee while John stripped down to a pair of swimming
trunks. Ian and I watched him running down the beach, his
scarred back paler than the rest of him, arms pumping. He
ran into the surf and yelled as the cold hit him, dived into a
breaking wave and swam out towards the volcanic arch. Then
he turned and waved, laughing, water crashing round him. I
tried to clear my head and wave back.

4 June 2000

John came into my bedroom this morning with a cup of
coffee, sat on the bed and told me everything that has
happened with Sonja. That it's over, that he's left her the
house, sold his interest in the business to Ian. I've known
for a long time that something was wrong but I didn't guess
the extent of it. Years ago he presented me with his decision
to marry as a *fait accompli* and now he's done the same with

his divorce. I remember Ellen telling me that John was always trying to protect me from sadness and, as usual, she was right. He never did take my advice. I told him to ask for help because he'd need it but he never has.

I'm ashamed to admit that I feel relieved. When he'd gone I lay in bed and tried to work out the source of that relief. Sonja – I never did work her out. John says she's been seeing a blind man, as it were. I can't even begin to work out what's going on in her head. Next week John will have his electrodes tuned and if everything works out he'll hear again, or at least he'll hear something. And it's at this moment in their lives she begins an affair with a blind man. Madness. Was it that she couldn't face the thought of John being whole? Does she have to substitute her own crazed sensibilities for someone else's? I don't know. It seems to me now that John didn't grow when he was with her, he just hid behind her, and I think she relished that.

9 June 2000

Ian and I sat for hours today in the ENT clinic, reading papers and jumping every time the door opened, waiting for John. I kept going for a cigarette but I'd only have a couple of drags because I wanted to be there when he came out. I wished Ellen could have been with us, wished John could have heard her voice. But even memories of Ellen couldn't keep my nervousness at bay. Ian kept jumping up and down, reading posters and pacing around. Nerves played havoc with my bladder and I went to the bathroom. When I walked back into the waiting room John was standing with his back to me, talking to Ian, and I did what I haven't done for so many years:

I called out to him and he turned round, grinning at the sound of his own name.

11 August 2000

A year ago Ellen sat here with me and watched the sun disappear. A year ago. It doesn't seem that long. Now she is dead and John is getting divorced. He left last week with Ian and two of the carpenters from Elemental, to drive through France in a camper-van. I think I can guess where he's heading. He asked if I wanted to join them but of course I didn't. I want him to start to have fun. I want him to grow into his new voice, his new world. I paid for the van to be fitted with a radio and CD player as a present, and the expression on his face when he saw it was the same as when I gave him the water-skis. I hope he gets more use out of them than he did out of the skis. I also gave him a CD of Peggy Lee's songs. He says he can't hear it clearly but he can hear enough of it and for days before they left he walked around the house singing, 'Is that all there is?' at the top of his tuneless voice.

20 August 2000

My new deck is stout and plain, made of limed ash with beech rails. I love it. The steps are smooth and deep, perfect for sitting and looking over the beach. I never told John about Ellen's deck, about how she waited on it, waited for Matt to come back from his fishing trip. I'm glad I never told him because he doesn't need to know. I'm glad, too, that he seems at last to have grabbed his life in both hands and shaken some sense into it. I want him to stay in that van and keep going. Drive through Europe, along the Mediterranean, down through Greece to Piraeus, jump on a ship and sail the world.

29 August 2000

When I was a girl I wanted the bombs to stop, I wanted the farm girl in the shelter not to be alone. I wanted my daddy to come home, and he did. When I was at university I wanted to be a Doctor of Philosophy, to understand the human heart and mind, how they work, how the language we have paints pictures of what they want, our hearts and minds. When I was with Dai Davies I wanted him to be happy, content, and he was. When John was Merboy I wanted him to love me; I wanted everyone to love me, to desire me, and they did. When I lived in the cottage I coveted this house, this house with its deck, its endless watery view, its gravitas. The emblem, the signifier, of all I had achieved. And then, when the bomb blew up in my face, all I wanted was to be left alone.

Be very, very careful what you wish for.

Author's Note

I would like to record my thanks to Peter Porter for permission to quote from his poem, 'The Great Poet comes here in Winter', as well as *Elementary Logic* by W.V.O. Quine, and the following songs: 'Is That All There Is' by Peggy Lee, 'Zing Went The Strings of My Heart' Hanley (Chappell & Co Ltd/MCPS), 'Sh-Boom – Life Could Be a Dream' by Keyes, Feafter, Edwards and McRae (Carlin Music Corps/MCPS) and 'The Boy from New York City' by The Ad Libs.